LOWFIELD

LOWFIELD

A Novel

MARK SAMPSON

| N₁ | O₂ | N₁ |
CANADA

Copyright © 2025 by Mark Sampson

All rights reserved. No part of this book may be used or reproduced in any manner whatsoever without the prior written permission of the publisher, except in the case of brief quotations embodied in reviews.

Publisher's note: This book is a work of fiction. Names, characters, places and incidents are either the product of the author's imagination or are used fictitiously, and any resemblance to actual persons living or dead is entirely coincidental.

Library and Archives Canada Cataloguing in Publication

Title: Lowfield : a novel / Mark Sampson.

Names: Sampson, Mark, 1975- author.

Identifiers: Canadiana (print) 20240534247 | Canadiana (ebook) 20240534255 | ISBN 9781989689813 (softcover) | ISBN 9781989689851 (EPUB)

Subjects: LCGFT: Horror fiction. | LCGFT: Paranormal fiction. | LCGFT: Novels.

Classification: LCC PS8637.A53853 L69 2025 | C813/.6—dc23

Printed and bound in Canada on 100% recycled paper.

Now Or Never Publishing
901, 163 Street
Surrey, British Columbia
Canada V4A 9T8

nonpublishing.com
Fighting Words.

We gratefully acknowledge the support of the Canada Council for the Arts and the British Columbia Arts Council for our publishing program.

For Aaron MacRae

Part 1: The Absentee Landlord

Chapter 1

The man stood at the rail of the ferry and stared out at what looked like a row of enormous tombstones rising out of the water. He knew this wasn't what they were. The huge, T-shaped pillars winding in a giant line across the Northumberland Strait were the first foundational pieces of a massive bridge under construction. Cranes climbed high into the air from their platforms and dangled their spindly, Tinker Toy arms out over the pillars. Rebar jutted like metallic intestines out of exposed concrete, and gulls bobbed in the air above with languid curiosity. But to the man, there at the ferry's rail, those pillars looked like headstones, like monuments in a lengthy, linear graveyard.

Riley Fuller was not prone to either moribund or metaphoric thinking, but as he took a drag on his cigarette and cast his hard, hazel eyes out over the Strait's expanse, he had to admit there was something spooky about a construction site in the middle of a body of water. It looked almost... *otherworldly*, as if the bridge were arising out of another dimension of space and time. The day didn't help his unease: the sky was dully overcast and the air out here was cold. The waves of the Strait looked like rippling silver and struck him as menacing, as if the water would gladly swallow him up, would carry him down into the depths if he gave it half a chance.

A couple of preteens raced past him on the ferry's deck. Riley turned and watched as the two of them, likely brother and sister, stopped about ten feet from where he stood, climbed up onto the first rung of the rail, and leaned over it. He could see that the kids each had a small fistful of pennies, probably given to them by their mother. They took turns fishing one of the coins out of their palm and dropping it with a dainty, dramatic release of thumb and finger over the side of the ship. They were trying to get each penny to land—and stay—on the lip of the hull below. They weren't having much luck. Some pennies sailed right past that black buttress and into the foaming green water beneath it. A few hit the lip before ricocheting off and vanishing into the spume. One penny bounced a couple times on the lip before tottering off the edge. "So *close*," the boy cried. "This one for sure!" squealed the girl as she dropped another coin toward the hull.

Riley took the last drag of his cigarette and then mimicked the kids, pinching the butt between his thumb and index finger and then suspending his hand over the rail. He released the cigarette, but it had no chance of reaching the hull two storeys below. The cold April wind snatched it up and sailed it off into the spritzing, rolling waves. *That could me*, he thought, his mind souring again. *In three quick steps I could be up and over this rail, pitching myself into the Strait, and I'd be gone. I'd disappear into that churn as anonymously as a cigarette butt. Wouldn't that be something? Maybe that's how I'm meant to go.*

He turned to his left, away from the kids, and saw that a gull had perched itself on the rail not four feet from his elbow. Riley flinched a little, but then collected himself and gazed coldly at the bird. The bird gazed back. Its feathers were an almost artful mix of white and charcoal. The gull shuffled on its feet and turned its narrow face in profile to Riley, its black eye staring at him with a kind of knowing, of *cunning*. Riley frowned. The gull peered at him a moment longer, then released a rhythmic, syllabic squawk. Riley thought of swinging out his arm to shoo it away. But then the bird lifted off on its own, taking flight with a surprising wingspan, then stroked and stroked and stroked out over the water. It sailed all the way to the nearest concrete pillar mounting out of the Strait, landed on its edge, and folded up its wings. The gull turned in profile again and once more found Riley's gaze, locking onto it across that wide expanse. The gull let out another screech. That staccato cry echoed out to the next pillar over, lined up to create a bridge that, in two years' time, would connect the Island looming in front of the ship to the mainland receding behind it.

Riley decided to go inside.

~

The *John Hamilton Gray* was an older ferry but a comfortable one. The crossing here, on the New Brunswick side, was Riley's sole option: the Nova Scotia ferry wouldn't start its season for another month yet. This crossing was shorter anyhow, just forty-five minutes, compared to seventy-five on the Nova Scotia side, which suited Riley just fine. His Maritime roots notwithstanding, he wasn't really good on the water. And now, stepping inside the ferry's main cabin area, he recalled yet again that he was no longer good with crowds, either.

It was still the off season but a Sunday, and the ship's cafeteria and lounges, and the narrow hallways connecting them, were moderately busy. In the corner just inside the door were two arcade machines, an ancient *Ms. Pac-Man* and a more contemporary-looking game, *Streetfighter II*. Teenagers were playing both, with more teens huddled around them to watch. Beyond this, Riley spotted the lineup in the cafeteria, that rat maze of metal piping. It was about halfway full, which made Riley nervous. His appetite, so capricious for so long, had made an appearance this afternoon, but he wondered if he could stand there long enough to get served. Maybe he could. He headed into the cramped café and checked out its board menus. He decided on a bit of chowder and a roll, and got in line. But as his eyes took a quick sweep around the seating area, Riley realized there was only one empty chair he could imagine himself sitting in. It was part of a vacant two-seater right against the nearby bulkhead, where he could park himself with his back against the wall and face the room. This was a necessary habit, these days. He didn't like people standing or sitting or walking up behind him. Riley thought about going over and throwing his plaid fleece jacket over the chair to reserve it, but then the line moved and he moved with it. He turned back to the servers behind the counter, and the cashier at the end. Could he pay for his chowder and get over to that seat fast enough to claim it?

He could not. By the time Riley got through the line and had his plastic tray in hand, the two-seater was taken. He considered ditching the food outright and just stealing back downstairs to the vehicle deck to sit in his Chevy Lumina and wait the crossing out, but he was hungry now. So instead, he put the tray and utensils back and just stood stiffly against the nearest wall with his chowder and his roll. He scarfed the bun in three bites and then began drinking the chowder out of its Styrofoam bowl instead of eating it, trying to do so as inconspicuously as possible.

He wasn't inconspicuous enough. A guy in a chewed-up Montreal Canadiens hat and Helly Hansen jacket, sitting at a table right in front of where Riley stood, turned up to look at him, his eyes narrowing. Did he recognize Riley? Did he know him? Had he maybe seen his picture in the Moncton newspaper with a series of articles that had run sixteen months ago, and was now trying to recall what those articles had been about? *Could* he place this man?

No. The guy merely looked awkward, uncomfortable at having this stranger stand so close to his table. "Hey buddy," he said. "Hey buddy. You okay?" The guy's jacket make a swishing sound as he twisted in his chair again to look up at Riley. "Hey buddy, you gonna find a seat or what?"

Riley glared at him over his Styrofoam bowl. "No. I'm fine here, thank you."

The guy looked more puzzled than angry at that, and turned away. Seeing the look in Riley's eyes, he wasn't going to argue the point.

~

After he finished eating, Riley did something he'd been putting off for the entire crossing. He moved to the lounge at the front of the ferry so he could look out at the approaching Island. As he stood near the corner of that wide row of windows, he could see how close they were to arriving, to pulling up to a huge iron and concrete terminal almost identical to the one they left behind. At this distance, the Island didn't look like an island at all. It looked like just another mainland, as characterless as the New Brunswick coast that the *John Hamilton Gray* had departed from.

Riley heard the ferry's engines gathering themselves, and a moment later some charmless music played and an announcement came over the PA. It instructed the passengers to return to their vehicles to prepare for—and here, used a term that struck Riley as comically baroque—*disembarkation*.

He waited for everyone else to file out of the lounges and cafeteria before he himself made his move. He wanted to be the last person entering the narrow, suffocating stairwells that led back down to the vehicle decks.

Chapter 2

Prince Edward Island did not wear early April well. Despite winter's official end nearly two weeks earlier, Riley could see—once he'd driven his Lumina off the ferry and hit the highway toward Charlottetown—that there were still crusts of ashen snow in the ditches here, and the trees appeared not only bare but somehow *battered*, weak and arthritic-looking. In another few months, the sight of these rolling fields and indented coastlines would attract tourists from around the world. But today, in very early spring, everything looked cold and wet and colourless. It was as if the whole Island, Riley thought, had been assaulted, utterly *gangbanged* by winter, and was still recovering. He sniffed at that, there at the wheel. *Gangbanged?* he thought. *Jesus, Fuller. Where did that come from?*

And then another, equally unbeckoned thought pressed into his mind: *I've been here before. Fuck me if I haven't.* He knew that was ridiculous; Riley, despite having lived all of his forty-five years in neighbouring New Brunswick, had never set foot on PEI prior to today. And yet the simple, rural landscape on either side of the highway seemed instantly familiar, as if a freshet of *déjà vu* had come rushing over him. The rolling hills, the red earth, the copses of spruce trees—it was like he knew their every detail. Like he had seen them before. *This place almost feels like home*, he thought. *My* new *home.* He didn't sniff at that. Not at all. He felt a pang of desire rise up in his gut instead.

A Rolling Stones compilation album was just wrapping up in the Lumina's tape deck, and when it did, Riley hauled the cassette out and tossed it onto the passenger seat. With one hand on the wheel and one eye on the road, he mashed his cigarette into the ashtray and then began rifling through other tapes gathered on the seat. There was Springsteen's *Nebraska* album, which was too downbeat for his mood, and a couple of bands from his youth, the Beatles and, later, The Doors, which wouldn't suit, either. *I should have brought more tunes for this trip*, he thought. He popped open the glove box, thinking he might find something else in there.

He did. Behind the thickets of insurance and registration papers and old Canadian Tire money, he located a sole cassette at the very back of the glove box. It had no case and was one of those tapes you could see clear through, a transparent silver plastic. He took it out and examined it, glancing back to the road as he did.

Oh Jesus, he thought. This was *not* one of his albums. It was one of Jane's. Michael Bolton's *Time, Love & Tenderness* to be exact. He squirmed under his seatbelt at the sight of it. Riley's ex-wife may have been the most comprehensively decent person he'd ever known, effortlessly kind and level-headed in every way—but *man* did she have shitty taste in music. How did *this* tape end up in *his* glove box? When would she have brought it into his car? He had a mind to chuck the cassette out the window, right then and there, as if it were diseased.

But he paused instead. What if she wanted this album back? And what if Riley told her that he'd already found the cassette and thrown it out? Would she see this as just another betrayal, a small treachery to go along with his larger ones, the secrets he had kept that, once exposed, had led to their divorce? Would this one thoughtless gesture just verify everything that she already knew about Riley Fuller, that *he* was not comprehensively decent, that he was, in fact, a bag of shit and always would be? He mulled on that as he set the tape down long enough to dig out a fresh du Maurier, stick it in his mouth, and get the cigarette lighter going.

By the time he had the smoke lit and taken the first drag, he'd made up his mind. *Fuck that shit,* he thought. *It's a new day. Maybe it'll be a new life for me, here on PEI. I can't spend any more time making up hypothetical reasons to grovel for Jane's forgiveness. I'm done with that.* He reached over and cranked down the passenger window. Taking the cassette up again, he stole another quick glance at the road before flicking his wrist, as if throwing a

Frisbee. The tape sailed out the open window and into the cold spring air. It cartwheeled out of the racing Lumina and landed in a weedy, soggy ditch not far from a town called, perhaps fittingly, Crapaud.

~

A half hour later, Riley pulled into the parking lot of the Charlottetown Best Western, navigated into a free spot, and turned the car off. He looked up at the hotel, a rambling, multi-angled structure, and frowned when he saw that it was only two storeys tall. *Shit,* he thought. *That's going to be a problem.* Riley kicked himself. *Should have checked that before I booked it.* His best friend, Sammy, had advised against staying here in the first place. Sammy had a queer beef with this chain of hotel, calling it the Worst Western, and thought Riley could do, and indeed deserved, better. But the truth was it was cheap, especially this time of year. Now, he realized he really should have ensured his hotel was more than two storeys high.

He checked in and found his room, a shabby little unit with two double beds and thick curtains over the window. It was, thankfully, on the far side of the first floor, away from the noises of the street—not that Riley thought he'd sleep any better here than at home. But the room was at least clean and he was allowed to smoke in it, which was good. He set his extra cigarette packs on the particle-board nightstand along with the bottle of Jim Beam he'd brought over from Moncton, a liquor that Sam had nicknamed Sweet Lady Bourbon. Riley had a drink, had a smoke, turned on the TV in its cabinet, saw that the cable channels here were almost identical to the ones back home, and then turned it off.

Then he picked up the room phone and dialed Dave Campbell, not bothering to worry about what the hotel would charge him for this call.

"Hello."

"Is that Dave Campbell?"

"Why, yes it is. Is that Riley Fuller?"

"Yep."

"Good stuff. Say, where are you?"

"I'm in Charlottetown. Just arrived."

Campbell chuckled at that. "You know, we have places to stay here in Montague, right?" The man, Riley noticed, pronounced the name of the town without the T.

"That's okay," he said. "I won't mind the drive back and forth. It'll give me a chance to see some of the Island."

"Fair enough."

"So what's the plan?"

"Well, I was thinking about that. The property is over in Glenning and a bit tricky to find if you don't know where it is. I think the best thing is for us to just meet in Montague tomorrow morning—say 10 o'clock?—and I'll take you over to the house myself. It's about nine miles northeast of here. Sound good?"

"Sounds good. Where in Montague should I meet you?"

Campbell chuckled again. "There is, you'll be shocked to learn, a Tim Hortons right on Main Street. Do you think you could find it?"

"Shouldn't be a problem."

"All right, then. I'll see you there tomorrow at ten. Have yourself a good night, sir. Sleep well."

"You, too."

After he hung up, Riley sat for a moment, or maybe longer than a moment, on the edge of the bed, staying very still, very quiet. He cleared his throat, breathed in and out, nice and slow, nice and easy, like he'd been taught. He could hear Campbell's last two words to him jangling in his head, almost taunting him. *Careful now*, he thought. *Don't* trigger *it, for Christsake*. But it was too late. Barely coming on dusk and Riley could already feel insomnia's first tickle, his brain set to maximum restlessness, and the sensation of a full-body ache, one that would, somehow, grow more languid *and* more kinetic with each passing hour. *Sleep well*, Dave Campbell had said. But Riley already knew that he wouldn't. Not tonight, nor possibly any night ever again.

Four shots from a pistol echoed through the deepest recesses of his memory. *POP! POP! POP! POP!*

He poured himself another drink.

~

If you need to roam, his social worker had told him, *then you bloody well roam.*

And so Riley had roamed. It had been okay, quite comfortable actually, to do it in his house, back when he still had a house, when he still lived in a nice, two-and-half storey home in a quiet Moncton suburb, a home he had shared with Jane for seventeen years. Even while they were working out the logistics of their divorce, Riley had followed the advice of his social worker, and roamed. When he first started this ritual, wandering up and down the floors of that house, Jane was still too upset with him, too upset in general, to ask what on earth he was doing. His behaviour struck her as weird, but perhaps understandable, considering what he'd been through. At a time in the evening when the average person might think about going to bed, Riley would ascend to the house's third-floor attic, then roam all the way down to its cozy, wood-paneled basement. And then he'd go all the way back up again. And then all the way back down. He needed to feel the stairs beneath his feet, the tension in his legs as he went up, the release in them as he went down. Over and over he would go, ascending and descending the floors of that big beautiful house he lived in with the woman he loved, a home that they had tried for years to fill with children, but couldn't.

After the divorce, Riley moved into a midrise apartment building closer to downtown. Nine storeys, which suited him just fine. His fellow tenants—many of whom, *most* of whom, he guessed, had an inkling about who he was, had seen his picture on the news—might find Riley in the stairwell in the evenings, doing the ritual: wandering all the way up to the top floor, which the elevator ludicrously labelled the "penthouse"; all the way back down to the laundry and boiler and storage rooms in the basement. The ritual caused these neighbours to stare at Riley, to look away when he passed, to whisper amongst themselves about his eccentricity, which made him self-conscious. But his social worker, to his credit, did not dissuade him. *If you need to roam, Mr. Christopher D. Bentley, BA, BSW, MSW, RSW*, had told him, *then you bloody well roam*.

The Worst Western, with its pathetic two floors and, as far as Riley could see, no public access to the basement, was just not going to cut it. And so, after darkness fell and Riley still couldn't sleep, he wandered out into the streets of Charlottetown.

It was fucking eerie, he thought, how empty they were at this hour. Was it just another symptom of the time of year, that nobody seemed to be out and about? It was, after all, early April of 1995, pre-tourism season *and* a school night. Still, he didn't mind the emptiness, not after the crowd-fear he experienced on the ferry, and he didn't mind Charlottetown itself. It was a small but pleasant little city. It carried none of the memories, none of the triggers that Riley now associated with every single block of the city he had lived in his whole life. The best thing about Charlottetown was that it wasn't Moncton. Which, he supposed, you could say about anywhere. You could say it about Charlottetown, or Montague, or that place that Dave Campbell had mentioned, Glenning, wherever *that* was. Really, anywhere on PEI felt good, felt like home, because it wasn't Moncton, and he let that feeling, that bloom of desire, swell up in him again.

Riley eventually found his way back to his hotel room. He sat in its shadowy grimness, there on the edge of one of the double beds, yet another glass of Sweet Lady Bourbon in his fist. Now that it was full dark, his mind would, of course, not let him rest. His daytime optimism was once again replaced by the shame, the disgrace, the reminders of what he had done that always came back to him so fiercely at night. *Why won't you let me sleep?* he asked his body. *I'm so fucking tired. I just want a few hours. I just want to get outside my own head for a little while. Can we not do that? Please? Can you please just let me sleep?*

His body's answer was emphatic.

Riley got up then, went to his suitcase, and took out the *other* thing he had brought from Moncton. He carried it back over to the bed, sat down, and rested it in his lap. Riley found the feel of it in his hand, the weight of it on his thigh, the grooves and ridges of its handle, almost as soothing as the ritual itself. The Glock was a perfectly engineered little machine, and had only one purpose. It was not Riley's service weapon—a supervisor at the RCMP, someone he had worked with for nearly twenty years, had come to his house and taken *that* piece away from him, as a precaution—but the Glock was his weapon just the same. Some nights, in the living room of the apartment that his divorce had banished him to, when his nocturnal roaming hadn't worked, he would just sit with the Glock in his lap, as he was doing now, with the magazine loaded and locked in the handle. It eased his mind just to know it was there. Sometimes, he'd even stick the muzzle in his mouth, the way he was doing now, feeling the oily heft of it on his tongue, and think about all the promises this gun had made to him. It was his nuclear option, his exit plan, the portal that would take him out of this world and, maybe, into another.

Was tonight the night? Was it?

No. He hauled the gun back out, its metal scraping on his teeth, the black muzzle now blacker with his saliva on it. No, not tonight. Tomorrow morning, Dave Campbell of Montague was going to take Riley up to see the closest thing he had to an ancestral home, and he didn't want to miss that.

So no. Not tonight. But maybe some other.

Chapter 3

Montague, on the eastern end of PEI, was a pretty if nondescript little town with a river running through the middle of it, and, as Dave Campbell predicted, Riley had no trouble locating its Tim Hortons. At 10 am, the coffee shop wasn't too busy, as it would have been even an hour earlier. Riley opened the shop's glass door and stepped onto its hard brown tiles. A man in a nearby seat, seeing him come in, rose immediately and smiled. Riley figured the guy knew it was him because he was the only person in the joint he didn't recognize.

"Riley Fuller?" he asked.

"Dave?"

The two men shook hands, and then Campbell gestured to the counter. "You want something here?"

"No, I'm good."

With his short, stocky build and balding head, his beady eyes behind thick glasses, Dave Campbell looked a bit like Jason Alexander, the actor who played George on *Seinfeld*. Riley wondered if he could make Campbell laugh, would he snort like a warthog, the way the character on the show sometimes did?

"So the house is about ten minutes away," Campbell said. "You can just leave your vehicle here. I'll drive us up and then take you back."

"Actually," Riley said, his mouth creasing downward, "if it's all the same, I'll follow you in my car."

"Oh?" Campbell asked with a little laugh. "Worried I might *kidnap* you, eh?" When Riley didn't return the chuckle, when his hazel eyes just stared back stonily at Dave and it became clear he didn't find that funny, a look of unease passed over Campbell's face. "Well, that's fine," he said with a pleasant, PEI shrug. "If that's what you want. You think you'll be able to tail me?"

"That shouldn't be a problem," Riley replied.

They headed back out to the parking lot and their respective vehicles, Campbell's a burgundy Honda Accord. The day's weather was even worse than yesterday's: a cold spring fog had rolled in during the early-morning hours, and the air was chilly enough to threaten snow. Riley drove behind Campbell as he turned north and followed Main Street as it quickly transformed into a simple country road leading out of town. Within five minutes they passed through something called Pooles Corner and then headed north up and up into an empty rural expanse. The fog made the farm fields here seem a bit creepy, a bit desolate. *Where the hell is he taking me?* Riley thought. But then he watched as Campbell slowed his car, signaled, and then turned east onto something called the Eight Mile Road. It was narrow and badly marked, an easy turnoff to miss. No wonder Campbell felt the need, Riley thought, to take him up here in person. They drove along this road for a bit, and soon passed through the community of Glenning. It wasn't *much* of a community: just a single crossroads with a derelict autobody shop on the northeast corner, about a half dozen tiny bungalows scattered about, and what looked like a dairy farm up on the hill. They went along the road for a while longer, quite a while actually, until they were *really* out in the middle of nowhere. It was all forest out here. But then Campbell signaled again, pulling onto the shoulder, and Riley followed suit. Where they stopped, Riley could see a dirt laneway coming out from between the trees.

They climbed out of their cars and met at the ditch's edge, Campbell bringing with him a large shoulder bag. Riley found himself excited to finally see what Campbell was about to show him. He could already spot part of it: there, above the spruces, was the very peak of what looked like an old turret.

To stall his emotions, Riley nodded at the ditch, at the long, blackened scab of snow there. "Quite a bit still on the ground," he said absently.

"Oh, that's probably left over from the big storm back on the 17th," Campbell replied. "PEI almost always has a blizzard on St. Paddy's Day. Kind of an Island tradition. It's the strangest thing."

"Must be tough on the leprechauns," Riley said.

Campbell laughed at that. No George Costanza snort.

"So you ready?" he asked.

Riley dug out his du Mauriers. He offered one to Campbell, who declined. Then he stuck a cigarette in his own mouth and lit it.

"Yep," he said with as much nonchalance as he could muster, though his insides were now roiling.

They headed across the laneway, which was cratered and weedy and unloved, and passed through the copse of spruces and onto the property, a one-acre lot carved into the woods. Riley looked up as he did, and finally saw what he'd come to Prince Edward Island to see.

The house, built well back from the road, was a large, Victorian-style structure, almost a mansion. It sat in an unkempt mélange of wild, ancient timothy grass, like an untended meadow, and what seemed like decades of rotten leaves that had fallen off nearby maples. From this distance, Riley thought the house looked as if it were made entirely of papier-mâché, a sinister, weather-beaten grey the colour of bird shit, of hornet's nest. At the front of the house was a large, shambling porch with crumbling slats of wood and battered columns on either side to prop up a canopy-like roof above it. To the right of the porch stood a three-storey Queen Anne turret, a few battered shingles clinging to the dunce cap of its roof. The rest of the house, all peaks and gables of varying heights, rambled away from this front-facing façade to end about a dozen yards from the wild, jungly forest at the very back of the property.

Riley and Campbell hiked their way up the foggy, J-shaped lane and soon stood at the edge of the manse. Riley cast his gaze all around it and noticed something peculiar right off the bat. All the windows, though blackened with grime and entirely opaque, were intact. Not a single shattered pane in any of those wooden frames. He nudged Campbell and nodded upward.

"No broken windows," he said. "What, they don't have vandals here in Glenning? No bored teenagers?"

Campbell shrugged. "Not a lot of people come this far up the Eight Mile Road," he said dismissively. "There's nothing else out here, and I doubt what few kids are around even know this place exists."

"Still, not one broken window, from a storm or anything?" Riley said, dropping his cigarette butt onto the mushy spring ground and stamping it out before lighting a fresh one. "That's fucking weird."

Something else was weird. While the elements had, over countless seasons, stripped all but a few flaking chips of paint off the sides of the house, Riley could see that there was still a touch of colour up in the highest gables. A bit of brown winked out there from each shadowy arch. No, it wasn't brown, he thought. It was red, a very old, very faded lick of scarlet paint, the colour of dried blood, up in each of those side-facing peaks.

"Red gables," he said, and pointed with his cigarette.

Campbell's gaze followed it up. "Oh yeah," he replied.

Riley gave a single, dry chuckle. "You'd think they'd be green, here on PEI."

Campbell didn't get this at first, but then he did. "Oh yeah," he said again, and then *did* snort like George Costanza. "If you moved in here, you'd be Riley of Red Gables."

The other thing that had caught his eye was on the near end of the lane, in the wheat-like tangles of yellow grass growing in what would have been the house's side lawn. Riley walked over to get a better look. There, he could see an oval loop of carefully arranged rocks forming a broad kidney shape on the ground, about nine feet long and four feet wide; and next to it, a second one of the same size and shape. In the first, he caught a glimpse of a crumbling stone sundial peeping through the weeds. It was practically disintegrating back down into the earth.

"There were gardens here, once," Riley said.

Campbell nodded. "You garden?"

"A bit. My ex-wife did most of it. She was the one with the green thumb. But I provided the muscle whenever she needed help."

A person would need a lot of muscle, Riley thought, *to get these two patches back in order so you could grow something.*

The wind picked up then, causing the branches of nearby maples and spruces to shutter and shake. The two men headed up and onto the house's front porch. With the exception of a few planks of wood having caved in on themselves, the floor there was sound. This surprised them both. The entire house—never mind the porch boards—should have rotted down to a pile of rubble by now, based on how long it had sat empty. Yet the manse, while badly dilapidated, was more or less intact. Riley looked up at the big, oaken front door with its rusted padlock, and, next to it, he could see a badly faded green-blue plaque nailed to the clapboard there. His brow furrowed as he read what looked like old-timey Celtic lettering:

APPLEGARTH

"The house has a name?" Riley asked. "They didn't tell me that, when I looked into it."

"Yeah, no, it's more of a colloquial thing," Campbell said. "Some of the older folks around here might even still know it as Applegarth. When my office first received your documents, I had to dig around a bit to figure out which property we were talking about."

Riley nodded at that. He leaned back against the wood-slat rail and looked to his right, to the grimy windows in the first storey of the Queen Anne turret.

"Dave, this property *does* belong to me, right?"

"Oh, very much," Campbell replied. "My office checked and triple checked all the documents, and your claim to Applegarth is solid. You're welcome to do whatever you want with it. You could sell, though it's hard to say what kind of price you'd get for the land. There's not much development out here, as you can see—though things may change once that," and here, Campbell rolled his eyes, "*stupid* bridge gets finished. If you do want to sell, I know a corker of a real estate agent in Montague who can help you. Don't use any of the ones in Charlottetown.

They're all crooks." Campbell threw a smile at Riley, but went on when he didn't toss one back. "If you do sell, try and sell to an Islander. People around here get squirrely about come-from-aways owning too much land. Old history and such."

Riley nodded at all this, though he didn't understand what Campbell meant.

"Did you want to see the inside?" Campbell asked, and patted his shoulder bag. "I did get the keys from the county office and I brought some good flashlights with me."

Riley felt his heart once again pick up pace as another fit of anticipation churned through him.

"Yes, I would," he said. "I would like that very much."

Campbell nodded, then unzipped his bag. He took out a small manila envelope, opened it, and poured a set of keys into his palm. He then took a couple of flashlights out of his bag and handed one to Riley. He turned and began trying keys in the big padlock on the door. The fifth one fit in, and Campbell began twisting hard to get it to open.

"This wouldn't have been the main entry into the house anyway," he said as he tried to get the rusted lock to pop. "Most people would have entered through the side door at the top of the lane. It's where the house's main foyer is, apparently."

Then the lock did release itself, and Campbell pulled it free and handed it to Riley. Then he gave the door a bump with his shoulder. It wobbled forward, slowly, reluctantly, squealing on hinges black with rust and probably as old as the house itself.

With the door open, Campbell looked back and nodded at Riley. "You may want to put your cigarette out," he said. "Wouldn't want to burn the place down."

Chapter 4

Campbell had been right. The lobby they stepped into felt like a false front, a parlour intended more for entertaining than a place of ingress and egress to the house itself. Their flashlight beams cut through shadows and motes of dust. Despite the darkness, Riley could see that the plaster walls here were mint green, a colour and texture that struck him as very nineteenth century. There was, he noticed, elaborate wainscoting that seemed to be holding up well despite its age.

The two men stepped through the front foyer and into an enormous kitchen. They could see a round wooden table, warped by moisture and peppered in rat droppings, standing in the kitchen's eating area. A single chair with a couple of spindles missing lay upturned on the floor next to it. A row of wooden counters and cupboards ran along one wall. Next to these was a door. Riley opened it and poked his head in. There, he saw the largest dining room he'd ever laid eyes on. The fact that it had a door that closed also struck him as very nineteenth century. He stepped inside and cast his flashlight up and around. The room contained a full dining table and chairs, capable of seating about a dozen people.

Riley came back out, closed the dining room door, and swept his flashlight around the rest of the kitchen. He saw a sink, a light switch, an outlet. He nudged Campbell again and nodded curiously at them.

"As you know, your grandfather occupied the house for only six months, back in 1930," Campbell explained, "but it was enough time to install contemporary wiring and plumbing. The electrical would likely be knob and tube, not that it would work now. Ditto for the plumbing. *If* you are interested in moving in to the place, that is. Har har." He actually said *har har*.

It was no laughing matter for Riley. Standing there in the kitchen that had once belonged to his grandfather, and to *his* grandfather before that, Riley felt a sensation wash over him. He couldn't place it at first, but it was something that he had felt before, though too long ago now to remember when. The feeling didn't frighten him. Quite the opposite. For the first time in ages, he actually felt calm. Peaceful. His thoughts were quieting. He was becoming... like himself again, his true self. The person he had once been.

The house creaked and settled all around them, even though he and Campbell were standing still.

"Shall we move on?" Campbell asked.

"Yep," Riley said simply.

At the southwest end of the kitchen was a large walk-in pantry, and Campbell opened its door to show Riley the space inside. At the very back of the pantry was a set of stone stairs that descended into what Campbell described as a large but unfinished basement. He closed the pantry door again and they headed out of the kitchen, through another massive arch, and into the main foyer that Campbell had mentioned before. There, facing the double doors that led outside, was a wide and ornate staircase that turned and twisted its way up to the second floor. They passed this and stepped through yet another wood-lined arch that led to the house's spacious living room. Against the far wall was a cold but immaculate fireplace, its grate sitting like a wrought-iron claw inside. Deeper into the living room, to their left, stood French doors leading to a solarium with large windows making up three of its four walls facing the backyard. Like the others in the house, these windows were the epitome of filth, but still intact.

The two men did a lap around the large living room, and as they turned to leave, Riley spotted something else. There, on the plaster wall next to the fireplace, crawled a huge and unsightly stain of mold. It looked like leopard prints, or maybe a tattoo, and climbed nearly halfway to the ceiling. It was the only blemish on the otherwise perfectly preserved room. Riley stared at it a moment, as if mesmerized.

"Some moisture must have seeped in," Campbell said.

"Looks like it," Riley agreed.

They headed back to the foyer to climb the huge staircase that led up to the second floor. Each step they took seemed to cause the entire house to crack and shift. At the top, they arrived at a huge, carpeted landing. On its left was the door leading to the master bedroom. Campbell opened it and let Riley peek inside. The huge room had windows facing the backyard and its own fireplace. Campbell closed the door again after Riley came out. Straight ahead on the landing was a small bathroom, and above its door, in the ceiling, was a pull-down stairwell that provided access to the attic. On the right was a hallway with a hardwood floor leading back up toward the front of the house. The two men roamed down it, their flashlight beams swinging and crossing. Here, Riley counted three bedrooms along the east side of the floor, and three on the west.

The hallway T-boned into a commodious library at the very front of the house. Its walls contained built-in wooden shelves loaded with old and dusty books—some lined up neatly with their spines facing out, others in manic piles scattered helter-skelter. Riley cast his flashlight over these leather-bound tomes. He didn't know books, not like Sammy did, but these, like so much else in the house, struck him as very nineteenth century.

In the far corner of the library sat an old and dusty writing desk. Beyond it was the archway into the turret's second floor. Riley popped his head in. This rounded shell of a room may have once formed a cozy reading nook, he thought. On the near side of the curved wall was another pull-down set of stairs leading up to the third level of the turret.

Coming back out, he and Campbell stood in the centre of the library.

"So this is Applegarth," Campbell said with an almost satisfied sigh. "What do you think?"

Riley was quiet for the longest time, but then rubbed his neck and shook his head. "I think it's in incredible shape, considering how old it is and how long it's sat empty."

"Yeah, I'm quite shocked, frankly," Campbell replied. "I expected the place to be falling down around us. I guess they just built homes better back in the day. I mean, there are lots of old, abandoned houses dotting PEI's countryside, but Applegarth is the best one I've ever seen, bar none."

Riley said nothing. That feeling had come over him again. That sense of calm, of being very relaxed here, very comfortable in his own skin. The house should have felt cold and drafty and unwelcoming, but instead it was like a huge and familiar blanket, a large duvet wrapping itself around him.

Campbell obviously didn't feel the same way, as he was now rubbing his triceps through his spring jacket to ward off the chill of the room. "Anyway," he said, "sell it, leave it empty, or whatever, but just let me know what you want to do. I'll try to help you out any way I can."

Riley nodded at that. "Thank you," he said. Then he looked up at Campbell. "Dave, do you mind if I... if I stay here for a bit today? I don't want to tie you up, but we did come in separate vehicles. I'd like to just... just hang out here for a while, if that's all right."

"Riley, this is *your* house. You're welcome to stay as long as you like. And hey, I don't blame you one bit. This is like your ancestral home. You're literally an absentee landlord laying eyes on what's yours for the first time."

"You mean absentee property owner," Riley corrected. "Landlord would imply I have tenants here."

At that, Campbell let out a strange and uneasy laugh. He rubbed his arms again.

"Anyway, you can keep the flashlight until I see you next," he said, "and, here, I'll give you the keys." He handed them to Riley. "You'll probably want to lock up when you do leave. It's not like we have *zero* vandals around these parts."

~

And so Riley stayed a while, sitting on the sill of the library windows and looking out. He didn't know how long he remained there after Campbell left, but the sun had clearly moved across the sky. The light had changed. The shadows had thickened. His craving for a cigarette raged like a fire.

He finally moved back out of the library and up the hall, past the bedrooms and toward the staircase. The floorboards creaked and cracked as he walked, as did the steps and banister as he made his descent to the ground level. In the foyer, Riley paused a moment to stare at the door that led out to the lane. As he did, a queer, improbable image flickered across his mind, one of himself having moved in to this house, moved in and coming through that door day in and day out. Taking his shoes off in this vestibule. Hanging up his coat in its closet. A great sense of purpose, warm as honey, spread through him then, the drive to reclaim a life that had once belonged to him but had been viciously, unceremoniously ripped away. *A man's entitled to a home*, he thought. *Fuck, I'm entitled to a home, a place to stake my claim. What happened back in Moncton doesn't change that.*

Something moved through the shadows to his left, there beyond the archway leading into the living room.

Riley swung his flashlight around in an instant. He barely needed it: now that the sun had moved over to the west side of the house, there was a good stream of light coming through the big bay window. He stepped deeper into the living room, looked around. Heard a rustle to his left, up where the French doors led out to the solarium. He cast his light over there. *Rats, probably*, he thought. *Rats scurrying on the floor. Or else in the walls.*

As he went to go, Riley panned his flashlight once more around the living room, slicing its beam across the fireplace. When he did, he stopped. Lingered his light on the wall next to the hearth. Took a step closer to it, his hard, narrow eyes squinting.

That was odd. The wall there was different. When he and Campbell had stood here before, the wall had had that huge, disturbing patch of mold growing through its plaster. They both had mentioned it. But now, the wall seemed fine. Well, not *fine*, Riley thought. There was still some mildew there, fainter and lower down, near the baseboards. He cast his light over it. But hadn't the blight been halfway to the ceiling before? Because it wasn't now. Most of it, the darkest parts, rose barely six inches off the floor.

What the hell? he thought. Had it been just a trick of the light, a prank of the shadows, that made him think that the mold was much worse before than it was now? But both he *and* Campbell had seen it, had pointed it out. "That is really fucking odd," Riley said out loud.

He headed back down the house, passing through the foyer, then into that massive kitchen, and finally reaching the parlour that led out to the porch. Riley didn't look back as he stepped outside. He shut the front door tight behind him, then locked it with the padlock before climbing back down off the porch and heading to his car.

Chapter 5

That evening, back at the Worst Western, Riley couldn't sleep. He'd tried going to bed early, to get a good night's rest, but soon found himself shifting and twisting in his hotel sheets, unable to nod off. It was as if that glimmer of ambition he'd felt while standing in Applegarth's foyer was now replaced by his usual shame, the most wretched, debilitating despair Riley could have imagined. The memory of what had happened in Moncton—*POP! POP! POP! POP!* went the pistol fire—overwhelmed him once again, and his disgrace, acute and piercing, grilled him like a sausage in his bed.

He eventually got up, put his clothes back on, and headed out into Charlottetown's streets as he had the night before. This time, he found a bar. It was a rundown old neighbourhood pub with a joker-like mascot on its sign, juggling balls, and what looked a set of apartments upstairs. He went into the pub and drank there until close, then staggered back to the hotel. In his room, he polished off the last of the Jim Beam, that Sweet Lady Bourbon, then splashed out on his bed, where he not so much fell asleep as passed out into a dreamless oblivion.

~

The next day, he drove back to Montague. He found a hardware store, and, on an impulse he didn't understand, bought a few implements there: a broom and dustpan, a big plastic garbage bucket, a metal rake.

He drove these items up and out of town. Aiming for the Eight Mile Road, Riley missed it the first time and had to double back. But then he found it, turned onto that old country road, then headed across Glenning and finally out to Applegarth.

When he got there, he steered into the laneway, the Lumina jostling over its crags and craters. Then he parked in front of the house and turned the engine off. He stared up at that big manse, just sitting there like a shabby, rotting hornet's nest in the middle of the wooded countryside.

He sat there a while, smoking a du Maurier. That feeling of calm, that sense of being himself again, had returned. He climbed out of the Lumina and made his way up to the house. Scaling its dilapidated porch, he went over and unlocked the padlock—it came apart more easily this time—and shouldered the door open. Soon, Riley found himself in Applegarth's kitchen. He set up the knocked-over chair and sat for a while at the filthy, warped table there. At one point he got up and looked under the old sink, where he found an ancient tin can, its label long lost to the decades. He brought it back to the table and used it as an ashtray, Campbell's warning be damned. Riley just sat there, smoking away, letting the house's presence wash over him.

After a while, he thought: *This is fucking stupid. You want to do it, so just do it.*

He returned to the car, took out the rake and bucket, the broom and dustpan. He started with the garden. It was warmer today than yesterday, and it was nice to work outside after so many months of apartment living. With hard, steady strokes of the rake, Riley tore away the grass and weeds that partially hid the stony formations on the ground. He navigated the rake's claw around the sundial near the edge of the first plot, and saw that the object wasn't in nearly as bad of shape as he thought yesterday. With the weeds pulled back, the sundial looked solid, almost stout.

He loaded the garbage bucket with his rakings, then hauled them to the edge of the property and dumped them into the woods. Coming back to the garden, Riley looked down at his work. *These plots really are sharp*, he thought. *I mean, the dirt here is shit; little more than grey clay. But with some good soil, these beds really could be something.* Riley knew that if Jane had been there, her mind would already be racing with ideas about the vegetables they could grow, and how to go about it. He found himself doing the same.

Next, he took the broom, dustpan and bucket into the house. It was midday now, and Applegarth was as bright with sunlight as it was going to be. Starting in the front parlour, Riley began to sweep, just to sweep, just to get the dust and rat droppings off the floor, to make the place a bit more pleasant. He worked his way from the parlour into the turret's first floor, then into the dining room, then into that enormous kitchen, and then on to the main foyer. As he did, Riley mused that there really wasn't as much dirt here as one would think. In fact, there seemed to be less dust and grit on the floor than there had been just yesterday, when he'd been here with Campbell.

Riley paused at the archway to the living room. His heart began to jump, his nerves jangling. He stepped in and immediately turned his back to the fireplace. He began to sweep, as he had done in the other rooms, whisking the broom along the floor as casually as he could, loading up his dustpan, then unloading it into the garbage bucket. This almost felt like his nocturnal roaming: an act that made little sense on the surface, but soothed him immeasurably in its execution.

Soon, however, Riley's curiosity got the better of him. It was as if his gaze were being turned to that corner of the living room against his will. He looked over at the fireplace, at the wall next to it. The western sun was now pouring through the bay window, and he once again wondered if that blaze of light were playing a hoax on him, a trick of the eye.

No, he thought. *No, it's not.* It was yesterday's shadows that had been pranking him. They must have been, because the wall there, that patch of plaster next to the stony, square hearth, looked pristine. Unmarked.

The mold that Riley thought he saw yesterday was nowhere to be found.

~

That night, back in the Worst Western, as he stood in the shower washing Applegarth's dust off him, Riley made a decision.

The forty-minute drive between Charlottetown and Glenning would no longer suit. After getting out of the shower, he gave Campbell a call.

"Dave, you twisted my rubber arm," he said, his voice uncharacteristically jovial. "I'm just picking away at Applegarth, and the drive's a nuisance. Any chance you could recommend somewhere to stay in your area? Preferably a room I could rent by the week?"

"So great to hear," Campbell replied, and suggested a few bed-and-breakfast spots in Montague and nearby Cardigan that would probably welcome Riley's business ahead of the tourism season.

~

The next day, he returned to the hardware store in Montague, this time to purchase a hammer, a box of nails, a box of screws, a collapsible ladder, a battery-powered drill, a handsaw and paint scraper. He tried not to think of *why* he had bought these items; he just put them in the trunk of his car before the decision had fully sunk in.

He checked into the B&B he had booked after speaking to Campbell, a place just on the outskirts of Montague called Camilla's Cottages and Lodge. After signing the register, he stayed just long enough to drop his bags in the cabin he had rented, then was out the door to drive back to Applegarth. He spent the rest of the afternoon there, doing the sort of tasks that his late father, Thomas, had called "pickin' and grinnin'": fixing a cupboard door here; scraping old paint off a wall there; hauling junk out of the house; more raking in the garden. Why was he doing this, Riley wondered, other than it seemed to calm his restless brain? If he were to sell the property, the new owner would likely demolish the old house and build something more modern in its place. Or, if Riley kept the land but let the house sit empty, as it had for the last sixty-five years, then the elements would eventually undo all the effort he'd put in over the last two days. So why put the effort in at all?

Because I want this place for myself, he thought. *Because I fucking deserve it, frankly. I can't spend all my time wallowing over happened back in Moncton. I can't just live in a one-bedroom apartment like a fucking student for the rest of my life, paying penance for what I did. I'm better than that. I am used to things a certain way, and I want those ways back in my life. I deserve them, despite everything. This house is my chance to turn a page, to seize the opportunity I've been given. I mean, why did I even come to PEI? It wasn't just to see Applegarth. It was to see what it could give me.*

These answers burned as bright as the sun, grew more crystalline as the afternoon went on and Riley swept all the floors upstairs and then cleaned out Applegarth's wooden gutters, which were shockingly free of rot. By the time dusk had arrived, he'd made up his mind.

That night, back at Camilla's, she let him use the lodge phone to call Campbell yet again.

"You're going to think I'm insane," Riley said.

"Tell me," Campbell replied, clearly smirking on the line.

So Riley told him.

"Wow, are you *sure*?" Campbell mused. "That place has sat empty since 1930. There's no way it's livable."

"It's totally livable," Riley countered. "though it'll need a ton of work before I can live in it. Do you think you could connect me with some tradespeople to help? Just keep track of your time and add it to my bill."

"Of course," Campbell replied. "But, Riley, I will say, if you're actually planning to move into Applegarth, that's going to attract some curiosity. I think your presence around here these last few days already has. Don't be surprised if the weekly paper in Montague wants to write something about you and the house. I know the guy who runs it. He's a bit of a shit disturber, but he's a good man and he *loves* publishing local stories that the paper in Charlottetown won't touch. If you move into that old pace, I suspect you'll end up on his radar, sooner or later."

Riley sniffed at that. He didn't really care for journalists. But then he found himself saying, "That's fine. Whatever." He sniffed again. "Oh, and one other thing, Dave."

"Shoot."

"I mean, this is fairly low down on my priority list, but I'm keen on getting those garden plots on the side lawn up and running. Any chance you could score me some topsoil?"

"I'll ask around," Campbell said. "I'm sure I can hook you up."

~

What surprised Riley was not the work involved to make Applegarth livable, but how little time all that work took. The days seemed to just glide by, and every day brought with it a fresh slew of progress, of accomplishment. Dave Campbell had been wrong about both the electrical and the plumbing. Inspectors arrived to look at the old knob-and-tube wiring, baffled that it was in such good shape, and before long the power company came out and got the electricity running. Riley ordered a few cords of wood for the stove in the kitchen, and a chimney cleaner to come out, and soon he had heat. Plumbers got the plumbing going, amazed that the old pipes hadn't so much as cracked over so many PEI winters of disuse. Riley bought new toilets for the bathroom, a tub and shower, various other fixtures. He also bought a water heater, which got installed in the basement next to a cobwebby pile of old cinder blocks, and he soon had hot water. A locksmith came out to update all the locks. Pavers arrived and turned the lane into a proper driveway. Riley installed a mailbox at the end of it and visited the Montague post office to figure out his address and get the house back on the local route. Landscapers showed up with a huge tractor mower and made short work of the timothy grass that hid the glory of Applegarth's lawn. Riley got the house onto the garbage collector's route. Soon the phone company came to install a phone, and in the process told Riley that he was just enough inside the community line to get access to dial-up internet, if he wanted it. He did, figuring it would provide important contact with the outside world. He bought a desktop computer from a guy in Georgetown. The machine was two years old but had some recent software programs installed on it, including one that would allow Riley to surf the world wide web. It also came with a large plastic covering, an opaque hood that he could pull down over the computer when he was done using it, to protect it from dust, of which there was still plenty in Applegarth. He set the computer up in the second-floor library, atop that old writing desk, which didn't seem nearly as decrepit as it had the first day he laid eyes on it. Riley soon registered for an email address, his very first. He used it to order some house insurance for Applegarth.

He was also surprised at how little time it took to shut down his life back in Moncton. He rented a moving van and was gone less than a day: he left early in the morning and was back by that night. To describe his Moncton apartment as spartan was an understatement. He packed up what few bits of furniture he had and the appliances that belonged to him; he paid the landlord for the remaining months on his lease; he called to cancel the phone and had the final bill forwarded to him on PEI. His circle of friends—with the exception of Sammy, who'd been living in Fredericton for more than a decade now—had all but vanished after the events of last year, and so Riley had literally nobody to say goodbye to. He didn't even bother contacting Jane to tell her where he was moving.

Back on PEI, Riley installed what furniture and appliances he had, and then went into Charlottetown to buy more: a fridge, a stove, a washer and dryer. He thought perhaps he'd also need to replace Applegarth's lengthy dining room table and accompanying chairs. But they soon proved, like so much else in the house, to be in far better shape than they first appeared, far better shape than they had any business being.

Applegarth was getting very close to being livable now. He put in his notice with Camilla at the B&B.

Chapter 6

It took some doing, but Dave Campbell tracked down someone who might have a bit of topsoil to give away: an old acquaintance, Mike Murphy, who lived with his wife and elderly mother-in-law in nearby Cardigan. Dave and Mike had curled together a few years back at the Montague Curling Club, and Dave decided to call him one Friday evening.

It was the mother-in-law who answered. "*'Ello!*" she bellowed into the receiver.

"Is that Mrs. Keating?"

"It is."

"It's Dave Campbell calling."

"*Who?!*"

Dave winced away from the phone. He knew Gladys Keating a little. Back when he first broke in to property law, he'd helped her sell a couple of vacant lots that her late husband had owned down in Murray River. Dave remembered Mrs. Keating as a sharp and suspicious woman, a walking, breathing genealogical record, a town chatterbox who knew everyone's business and always had some gossip, as juicy as a peach, to share. She was also, he remembered, a cranky old widow determined not be taken advantage of, especially now that her idiot husband was no longer around calling the shots. Yet, on this occasion, Dave wondered whether she was going soft in the ears, if not in the mind. How old would she be now? Eighty? No, she had to be closer to eighty-five.

"I said it's Dave Campbell, from Montague."

"Well hello there young fella," she said. "Long time no chat."

"Same to you. Listen, is your lovely son-in-law home?"

"No. He went up west for the weekend to see he's brother."

"Oh, I'm sorry I missed him. Listen, does he still have any of that there good topsoil he had before?"

Mrs. Keating let out a sound that was sort of a mix between *what* and *huh*. "Wha-uh?"

"Topsoil," Dave repeated. "Does he have any topsoil left?"

"Well, I'd *imagine*," she said. "There's still a big jeezly pile out in the backyard. I've been trying to convince him since last summer to just get rid of it."

"Great stuff. Listen, do you think he'd mind dropping off a truckload to a guy moving into a house over in Glenning?"

"Glenning?" she asked, and then paused. Paused for a quite a while. "There ain't been no houses for sale over in Glenning. None under construction neither. Not recently."

Oh, Mrs. Keating, you're just as gossip-sodden as ever. And definitely not *going mushy in the head.* "No, it's the owner of the older house further up the Eight Mile Road," he said. "The big place there. They used to call it Applegarth. Do you know it?"

She said nothing. The line went silent. Had she fallen asleep? Might she petition him again to repeat himself?

"Anyway," he went on, "he's moving into it and he wants to do some gardening." Still nothing on line. Dave wondered if the call had dropped. "Mrs. Keating?"

"Who might that be?" she asked darkly, and paused again. "What's he's name?"

"His name?" Dave asked with a laugh. This struck him as a weird question. "Fuller. Riley Fuller. Of *Moncton*," he added, just to disabuse her of the notion that she might know him. But then she let out a small sound on the line, a tiny gasp, as if she *did* know him, as if she did recognize that name. There was another, even lengthier pause on the line.

"So do you think Mike could bring him some topsoil?" Dave asked.

"No," Mrs. Keating replied finally. "No. I won't be sending Mikey up there. And certainly not Edna neither." She cleared her throat. "You tell Mr. Fuller that he'll need to get he's topsoil someplace else."

"Well, I must say, Mrs. Keating, that's not very neighbourly."

"Neighbourly?" she asked, her voice now like an engine revving. "Neighbourly, you say? Well tell me this, Dave Campbell of Montague. Is it neighbourly, I say, to *hypnotize* people against their will?" She herself sounded like she'd slipped into a trance. "Hypnotize them, and make them do things they don't want to do? Horrible, unspeakable things? To make like lie with like? Is it neighbourly, I say, to grow toxic crops off your land? Or to summon at your will the fox in the forest, the crow in the air, the jellyfish in the sea—all to do your awful, sinful bidding? Is that very *neighbourly*, Mr. Dave Campbell of Montague? You tell me that."

Dave swallowed. *What in the bloody blue Jesus was she going on about? Maybe she was going mushy in the head.*

"Mrs. Keating…?"

"I'm gonna go now," she said. "I gotta take me pills, and then I gotta get ready for bed. Not that I'll sleep well tonight, thanks to *you*."

And then she hung up on him.

~

April 28, 1995
Dear Sammy,
No, your eyes aren't playing tricks on you, buddy. That's my name in your inbox. Yep, it's true. After months of dragging my feet, I'm finally on the email bandwagon. I hope you get this message, as I'm still a little mistrustful of the whole "information superhighway." It feels like I'm talking into the ether.

How are you, my friend? I know you've been worried about me these last few months, so please consider this message an act of rumour control—especially if you're talking to the old gang back in Moncton. No, I have *not* driven off into the woods to kill myself. (At least not yet, haha.) Yes, I *have* moved to Prince Edward

Island. I think it's good for me to get some distance from Moncton. Bentley, my social worker, told me that might be the case, and he's right.

Sam, let me tell you how I ended up here, as I know you're probably curious. When a guy is both freshly divorced *and* on Off Duty Sick from his job, he has a lot of free time on his hands. I spent that time going through some old papers of my parents, and found that Pop had this deed to a property in eastern PEI that he never told me about or included in his estate. I checked, and sure enough it legitly belonged to him, which means it now legitly belongs to me. I didn't know anything about this old place before I got a couple of property lawyers here and in Moncton to help me with my research. I learned that the last person to occupy "Applegarth," as the house is called, was my grandfather, James Fuller, back in 1930. And I found out that it was built by *his* grandfather, whose name, believe it or not, was also Riley Fuller—and his brother, Robert, which is my middle name, oddly enough. Those two were business partners, apparently, and they built this place in the early 1860s. It eventually got passed down to James, who in turned passed it on to Dad.

But I must have a touch of James in me, because like me he also got divorced. He was an Anglican minister in Halifax but moved here in 1930 after he split up with my grandmother and she and my dad moved to Moncton. The story always went that James was a bit screwy in the head, and, as it turns out, actually killed himself in this house about six or seven months after moving into it. Nobody knows why. But before he died, he left it to my dad, who was just a little kid at the time, putting the property in a trust for him. But Pop didn't have much interest in it, I guess, and as far as I know, he never set foot on PEI. He didn't like to leave Moncton very often. Anyway, when Pop died four years ago, Applegarth legally became mine. I am the first person to occupy this house since 1930. It was just left to rot in the PEI countryside for sixty-five years.

Except it isn't rotting. For an old abandoned house, it's scary how sound it is. And huge. Holy shit, Sams. Seven bedrooms upstairs, plus this enormous library, which is where I'm writing this email from. You'd love this room, buddy—there's got to be 2,000 old books on the shelves up here. The dining room, on the first floor, is massive, as is the kitchen and living room. I've barely scratched the surface of the unfinished basement, and I haven't even been up to the attic yet. Still so much to explore.

But the house is old, don't get me wrong. It's taken all of April, and a lot of money, just to get it into good enough shape to move into. But at least I have lights over my head now, a toilet to shit in, and outlets that work. In fact, this will be my first night sleeping here, which I'm excited about. There's still so much work to do, but at least it's keeping my hands busy and my mind occupied, haha.

I will say, my move in here has attracted some attention from the locals, what with me ordering so many tradespeople and whatnot to come by and do stuff around the property. Apparently there's a little weekly newspaper over in Montague, and they're sending a reporter over next week to write a profile of me. I'm not looking forward to it. I hate talking, as you well know, and I hate talking about myself even more. But I agreed to it because I want to make nice with my curious neighbours, and I think most of the reporter's questions will be about the house anyway.

Okay. First email done. Please write back and tell me all your news. I hope things are well with Joan and the kids. What are the boys doing for the summer? Presumably soccer camp again? I miss you, brother. Here's my new mailing address, for your records:

Riley Fuller
Applegarth
RR#4, Glenning PE
C0A 1G0 Canada

Take care,
Riley

He hit SEND and watched as a little digital envelope with flapping angel wings fluttered across the screen and disappeared into the Outbox. Would Sammy get the message? Email seemed so mysterious to Riley, a phenomenon he wouldn't quite believe in until he saw his friend's reply come back. He shifted in his chair, which he had hauled up from the dining room. It wasn't the least bit comfortable, and Riley figured if he was going to spend a lot of time in front of this computer, he should invest in a proper office chair, with little arm rests and a cushioned seat.

Was he planning to spend a lot of time here? The question made him think once again of Bentley. At the very beginning of their relationship, when Riley's mental state had been at its worst, the social worker had given him some techniques to deal with things: a few breathing exercises and a relatively new treatment called Eye Movement Desensitization and Reprocessing (or EMDR), neither of which seemed to help. But Bentley had also asked: *Have you ever considered journaling?* Not only had Riley not considered journaling, but he hadn't even considered *journal* a verb. The idea of scribbling his thoughts into a diary made him think of writing end-of-term exams back when he was a teen and the hand cramps they caused. But this computer would eliminate that problem. *Could* he write his feelings down? Could he work through what... what had *happened* in Moncton, the events that still rippled like waves through his memory? Could he write about the disgrace of it all? Could he write about... about *her*? About her, and what she had done? Was that something he even wanted to do? It was worth considering, at least.

In the meantime, Riley booted down the computer, pulled its plastic shroud back over it, and thought about getting ready for bed.

Behind him, through the library's archway and down the hall, he thought he heard a sudden rustle. He stood and turned, his brow furrowing, and headed in the sound's direction. Moving through the long upstairs hall, its hardwood floor creaking and twisting beneath Riley's feet, he heard the sound again, louder than before. A crackle. A shuffle. A lurch. It seemed to be coming from near, or possibly above, the door leading into his bedroom. He looked up and around this space, the large landing at the top of the spiraling stairs, in front of the bathroom and just below the pull-down steps for the attic.

He heard the sound again.

Rats in the walls, he thought. *It's got to be that. I'll have to track down an exterminator to come here and deal with them. One more thing to put on my list.*

He headed to the ground floor to make sure all the doors were locked, a habit he'd developed while living in his downtown Moncton apartment. Then, returning to the spiral stairs and making his ascent, he looked up at the splash of radiance, a wide, pale octagon of luminance cast on the staircase's rear wall from the landing's light, a bulb Riley had installed barely a week ago.

Within that octagon, he saw what was clearly the silhouette of a man's legs dangling in the air.

Riley froze. His eyes widened. His hand moved reflexively to his hip, though there was no weapon there. He stopped and stared at those legs as they swayed ever so gently before him, like a hypnotist's pendulum. The sound he had heard before now returned. Not a crackle. Or a shuffle. Or a lurch. It was the sound of a hemp rope, stricken by a man's weight, creaking against a wooden beam. Riley knew that his grandfather, James Fuller, had killed himself, had *hanged himself*, in this house back in 1930. That fact, if Riley were honest, had never been far from his mind from the moment he set foot on PEI. And now, he was staring up at the shadowy shape of those dead limbs, the black, looming figure of—

The legs suddenly juddered downward, a scarecrow's dance, as the attic's collapsible stairs crashed open like an accordion toward the landing floor. The sound peeled across Riley's ears and filled the house like a shotgun blast.

He rushed up the rest of the stairs, making the turn toward the landing, fully expecting to see the corpse of James Fuller suspended from those rickety steps. It was such a horror movie cliché, he thought, what he was about to see: the bloated face purple with rot, the old-timey clothes, the neck twisted at a ghoulish, unholy angle, the deep, hollow eyes staring out as if in accusation. In one instant, Riley was prepared to submit himself to utter madness at such a sight.

He reached the top of the landing, and found nothing there. The space was as empty as he'd left it. The attic steps were still in the ceiling. Nothing floated before the lightbulb's sodium glow. There was a slight *crick-crick-cricking* sound coming from behind the landing's plaster, but that was all. *Rats in the walls*, Riley thought, and allowed himself a short, harsh swallow. Then he laughed. Actually laughed. *You fucking moron,* he said to himself. *You're going to scare yourself half to death.*

~

That night, his first sleeping under Applegarth's roof, Riley did something that he hadn't done in a long, long time. He jerked off. He hadn't planned to, hadn't felt the urge until after he'd settled under the sheets. But then, behind his closed and twitching eyes, images began to flicker and surge through his brain. They weren't quite like porn, not that he'd seen a lot of porn in his day. They were something else. The women in these visions—and there were multiple women—were gorgeous, nubile girls barely out of their teens, and yet… and yet also like old friends, like people Riley had known all his life in some other world. Soon they were all over him in the dream, these stranger-friends, all over him and other men who abruptly joined Riley in the vision. Soon they were all together, being together, everyone together. This was not anything Riley had fantasized about before, but he surrendered over to it now, yielding with great relish to what the theatre of his mind suddenly wanted to show him. *God*, he thought. *God… DAMN.*

Riley first touched himself, then stroked himself, then pounded himself, there in the bed. It took no time at all. He cried out, louder than he thought possible, his body rising up in a torqued arch before collapsing back down onto the mattress.

Afterward, still heaving breathlessly in the sheets, he couldn't even bring himself to go to the bathroom and clean up. He just fell into a sticky, delicious sleep, the best he'd had in longer than he could remember.

~

The next day, a Saturday, Riley drove into Charlottetown to visit the big Canadian Tire there and make a few larger purchases he'd need delivered to the house: a ride-on mower (the lawn was already starting to go wild again), a wheel barrow, a swing seat he wanted to install on Applegarth's porch. He also popped by the local Zellers—there were countless household items that he kept realizing he needed: a fresh dish rack (the one he'd brought over from Moncton was getting funky), a pair of oven mitts, hooks for the bathroom, a couple of stand-up fans for when summer came and the days got hot. He loaded these items into the Lumina's trunk and then drove back to Glenning via a more scenic route, cruising along PEI's north shore before passing through places with names like Saint Peters Bay and Albion Cross. *Frig, the Island is pretty*, Riley thought, clasping a cigarette out of the side of his mouth and blaring the Eagles from the car's tape deck as he drove. He was struck once again by that daylight feeling he now frequently had: that PEI was his new domain, that he was the master of his life once again, that he had put the traumas of Moncton behind him and embraced a new and welcome chapter to his days.

He eventually found his way back to the more desolate Eight Mile Road, pulled up to the top of Applegarth's long driveway, parked and killed the engine. Popping the trunk and getting out, Riley moved to fetch out his purchases.

As he did, his gaze panned across the driveway and over to the side lawn. And that's when he saw them.

Riley paused a moment, sort of blinked, and then gave a half smile.

He walked over and stood before the two garden plots there, the stone rings forming their kidney shapes on the ground. Inside those shapes, raked to perfect smoothness, were two long, glorious beds of topsoil. Riley squatted down in front of the nearest one, clawed a casual hand through the dirt, and marveled at the sight before him. *You're a good man, Dave Campbell,* he thought. *I had a feeling you'd pull through for me.*

This was, Riley thought, really excellent topsoil. Some good PEI dirt. It was, in fact, the rusty-red colour that the Island's dirt was famous for.

He went back to the Lumina, hauled out his purchases and brought them into the house, then went to the phone to call Campbell in Montague. Being Saturday, he wouldn't get him at the office, but Campbell had also given Riley his home number, and that's where he reached him now.

"Dave? Hey, it's Riley Fuller calling."

"Well hello there," Campbell replied. "You know, *I* was just thinking of calling *you*. Brilliant minds."

"Listen, I wanted to thank you for scoring me the topsoil. I can't believe how much is out there. You really came through."

There was a pause on the line. A long one.

"I'm sorry?" Campbell asked.

"Just thanking you for the topsoil."

"Riley, I wasn't able to get you any topsoil."

"What?" Riley asked, baffled. "What do you mean?"

"No, my friend, I ran into an issue with the person I'd thought could give you some. It was the weirdest thing. That's what I was going to call you about."

Riley sort of blinked. "Well, *somebody* gave me topsoil."

There was another briefer silence on the phone. "You're pulling my chain, right?" Campbell asked.

"No. I'm telling you—there are two big mounds of it out in my garden."

"Well, that's a hell of a thing. I don't know who else I might have told that you needed topsoil. I'm trying to think. I must have blabbed it to somebody here in Montague, I guess. Whoever it was must have found you some and brought it over."

"They did more than that," Riley said. "They poured it right into the plots, raked it, smoothed it all out for me. It looks fucking fantastic." It was Riley's turn to pause. He swallowed. Cleared his throat. "Dave, you're pulling *my* chain, right?"

"No way. I'm telling you. I don't know who brought you that soil."

Riley just blinked again. He couldn't believe it. He had wanted some topsoil, and the universe had provided him some—as if it were an entitlement. It *felt* like an entitlement.

"Anyway," Campbell went on, "here's to neighbours who do nice things without getting caught."

"I should let you go," Riley said.

"Okay, but if you solve the mystery of the magically appearing soil, you let me know."

But Riley didn't reply. He just hung up. Standing there next to the living room end table where he'd set up the phone, his breath grew uneven. The late April light coming through the windows had turned faint, silvery, ominous. He took another shaky inhale, then left the living room, crossed the foyer, and headed out the doors. He walked over the driveway to the side lawn. Stood before the garden there, the garden he had barely touched, and yet looked so incredibly perfect now.

The soil really was gorgeous, he thought. It spread out evenly across both beds, ready for seeding and tending and growth. The dirt almost seemed to breathe.

Riley squatted down in front of the plots again, his back to Applegarth. His eye caught something it hadn't before. He leaned in to get a closer look, puzzlement narrowing his hazel eyes.

There, in one small part of the nearest plot, he could see a tiny row of... of sprouts, already poking up through the rich red soil. They were almost imperceptible, easy enough to miss when he'd first examined this strange new garden. But there they were, the tiniest greens, like little verdant threads, reaching up and out of the Island dirt, looking just as delicate as you please. There were sprouts growing there despite the early season, the still-chilly air, and the fact that this soil hadn't even *been* there three hours earlier, when Riley had left for town. *Well I'll be*, he thought.

He stood up again and turned back to face the house.

His eyes were hauled upward then, to the heights of Applegarth's rambling, shambling roof.

He froze.

There was suddenly no breath in his lungs, no strength in his legs at the sight in front of him. How could he have missed these before, when he'd pulled up the driveway? Were his eyes failing him? Was he going crazy?

Riley could see that the gables of Applegarth gleamed with fresh red paint.

The rest of the house was still that hornet's nest grey, that anti-colour left by dozens of battering PEI winters. But the gables shone like new. The paint there, a deep velvety red, almost matched the colour of the garden's soil.

Riley's mouth fell open. For one moment, he thought again that the light was playing pranks on him. Or was it maybe neighbourhood kids? Punks over in Glenning or Cardigan who came onto your property and, instead of smashing your windows and toilet-papering your trees, painted your gables for you and planted a garden? A garden that could grow sprouts instantly?

No, Riley mused. That was a ridiculous thought. But some less ridiculous thoughts came pushing into his mind then. *I am the absentee landlord here, just like Dave Campbell said. And my tenants are trying to please me. Please me by planting a garden and painting my gables and... and filling my head with* certain kinds of visions *when I slip into bed at night.*

These notions felt like an entitlement, too. Things he was owed for what he had lost, what he had cost himself, back in Moncton. They too felt like a gift from the universe, which is why, standing there in his yard, Riley was able to put them out of his mind and go back inside.

CHAPTER 7

A baby blue Dodge Caravan turned into Applegarth's driveway, pulled up close to the house, and parked. To Riley's eyes, the rusty, worn-down vehicle looked about seven or eight years old, and the girl who climbed out of it, no more than twenty. She wore shiny brown boots that went nearly to her knees, deep-navy jeans, and a puffy nylon vest for spring. Her wavy, crow-black hair was parted on one side and tucked behind her ears. From the swing seat he had just finished installing on Applegarth's porch, Riley watched as the girl took a small canvas kitbag with her from the van, slinging it over one shoulder after she slammed the driver door shut.

She came up the front lawn and approached the porch. "Mr. Fuller?" she called over.

"That would be me."

"Hi. I'm Jessie MacIntosh, from the *Eastern Pioneer*. You spoke to my boss, Jack Mackenzie, last week?"

"I did."

"Are you still okay to talk today?"

Riley took a drag on his cigarette. "Good a time as any," he answered, eying her closely as she scaled the porch. He sat forward a little in the swing seat, its frame tipping under his weight. "I hope you don't mind me asking," he said, "but how old are you? You seem a bit young to be a journalist."

She laughed this off. "I get that a lot. I'm twenty. I just wrapped up my second year of journalism school in Halifax. I'm home for the summer and working for the *Pioneer*. Jack's been great to give me a chance. I've been hounding him for a reporter job since my last year of high school."

Riley nodded at that and crushed out his cigarette into the ashtray on the swing seat's arm. He offered Jessie the pack.

"Oh, no thank you. I don't smoke." She set her kitbag down on the floor of the porch, undid its straps, and took out a steno pad and pen. She flipped over the steno's first few pages. "I'm actually very excited to talk to you today," she said. "I've lived in Glenning my whole life and nobody has ever occupied this house, not since before my parents were born. You moving in has been the most exciting thing to happen around here in a while." She turned then, briefly, to look behind her. "Say, is that porch rail stable enough to sit on?"

Riley shrugged. "Only one way to find out."

He watched as she hopped up onto it with ease, a lithe, almost athletic move. The rail wobbled for a moment under her slim weight but then held firm—something Riley couldn't have imagined it doing on his first day at this house, though he'd done no work to strengthen or repair the rail since. In spite of himself, he eyed up Jessie again as she sat there with her legs now dangling and the opened steno resting on her thigh. She *was* young, looked even younger than twenty. She could almost pass for seventeen.

Jessie uncapped the pen and hovered it over her notepad. "Just to begin," she said, "can you confirm the spelling of your first and last name?"

Riley did, reciting each letter in turn. She wrote them down.

"And how old are *you*?" she asked, looking up.

"Forty-five."

"And where are you from, originally?"

"Moncton."

"And what do you do for a living?"

Riley plucked a fresh smoke from his pack, lit it. "I was RCMP," he said, and watched as she again lifted her gaze from the pad and locked onto him. It was then that he noticed Jessie's eye colour—a steely, striking grey, with the tiniest black pupils, which matched her hair colour, in the centre. "Sorry, I *am* RCMP," he corrected.

Had he already said too much? She was staring at him intently now. Would this girl know about what had happened in Moncton, the shit that had gone down there? Might she have heard or read about it in the news? Jessie would have been in her first year of journalism school then, he calculated. So probably.

"*Was* or *am*?" she asked.

"I'm on what's called Off Duty Sick, or ODS," he said. "It's sort of like long-term disability."

She looked at him even more intently. He could see her mind turning, trying to connect distant dots in her brain. He had been wrong, he now realized, to mistake her for even younger than twenty. There was a cool, youthful wisdom in that Cheshire stare of hers. A reporter's stare. He thought: she's going to figure it out, and suddenly her story is going to be very different than the one she came here to write.

But just as quickly as it arrived, Jessie's frigid curiosity melted away. She was a kid again. "ODS?" she asked, and gave him another little smile. "Sounds rather *odious*, right?"

"Huh. That's funny," Riley said without laughing.

"So tell me: how did you come to move into," and here, she nodded to the wooden blue plaque nailed to the porch wall, "*Applegarth*?"

So he recounted the story for her, the same one he told Sammy in that first email. Jessie scribbled and scribbled.

"And what's it like moving into an abandoned house this old?" she asked. "What have been the challenges to making it livable?"

He told her about his long parade of renos on Applegarth over the last few weeks. For every one problem he solved, he said, about five more seemed to crop up in its place. Which was fine by him, since he had the time and inclination to put the effort in.

"And what's it like living in what is essentially your ancestral home?" Jessie asked. "Is there anything special you've noticed about the house? Anything that caught you off guard?"

Riley almost laughed at her. "Oh well, these old places keep a lot of secrets," he said, taking a long and thoughtful drag on his cigarette. He knew, from watching his fellow officers or the PR people on the force talk to journalists, that the answer he gave to this question would become the heart of the story. Reporters were like that, Riley knew. They asked you two or three Nerf-Ball questions off the top to soften you up, to make you feel comfortable, and then the fourth or fifth question, and the answers you provided, became the information relayed in the lead paragraph, if not the guts of the whole article. That was how it worked. He cleared his throat. "Applegarth's secrets seem to be in its very floorboards," he went on. "Every step I take makes the whole house twist and creak. It's a little eerie, but you know what? I feel comfortable here. Very much like my old self. I *do* sense my family's presence inside these walls, even though I never met them. It calms me to be under Applegarth's roof."

Jessie looked up from her pad. "So any chance I could get a tour?" she asked.

Riley shrugged, crushed out his cigarette, and stood up. He opened Applegarth's front door and made a gesture to welcome her in. Jessie hopped down off the porch rail, grabbed her bag, and headed through the threshold. Starting with the parlour, Riley gave her essentially the same tour Campbell had given him. He allowed Jessie to take the lead as they went, not only to let her encounter each room and alcove without his editorializing, but also because he *still*, even now, didn't like people coming up behind him. As they moved through the house, he became self-conscious of how incredibly shabby and run down it still was. From certain angles, the walls appeared to be on the brink of crumbling. Dust coated countless surfaces. A musty, almost fecal smell he still hadn't managed to flush out clung faintly to the air. It often took having somebody in your personal space, he thought, to make you aware of everything wrong with it.

Still, the girl seemed genuinely intrigued by Applegarth, once again tucking her hair behind her ear as she gazed at the ceilings and wainscoting, the floor and baseboards, and the wide wooden archways throughout the house. "So sorry, can you remind me," she asked, "who helped you move into Applegarth in the first place?"

"Dave Campbell, the property lawyer in Montague. He worked with my Moncton guy to confirm that the deed I had was legit, and he did a bunch of other stuff for me, too."

"Do you think I could speak to him for my story?"

"I doubt that would be a problem."

She asked Riley more questions as they wandered, jotting the occasional answer in her notepad. Finally, they arrived at the house's huge second-floor library. Riley could already tell this was going to be Jessie's favourite room.

"Oh wow," she said, drifting into its wide and welcoming centre, then turning and turning, almost like a kitten chasing its tail. "Look at these shelves—look at these old books!" Her grey eyes lit up.

"They were here when I moved in," he told her.

"Wow," she said again. "What a fantastic space."

"I do like it up here," Riley said. "I mean, I'm not much of a reader, but it's a cozy spot to retreat to after a long day."

She nodded toward the big writing desk in the corner. "And the computer?" she asked, gesturing with a smile to the hulking machine under its plastic shroud. "I'm assuming that didn't come with the house."

"No, I *just* bought that. Finally got myself on email and the web. I'm probably the last person to do so."

She turned around once more to face Riley. "Can *I* have your email address?" she asked. "In case I think of more questions to ask later?"

A sudden, unwelcome warmth burst in Riley's gut, a certain pleasant tightening, a lift in his nether regions as Jessie stared, waiting for his answer. In spite of himself, Riley began thinking thoughts, little visions akin to the sexualized cinema that had flashed and flickered through his mind on the first night he had slept under this roof. But then he pushed them away, mildly disgusted with himself. *Jesus, Fuller*, he thought, *what the fuck's the matter with you? Seriously, she's less than half your age. Knock it off.*

Applegarth settled onto itself then, creaking and cracking all on its own.

"Sure thing," Riley said, and recited the address to her so she could write it in her steno.

They soon began making their way down through the house and eventually back onto the porch. "Do you mind if I take your photo for the article?" Jessie asked when they did.

"I suppose that would be fine."

So she squatted on the porch floor with her bag and dug out what looked like a relatively inexpensive Nikon. She twisted dials with her thumbs and then stood, raising the camera to her face and pointing it at him. Riley shifted on one foot, sort of grimaced. No, it was more than that. He flinched. He didn't like having things pointed at him. Not at all.

Jessie lifted her face above the camera, managed to both smile and furrow her brow at him, then lowered it back down. She did this a second time. "Look, I didn't bring any sock puppets with me today," she said behind the lens, "but do you think you could smile anyhow?"

Riley couldn't help himself. He burst out laughing at that. Jesus, she *was* cheeky. He sort of loved how forward she was with him.

SNAP SNAP SNAP went the camera.

He settled into a more austere grin, his cheeks barely ballooning toward his eyes.

SNAP SNAP SNAP went the camera, and then Jessie lowered it again. "Thanks, that's great," she said.

After they were done, Riley walked her back to her vehicle. It really was an old beater of a minivan: he could see a large scab of rust over the back driver-side wheel well, a giant burgundy P. He and Jessie stood there for a bit, chatting idly, but he soon realized how she was squeezing other details, with cagey nonchalance, out of him—that he was recently divorced, that he had no kids, that he was thinking seriously of staying on PEI but had made no moves to transfer to one of the RCMP detachments here. Of course, they were still on the record, and he wondered again what sort of story she might write.

"Anyway," she said, popping open the minivan's door and chucking her kitbag back in, "if I think of anything else to ask, can I give you a call, or maybe send you an email?"

"Sure, whatever you want," he replied, pulling out his pack of smokes and sticking one in his mouth. "Say, when will the article run?"

"Well, it's too late to make it into this week's edition, but next week for sure. You'll find lots of copies around Montague."

"Okay."

"Thanks again for speaking to me," she said as she scooted up into the driver's seat. "Jack and I really appreciate it."

She shut the door and started the engine. Then she gave him a wave, a little twiddle of her fingers that made Riley's heart lurch. Before he could wave back, she turned over her shoulder with a look of more earnest care and began backing her Caravan down the long driveway to the road.

After she was gone, Riley stood there and finished his cigarette before heading back inside the house. He knew what he was going to do next. He knew exactly. God, it was so gross. What was wrong with him? She was just a *kid*. Still, did it matter? There was nobody here to see or hear him; nobody to judge his actions. He headed upstairs and into his room. Standing before the bed, he pulled his shirt up and off himself, then unbuckled his jeans and lowered them, along with his boxer shorts, to his ankles. Then he turned and lay himself atop the duvet, his long, thick legs dangling over the side of the mattress.

After he finished, he thought: *Jesus, Fuller. That's like, three times in one week. What are you, some kind of horny teenage boy again? Jesus. What is the* matter *with you?*

~

By nightfall, that tickle of revulsion had turned into all-out self-loathing, as bad as any he had felt before. So Riley decided to roam, to wander Applegarth's nooks and hallways, to move up and down through the house, ascending and descending the spiral staircase and the stone steps that led to the basement, then all the way back up again. *If you need to roam*, Bentley had said, *then you bloody well roam.*

It didn't help. How could it? *You practically undressed that girl with your eyes today*, Riley chastised himself, *thinking your filthy little thoughts. You envisioned the sort of behaviour—the* exact *sort of behaviour, Riley—that got you into this mess in the first place, that destroyed everything with Jane. How could you do that? Have you learned nothing from what happened in Moncton, you piece of shit? How could you fucking do that?*

The crackle of pistol fire shook through his memory. *POP! POP! POP! POP!* Behind Riley's eyes, three of his colleagues fell to the winter ground, splaying out in a circle around him, their blood spreading like giant Rorschach tests through the snow.

He flinched at this vision in mid-descent. He had to grab the staircase's banister to steady himself.

No.

No amount of roaming could banish all this from his head. Those thoughts were like a rotting tooth, a decay inside his brain. After a breath, Riley continued down into the kitchen and opened the drawer where he kept the Glock. He took it out, picked up the magazine—laden with tightly stacked rounds, ready to go—and palmed it into the handle with one quick slap. He shuffled, almost zombie-like, with the now loaded Glock into Applegarth's living room and sat on his floral-patterned couch. Resting the weapon on his thigh, as he had done on so many nights before, Riley slowly counted his inhales and exhales. Was he really going to shoot himself, here in this house? Could he join his grandfather, James, in an act of suicide? Would it feel right? Or would it, he wondered, feel like a failure?

You're stalling, he thought. *What are you waiting for? Do you think things are going to get better, if you just butch it out? Do you think these thoughts are ever going to leave you? You fucking piece of shit. Do you honestly think you're a better man than you were three years go? Fuck you. You proved today that you are not. So what are you waiting for? What do you think is going to happen? What do you think is going to change? This Glock is your answer. It's your escape hatch.*

He raised the gun, tucked the muzzle under his chin, and looked at the ceiling.

But then he heard Bentley's voice once again: *Have you ever considered journaling?*

Riley turned his thoughts to the second floor, to the library at the other end of the house. He slowly lowered the Glock. After a moment, he released the magazine and cleared the chamber. After another moment, he got up and carried the weapon back to the kitchen and returned it to its drawer. Then he headed upstairs to the library. Going inside, he stood in front of the desk, the computer, for a few seconds before lifting the plastic cover off and settling in. He booted up that big grey machine. It took forever, the hard drive whirling and spluttering. While he waited, Riley thought: *Wow, this really does feel like a therapy of last resort. How will I even begin? This this be like writing just another police report?* Eventually, he found his way into the computer's word-processing program, and launched a fresh document. Then he rested his fingers on the keyboard's fat, plastic keys. He took a breath. Then he just started typing.

May 2, 1995
Dear Diary, or Journal, or whatever the fuck you are,
Day 5 in Applegarth: I am feeling very low tonight.
Fact: I am a piece of fucking garbage. I am shit.
Fact: I have betrayed *everything* that meant anything to me. My wife, my friendships, my colleagues, my name.
Fact: There is nothing I can do, not one fucking thing, to take back all the hurt I caused. Fact: there is nothing I can do to bring back the men killed, the lives that were taken, and all the other lives that were ruined, because of the terrible decisions I made.
Especially hers. My sweet Marigold. *Her* ruined life.
Fact: Chris Bentley, my social worker, advises that writing all this down might help. *Have you ever considered journaling?* he once asked me. So here I am, journaling.
Question: What good can it do?
Question: Will I ever not feel ashamed? Will ever be able to let go of what I have done, no matter how much distance I get from it?
Fact: This house may have something to say about that.

Riley stopped typing and looked over what he wrote. Should he delete it? Part of him wanted to, but another part told him he shouldn't.
Leave it. Just... leave it, for posterity.

He clicked on the little floppy-disk icon to save what he'd written, the hard drive pumping and whirring like a washing machine. He named the file that popped up JOURNALING.

Chapter 8

Jessie MacIntosh sat in front of a Macintosh, her face illuminated by the blue-white glow of its screen. She poised her fingers over the keyboard as she struggled to type the next sentence of her story. No matter how long she stared at that thick blinking cursor, it simply refused to dance. This was strange. In the two years since becoming a journalism student in Halifax, and, now, as a summer intern back on PEI, she'd *never* gotten writer's block, especially when on a deadline. What was wrong with her tonight? Here, in the early evening hours, she had the office of the *Eastern Pioneer* weekly newspaper (*The Voice of Kings & Eastern Queens County!*) to herself. The person she shared this computer with—a pug-faced, middle-aged woman named Maggie McKenna, the only other dedicated full-time reporter on staff—had already gone home for the night, and their boss, publisher Jack Mackenzie, had driven to Charlottetown to chase some story or other. The office's quietude should have liberated Jessie's mind and hands, but tonight, it seemed to do the opposite.

"Office" was a bit of misnomer. Located on the second floor of a two-storey building on Main Street in Montague, the *Pioneer*'s space closely resembled a barn loft. At the very back of the floor was Jack's small, squat office. Three of his four walls were glass, so that he could look out over his "newsroom," and the fourth, the wood-paneling behind where he sat, looked from a distance like a green and red fresco, a kind of Christmasy mural. In actuality, it was a museum-like display that Jack had set up of the now-faded political buttons and stickers—YES and NO—from the plebiscite held seven years ago about whether the Island should build that bridge to the mainland. Jessie knew that Jack considered the bridge to be the defining issue of PEI's recent history, one that divided Islanders so contentiously. She'd learned while still in high school that Jack had written no fewer than *forty* stories about the bridge debate in the six weeks leading up to the plebiscite, a one-man editorial machine. She knew then that she just *had* to work for him.

Now that she did, she learned that Jack was a true Jack of all trades: he did a little bit of everything for the paper—wrote news articles, wrote opinion pieces, sold advertising, laid the paper out, and even drove bundles of it around in his car after it was printed, delivering copies to subscribers and businesses. Just outside his office, near the centre of the floor, was a desk used by his wife, Helen, who came in two or three days a week to sell ads, type up the classifieds, and do whatever office management needed doing. Directly across from her was the desk that Jessie sat at now, grappling with her story. At the front of the floor, near the steps leading up from the entry downstairs, was the *Pioneer*'s "lobby." Here were the wooden cubbyholes where a tiny stable of freelance columnists could drop off their monthly pieces. Most came as typed-up pages in a manila envelope, but a couple of the writers had recently switched to computers and dropped off a floppy disk instead. All of the freelancers were retirees and didn't really need the 7¢ a word Jack was paying them. A couple of the columnists would occasionally bring their portable typewriters to the office and set themselves up to write on the spare desk in the far corner. Jessie *loved* those days. With the columnist clacking and smoking away, Jessie and Maggie sharing the computer in between phone interviews, Helen selling ads, and Jack in his office, puffing away on his pipe as he worked, the joint felt like a real newspaper, a viable business.

There was none of that energy tonight. Inside the upped hood of her sweatshirt, Jessie wore the headphones of her Discman as she worked, but considered moving the album she was listening to (Hole's *Live through This*) to the boom box she'd set up on the brick ledge behind her, now that she had the place to herself. She *loved* listening to music, the louder the better, when she was pounding out a story, and didn't understand other writers—her coworkers here at the paper, or her classmates back in Halifax—who didn't. Immigrating the CD to the boom box would give Jessie an excuse to get up and move her body, to mosh around a bit and get the juices flowing. But she decided against it. Jack could walk in any minute, and he'd *hate* Courtney Love, her raging songs.

Jessie hit SAVE on her story yet again despite having written only half a sentence in the last twenty minutes. Usually, if she gave herself ninety minutes to write an article, she'd need half that time to get the lede just right, but then the other four or five paragraphs would flow pretty quickly after that. But not with this piece. MAN MOVES INTO HOUSE wasn't exactly a scintillating news hook, especially for the *Pioneer*, a scrappy, award-winning local weekly that kept the puff pieces and "grip and grins" to a minimum. The problem was that Jessie couldn't figure out the focus of the story. Was it Riley Fuller, or the house he'd moved into? Fuller *did* divulge some interesting facts about himself—that he was on long-term disability from the Moncton RCMP (what was up with *that*?), that he was divorced, that he might very well stay permanently on PEI. But would all that, as Jack might put it, make for "a *dinger* of a story," one with broad appeal to the community? And yes, the abandoned house he'd moved into, the place called Applegarth, was big and rambling and older than salt, but it was also way out on the arse end of Glenning's Eight Mile Road, and few locals would even know it existed. Was the fact that it was occupied again after so many decades really *newsworthy*?

Jessie understood that the guts of the article would be the connection between Fuller's story and Applegarth's, but so far that intersection had eluded her. She'd need to figure it out, and fast: she was meeting her friends at the Boar's Head Pub up the street in an hour and didn't want to be late. The plan was to have a couple of drinks and then head out to Petit Point for a bonfire. They were all counting on Jessie to get them out there: she was the one with wheels, and a minivan no less.

The album ended and she hit the OPEN button on her Discman, popping it apart like a clam shell. She gingerly pulled the CD free and returned it to its case. Just as she was thinking about what to play next, she heard the door downstairs open and close, and then someone was hustling up the steps.

It was Jack. He came puffing into the office and over to where she sat. He had, she noticed, a folder under his arm and an urgent look on his face.

"Jessie-Mac," he said as he approached, the slightest hint of a Scotsman's brogue on his voice, "have you written your story about the cop moving into that old house over in Glenning yet?"

"I'm just hacking it out now. Why?"

He slapped the folder onto her desk. "Check that out," he said.

Jessie looked at him curiously, then opened the folder. Inside, she found photocopies Jack had made of the Moncton *Times & Transcript*. Front-page stories from seventeen months ago.

"When you told me he was Moncton RCMP," Jack said, "I bloody *knew* there was more to his story than he was letting on."

Jessie's eyes grew wide as she read over those blaring headlines and the sensational ledes beneath them.

"Holy shit," she said, looking back up at Jack. She realized then that there was no way she'd be meeting up with her friends at the Boar's Head tonight.

~

May 8, 1995
Dear Sammy,
Just a quick email to say your housewarming gift arrived in the mail today. Thanks for that. You know I'm not much of a reader, especially of poetry, but I will give these books a try if you vouch for them.

Sorry to hear your trip to Toronto was such a bust. Wow, it's a real shame that someone would pay good money to fly you out there and then have only 10 people show up for your thing. I hope your ego isn't too stung by that.

Thanks for asking about the house. The renos and repairs feel endless. I spent part of the weekend buying a bed and dresser for one of the *six* spare rooms up here, in case you and Joan might want to pop over for a visit this summer. I set them up in the room closest to the library. I thought you'd appreciate that, haha. But, to be fair, there's still so much work to do on Applegarth before I can host overnight company.

Anyway, Sams, write me back when you get a chance. I love this email thing. It makes me feel less alone.

Best,
Riley

After reading the note over, he hit SEND and watched it flutter off and disappear into the Outbox. Riley then shut the computer down and got up from the desk. He took the small pile of books Sammy had sent and tried to find some shelf space where he could put them. There was very little here in the library proper, but inside the second-storey turret, against its back wall, there was a bookcase that still had a bit of room. Riley went inside and put the books on the shelf there, laying them flat and perpendicular to the wall, instead of standing them up, as a reminder to read them. He'd be able to see the books through the turret's archway from where he sat at the desk, a visual cue that he needed to give them a try once he had a bit of time.

Riley started to go, but just as he did, there came another loud, lumbering lurch. It shuttered outward from behind the bookshelf, somewhere beyond its back wall. The sound seemed to rattle the very shell of the turret, almost echoed through it like a voice. He stopped, there in the archway, and looked back.

Returning to the shelf, to where he had set Sammy's books down, Riley looked over at the stack of vertical texts next to them. The noise seemed to have come from there. These volumes, he could now see, were not actually books at all. They were hardback leather-bound journals, three of them, standing dustily on the shelf with a number on each of their spines, handwritten on the little baby-blue label there: one to three. Riley looked at them curiously. Had he not seen these before, when he was in here to clean? They did look inconspicuous, their spines roughly the same colour as the other volumes here, that swampy, black-green shade of leather that was everywhere in this library. Only their slimness and the handwritten number on their spines gave them away as journals.

Riley reached up and pulled down the third volume, turned it over in his hands, and looked at the front cover. There, in the centre of it, he saw another, larger label, the same shade of faint blue as the one on the spine. On this label was written:

The private diary
of
Riley Fuller

He recoiled a little at the sight of it, hauling a deep intake of air through his nostrils. Staring at those words, Riley thought, was like looking into a mirror and seeing a face that wasn't quite your own. He knew that his grandfather's grandfather, one of the two men who had built Applegarth, was also named Riley Fuller.

Very carefully, Riley opened the cover and looked at the first page inside. There, on the top line, in thin, spidery ink, aged but still legible, was a date:

13 September 1863

Below that were the words *Dear Diary*, and below *them* was a manic, frantic block of handwritten text.

Riley looked over the words without really reading them, then cast his eyes back up to the shelf. Had these volumes been sitting here for nearly a century and a half? Riley guessed that they had. He lowered his eyes back to the open page in his hands, read the first few sentences of that first entry, but couldn't make sense of them. They began *in medias res*—a term Sammy had taught him—and seemed a bit panicked. Riley had no context for what he was reading. So he closed the volume and carefully put it back in its place on the shelf, and then took down the journal on the far-left side of the set, the one labeled "1." On its cover was the same note: *The Private Diary of Riley Fuller*. He opened it—again, very carefully—and looked at the date on the first page:

28 April 1862

There was, of course, another block of handwritten text here, though less desperately scribbled than in the third volume. Riley read the first few words below that date.

Dear Diary,
Today, Robert and I finally completed our move into Applegarth. We are in our new home at last.

Riley stopped reading, right then and there. Something in those words had unsettled him, had caused a queer, kinetic bolt of unease to race up his spine.

It was the date. The date at the top of that first entry in that first volume.

It took him less than a second to realize the coincidence. Hadn't he too moved into Applegarth on April 28? He had. He had spent his first night under this roof exactly 133 years after his grandfather's grandfather had—*to the day.*

And suddenly, it didn't feel like a coincidence at all. A chill came over Riley then. He tried to shake it off. *Fucking ridiculous*, he thought. *What are you telling yourself, Fuller? What is your mind trying to imply?*

He closed the volume and shoved it back into its place on the bookshelf. It and the other two journals stared back, taunting him with their windows into another world.

He shambled out of the library and headed back downstairs. There was a bottle of Jim Beam, that Sweet Lady Bourbon, waiting for him in the kitchen. He would drink the whole thing before this night was through.

Chapter 9

From the Montague *Eastern Pioneer*. May 11, 1995:

RCMP OFFICER INVOLVED IN MONCTON ATTACK MOVES TO GLENNING
by Jessica MacIntosh—summer intern

A Moncton RCMP officer at the heart of the December 1993 shooting that left three of his colleagues dead has moved to the community of Glenning, the *Eastern Pioneer* has learned.

Riley Fuller, 45, settled into the large, Victorian-style home out on the Eight Mile Road in late April. Fuller inherited the house, which is known colloquially as Applegarth, from the estate of his father, who passed away in 1991. The house, which was built in the early 1860s, has sat abandoned for 65 years. It was last inhabited by Fuller's grandfather, who occupied it briefly in 1930.

Fuller made headlines in late 1993 and early 1994 following an attack at the RCMP headquarters on Main Street in Moncton, an event that shook that city to its core. Marigold Burque, 25, originally from Bouctouche, NB, shot and killed three officers on the night of December 13, 1993—Csts Roy Nadon, Howard (Howie) Doodnaught, and Dale Sloka—as they enjoyed a cigarette break in the parking lot behind the headquarters. Fuller was with the other officers at the time but Burque did not shoot him, and he did not draw his service weapon on her.

It came to light as part of the investigation that Fuller had been involved in an extramarital affair with

Burque dating back to early 1992, and this most likely explained why she didn't kill him as well.

The motive behind the attack remains unclear, though there was speculation that Burque—who had had several run-ins with Moncton police dating back to her early teens—had been sexually assaulted by a group of RCMP officers approximately ten days before the shooting. She is currently serving three consecutive life sentences at the New Brunswick Women's Correctional Centre in Chatham, NB.

Fuller, now divorced from his wife and on long-term leave from the RCMP, has stayed tight-lipped about his role in the tragedy. He may very well have moved to Prince Edward Island to put the awful events of that night behind him. "I feel very comfortable here," he says of the old house in Glenning, "very much like my old self. I *do* sense my family's presence inside these walls, even though I never met them. It calms me to be under Applegarth's roof."

The house has remained in Fuller's bloodline since its construction, and he has spent the last month restoring it. The manse contains seven bedrooms, a solarium, a grand dining room, and a large library. "It's been a lot of work," Fuller says, "but that's okay. It's kept my mind and my hands busy."

David Campbell, a property lawyer in Montague, assisted Fuller in confirming the legitimacy of the deed Fuller had found in his deceased father's papers, and has helped him with other aspects of the move into Applegarth. "I was shocked by how good of shape the house was in," Campbell says. "For an old place that has sat empty for most of the last century, it's held up surprisingly well." Campbell says he had no knowledge of Fuller's involvement in the Moncton shooting prior to speaking to the *Pioneer*.

It is unknown whether Fuller will remain permanently on PEI, or whether he will ever return to active service with the Mounties. For now, he says he is happy to spend his days just "pickin' and grinnin'" away at Applegarth. "It's a good, solid house, despite how many PEI winters it has sat abandoned," he says. "The damage appears to be minimal."

Chapter 10

Riley pulled into the big hardware store on Main Street in Montague, a place he had grown intimately familiar with in the last month. He killed the engine, silencing the Springsteen that rollicked out of the tape deck, got out, and locked the car. Instead of heading into the hardware store, as he normally would, Riley crossed the street to the offices of the *Eastern Pioneer*. He had a copy of that week's edition, which splashed his photo across its front page, tucked under his arm.

Opening the building's glass door, he was confronted by a steep set of stairs leading up to the second floor. He took the steps two at a time and soon arrived into the wide, barn-like space that was the *Pioneer*'s offices, a light soak of adrenalin entering his bloodstream. In spite of himself, his anger, Riley thought: *Am I going to get to see her? Is she in today, I wonder?*

She was not. The place was quiet for a Friday morning. The couple of desks that were scattered about were empty, as was the glass office at the very back of the room. But somebody *had* to be here, Riley thought. Otherwise the door downstairs would have been locked. He craned his neck and looked around. "Hell-*lo!*" he called out.

From behind him, he heard the sound of a toilet flushing. He turned to face a door to a little room near the lobby, and listened to the sound of someone washing their hands behind it. *Will that be Jessie?* he wondered. But a moment later the door opened and a man emerged. He looked to be in his late fifties, with a fluffy ducktail of grey hair and a salt-and-pepper beard. He wore a simple work shirt with the sleeves rolled up and its breast pocket loaded with cheap pens and a little notepad. He stopped when he saw he had a visitor.

"Jack Mackenzie?" Riley asked.

"Aye. That'd be me."

"I'm assuming you recognize *my* face." He held up the newspaper to show him the front page.

"Mr. Fuller," Jack replied. He seemed in no way concerned that this large, disgruntled man was suddenly standing in front of him. "Welcome to the *Eastern Pioneer*."

"We need to talk," Riley said.

~

They settled into the cramped fishbowl of Jack's office, with Riley easing himself into its ancient guest chair. He took a look around, at the old manual typewriter on Jack's desk, the stacks of pages next to it; the filing cabinet and piles of folders on the floor; the back wall with its green and red YES and NO stickers facing him. He cleared his throat before beginning. "I didn't realize you were going to run that profile of me on your front page," he said. "I was pretty shocked to see it there, to be honest."

While Riley spoke, Jack took up the pipe on his desk. From the pack of tobacco next to where it sat, he grabbed a generous pinch and tamped it into the bowl before fishing a wooden match out of his crowded breast pocket. After a single flick of Jack's thumb, the match burst to life, and he angled it into the pipe, sucking and smacking his lips to get it going. "Yeah, no," he said, flicking his wrist to put the match out, "we don't normally run our layout decisions by the people we interview."

This could have come off as snarky, except Jack said it with a big affable grin over the pipe's stem. Riley frowned back, but eyed the pipe as it filled the room with its pleasant, old-gentleman smell. "Do you mind if I smoke in here, too?" he asked with a scowl.

"By all means," Jack said with a welcoming sweep of his hand.

Riley pulled out his du Mauriers and lit one. "And another thing," he said, taking a drag. "That little chick you sent over to interview me? Jessie? Jessica?"

"Jessie-Mac," Jack said cheerfully. "Great kid. Love her."

"I'll have you know, she never asked me *one* question about the shooting. Not one. And yet it's, like, the whole top half of the story, plus the headline. If she *had* asked me some questions about it, I would've answered them. I've got nothing to hide, and I don't bullshit people."

"Neither do I," Jack replied. Tobacco sizzled in the pipe as he puffed. "So let me be up front with you, Riley. May I call you Riley? Jessie-Mac didn't *know* about your involvement in the shooting at the time she interviewed you. She's still a kid, still learning, and she just hadn't connected the dots. But I got a hunch when she told me you were Moncton RCMP, and so I pulled some old articles from the *Times & Transcript*. I helped her out with that part."

"She could've called or emailed me with some follow-up questions. She even said she might."

"There was no time by that point. We were on a deadline." And here, Jack nodded toward the rest of the office. "As you can see, we run a pretty shoestring operation around here. It's a mad scramble every week to put the paper out."

Riley just shook his head and tapped his cigarette into the ceramic ashtray on the desk. "It still doesn't seem right."

"Is there anything... inaccurate in the article?"

Riley didn't answer right away. He thought it over for a moment. "It's structured like she and I *did* talk about the shooting," he said finally. "Which we didn't."

"You want to write a letter to the editor and clarify? I'll print it. I'd be happy for the ink."

Riley just huffed at that, his hackles raising. "Is that how journalism works around here? You just publish whatever you want and let your sources correct your mistakes after the fact?"

"Hey, I'm doing the best I can with the resources I have," Jack shrugged. The two men—one still cordial, one still seething—stared at each other over their respective smokes before Jack went on. "Look, I can tell you're upset."

"I'm fucking pissed," Riley concurred. "I live in this community now. I don't want people judging me. I don't want some religious whack job egging my house because I was an adulterer."

This struck Jack as hilarious, and he let out a big jolly chortle. But when Riley didn't join in, he stopped. "Okay, you're pissed," he said, resigned. "I get that. But don't be too pissed at Jessie-Mac. She's the best intern we've had around here in, like, fifteen years. She works her little butt off, she can write like a motherfucker, and she's going to be a great journalist one day. A real force of nature. I honestly don't think that—" But then Jack perked in his chair, looking out and behind Riley through the glass walls of his office. "Oh, speak of the devil."

Riley turned and saw that Jessie had just come up the stairs, dropped her bag on the desk with the computer on it, and was heading toward them. He realized—again—how much he'd hoped to see her, to catch a glimpse of her, on this visit. That feeling suddenly burned warm in his chest as she approached. *What the fuck is the matter with you?* he thought, pushing it away. *She's twenty. You're being gross. And besides, you're supposed to be mad at her.*

"Knock, knock," Jessie said without knocking, and entered.

"Hell-ooo Jessie-Mac," crooned Jack.

"Riley Fuller," she said, turning to Riley. She seemed surprised to see him. Then she motioned to both men. "No, no, lads—don't get up!"

Before Riley could even offer her his seat, she parked herself atop the mid-size filing cabinet in the corner, like she had on the porch rail at Applegarth. *She likes that*, Riley thought. *She likes sitting a bit higher than people and getting a good bird's-eye view on things.*

"So I assume you saw the article," Jessie said to him.

"I did," Riley replied. He took the last drag on his cigarette and crushed it out. "I think it's pretty fucking shitty, what you did."

Jack gave a little groan behind his desk.

Jessie looked at her boss, then back at Riley. "I'm *sorry*?"

"I think it's a fucking shitty piece of work."

Shock and anger flashed through Jessie's grey eyes, and suddenly she looked very young and very old at the same time. "Are you *kidding*?" she asked. "That's an *excellent* piece of work. One of the best I've ever done. Other than all the passive verbs that sneaked in because I was in such a rush, that's a portfolio-worthy article."

"Okay, okay," Jack said in an attempt to calm them both down.

"We didn't talk about the shooting," Riley said. "You didn't ask any questions about the shooting. And yet you fucking wrote about the shooting."

"All the stuff was in the public domain anyway," she replied. "We just recapped it. I wrote the story that was a story."

"That's not the story you came to my house to write."

"Oh, I'm *sorry*," she said. "Did I approach you under false pretenses? Did I say what kind of story it would be? Did I call you up and be all like…" And here she flung her hair and sing-sang at him in a deep-south, *Gone with the Wind* accent. "Well hello there, Mr. Fuller. This is Debbie Dumbitch, *Eastern Pioneer* society columnist. I'd just *love* to write a puffy little profile of *yoo-ooo*." She batted her eyelashes and sashayed her shoulders at him. "Do you think you could explain your big home reno to little ol' me?"

"Jessie-Mac," Jack admonished quietly, pursing his lips and making a *Let's take it back a notch* gesture with his hands.

But Riley, much to his surprise, found himself softening, ever so slightly, toward her. *Debbie Dumbitch,* he thought, suppressing a chuckle. *That's actually pretty fucking adorable.*

"Is there anything inaccurate about the piece?" Jessie asked, parroting the question Jack had asked earlier. Her words were as thin as ice shavings.

"There is… there is…" What Riley wanted to say, but couldn't quite, was: *There is a big difference between accuracy and the truth. You're a bit young to see that right now, but maybe one day you won't be. Maybe something shitty will happen to you and you'll realize that the "truth" is far more complicated than that.*

He felt his eyes start to burn. The *fuck* he was going to cry in front of these people.

"Look, Riley, I'm sorry you're pissed," Jessie said, sounding not sorry at all, "but I wrote the story *that was a story*."

"Fine. You wrote my story. Congratulations." He stood up. "Jack, thank you for letting me smoke in your office. Jessie-Mac, go fuck yourself. In fact, you can both go fuck yourselves as you put out your shitty, sensationalist rag of a newspaper."

"*Och aye*, Riley, c'mon," Jack crooned. "Have a seat. We can talk this through."

But Riley was already on the move. He walked out of Jack's office and across the newsroom floor, then went clopping back down the stairs without looking back.

Chapter 11

Mid-May brought the first truly warm afternoon of the year, and Riley spent it working in the garden that was growing all on its own. If he'd had close neighbours this far out on the Eight Mile Road, they would have been astounded by—even jealous of—what these two large plots had already started to produce. Not that there was much chance of a casual gawker to glimpse them. These crops had all the privacy they needed as they flourished.

What exactly was growing here? Carrots and snow peas were definitely coming up, he saw as he raked and hoed and stooped to pull the few weeds that encroached out of the ruddy red soil. He also spotted the first signs of what looked like a strawberry patch sprouting in the middle of the second plot. And what was that over there, rising up in the corner near the stone sundial in the first? Zucchini? Zucchini always came on like gangbusters. He remembered that from the garden that Jane had kept, year after year. But no. These were something darker, richer in the body. Eggplant? Yes, his garden was growing eggplant.

Riley had sown none of these things. They just slowly began to appear, day after day, as if an invisible force were pushing them up from beneath the earth. Riley had even driven out to a well-known seed store over in York to buy his own stuff to plant—red potatoes, pumpkin, butternut squash, a bit of corn—plus some peat moss and a few plastic, pillow-like bags of a local fertilizer called Mussel Mud. He wondered whether the plots would reject all this, like how the human body might reject a transplanted organ. But the garden welcomed these additions, and soon Riley's own plants were thriving right alongside the ones he had nothing to do with.

All of this should have freaked him out. But as with the house, working in the garden seemed to calm Riley's mind. It felt—paradoxically, he supposed—so *normal* to be out here, lightly toiling among these magical rows, just as it felt normal to be restoring Applegarth, or, more accurately, helping it restore itself. Like so much else on PEI, the house's repairs, the garden's bounty, felt like something the universe owed to Riley. He had suffered, he had lost everything back on the mainland. But here, finally, he was succeeding in turning the page, and this was his reward.

By late afternoon, he had actually gotten a sweat on; and after finishing the day's effort, he felt a satisfaction he hadn't in a long time. He went into the house, washed his hands in the kitchen sink, then fetched a six-pack of Alpine lager from the fridge. He took it and his du Mauriers out to the porch to just sit in the swing seat there, to smoke and drink and watch the evening come on while he thought about what to make for supper. Riley actually felt *good*, almost youthful as he sucked back the beer and smoked away. The aches and pains that often plagued his forty-five-year-old body were nowhere to be found tonight, despite all the work he'd done in the garden, and his mind felt sharp and active, his mood high and playful. He wondered if this meant that he'd be visited again tonight by the sexy dreams—now, almost always starring Jessie-Mac herself—that had begun making regular appearances in the theatre of his mind while he lay upstairs in Applegarth's master bedroom. Each night's vision seemed raunchier, more vivid than the last—not that Riley cared. Who gave a fuck what he imagined, or did to himself, he thought, in the privacy of his own bed?

The early evening light began to soften. Sparrows and grackles flittered around the woods that surrounded the property. Riley was just pulling the fifth bottle of Alpine from the box when he saw, down there on the road through the dense curtain of spruce trees, a vehicle slow suddenly and then come swinging onto his driveway. It was a caramel-coloured pickup truck, old and muddy. It pulled about halfway up the lane before coming to a stop. Riley watched as three young guys, maybe in their early twenties, got out, took a long look around, saw him on the porch, and began to approach.

Had Riley only had *two* beer in him, or even three, he may have grown nervous, defensive even, at the sight of these strangers arriving uninvited onto his land. But Riley had *four* beer in him, and was feeling loose and foggy, light and hospitable. He leaned back on the swing seat and spread his arms out, as if putting them around two gorgeous, invisible showgirls.

"Hey there fellas," he called over.

They stopped in front of the porch. The guy who had been driving the truck looked up and above him then, at the house itself. His eyes betrayed a brief but unmissable look of dread. Riley could tell exactly what the kid was staring at: Applegarth's gleaming, blood-red gables high above them. They *were* rather arresting. He wondered then if the kid noticed the *other* thing. Was it even noticeable? When Riley had first laid eyes on the house, six weeks ago, every square inch of its clapboard siding had been stripped bare by the elements. That was no longer the case, even though he had yet to hire a single painter to come by. The white, flaking paint was coming back, gradually, all on its own, all over the house. It arrived on the siding, almost *growing* there in scaly, checkered patterns. Riley figured in another couple of weeks, the entire siding would be filled in by that white paint, and, with those red gables, the house would look as good as new.

The kid lowered his eyes back to the porch. "You're Riley Fuller," he said. It wasn't a question.

"I am," Riley replied cheerily, eyeing his visitor up. The kid wore a cut-off denim jacket over a Guns N' Roses tee-shirt, and had a pair of skinny, acid-washed jeans hugging his hips and legs. He also had a huge dimple right in the middle of his chin, as if someone had stabbed him there with a pencil. But these were not what captured Riley's attention the most. It was the kid's hair. The kid's hair was a fucking joke. It was the epitome, the very apotheosis, of a small-town mullet—business casual in the front, and a huge party in the back. It looked like a lion's mane, and matched the leonine look in the kid's eyes. That great helmet of hair might have elicited a laugh from Riley, had he had all six beer in him. Instead, he just asked: "And who might you boys be?"

"I'm Danny MacPherson," said the one with the mullet. He nodded to the kid standing at his right. "This here's Calvin Beck, and this," and he nodded to the third guy, standing on his left, "is Tony Gallant. We're from Montague." Like Dave Campbell, Danny pronounced the name of the town without the *t*.

"Well, welcome," Riley said. "I only got the one beer left, but you're welcome to split it if you's want."

The boys said nothing.

"So what can I do you for?" Riley asked.

"I read Jessie-Mac's story on you in last week's *Pioneer*," Danny said.

Riley found himself bristling, ever so slightly, at the kid's use of Jessie's nickname. *He knows her*, he thought. A memory of his latest night vision carouselled through his head: of Jessie's ice-grey eyes staring playfully at him while her twenty-year-old mouth, open just a little and smiling, hovered near the bulging tip of his middle-aged cock.

"That so?" he asked simply.

"That is so," Danny replied. "I just wanted to pop by and see how your reno's comin' along. Looks like you're making lots of headway."

"I am," Riley said. He felt the first ping of alarm, like a depth charge, go off in his gut.

"You're gonna sell this property after you're done," Danny added. This, too, wasn't a question.

Riley just shrugged. "Maybe I will and maybe I won't. As the article said, I haven't decided yet."

"No, you're gonna sell after you're done," Danny stressed. His voice was like ice.

The invisible showgirls disappeared and Riley lowered his arms. "*Excuse* me?"

Even Danny's buddies seemed taken aback, confused by what he said. This visit had obviously been a spur-of-the-moment thing, an impulse decision Danny had made while out tooling around with his friends in his truck. He clearly hadn't given them advance warning about popping by this property and harassing its owner.

"I said you'll sell it," Danny repeated. "You won't get a ton of money, but enough to set yourself up someplace else."

Riley laughed awkwardly. This kid was curdling his good mood, and he didn't want that. To keep things light, he took another mocking glance at Danny's mullet. It was like a lava lamp, the way it drew his eye. "What, *you* want this land, kid? You wanna buy me out?"

"I don't want this fucking land," Danny replied darkly. He took another glance up at Applegarth, and Riley realized he wasn't looking at it with dread. He was looking at it with disgust. Like he *knew* the kind of visions and fantasies it had been putting in Riley's head.

"Get the fuck out of here," Riley said. "Seriously, you couldn't *afford* what I'd want for this property."

"You don't belong here," Danny said, his words like a stone he had chucked at Riley's head.

The guy he called Tony gave him another sideways glance. "Danny, Jesus," he said under his breath.

"The fuck I don't," Riley replied. He stood up from the swing seat. It banged lightly against the back of the porch. "My granddaddy lived here, and his granddaddy before him. *He* built this place."

"Oh, I know," Danny said with a definitive nod. It came out as if he'd learned this, not from Jessie's story, but from somewhere else.

That certitude sent a chill right through Riley. He didn't want to go into fight mode right now; he'd been having such a pleasant evening. He tried smiling again. "What are you boys trying to pull, anyway? The whole," and here Riley made a *clicky-clicky* noise with his mouth, "'scare the come-from-away out of town' routine?"

"You know, Jessie-Mac's article made you sound pretty pathetic," Danny said. "Don't you think you'd be better off being pathetic someplace else? Charlottetown, maybe? Or back in Moncton? Or Timuktu, for all I give a fuck?"

Riley just grinned at him like a wolf. "Yeah, yeah. Oh, and speaking of pathetic, Danny," he said, "1982 called—it wants its hairstyle back." When none of them laughed at what Riley thought was a very good joke, he just chortled to himself and added, "Seriously, kids, get the fuck off my land."

"This isn't your land," Danny said. "It doesn't belong to you. *You* belong to *it*. Haven't you figured that out yet?"

Ice water raced through Riley's veins.

The two other guys looked stunned by their friend's behaviour, and very ready to hustle back to the truck.

"Thanks for coming by, boys," Riley said to nudge them along, his voice now sour with scorn.

Calvin and Tony started to head back to the truck, but Danny didn't follow them at first. He just continued staring up with a look Riley couldn't read. "Think about what I said," Danny called over before slowly turning to join his friends.

And that's when Riley felt it surge up in him, a great comic force even stronger than the crack he'd made about the mullet. In one second, he felt—strangely, but with absolute certainty—as if the *house* were speaking through him, as if Applegarth itself were forcing words involuntarily out of his mouth. "Oh, and Danny," he yelled as the kid strolled away, a sinister grin peeling back Riley's lips, "tell your mom the boys all say thanks for a *grrreat* weekend!"

The kid was up, over, and onto the porch in a flash. He slammed into Riley and drove him against the back wall, next to the little blue APPLEGARTH plaque there. Riley was caught off guard by the kid's strength: he himself was six-foot-three and thick through the shoulders and chest, while Danny looked a lanky five-ten. Yet the kid pinned him there, against that clapboard siding, and shoved his forearm up under Riley's chin and into his throat. Danny's eyes blazed like gas fires, and Riley was certain he was going to scream words in his face like *What'd you say about my mom?!* or *Shut your filthy mouth!* Instead, he said something wholly cryptic, utterly unexpected—words that sent another harrowing chill through Riley.

"*This isn't who you really are!*"

Riley froze a moment in utter paralysis, and locked eyes with Danny, who was himself tremulous. It was like they were both under a spell cast by that perplexing exclamation.

But just as quickly as he entered that trance, Riley snapped out of it.

"Get the fuck *offa me!*" he said, and gave Danny a great good shove. The kid went pinwheeling backward off the porch and into the arms of his friends, who had come racing back at the first sound of this commotion. Riley was panting now. "You come on this property again," he said, "and I will blow your fucking heads off. I am a cop. Don't doubt I have the means to do it."

Danny began shambling back toward the pickup, his friends following. "You don't belong here," he repeated back at Riley over his shoulder, but without as much conviction as before. As they went, Riley heard Calvin say: "What the *fuck* was that all about, Dan?"

They climbed into the cab of the truck, and a moment later went pealing back down the driveway and onto the Eight Mile Road. Riley stayed standing on his porch long after he was certain they were gone.

Chapter 12

That night, Riley knew he was going to get very little sleep. The entire incident had left him manic, his insides drenched in rancid, unwanted adrenalin. As evening turned to night, Riley paced up and down the halls and stairways of Applegarth, the old floorboards twisting and screaming beneath his feet, but it did no good. In the kitchen, he polished off his latest bottle of Jim Beam, which did nothing to relax him. In the living room, he sat for a while with the loaded Glock on his lap, wanting to shoot something—the TV, the VCR, himself—before unloading it again and putting it back in its kitchen drawer.

Eventually, Riley found his way back upstairs, to the library. He pulled off the computer's plastic hood, set it on the floor, sat down, and turned the machine on. After it finished booting up, Riley dialed into the modem and then checked to see if an email had come in from Sammy. One had not. Then he stared awhile at the WordPerfect file he had labeled JOURNALING. Might it help? Might it get him to calm down, to flush out all the thoughts that Danny MacPherson's visit had shoved into his brain?

He launched the document, causing the hard drive to whir. After it loaded and was open, he scrolled down to the bottom of the previous entry, and put his fingers on the keys.

May 16, 1995
Dear Diary, or Journal, or whatever the fuck you are,
Fact: Today, some local shithead came by my house and tried to scare me off my land. This asshole, with two of his buddies in tow, showed up in a dirty old truck and started threatening me and telling me I should sell Applegarth and move someplace else. After that profile of me ran last week in the local paper, I figured I'd get

the stink-eye from a few folks around here, at least for a while. I expected some of them to shun me in the grocery store or give me queer looks in line at the post office. I did not expect this.

The kid, this Danny MacPherson, shouldn't have been able to get my goat like that. There was nothing to him—I could have broken him over my knee like a stick—but he really wriggled under my skin, and things escalated so quickly that I was caught off guard. I said something to him that was totally out of character for me, something truly vile about his mom. I hadn't said *anything* that juvenile since I was a teen. It was the strangest feeling, to have those words bubble up from my mouth against my will. I would never admit this to anyone out loud—they'd think I've lost my marbles—but I guess I can confess it here, in the privacy of this journal: I am almost certain that it was the house that made me say what I said to Danny. That it was Applegarth, which has given me so many moments of peace since I moved in last month, not to mention some frightfully vivid (if pleasurable!) dreams, that put those horrible words in my mouth. *Tell your mom the boys all say thanks for a* grrreat *weekend*. I mean, Jesus, who even says that?

And this Danny MacPherson, a guy I didn't even know five minutes earlier, said something equally disturbing to me when he should have been trying to punch me in the face.

This isn't who you really are!

Fact: That, more than anything, froze me right in my bones. Who the *fuck* was he to say who I really am? He doesn't know the first thing about me. Where did he get off saying that, and with such conviction?

And yet he did. *This isn't who you really are.* I haven't been able to stop thinking about that. Because that is the question, isn't it? It has *been* the question for what seems like forever. Who I really am has been in doubt for longer than I can bring myself to remember. It was at the heart of my... my *entanglement* with Marigold Burque, and everything that came after.

This isn't who you really are.

Well then, who am I? I'm certainly not going to get the answer from a local scumbag like Danny MacPherson. So then where? Where do I get that answer?

But then, there in his desk chair, he turned to his left and stared through the archway of Applegarth's second-storey turret, at the bookcase on the back wall. He got up and went to it, standing before those shelves like a child in the throes of wonder. His eyes were drawn not to the small pile of poetry books that Sammy had sent him, still unread, but to the row of diaries standing next to it. The private journals of his grandfather's grandfather, the original Riley Fuller. Diaries that no doubt captured his thoughts and feelings upon building Applegarth and moving into it with his brother.

Riley pulled down the volume labeled number 1.

He took it back out to the library proper, settled into the reading chair he had set up in the corner opposite the writing desk, and popped on the standing lamp next to it. Cracking open the cover of the journal, Riley took a moment to flip through the pages inside. His ancestor's handwriting was small and spidery, etched in thin black ink, but still quite legible. In some sections, he could see that the man had added a new entry every few days; in others, he had gone weeks or more without writing anything.

He turned back to the first page. With a sigh, Riley reread the opening gambit he had found there before, and then pressed several paragraphs beyond it. The entry was a kind of time capsule, recapping details around the construction of Applegarth in 1861-62 and the brothers' move into it, along with Robert's nine-year-old daughter, Miriam. The house's moniker, Riley learned, was taken from the maiden name of Robert's dead wife, Claire, whom he was still mourning in the spring of 1862. The brothers had moved themselves and their import-export business to PEI for a fresh start. Queerly enough, the land upon which Applegarth was built was bequeathed to them from a dead cousin they had never met who had lived in the nearby village of Lowfield, where the boys' mother, Melinda Fuller, had grown up. Lowfield, according to the diary, was a bit of a shunned village in the broader community, but it resided less than two miles directly behind the plot of land where Applegarth was built?

Is that true? Riley thought. He had been in the area six weeks now, and had not heard a single mention of this place. He knew there were dozens of tiny communities spread all over PEI, many of which were nothing more than a sign on the side of the road; and some of these places even had a deserted house in them, rotting away in the countryside, just like Applegarth had been. Could Lowfield be one of these places?

He set the journal aside, got up from the chair, and headed downstairs. He went outside, to the driveway. He hustled around to open his car's passenger door and dug out the gas-station map of PEI that was in the glovebox amidst all his cassettes. He took the map back into the house, went to the dining room, and unfolded it out onto the table there.

Lowfield resides less than two miles directly behind Applegarth, the diary had said. Riley studied the map until he located the Eight Mile Road and roughly where Applegarth sat upon it. He traced his finger backward from the spot. Stared where it landed. There was no village marked within two miles behind his house, as far as he could see. Riley always just assumed there was nothing back there but woods, which the map seemed to confirm. Other, familiar places were labeled all around that location—Cardigan and Cardigan North, Glenning and Montague, Georgetown and Petit Point. But no Lowfield.

He flipped to the legend on the flap, which listed every community on PEI in alphabetical order and their place on the map's letter-number grid. His eyes traced down the list, which included lots of places he knew or knew of—Bedeque and Blooming Point, Cavendish and Charlottetown, Crapaud and Kensington. But no Lowfield.

Why would the diary mention a place that did not exist? Or *had* it existed, at one time?

Riley took a long, slow breath.

Lowfield resides less than two miles directly behind Applegarth, his grandfather's grandfather had written. *We can easily hike there and back in a day*, he had said. *We know we still have kin in that village—perhaps many kin...*

Applegarth settled onto itself then, creaking and shuddering as an idea arrived in Riley's mind.

Part II: The Grimoire of Shaal

Chapter 13

May 18, 1995
Dear Sammy,

Thanks for the email, brother. No, sorry, I haven't had a chance to crack any of the books you sent. I will, I promise. Truth is, I found something else here in the library at Applegarth that I'll want to read first. It's a bit of an unbelievable find, actually: the private diaries of my grandfather's grandfather, whose name was also Riley Fuller. Three volumes of them, to be exact. It would appear they've been sitting up here since the early 1860s. I can't tell whether my grandfather, James, who was the last person to live in Applegarth before me, would have found these journals. But if he did, he left them in the correct order in the bookcase and in good condition for me to find.

Since discovering them the other night, I've only read the first entry in the first volume, which is quite lengthy and outlines Riley's thoughts and feelings after moving here with his brother, Robert. He mentioned a few of the communities in the area—one of which may no longer exist—as well as the fact that Robert was a widower and brought his nine-year-old daughter, Miriam, with them to PEI, which is all news to me. Anyway, I'm not a big reader, as you know, but I do plan to work my way through these volumes over the coming weeks. Once I do, I'll crack open your stuff, I promise.

To answer your other question, no, I haven't heard from any of the old gang back in Moncton. It's okay. I understand why people don't want to talk to me. I wouldn't either if I were them. But I really appreciate your advice about needing to forge relationships here on PEI if I plan to stay long-term. Wise words as usual, Sams. Having said that, I do find it harder and harder to make new friendships the older I get. My father was like that, too. Thomas *hated* meeting new people, especially after my mother died.

Anyway, I'll try to make friends here, though it'll be tricky. A profile of me ran in the local paper last week, and it aired a lot of my dirty laundry. I now have serious doubts about how welcoming Islanders actually are.

Best,
Riley

~

On a sunny Saturday afternoon, Riley pulled into a sporting goods store in Montague to buy himself a pair of good, reliable hiking boots for the idea he had. Neil Young's "Old Man" was knuckle-dragging out of the Lumina's tape deck, a tune that always made Riley think of his own old man, and he let it play through before killing the engine. Getting out, he stood squinting in the blare of the day and looking out across the street. There, on the other side of it, he could see a small, narrow park rolling downhill away from the road and toward the river. It wasn't *much* of a park. It had some willows and birch trees, a few benches and a gazebo. But the place was jumping as people were out enjoying the warm weather's long-awaited return.

Riley could see, from where he stood, that Jessie MacIntosh was among them.

She sat crouched like a cat atop the gazebo's rail, looking down at a clique of young people who were obviously her friends. They had just wrapped up a game of frisbee and had now begun their long goodbyeing for the afternoon. Riley just lit a du Maurier and stood in front of his car awhile to watch them. Some in the group still wore fleeces or spring jackets despite the warmth of the day. Another, a slim girl with a pixie haircut, wore a dark-green tank top and cargo shorts and—what was that around her neck? Dog tags? Yes, they looked like dog tags. She glanced up and said something to Jessie, and Jessie laughed uproariously.

Soon the friends began drifting away, one by one, and Jessie gave each a wave from the gazebo rail as they did. *How great it must feel*, Riley thought, *to be that comfortable, that at ease with people, to not have your hackles up all the time or want to press your back against a wall and retreat into yourself. How delightful,* he thought, *to be twenty years old again and be that open with folks, that unguarded.*

Eventually the friends were all gone save for one, a young man with his hands in his pockets. When they were alone, Jessie hopped down off the gazebo rail and stood before him. Strapped to her back was the same canvas kitbag she'd brought with her on the day she visited Applegarth.

The guy she was talking to, Riley could see, was Danny MacPherson. He'd recognize that mullet anywhere.

Tell your mom the boys all say thanks for a grrreat *weekend.*

Riley lit another smoke and watched them. The two young people stood maybe four or five feet apart as they talked. The wind was up and Riley couldn't catch even a whiff of what they said to each other. Jessie had her arms folded lightly over her chest, and Danny's hands stayed in his pockets. Their body language was impossible to read from this distance. At one point, Riley thought they had a real intimacy; at another, they looked like gunfighters squaring off. Jessie perhaps said something droll, which caused Danny to chuckle lightly. She went over and hugged him then. It wasn't exactly a platonic hug, but it wasn't exactly *not* a platonic hug. Riley felt his stomach stir, his shoulders clench. He watched as Danny turned to go, and Jessie touched his jean-jacketed back as he did, giving him a little rub there to send him on his way. When he was gone, she went over and flounced herself into a nearby bench, twisting her kitbag around into her lap to begin rifling through it.

What the ever-loving fuck is she doing with that *asshole?* Riley thought.

He decided that, if she was still on that bench by the time he came out of the sporting goods store, he would go over and talk to her. He figured he owed her an apology for how he'd behaved at the *Eastern Pioneer* offices.

He went inside and found a sales assistant to help him pick out a pair of suitable boots for his purposes—durable, waterproof, and with a good set of rubber cleats on the soles. He made his purchase and then came back out to the Lumina, tossing the boxed-up boots in their giant plastic bang onto the passenger seat. Then he looked back across the road to the park. Jessie was still sitting on her bench, her head now down in what looked like prayer. Riley shut the car door and strolled over toward her.

When he got there, he saw that she wasn't praying, of course. She was listening to music. Over her hair rested a little metallic set of headphones, its cord attached to a Discman set up on the bench next to her thigh. The music was just loud enough for Riley to hear a garbled hiss from where he stood. Jessie was reading a paperback very intently as she listened. Riley could see the title of the book: *Skinny Legs and All*.

He took a step closer to the bench, and Jessie looked up. When she saw him, she reached down and hit the PLAY/PAUSE button on her Discman, then took the headphones off and draped them around her neck. The look she gave him, Riley was relieved to see, was not hostile. It was impersonal. It just said: Oh, hey, if it isn't *you*.

"Excuse me," he addressed her, trying to smile, "but aren't you *Eastern Pioneer* society columnist Debbie Dumbitch?"

Her expression remained neutral for just a second, but then she smiled broadly and chuckled. "Debbie Dumbitch," she repeated with a gleeful shake of her hair. "Jesus."

"I swear, that was one of the cleverest things I've ever heard," Riley went on. "I've been replaying it in my head ever since you said it."

"And to think I came up with that right on the spot," she beamed. She bookmarked her novel and put it back in her bag, then picked up her Discman and rested it on her lap before scooching over on the bench. "You wanna sit?"

"Sure," he replied, and lowered his hulking frame there next to her tiny one. He turned and looked briefly into Jessie's face.

"Look, I owe you an apology," he said. "Your story really pissed me off, but I didn't need to come aboard of you like that. I'm sorry. You were just doing your job."

"That's okay. Apology accepted. And actually, Jack and I had a long talk about that article after you left."

"Did you now?"

"Yep. He said that, in hindsight, he now agrees with you, that it wasn't fair. That we shouldn't have rushed that piece into print before we got a chance to talk to you about the Moncton shooting. I, of course, disagree. That stuff was in the public domain and we were totally within our right to use it."

He nodded, almost laughed. "That's fine. We can agree to disagree. I still feel bad. You're only twenty. I shouldn't have told you to go fuck yourself." But when he said this, a sudden and unwelcome quip forced its way into Riley's mind. *And besides, you really shouldn't have to fuck yourself. You should have someone to do that for you, there Jessie-Mac. Tell me, is that Danny MacPherson's job?* But he banished those thoughts as soon as they came. He felt like a dirty old man for even thinking them.

"It's okay," Jessie went on, "I get it. And you *were* right about one thing—you *do* have to live in this community." She cast her eyes down. "I *know* what it's like to have people around here all up in your business. Believe me."

Riley looked at her quizzically. What did she mean by *that*? He waited for her to explain herself, but she didn't. So he just shrugged instead. "Friends?" he said.

"Friends."

"And for the record," he added, taking out his du Mauriers, "I don't think you're a dumb bitch. I think you're a very smart bitch, actually."

"Awhh—*thank you!*" She reached over and gave his knee a good hearty jostle. The feel of her touch forced Riley to pull in a long, thin breath through his nose.

He popped a cigarette into his mouth and lit it. "Though I question *how* smart," he went on, "if Danny MacPherson is your boyfriend."

"Excuse me?"

"I spotted you two chatting earlier."

"How do *you* know Danny?"

Riley looked at her as he took a drag, hesitating. But then he told her how Danny had shown up at Applegarth after reading Jessie's story, how he threatened Riley and tried to scare him off his own property.

"No," she said with a slow shake of her head when he finished. "No, that's not right. Danny would never do that."

"He did. Showed up in his truck with two other goons—a kid named Calvin somebody, and another guy named Tony. They had no idea *what* he was going on about, but he was adamant that I should leave the area. Things got pretty heated, and he tackled me at one point."

Jessie cupped her hands over her mouth. "I... I can't believe that," she said through her fingers.

"Well, believe it. So I'm a bit surprised that someone as bright as you is dating a skeezer like that."

"Okay, first of all," she said, lowering her hands again, "'skeezer' is a term for a girl, not a guy."

"Fine. Skeezoid. Hayseed. Dirt nugget. Fucking lowlife, is what he is."

"Second of all, Danny's not my boyfriend. He's my *ex*-boyfriend. We're still friends, obviously. And he's not a lowlife. Danny's a good egg. One of the best."

"Oh really?"

"Yes, really. Did you know he lives with his grandmother, and takes care of her? She's *ninety-seven*. He does everything for her. They're very close. How can someone like that be a lowlife?"

"So then why did you two break up?"

Jessie looked at Riley for a moment, then turned away, letting her dark hair fall in her face. She let out a heavy sigh. "Okay, tell you what. Since I know something very intimate about you, after writing that story," she said slowly, "I'm going to share something very intimate about me." She looked back up at him, but then hesitated.

Riley felt another pang of desire stir deep within him. He swallowed. "You know, you don't have to tell me. If you don't want."

"No, it's fine. I want to tell you." She took another big breath. "So... Danny got me pregnant back in Grade 11. Needless to say, it messed me right up. I was *just* getting interested in journalism at that point, and so bringing a kid into this world was *not* on. Not at all." She made a face, as if procreation were something slightly disgusting.

Riley nodded and waited for her to continue. When she didn't, he said, "So you got an abortion."

"Yeah, I did. But not here. You can't *get* an abortion anywhere on PEI."

"Oh no?"

"Nope. We're a pro-life province, baby. Resolution 17. Life begins at conception. That's official government policy here on the Island."

"You serious?"

"Fucking serious. The Catholic Church has controlled what girls here can do with their uteruses *for years*. There hasn't been a single abortion on PEI since 1982. Which I didn't even know until I needed one. Those assholes have driven out every pro-choice movement on the Island. They've threatened elected officials. They've harassed pro-choice journalists, including one of our own columnists at the *Pioneer*." She practically shook with anger. "Anyway, I was so fucking scared when I learned all this. To get the procedure, I had to go to Montreal. On the *bus*. Do you have any idea how long it takes to go from PEI to Montreal on the bus? Do you know what it *costs*?"

Riley shook his head.

"Me neither, actually," she went on, "and that's my point. Danny paid for it all. He took care of everything. So he's not a lowlife, Riley. Not at all."

So then why did he come to my house and threaten me? he wanted to ask. He could not reconcile the guy who did that with the guy who looked after his ninety-seven-year-old grandmother and took care of his knocked-up girlfriend. But instead, Riley just repeated his other question. "So then why did you break up with him?"

To his surprise, Jessie smiled. "How do you know *I* broke up with *him*?"

"Oh please," Riley scoffed. "Guys like *that* don't break up with girls like *you*."

He was pleased to see her flush a little at the flattery. "*Anyway*," she said with a sideward glance, "as I neared graduation, he started going on about wanting to get married and have 'real babies' with me. But I just, I don't know, resisted all that talk. After I got accepted into journalism school in Halifax, I knew things would... would change between us." Here she paused, as if the decision she had to make still made her sad. "I'd be over there for eight months of the year, meeting new people and having new experiences, and it wouldn't be fair to him. I'd be growing in one direction and he'd be growing in another. So I broke things off the summer after grad, which felt less shitty than waiting until my first Thanksgiving or Christmas home to do it."

Riley nodded. "That makes sense. You'll be leaving us all in the dust once you start writing for the *New York Times*."

It was Jessie's turn to scoff. "Um, no. Believe it or not, I don't want to work off Island. My goal, modest as it sounds, is to be a reporter at the Charlottetown *Guardian* once I finish my degree. The *Pioneer* internship will certainly help with that. As much as this backward province drives me crazy sometimes, I do love it and want to build my career here."

"I'm sure you can do whatever you want," he told her.

"Of course, that goal will interfere with my *other* ambition," she said with a smile, and petted the Discman there in her lap, "which is to marry Michael Stipe."

"Who's he?" Riley asked. "Another local dirt nugget?"

Jessie burst out laughing, but then looked at him. "What, are you *serious*?" She reached down and began digging around in her knapsack until she pulled out an orange CD case and handed it to him. It had what looked like the pixilated image of a cat's face on the cover, and the word MONSTER written in red in the top left-hand corner.

That's what I am, he thought absently as he looked at it. *That's me. I'm a monster.*

"I've been playing this album into the ground since it came out last fall," she said. "Here, take a listen."

She lifted the metal headphones and up over her head, then shifted closer to Riley on the bench so she could maneuver them onto his. Which she didn't need to do, he thought. She could have just handed him the headset and let him put it on himself. But she took great care in adjusting the headphones over his ears so he'd be comfortable, looking into his face as she did. Riley became very aware of her close proximity. Felt himself stir and solidify. He fought like mad to defy the urge that suddenly came geysering up in him. Her mouth was very close to his.

"You ready?" she asked.

"Sure."

She hit play, and the music, such as it was, came hissing into his ears. He tried to take in a few bars but was instantly annoyed. "*Fock!*" he said with a flinch. What the hell was he listening to? This singer that Jessie-Mac was so madly in love with was actually *whimpering* into the microphone, raising his voice into a prissy falsetto and talking about how he doesn't sleep, he *dreams*. Riley let the song play for a few bars more before reaching over to her lap and pressing the PLAY/PAUSE button.

"Enough of *that* foolishness," he said, taking the headphones off and handing them back to her. "Guy's a fucking whiner, Jessie-Mac. Why do you want to go and marry such a whiner?" He gave her a wry smile. "What is it with you kids and your terrible taste in music?"

"Yeah, yeah," she replied, putting the CD case back in her bag. "This from the generation that *lost its shit* over The Monkees."

She's quick, he thought. *Fuck she's quick*.

He laughed at her and she laughed at him.

"Anyway, I should go," he said, standing up from the bench. "I've got more work to do on Applegarth."

"Sure thing," she replied. "Oh, and Riley?"

"Yeah?"

"You know, you also told Jack to go fuck himself. Maybe you could apologize to him, too. Give him a call. He'd appreciate that. He's a good man. He puts out a kick-ass newspaper."

Riley nodded. "I will. I promise." He took in another breath and thought of the hiking boots back in his Lumina. *I just have something to take care of out behind my property first*, he thought.

Chapter 14

May 21, 1995
Dear Diary, or Journal, or whatever the fuck you are,
I know I'm supposed to come here to work out everything I'm still dealing with about the shooting, to grapple with whatever shame or "survivor guilt" I continue to feel. I could talk about that, outlining my Facts and my Questions. Or I could outline my encounter with Jessie MacIntosh in that Montague park yesterday afternoon, or the vivid fantasies I had about her *again* last night in bed as I floated somewhere between sleeping and dreaming. I could talk about all the vile things I did to myself as I imagined Jessie there with me. I could write about *that* guilt, the remorse I felt even though I did what I did in the privacy of my own home, my own head.

But I'm not going to talk about either of those things to you Diary, or Journal, or whatever the fuck you are. Instead, I'm going to tell a story. A story about what happened to me earlier today, events I'm still struggling to make sense of. This tale is literally unbelievable—or would be, if not for the rest of the unbelievable things that have been occurring from the very first day I set foot in this house. I've only just now settled my nerves enough to sit at this computer and begin typing it out. I've had many tense and harrowing moments over my twenty-one years as an RCMP officer, but nothing compares to what I saw, what I went through, in the last few hours.

My goal yesterday, prior to the run-in with Jessie, was to acquire a pair of hiking boots for the trek I wanted to make through the thickly wooded area directly behind Applegarth. According to the diary kept by my grandfather's grandfather, whose name was also Riley Fuller, there is supposed to be—or, at least, once was—an entire village back there, less than two miles behind my property. The place, called Lowfield, is not on any map I've seen. But my ancestor wrote about it exactly as he did of Glenning and Cardigan, of Georgetown and Petit Point—all places in this area that *do* exist. I wanted to know what I might find if I went rambling back there.

So that's what I did.

Let me tell you, off the bat, that trudging through an overgrown forest is not easy, especially if you're forty-five and haven't gotten any real exercise (save for a bit of yardwork around Applegarth) in a year and a half. It was hard going right from the start, and within ten minutes I was puffing and wheezing as I pushed through dense brush and stepped over thick tree roots and tried not to get slapped in the face by branches. What, I wondered, did I expect to find out here? What if I went wildly off course? I hadn't brought a compass with me but was fairly certain I was still heading due south. At the very worst I would push through all the way to route 319 and come out at Cardigan North.

Nearly forty-five minutes passed and I had all but given up on seeing anything out there. Whatever that other Riley Fuller had been writing about, I thought, was long gone. But then, the forest began to... began to *change* the deeper I went into it. Hardwood gave way to spruce timber and ancient apple trees, though I had no idea what this meant. The undergrowth began to ease up a little as I hiked through it. I looked down and over, and sure enough I could see, peeping through the mossy, weedy ground, a row of old and tightly packed wooden boards, faded to the ashiest grey I'd ever seen, leading off deeper into the forest. This was, beyond a doubt, the remnants of an old-timey corduroy road. It seemed to appear there like an apparition, to emerge out of and run along the uneven earth like something out of a fairy tale. I was alarmed to see it. Wouldn't such a thing have rotted away decades ago? Even the iron spikes holding it together should have rusted down to nothingness by now. I nonetheless began following it, overcome with curiosity. As I did, the woods started to recede a little, making the walk easier and giving my now sore and battered ankles a much-needed break.

It took another five minutes, but then the clearing grew even wider, and I soon came upon what I had trekked out here to find. Off in the distance, as the ground sloped into a gentle incline, I could see a smattering of weather-beaten structures peeping through the trees. I approached, my heart rate increasing with the pace of my steps. These buildings were just sitting there, crouched in the woods like giant old mushrooms, an entire village undisturbed. The corduroy road passed right up through the middle of it like a thoroughfare. I paused at the mouth of this abruptly appearing place, feeling like an intruder. But then I began strolling down among those structures. Some were clearly tiny homes, not much more than shacks—low and dark, covered in clapboard siding and rotting wooden shingles. Others were crude commercial buildings, a blacksmith perhaps, a feed store, a tavern. There were more small homes behind them, crouched in the tall grass and under wild, slanting trees.

This was, I had no doubt, the village of Lowfield. I was now standing in the middle of it.

I can barely describe how eerie it was. The woods, this deep in, were perfectly silent, perfectly still, with not so much as a bird's cry or a wind rippling the leaves. The mosquitoes that had hounded me on my way here had suddenly left me alone. The sunlight, pushing through the trees, seemed somehow grey now, like slate. If Applegarth felt secluded, out on the arse end of the

Eight Mile Road, this place felt utterly isolated, as if existing in another dimension of reality altogether. As I wandered down the main drag, the air there felt leaden, heavy as I took it into my lungs. The homes and buildings stared at me as if with eyes. Their windows still had glass in them: like Applegarth's, they had not been damaged by weather or vandals. The whole place, though feeling ancient, looked intact. Much like Applegarth had. This sudden thought caused me to shudder.

I continued to walk and soon saw, there at the far end of the main drag, the most dominant structure in Lowfield. A small, rambling church sat in the long grass, looking somehow both squat and angular. Its siding still held thin flakes of paint, its steeple not quite clearing the height of the trees on either side of it. There, in the middle of the church's clapboard face, were tall double iron doors forming a black, frowning mouth. Those doors, as far as I could see, were the only ones in the village that were slightly ajar.

Diary, or Journal, or whatever the fuck you are: I admit that what I did next will sound improbable, but it was like I couldn't help myself. I wandered over to that battered place of worship, drawn there as if by a magnet. I climbed its steps and reached out to grasp the door's iron handle, which must have had copper in it because it had turned a sickly mint green with age. I pulled, and at first the hinges would not relent. So I pulled harder, and the door did give way, squealing like a sow as I hauled it open. The air that came rushing out had a putrid smell, like rotten wet leaves, or a dead animal trapped in a chimney. I should have turned back then, but by now I was almost in a trance. I squeezed through the door and stepped inside that abandoned, decaying church.

The floorboards of the narthex were coated in dust, and my hiking boots kicked some up as I wandered slowly in. On the far side of the narthex was a large archway, not that dissimilar from the ones peppered throughout Applegarth. It led into the main chamber of the church. I walked in and meandered up its dust-choked aisle between the long rows of pews. Some were knocked over; others had collapsed onto themselves with rot. As I moved toward the altar, my very breath seemed to echo up through that low yet vaulted ceiling. I looked to my right and left, at the stain-glass windows on either side, letting in the same sewage-grey light I'd seen outside.

I approached and then stepped up onto the altar. On the back wall hung a huge gold cross, its face inscribed by what I can only describe as an intricately Celtic pattern. The icon seemed to loom over the whole church like a beacon. There, on the wooden wall below it, was a dark, faded shape, like a shadow. Looking at it, I had no doubt as to what it was; my years in the RCMP had trained me to recognize it. It was a giant blood stain. Very old, true—maybe as old as Applegarth itself—but unmistakable. I looked at the floor of the wall. It too was stained with an ancient blood splatter. Something terrible, I knew, must have happened here.

I turned then to the high wooden pulpit there at the altar's edge. Walking over to it, I could feel my heart racing even faster than before. There seemed to be an energy, an almost magnetic force drawing me toward that pulpit. There, on that wide, ornately carved lectern, I could see that there was not one book but two. I looked down at them. The one on the right was a standard King James Bible. I turned open its hard leather cover and saw inside the bible's thin, almost translucent pages, gilded along the edges and holding the tiniest of print. My random flip had taken me to verses of Deuteronomy, which I recognized from my Sunday school days. I closed it again and turned to the other book, which sat at what would have been the preacher's left hand. This tome was not a bible, nor a prayer book, nor a hymnal. On its sickly brown cover, embossed in black, were the following words:

The Grimoire of Shaal

This expression meant nothing to me, but I was overcome by a curiosity to see what was written inside. I reached out and touched the book's cover, ready to peel it open as I had with the bible and see the pages below.

What I am about to write here is not a lie. I am *not* shitting you Diary, or Journal, or whatever the fuck you are.

That book was warm to the touch.

No, it was even more than that. It was hot. The book radiated heat, like a living body suffering from fever. I wanted to move my hand away but couldn't. It was like the book seized it there in its strange grip. I lifted the cover, turned it open, then flipped a few of the book's pages over to expose the words written inside. As with the bible, the text on each page was broken up into two columns, only they weren't in the same language. The one on the left contained an alphabet I didn't recognize. It wasn't Latin or Greek, but something that seemed much older, letters that looked almost Asiatic, or like druidic runes. On the right was English text, though it spelt out words that came from no language I'd ever heard before. I traced my finger under a line on that page, the paper nearly scalding below my touch. I read the phrase written there:

...*ti Ghroyan shuun dorn, dos maya Shaal huit, Shaal huit.*

As soon as my eyes passed over these words, there came a great groaning shudder, a moan that seemed to originate inside the pulpit itself. I froze. I couldn't move. Behind me came another sound, a noise like metal screaming, twisting itself and scraping loudly against wood. I didn't want to turn around. I didn't want to cast my gaze back to that wall behind me. But I couldn't help myself. My head rotated slowly, almost involuntarily there on my neck, and I looked.

The big gold cross was, of course, still there. Only now, it was hanging upside down.

I fucking ran. I fled the church as quickly as I could, prying the door back open and stumbling out into the late spring air, practically tripping over the church steps that led down to the ground. I hurried back up the corduroy road through the centre of Lowfield and toward the woods that would lead my home. Unlike before, the forest was now alive with noise: multiple types of birds—crows and sparrows and warblers—brayed at each other through the trees; trunks and branches seemed to now crawl with squirrels and chipmunks that nattered at each other in piercing wails. The brush under my feet began to shuffle and lurch with some larger, unseen animals.

I hurried through the tangles as best I could, the noises driving me almost to insanity. It took seemingly forever to push my way through all that wild and overgrown terrain, nearly two miles of it, but finally I re-emerged out of the woods and onto my own back lawn.

Panting and shaking, I stooped with my hands on my thighs and sucked in great gulps of air. Then I returned to the house, not sure what to do with myself. I paced around Applegarth for a while, roaming as I've done on many nights when I can't sleep, and then headed upstairs to the library. I parked myself in front of this computer and booted it up. I knew I just had to get this incredible story down.

Riley stopped typing. He reached over and cupped the mouse to click SAVE. The hard drive droned a moment before growing silent again. He took in a long breath, then began reading what he had written.

Had he written this? Looking at each sentence in turn, Riley could hardly believe that he had composed them. He knew from years of putting together reports and summaries of his police work that he had no flair for narrative—his bosses had often criticized him on this point. But what he had written here was a long and lucid story. The voice captured in these sentences was, for the most part, foreign to him. Except for a few parts here and there, it in no way resembled the syntax, the grammar of his thoughts. And what was with the vocabulary he used? *Apparition… putrid… druidic ruins.* These words were not in regular rotation inside his mind. And what about the alien phrase from that strange, unholy book on the pulpit? He had glimpsed it for only a few seconds inside that moldering church, and yet he captured it here… *verbatim*. He somehow *knew* that he had.

It felt then as if these words had not so much come from Riley as passed through him, as if he were merely a conduit for getting them down. *I've written this*, he thought, *for somebody else. I'm leaving a record behind… for someone.*

All of a sudden, he was tempted to delete the entire journal. He took in another deep, nasally breath and stared at the screen.

No. He shook his head and hit SAVE again. He'd keep this. These *were* his thoughts. He would preserve them for posterity.

Looking up from his desk, he could see that night had fallen. It was late now. What had happened to him in that deserted village already felt like a dream, like the whole thing had occurred to someone else. Riley looked to his right, to the reading chair he had set up on the other side of the library. On it rested the first volume of his grandfather's grandfather's diary, a bookmark stuck into the place where Riley had read to. He turned to his left, to look through the archway of the turret. There, he could see the other two volumes of that diary standing upright on their shelf. No doubt their pages would contain more details about the village of Lowfield, about whatever that *other* Riley Fuller and his brother, Robert, had found there. But Riley couldn't bear to read more of them, not tonight. He had seen and learned enough for now.

He got up from the desk, went into the turret, and looked through one of its windows and at his garden below. A stiff spring breeze had come up, and even from here Riley caught the sound of it rustling and whispering through the plants growing in rows down there. How soon would those vegetables be ready for harvest? Much sooner than should have been possible, he thought.

He went back out of the turret, passed through the library, went into the hall beyond it, and followed it down to his bedroom at the other end. He would sleep tonight. He had to—he was very tired now. Riley would try to nod off, no matter what filthy and degenerate dreams, what pornographic night visions, plagued him through the hours that would come.

Chapter 15

Two nights later, as he grappled with one of the worst cases of insomnia he'd had thus far, Riley Fuller did something that he had been putting off for several days: he called Jack Mackenzie to apologize.

Riley knew what he was apologizing for: not just for telling Jack to go fuck himself, but for calling the *Eastern Pioneer* a sensationalist little rag. This, he had discovered, was not true. Since that day, Riley had read the issue with his profile on the front page cover to cover, and he read the next week's edition as well. It was, as Jessie-Mac had indicated, a scrappy, spirited little newspaper. The main story in the most recent issue was an investigative piece that Jessie had written, about pay inequality at a nursing home in Souris. The male orderlies there, she uncovered, earned an average of twenty per cent more than the female ones. Neither the *Guardian* nor the CBC in Charlottetown had caught the discrepancy when the salaries had been published in a bland health-care sector report, but they both ran pieces on it *after* Jessie did—a huge coup for a summer intern. There were other treasures in the *Pioneer*. The columnists in that issue took to task various MLAs in Charlottetown about various small-town concerns, going after the elected officials with combative relish. There was also a regular update on the construction of the bridge to New Brunswick, written by Jack himself, clearly intended to hold various feet to the fire and make sure the people in charge completed the massive project on time. All in all, Riley thought it was amazing that Jack could put out such a compulsively readable newspaper with his tiny, shoestring operation. This little weekly out of Montague, he had to admit, did not fuck around. Even without Jessie's prompting, he wanted to make amends with Jack for saying otherwise.

But still, he was finding it hard tonight to actually say *I'm sorry*. He always found saying *I'm sorry* hard. He chalked thus up to a trait he inherited from his father, Thomas, who could never seem to admit he was wrong, no matter what the circumstances. Riley had that attitude in him, too. So instead, he came up with a compromise. It was, by any measure, the middle of the night now, and he decided to call the *Pioneer*'s office and leave his apology on the answering machine for Jack. A bit spineless, but it was all he could bring himself to do.

He sat on the living room couch with PEI's (surprisingly slim) phone book flipped open on his lap and dialed the number. He was caught off guard when somebody picked up on the third ring.

"Uh, hello? *Eastern Pioneer*."

Riley blinked. "Um, hi. Uh, yeah, is that... Jack?"

"Aye, it t's."

"Hi Jack. It's Riley Fuller calling."

"Well, a good evening to you, sir."

"Wow, I'm surprised there's anyone there at this hour. I was expecting to speak to your answering machine."

"Were you now?" Jack said. "No, I'm here. This is production night. We just finished putting this week's *Pioneer* to bed. It's a real *dinger* of an issue, too, if I dare say so. One of the best we've done in a while. I'm very excited about it."

"Good to hear."

"You're up late," Jack said, his voice angled.

"Couldn't sleep."

"Sorry to hear that." There was a pause, and then Jack added, "So, what did you want to talk to my answering machine about?"

God, Riley thought, *that* did *sound awful. An awful, cowardly cop-out.* "Look," he plowed forward, "I wanted to apologize for blowing up at you in your office. I'm sorry I lost my cool."

"Ah, hell," Jack said, "that's okay. Jessie-Mac told me yesterday about your chat in the park. It's fine. I get yelled at a lot. You know, I'm always telling my journalists, if you're not pissing somebody off you're not doing your job."

"Fair enough."

"I also know she mentioned to you that we chatted about that article after you left. In hindsight, I now think it was wrong to run the stuff about the shooting without your comment. She disagrees, of course. Leave it to a third-year journalism student to be puritanical in her ethics."

"I hear that."

"You're still welcome to submit a letter to the editor about it, if you want."

"No, that's okay," Riley replied. "I'm not much of a writer." But then he thought: *Or am I?* He cast his mind briefly up to the computer in his library, to the journaling he'd been doing, to the narrative torque he'd rendered onto those digital pages.

"There was something else about that story, actually," Jack went on. "I wanted to tell you why I was so hasty in jumping on your background in the first place. But it's probably better to have that chat in person." He cleared his throat. "Say, what are you doing right now?"

Riley blinked again. "Me? Going fifteen rounds with my insomnia. Why?"

"Whenever we put a dandy issue of the *Pioneer* to bed, like the one tonight, I go home and celebrate by having a Scotch or three and watching the sun come up over the Strait from my back deck. Care to join me?"

That made Riley think about his friend Sammy's advice in his most recent emails, about the importance of Riley making friends and creating social connections there on PEI, if he planned to stay long-term. "Yeah, actually, I'd like that a lot. Where are you?"

"We're out in Petit Point. You know where the old Sanderson farm used to be?"

"Jack, I just moved here in April."

"Oh right," he laughed. "I forgot. Sorry, it's an Island thing. Here, look: Just follow your Eight Mile Road east all the way to the end. Take a right at the T and go about a mile, then bang a left onto what's called the Old Loyalist Road. Follow that all the way to the shore. We're the second last house from the end. The big green one on the right. Park as quiet as you can and walk round the back, so you don't wake up my wife."

"Got it. When should I meet you?"

"I got a couple things to wrap up here. Gimme half an hour."

~

Riley found Jack's place with no trouble at all. He parked along the side of the road and then wandered up the long driveway to the big green house. He felt almost like a burglar as he navigated along the home's left-hand side, passing through the shadows there and over a drainage ditch, but he soon emerged in the backyard and saw the light beaming out from the deck. There was Jack, sitting at some modest patio furniture, smoking his pipe and sipping a Scotch. He appeared to be looking contemplatively out beyond his property to the water there, hidden for now by the deep dark night. Riley could hear but not see the surf as it roiled and sighed along the shore.

"Hello there," he said as gently as he could, as not to startle Jack or wake the house.

"*Och aye*, there he is!" Jack replied, raising his glass in salute as Riley climbed up onto the deck. "I was hoping you'd come out. Welcome, lad."

"Thanks for having me."

"You a Scotch man?"

"More bourbon that Scotch," Riley shrugged, sitting himself into one of the plastic chairs at the glass deck table. The evening was cool, almost cold. "Jim Beam, mostly," he added.

Jack made a face. "Ugh. Here. You need to try a real whisky." He picked up the bottle, which Riley could see was for something called Glenmorangie, and poured a generous glug into the second rocks glass that Jack had set out. Riley picked it up and took a sip, rolled the lively liquid around on his tongue. *Shit*, he thought. The stuff *was* smooth. It went down his throat like honey. Jack then pushed the ashtray in the middle of the table toward Riley in invitation.

Riley took out his du Mauriers, lit one, and looked back at the house. "Nice place you got," he said.

"Thanks. We like it. It was a great spot to raise five kids, let me tell you."

"Wow, five kids," Riley said, and felt a distant ache in his gut, a long-ago pain. "Five kids and your own small business. That's wild."

"What can I say?" Jack grinned as he ran a hand over his salt-and-pepper beard. "I earned every one of these here grey hairs. Our youngest three were born right up there, actually." He pointed with his pipe to a bedroom window on the second floor directly above their heads. "Home births with a midwife. You can't beat it with a stick. Caught them myself as they came into the world." Jack chuckled, but then grew pensive. "Now that they're all out and on their own, the Mrs. wants to sell and move closer to Montague. But I'm not quite ready for that." He gestured toward the back of the property. "You'll see why, once that sun comes up."

Riley just nodded.

Jack looked at him then, as if he were some exotic artifact. "You have kids?"

"Nope," Riley said, taking a drag and then tapping his ash. "Not at all. My wife and I... pardon me, my *ex*-wife and I, we tried for a long time, but we could never... bring one to term."

"Ugh. Sorry to hear it. That's shite."

"Yep. It is." Riley just took another drag.

Jack looked at him for a bit, and then said, "So, anyway, I usually just sit out here and play Solitaire and watch the sun rise. But I'm happy for the company." He picked up a deck of cards that was sitting on the table. They looked warped and weather-beaten, like they'd been left out in the rain. Jack freed them from their pack and began shuffling. "You play cards?"

"I know only one game," Riley said. "Scat. Do you know it?"

"Ah, love scat! Let's play."

"All right."

Jack dug three coins out of his pocket and Riley did the same, and they each set them on the table in front of them. Jack shuffled the cards some more and then dealt, three cards each. He set the remaining deck face down before lifting the top card and setting it face down next to it. Riley took the card up, looked at it, claimed it for his hand, and put down one he didn't want, a two of clubs. Jack had no use for that one, so he drew from the deck, looked at the card, and threw that one away too, a five of diamonds.

"My grandmother, my mom's mom, taught me this game," Riley said as they played. "She was vicious at it. She'd lose three hands in a row and be on her face, make you all cocky and think you had her on the ropes, then she'd come storming back and cream you four hands in a row. Every fucking time. It was a marvel to watch."

"That's hilarious," Jack laughed, puffing his pipe. On his turn, he drew from the deck, kept what he got, and threw away a nine of hearts. Taking the bait, Riley picked it up and added to his hand, throwing away a queen of spades. Jack immediately picked that one up and chucked out a four of diamonds. "That's scat," he declared, and dropped his three cards to reveal he'd had the king and ace of spades to go along with the queen. "Never throw away a face card if you can help it," he said. "Even for a nine."

"I'm rusty," Riley replied, pushing one of his coins into the centre of the table to form the kitty. Then he began gathering up the cards to shuffle them for the second hand. After a couple rounds in, he watched as Jack took up a two of hearts. "You must be working on threes," Riley said absently.

"Perhaps, I am," Jack smiled, "or maybe that's what I *want* you to think."

"So what did you want to tell me?" Riley asked as they played. "What was the thing you thought best to say to me in person?"

Jack hesitated for a bit, let a round or two go by before he spoke. "I thought you should know *why* I targeted you in that story, why I acted on my hunch about you after Jessie-Mac mentioned you were RCMP. It had nothing to do with the Moncton shooting. Not really. Truth is, I've had an axe to grind with the Mounties for a while now, and I probably jumped the gun to publish something else embarrassing about them in my paper."

"Why's that?" Riley asked, taking up a ten of diamonds that Jack had thrown away. He *was* working on three of a kind.

Jack sighed. "About four years ago, there was a Mountie in Charlottetown who enjoyed a few too many beers one night in the officers' mess there, but decided to drive home anyhow. On the way, he hit a high school kid with his car, right on the city's main drag. Killed him. There was a trial, but the cop got acquitted on all charges—his colleagues had closed ranks around him, of course. The story just *enraged* me. I couldn't stop thinking about that poor boy's parents and how they got no justice at all. I must have written three or four editorials about it during that time, each one angrier than the last. By the end, I was ranting about how the RCMP was the most corrupt employer in the country and could not be trusted to hold itself to account. Truth is, though, I'd had my own run-in with the Mounties about a year before that."

"Did you now?" Riley asked.

"Yes, sir. I got myself busted on a DUI while over in Nova Scotia. Just like that cop, I could have easily hit and killed somebody that night. I *didn't*, thank God, but I could have. I was convicted, as I should have been, and lost my license for six months. But do you know what I did when that happened?"

"What's that?" Riley asked, looking down at his hand. He had twenty-six points: the ten, plus a nine and a seven, all of diamonds. If Jack was still holding out for three of a kind, he'd be vulnerable. Riley decided he probably had enough points to win the hand, and so knocked on his next turn.

"I came home and ran a story about my own conviction on the front page of the *Pioneer*," Jack replied.

"Seriously?" Riley asked, perking a bit.

"Yes, sir. My thinking was: our paper should keep all the big shots in this community accountable, including its own publisher. It was the right thing to do."

"Wow. That's brassy." Riley sipped his Scotch, felt it warm up his chest. He had to admit, he was really starting to like Jack Mackenzie. Riley had dealt with a few small-town journalists over his years as a cop, and most of them, he'd found, were sanctimonious little rats. He didn't think any of them would have done something similar had *they* been convicted of a DUI.

"So I believe we're all responsible for our own actions," Jack went on. "Which is why I just couldn't get over what that Mountie did, and how he got away with it. I still have a chip on my shoulder, which is why I published your dirty laundry when maybe I shouldn't have."

"We RCMP have a bad reputation," Riley said. His mind flung briefly back to a year and a half earlier. "Not all of it undeserved," he added.

Jack looked down at the table. "Whose go is it anyhow? I've lost track."

"I knocked. It's your turn."

Jack drew a card off the deck and looked at it. "Well, frig me," he said, "wouldn't you know it." He added the card to his hand, chucked away an eight, and showed Riley what he had: three twos, which were worth thirty points. "That's just luck of the draw," he said. "I was chasing that two all hand."

"Shit," Riley smiled, showing him his twenty-six and then pushing his second coin into the kitty. "You got me on the ropes now."

As Jack shuffled and dealt for the next hand, he eyed up Riley as if searching his face for emotions that weren't quite there. "So you went through some bad shit in Moncton, didn't you?"

"The worst," Riley said. "You can't even imagine."

"You wanna talk about it? We're totally off the record if you do."

The truth was Riley did want to talk about it, but was worried how Jack might react if he knew the story, the *whole* story. Would he still want to be Riley's friend? Would he even still want him sitting here at his table and drinking his fancy Scotch?

Riley opened his mouth to start talking.

But just then, a slash of headlights came caroming across the backyard. Jack furrowed his brow in a *Who could that be at this hour?* expression. They heard a vehicle break on the sandy shoulder out front, an engine being killed, a door opening and then slamming shut. A moment later, the person appeared around the side of the house, taking the same path Riley had.

It was Jessie-Mac. With her appearance, the two men agreed—without exchanging a word—that their chat about the Moncton shooting was over.

"Oh good, you're still up," Jessie called over as she approached. She had her hoodie on, her black hair spread all over its shoulders. Both her hands were buried in the pouch pocket and she had what looked like a manila envelope pinched in her armpit. She trotted up the steps of the deck. "And Riley Fuller—you *did* decide to come out. I knew you two'd become fast friends if you just let it happen."

"Jessie-Mac, I told you to go home to bed," Jack admonished. "Darlin', it's late. Aren't you interviewing the post office manager in Georgetown at ten tomorrow morning?" He looked at his watch. "Excuse me, ten *this* morning?"

"Bah—I'll sleep when I'm dead," she replied, and flounced into one of the other chairs at the deck table. "Besides, once I started thinking my mom might still have that stuff I was telling you about, I couldn't *stop* thinking about it. I went home and dug around in the basement, and sure enough I found them." She passed Jack the manila envelope. "They're letters my great aunt wrote to my great grandmother, which my mom kept. They might be nothing, but they might help with that enquiry we got. They're certainly from the right time period."

Jack picked up the envelope, peeked his nose inside. "We could do a little retrospective feature about what happened back then."

"Or a series of them, if what the old lady who pitched the idea said was true." Jessie nodded at the envelope. "I'll need those back when you're done, obviously. They're like family heirlooms, so be careful with them."

"Your mom won't mind me reading these?"

"Not once I ask her."

Jack chuckled. "Well, I appreciate it. But you could've given these to me tomorrow, or next week?"

She shrugged and showed her palms to the still-dark sky, a gesture that said, *Well I'm here now.* Then she turned to Riley. "Sorry, shop talk. Blah blah blah." She nodded at the cards on the table. "Say, what are you gents playing?"

"It's called scat," Riley replied. "Do you know it?"

"Nope, but I learn fast. Can you teach me and then deal me in?"

"Why don't you watch a few hands and we'll explain the rules."

So that's what they did. As they played, Riley and Jack outlined how the goal was to get at or as close to thirty-one points, all of the same suit, while keeping only three cards in their hand at all times—no more, no less. During the explanation, Riley finally won a hand after knocking early with twenty-eight points, and Jack, having revealed he had only seventeen, shoved a coin into the kitty. But then Jack took the next hand, putting Riley on his face, as well as the hand after that, thus winning the game. "Make sense?" he asked Jessie as he redistributed the coins in the kitty and fished out three more from his pocket to give to her.

"Got it," she replied.

But it soon became apparent that she didn't quite have it. Not yet. She knocked earlier than she should have, forgetting that for points to count they had to come from the same suit.

"No, that's only sixteen, sweetheart," Jack pointed out when she revealed her hand, "not twenty-six. I've got twenty-two and Riley's got twenty. So you lose. Put a coin in the kitty."

"Oh shoot!" she said.

For the next hand, she stared at her cards more intently and the three of them played in silence for a while. But then she looked at Riley. "So did Jack tell you he's letting me write an opinion piece for the paper? It'll be my very first one."

"He did not," Riley replied, chucking a seven of hearts he drew from the deck. "Congratulations. What's it on?"

"My abortion," Jessie replied.

Riley raised his eyes up from his cards. "Really?"

"Yep. After our chat in the park that day, I decided I wanted to write about it. I've never talked about my abortion with people around here, but enough's enough. I'm not afraid. What I'm doing to do is tie it in with the construction of the bridge to the mainland."

"How's that?" Riley asked.

"Well, I figure once the bridge is done, it'll be a real boon for women's reproductive health here on the Island. Even if abortions are still banned on PEI, at least it'll be easier for women to get one out-of-province. They won't have to go through *quite* as much as I did."

At that, Jessie discarded the ace of spades after drawing it from the deck.

"Ooh, never throw away an ace," Riley said. "Bad move."

"But it's not the suit I'm working on."

"Doesn't matter. It should *become* the suit you're working on. That's just good strategy."

"And now, because it's my turn," Jack said, "I can claim that ace, and you've just given me scat." He chucked a four of diamonds from his hand and laid down his other two cards, the king and queen of spades. "And you *knew* I was working on spades because you saw me pick up the king you threw away three rounds ago. And because I got scat, you *both* have to pay the kitty."

"Oh *shoot*," Jessie exclaimed.

"Scat's all about watching for which suit the other person is working on and switching your own on the fly if it means not helping them." Riley gathered up the cards to shuffle and deal. As he did, he looked at Jack. "So you're okay with her doing this piece for the *Pioneer*?"

"I don't normally let interns write editorials," he replied, relighting his pipe before picking up the cards Riley had dealt him. "Reporters need to learn how to dig up the news before they learn how to comment on it. But I'm making an exception for Jessie-Mac. You're *that good*, little lady. Plus, a piece like that is gonna piss off all the right people around here."

Jessie beamed at the compliment, then shrugged at Riley. "Jack's got all kinds of crazy rules for his journalists. Did you know he won't let us attend press conferences? Calls them—what is it again, Jack? Orchestrated theatrics?"

"You go to the same press conference as all the other reporters," he said, examining his cards, "you write the same story as all the other reporters."

"And he wants us to talk to fifty people a day. Fifty! That's where we get 'real news,' he says."

"Just good community journalism," Jack shrugged. "That's how I learned about you moving into Applegarth, Riley—by bending Dave Campbell's ear in the Boar's Head one night."

The mention of the house caused Riley to brood. The memory of his hike into the woods behind it squelched up in his mind like black tar. "Can I ask you guys a question?" he said, staring at his hand. He held two fives, and so would work on threes rather than build on a suit.

"Sure thing," Jack replied, his lips smacking over his pipe as he examined his own cards.

"You ever hear of a place in the area called Lowfield?"

Jessie and Jack looked at each other quizzically, then shrugged.

"No, never," Jessie replied.

"Me neither," Jack said. "Why? What is it?"

Riley didn't answer right away. How much did he want to get into this with them? If they asked about the place and whether he'd been there, would he lie? Riley flicked absently at his cards with this thumb, waiting for his turn. No, he wouldn't. He wouldn't lie to these people. "It's an abandoned village," he went on tentatively. "It's probably been unincorporated or whatever, because it's not on any PEI map."

Jack just shook his head again and scratched his salt-and-pepper beard. "News to me. Of course, I didn't grow up around here. I immigrated to Canada as a young man—from Scotland, in case the accent didn't give me away."

"How about you, Jessie?" Riley asked. "Ever heard the word Lowfield. Maybe from some old timer around Glenning?"

"Can't say that I have," she replied. "How did you find out about it?"

"From a diary I found in Applegarth's library. I think a few of my ancestors lived in Lowfield before it became deserted."

"Where is it?" Jack asked. "Or should I say, where *was* it?"

Riley cleared his throat. "According to the diary, just shy of two miles back behind my property."

The next obvious question from these two journalists was of course, *Have you been there?* And if they asked that, they'd also ask what Riley had seen when he had. He suddenly wished he'd never brought up the topic. He no more wanted to talk about Lowfield than he did the Moncton shooting. These two people were quickly becoming his friends, and he didn't want to spoil that by bringing such dark topics into the conversation.

"Well, like I say, it's news to me," Jack said, drawing from the deck, "but I can ask around if you like. If it did exist, *somebody* must have heard of it."

"No, don't bother," Riley said. He had a vision of both Jack and Jessie traipsing through the woods behind Applegarth and stumbling upon Lowfield. And that, he thought, would somehow... put them in danger. "It's fine. It's okay. Just a bit of family lore I was curious about. It's no big deal."

Riley drew from the deck and got one of the other fives. He added it to his hand and discarded an eight of clubs, which Jessie picked up. On his next turn, he knocked.

"Oh no, you're *knocking*?" Jessie asked. "So soon? I just started building on a new suit. I'm not ready!"

"Them's the breaks," Jack said over his pipe.

He and Jessie got one more turn each, and then they all revealed their cards. With his three fives, Riley had thirty points. Jack had twenty-eight. Jessie, perhaps learning her lesson from the previous hand, did have an ace, as well as the eight Riley had tossed, and a four—but they were all from different suits. Eleven points was all she had. She glumly pushed her last coin into the kitty.

"You're on your face," Riley said to her.

As he said this, Jack glanced out beyond the deck's rail. "There it is!" he said suddenly, his bearded face squeezing upward into a grin. "Now *that's* what I'm talking about."

Riley and Jessie both turned to look.

The horizon line beyond Jack's backyard, for so long the deep cobalt of a barber's jar of disinfectant, abruptly burst into a wild smear of bright orange light. Those searing rays brought the shores of Petit Point to life in an instant, articulating their deep-red sands, the misty-blue waters, the fragile Island dunes with their long grasses swaying in the breeze. What had been pitch blackness a moment before, a sort of death, was now fervently and gorgeously alive. It almost seemed like there was some flourishing presence, as ancient as time itself, living and thriving right below the surface of those glittering waves as they rolled in from the Northumberland Strait. The three of them watched as a colony of gulls dunked and bobbed through the air at the place where the water met the land.

"Life is good, eh?" Jack said, raising his whisky glass and nodding it toward his companions. "Ah, that we should live so well."

"Frig, it is beautiful here," Riley concurred, sticking another du Maurier in his mouth and lighting it. He felt a swell of closeness to Jack and Jessie overtake him then. They *were* his friends, he thought.

"You're a very lucky man, Jack Mackenzie," Jessie said.

"Aye, I am."

They finished their game. Jessie managed to stay in for one more hand when she got scat after a couple rounds in, but after that she was done. By the time Jack got Riley on his face and then eliminated him to win the game, his wife Helen was awake and had shuffled out into the kitchen in her bathrobe. She waved to her husband through the glass door leading to the deck, looking unperturbed by the fact that he was out there drinking Scotch with Jessie and a stranger at dawn.

"Well this has been fun, gents, but I need to sleep," Jessie said, getting up. "I got that ten a.m. interview."

"I'll walk you to your car," Riley said, also getting up. "Jack, this has been fun."

"It has. I hope you'll both come again."

Out on the road, Riley led Jessie to her pale-blue minivan parked on the shoulder. He once again spotted the P-shaped scab of rust over its back wheel well.

"Good luck with your interview later," he said as they stood before the driver-side door. "I'm sure you'll do fine."

"Thanks," she replied, and then she did something totally unexpected. She hopped up and gave him a hug. Her small, lithe presence in his arms caught Riley off guard, and he nearly fell over. But before he could even absorb the hug, before he could fully appreciate it, it was over. Back on both feet, Jessie pulled open the Caravan's door and climbed in behind the wheel. "Try to get some sleep, Riley," she said with a smile. "You look like shit on a cracker."

He just waved as she drove off.

~

He thought about that hug all the way back to Glenning—the feel of it, its contours, its closeness. He could practically smell Jessie's soft scent, almost like baby powder, on his clothes the entire drive back. How long had it been since any female had touched him?

Riley pulled up his long driveway and parked in his usual spot, just next to the house's Queen Anne turret. He sat there in the Lumina for a long time, looking up at Applegarth, and at the dense forest behind it. His unholy garden, there on his right, swayed and shushed in the breeze. He didn't want to go in the house. He knew what would happen, what would come over him, if it did.

She's my friend now. She's my friend.

Yeah, but you're imagining lots of unfriendly things you'd like to do to her.

She's only twenty. She's just a kid.

Yeah, but she's got a body built for fucking.

Stop it!

He couldn't help himself. There was no place else to go.

He climbed out of the Lumina and went into Applegarth through its side entry. He kicked off his shoes in that enormous foyer and headed straight up the winding staircase, its wood cracking and twisting under his weight. He went into his room, stripped off his clothes and climbed into the bed. Once there, he masturbated wildly, feverishly into the sheets, his voice booming against the old plaster walls as he did.

Afterward, he just lay there, drenched in a sticky, salty remorse. *You fucking asshole,* he thought, disgusted with himself. *You fucking prick. She's just a kid. She's just a kid. You know exactly what all of this reminds you of.* And before he could stop it, Riley's memory pitched backward, returning him to more than three years earlier, the recollections bursting in his brain with perfect clarity. *You piece of garbage. This is the sort of shit, Riley, that cost you EVERYTHING.*

Chapter 16

"*We're taking this one to go see Queen Victoria.*"
"*Comeback, 418? Oh, wait. Har har. Got it.*"

On a cold and cloudless night in January 1992, Riley Fuller listened to this exchange on his squad car's CB radio as he sat parked and idling at a Moncton Tim Hortons. He had a medium double-double in one hand, a cigarette in the other, and very few thoughts in his head. As he sat there, the heater filling the car with warmth, Riley was looking forward to the end of his shift, though dreaded the idea of going home. He wasn't really listening to the CB radio, or at least he didn't *think* he was. But then he jolted lightly in his seat, squirmed a bit at the sound of those four words, *go see Queen Victoria*, as they crackled out of the speaker. Had that idiot just said them aloud, over the radio, to the dispatch? Riley knew the officer who had spoken them, a guy named Sloka. Dale Sloka was exactly the sort of cop who would use that phrase over the CB.

Riley took a long, hard drag on his cigarette. Sipped his coffee.

By this point in his career, Riley knew all the slang, all the lingo spoken on the CB and off. His favourite, by far, was the idiom *Can you call me a buffalo taxi?* This was what you said to the dispatch if you called him—or, more increasingly, her—from a payphone because you were off duty and downtown drinking and didn't want to pay for a cab to take you home. *Call me a buffalo taxi* meant: Can you please find a couple of officers with nothing better to do to come by and pick me up? And if the dispatch could, then your colleagues would drive over in their squad car, with the RCMP's buffalo logo on its doors, to whatever bar you were at and chauffer you home safely. It was one of the few perks of being a cop in a rough little city like Moncton.

The euphemism *Go see Queen Victoria* was another matter entirely—perhaps the very *opposite* matter. It didn't apply to officers. It applied to certain types that officers sometimes encountered on the street. Riley knew that Mounties around the country had different terms for it. On a clear night, like tonight, some might call it the Starlight Tour. Others might dub it the Long Walk. In Moncton, it was called Going to See Queen Victoria, on account of the stretch of road, well north of the city, that the more impatient officers in their detachment had picked out for such a purpose. Victoria Road, running between the backwater communities of Shaw Brook and New Scotland, was one of the most desolate places in the area, a lengthy stretch of rural Maritime nothingness: no street lamps, few houses, no real civilization of any kind, for several miles. To drive up there from downtown took about twenty-five minutes. But for an inebriated perp to *walk* back, after the RCMP dumped him or her on the side of that weedy, empty road, took more than four hours. Enough time to sober up and have a good think about your life decisions—or, on a night like tonight, which was minus-18 with the wind chill, have something far worse happen.

Riley sipped his coffee. Thrummed his fingers absently on the steering wheel. Fidgeted again.

The incident downtown that sparked all this had been, according to a previous exchange on the CB, a fairly standard drunk and disorderly. Sloka and his partner had been summoned to the corner of Main and Robinson. Some little chickee had had too much to drink at a dive bar on Robinson Street, gotten into a fight, broken a glass or two, been thrown out onto the sidewalk. While other details coming over the CB were sketchy, the arrival of the cops seemed to have resulted in a belligerence that achieved almost callisthenic proportions, plus some vomiting. Maybe Sloka was having a bad night, or a bad week. Maybe the girl had puked *on* him. But for whatever reason he and his partner decided that a night in the drunk tank was too good for her. *We're taking this one to go see Queen Victoria*, the moron had said moronically into the CB. Fuck he was a moron, Riley thought.

But he wasn't really dwelling on Dale Sloka. He was thinking about the girl. The dialogue on the CB had given no indication as to what she was wearing, though on a night like tonight, it probably wouldn't matter. Four or five hours out in this cold would be brutal, maybe even fatal. Riley knew what he *should* do, and the fact that doing it would stick it to Sloka was just the cherry on the sundae. Riley set his coffee in the cup holder and reached for the gear shift, but then lowered his hand again. A scenario, not all that unlikely, flickered through his head—of word getting around the detachment that he had undone Sloka's knee-jerk decision, had intervened in somebody's visit to Queen Victoria.

But still. It was minus-18 out.

In the end, it was Jane's voice, ricocheting through his head, that cast the deciding vote—telling him to do what he *knew* was right.

Riley waited ten more minutes, to ensure that his fellow officers would be long gone from Victoria Road by the time he himself got up there. Then he put his squad car in gear. Before he left, he went through the Tim Hortons' drive-thru to get another coffee. Only this one was black, extra-large, and piping hot.

~

When he arrived at the top of Victoria Road, Riley wondered if maybe he'd wasted his time coming up here. The girl was nowhere to be found at first. Had Sloka and his partner dropped her off someplace else? Had they changed their minds? But as he drove along that bleakly wooded and isolated stretch, he eventually spotted her marching up the road's snowy shoulder, the pompoms on her winter boots swinging, her breath a tornado-like plume pumping out in gusts from her hooded head. Sloka had, Riley could see as he pulled up behind her, let the girl keep her jacket at least. This didn't always happen. A Mountie somewhere out in the Prairies, maybe in Saskatoon or Winnipeg, had gotten into a spot of trouble a couple of winters back after stripping some kid of his jacket during a Starlight Tour, and got charged with (though eventually acquitted of) second-degree murder.

He gave the siren a squirt to get the girl's attention, but she didn't turn around.

So he pulled up next to her and slowed even more before reaching across to roll down the passenger window. A sledgehammer of cold air slammed into his face when he did.

"Get in," he called to the girl, and braked.

"*Fuck you!*" Her voice was slobbery with tears and snot.

She marched on, and he pulled ahead to catch up with her. "Seriously, get in. You'll freeze to death."

The girl stopped in a huff and turned to him. Her eyes and cheeks glowed wetly in the shadows of her hood. The jacket she wore looked old, flimsy. Not a proper winter coat. Her leggings made her thighs and shins look like sticks. She seemed to shiver from the crown of her head all the way to her ankles.

He popped open the passenger door. "Come on. Get in. I'll even let you sit up front with me."

She considered this. She turned and looked further down the dark, tree-lined throat of Victoria Road, to where it eventually T-boned at Indian Mountain Road, which would eventually lead in either direction to a couple of minor highways back into town. The Long Walk, indeed.

She wiped her nose with her sleeve, hesitated again, but then got in, flouncing into the passenger seat and slamming the door once her feet were safely in the bucket.

Riley drove on.

The girl said nothing. She just sat there, her wrist crushed into her dripping nose, her chest heaving. But then, with one swipe of her arm, she lowered her icy hood. Riley looked over.

She was pretty. Jesus fuck. If she'd were any prettier, Riley thought, she'd have to be on the cover of a magazine. Too pretty to be messing around in that dive bar on Robinson and getting picked up by the cops.

He nodded at the extra-large Tim Hortons in its cup holder. "That's for you," he said. "It should still be fairly hot."

She looked down at it, her black hair coming loose of her coat. Moving his eyes back and forth from the road to the girl, Riley watched as she lifted off the lid, took an exploratory glance inside, made a face, but then clasped the cup and raised it to her chapped lips. She grimaced again. "What, no milk and sugar?"

"I—I... sorry," Riley stammered. "I, I didn't know what you took it in." He almost had to chuckle.

"Asshole," she said, but then stole another, greedier gulp.

He liked her instantly.

~

On the drive back into town, Riley cajoled a few details out of her. Her name was Marigold Burque. She was originally from Bouctouche but was currently living rough in some flophouse in the sketchy Moncton neighbourhood of Parkton. Tonight was actually her twenty-fourth birthday, she told him, though the evening had, obviously, not gone as planned. He was somewhat incredulous when she said that she'd been living in Moncton off and on for nearly ten years, as he could not recall ever seeing her around town. It also wasn't clear what her relationship was with her Bouctouche people. In one breath, Marigold indicated she was estranged from them, that they were all drunks and layabouts and "total abusive fucks." In another, she spoke of her extended family with a kind of spooky reverence, as if they were gods instead of people. It sort of freaked him out.

By the time Riley parked the squad car out front of her building in Parkton, neither of them were quite ready to stop talking. There was a queer connection between them, right from the beginning. Even then, he knew this was wrong. He felt helpless as she charmed certain details out of him, too.

How long you been a pig?

He grinned at that, at the ridiculousness of the term. *Eighteen years this April.*

You married?

Yeah, but not happily.

Jesus. Why did he tell her that? He really shouldn't have told her that.

Eventually, she got out of his car. He was sad to see her go.

"Thanks again for, you know, saving my life or whatever."

"You're welcome," he said. "Happy birthday, Marigold."

"Thanks. I'll see you around, asshole."

~

And see her around, he did. It was so weird: she had lived in Moncton a decade and did, it turned out, have a lengthy rap sheet with police, and yet he'd never heard of her. Now, in the days and weeks following her visit to Victoria Road, he saw Marigold around all the time.

If he was alone, he'd stop and talk to her. She'd clam up at first, but then eventually warm to him. He started showing up in places he thought she'd be so he'd run into her, places he wouldn't normally be caught dead in, including the dive bar on Robinson Street that had gotten her into so much trouble. Riley knew this was wrong, too, but he couldn't help himself. It was like a compulsion, a game he'd play, seeing how many times he could encounter this person on Moncton's streets if he tried.

They started going for drives together in his Lumina. Up to Shediac or down to Elgin, where nobody knew them.

The first time they kissed was in the parking lot of the Shediac Tim Hortons. Riley knew, even in that moment's sweet delirium, that he was betraying his marriage, that he was humiliating Jane. But those thoughts seemed very distant as Marigold's mouth embraced his, her chest pressing into him as he reached for her across the Lumina's seats. She was a reluctant kisser until she wasn't.

The first time they fucked was in a roadside motel near Sackville, close to the Nova Scotia border. Riley seemed to know the routine by instinct: Go in first by himself and pay for a room with cash, signing in under a false name; then go back out to the car and retrieve his overnight bag and Marigold. Behind the dour motel room's now locked and chained door, they were wary with each other for a while, not quite believing that they had come this far. Riley was shy with her at first. He was still in okay shape back then—only a slight paunch to his gut, not much grey yet in his beard—but still, Marigold was indisputably cuter than he was. They just talked for a while. But talking soon led to kissing, which led to touching, which led to more. It amazed him how fluidly she moved from ambivalent hesitation to enthusiastic consent.

On their second night in a hotel room, the sex took less time to begin. And on the third, even less.

Their conversations remained almost as good as the sex, though Riley was baffled to explain why. Despite her eighth-grade education, Marigold was quick-witted and had a real way with words. Riley often couldn't believe the creative indelicacies that came out of her mouth. *A dick in the butt is worth two in the bush,* she'd said crassly after the first time they had anal and he made her squirt. Jane had never said—or done—anything like that.

He and Marigold didn't really go on dates. Their encounters involved mostly coffee at the Tims in Shediac and sex in the motel in Sackville. They once drove to Fredericton to take in a movie, a ridiculous-looking adaptation of a Stephen King story that Marigold loved, but had to bail when Riley thought he saw someone he knew going into the theatre. The only proper date they ever had was when, upon Riley giving her a tour of his service weapon, she said she wanted to learn how to shoot, and so, on the first halfway warm weekend of 1992, they drove down to an outdoor shooting range near Saint John. If Marigold was uncomfortable being around a bunch of beer-bellied, middle-class guys and their surly teenaged sons, all sporting firearms and decked out in camo gear, she didn't let on. As soon as Riley put his private pistol, the Glock, in her hands, her face lit up with a smile that made him love her a little. "Oh, I gotta get me one of *these*," she said, clasping the gun in both hands and swinging it recklessly from side to side, as if she wanted to waste every motherfucker in sight. "Target's over there, chickie," Riley said, guiding her wrists toward the paper human dangling at the other end of her lane.

To his surprise, she was an excellent shot right off the bat. Shockingly so. He'd never seen a beginner with such good aim. It was almost like Marigold had eyes in her fingers. He'd remember that, later.

Not long after that, Sammy came up from Fredericton for a visit after the end of semester. Riley asked that they meet at a roughneck bar over on Lewisville Road that he knew would be empty in the middle of the day. There, less than one bourbon in, Riley confessed the whole affair to his best friend.

When Riley finished, Sam assumed his usual posture of wisdom—elbows up on the bar table, his brown eyes large and locked onto his buddy, his thick eyebrows knitted together. "Okay, first thing's first," he said, almost smiling. "This may shock you to hear, Riley Fuller, but you're *not* the first 42-year-old man in history to get the hots for a 24-year-old woman. Okay?" Riley gave that an acrid chuckle. "All over this city, all over this *world*," Sam continued, "people are stepping out on their marriages—men *and* women. It happens every fucking day of the year. So on one level, what you've done is not out of the ordinary. Okay? You're not special."

"Okay," Riley said, looking down.

Sammy squinted at him. "Let me ask you a question. Do you read a lot of books about World War I."

Riley sort of blinked at him, confused. "No, not really."

"Me neither. I'm not a big fan of military history. I certainly don't write the stuff. But everybody knows that during World War I, the worst place a soldier could be on the battlefield was in no-man's land. You're ex-military; you know what I'm talking about."

Riley nodded. "Yeah, of course."

"You get up out of your trench and try to reach the enemy's, but you're trapped in that place in between. And it's a horrible spot to be. No man's land is where you get sniped at. It's where you feel helpless and pinned down. It's where the story ends very badly for you."

"Right," Riley said, starting to understand.

"That's where you are, right now. You're in no-man's land. You've gotten up out of the trench you've dug with Jane, but you're not all the way over to Marigold's. You're trapped in between. You want my advice? You want to be able to sleep at night? Get out of no-man's land. Either come all the way back to Jane—retreat into the trench you've dug with her, and *be* there. Whether you guys *ever* get pregnant, it doesn't matter. You love her. You be the man you want to be… *for her.*" Sam cleared his throat. "*Or,* if you really see a future with this other girl, then be with her. Go all in. Marigold isn't just a fuck toy to you. That's obvious. You care about her. So tell Jane you've met somebody else, and that's it."

Riley stared at the table. Shame set his ears and neck ablaze.

Sammy squinted at him again. "Let me ask: *do* you see a future with Marigold?"

Riley scoffed at that. "Most days I don't think *she* has a future," he said. "She lives pretty rough, and probably always will. Talk about a story ending very badly for someone."

"Well, I think that's your answer," Sam said. "Do you think you're going to *help* her situation by having an affair with her?"

Riley hesitated before he answered, but not for very long. "No," he said.

"Well, then? If you care about her, then do what's best for her. I think you know what that is."

Riley nodded. Sams, with his usual way with words, had given him another set of eyes to see view the world with.

~

Marigold must have known something was up, because Riley asked for them to meet at a Moncton Tim Hortons—a huge risk of being spotted together by someone they knew—rather than drive up in his Lumina to the one in Shediac.

She must have known something was up, because when she came into the Tims and joined him at his table, Riley didn't look at or greet her in his normal way. She was twenty minutes late, which was fine—she was always twenty minutes late, for everything. He already had their usual set out for them: two medium double-doubles, a chocolate dip donut for her and a bear claw for him.

She must have known something was up, because she already seemed a touch queasy, a bit green in the face, before Riley had even opened his mouth. In fact, she didn't touch her coffee or donut at all. She just looked at him in anticipation. *Fuck, she's going to take this hard,* he thought before he began.

But in the end, she didn't take it hard, or didn't seem to. Marigold just cast her eyes down as Riley held his coffee without drinking it and told her how things were going to be. The May morning sun beamed in through the window next to their table, tossing a triangle of light on its surface.

"I'm sorry," Riley said when he finished, and finally took a sip. Just a small one. "I really am."

She stared at the tabletop for a while longer, but then, much to his surprise, she looked up and gave her little shoulders a *whatcha gonna do?* jostle. "I guess I knew this would happen," she said. "All good shit comes to an end, ain't I right? It's probably for the best." And here, she gave him a wry smile. "I mean, I've been worried sick these last three months. If word gets around Parkton that I've been," and here, she lowered her voice in mock disgust, "*shagging a pig*, I'll never live it down."

He laughed at that. One dry hitch of his chest. "I'm sorry," he said again. "I should be helping you, Marigold, but this, this thing between us, is just causing you more harm."

"Nobody can help me," she said.

Her words chilled him right to his spine. He wanted to say something to refute her, to tell her things could be different, that there were many roads in life. But before he could, she told him, rather abruptly, that she had to go to the bathroom. She got up and went, and was gone a long time—a *very* long time. So long, in fact, that Riley began to worry, began to think that maybe he should get a Tims staff member to go check on her. But eventually she returned, scooting back into the seat across from him. He watched as she took some napkins out of their stainless steel holder on the table and wiped her mouth.

"I'm not really up for food or drink today," she said when she finished. "Sorry you wasted your money. But can you still give me a lift home? I don't have enough change for the bus back."

"Of course," he said with a nod. "Let's go."

~

Strangely, he didn't see Marigold Burque around town for a long while after that. In fact, a few months following their breakup, Riley heard that she was no longer living in Moncton at all. She must have reconciled with part or all of her people back in Bouctouche, because that's where she'd been since the middle of summer.

Then, about a year after that, Riley arrested one of her old pool-hall buddies on a drug possession charge. During their police station chat, the guy mentioned to Riley that Marigold had recently moved back to Moncton. Moved back, and had gotten herself a *job* no less. She was working, the guy said, as a chambermaid at the Red King Hotel over on Mountain Road. Word was she might even try going for her GED come that fall.

Warmth spread all through Riley when he heard this. *Good on ya, girl*, he thought. *Good on ya. Nobody can help you? Sounds like you're trying to help yourself.*

Little did he know that the Red King Hotel would prove to be the very gullet of the beast for Marigold. Something far worse than their affair, their brief, consensual tryst, loomed on her horizon. On Riley's, too.

Chapter 17

June 8, 1995,
Dear Sammy,

So glad to hear my little package arrived to you, and on time no less. Happy birthday, brother. To answer your question, I found that album at the big flea market held every Sunday at the Charlottetown Mall. I remembered you saying how you'd lost your own copy years ago and had to replace it on cassette, which just didn't sound the same. To answer your *other* question, my favourite track has always been the last one, "Jungleland." It's so epic, and not in a cheesy Meatloaf sort of way. I also made a purchase for myself at the flea market, one that finally drags me into the late 20th century: a CD player. I know, I know. I still keep tapes in the car, but I need something here in the house to listen to while I potter around and do my renos. The boom box I bought is a combo CD player, AM/FM radio, and tape deck, and I got it for cheap! I managed to pick up some Gordon Lightfoot and CCR at the flea market as well, to kick my collection off. It's a start.

Speaking of home renos, I've made lots of progress on Applegarth since my last email. What seemed like a rotting, dilapidated shell of a house two months ago now feels downright cozy, like a proper home. It's amazing how new hardwood floors in the living room, new cupboards in the kitchen, and some fresh paint on the walls will bring a place back to life. Still, I have so much work left to do. Yesterday I spent an hour in the dirt-floor basement trying to decide whether I can find a use for the pile of old cinder blocks down there. And hard as it is to believe, I *still* haven't ventured into the attic yet. There must be rats up there, or worse. I can hear them shuffling around all night and day behind the walls. The sound makes the house feel... I don't know, *unclean* somehow.

What I'm saying is, I would love for you and Joan to come visit, but I don't think the house is ready for that yet. I want you to be comfortable; I don't want you guys staying one night and then feeling compelled to check into a hotel for the rest of your visit because it's still sort of gross here. So maybe later this summer? I'll let you know.

But Sammy, please believe me when I say I have followed your advice. I am starting to lay down some roots here, and have even made a couple of friends, people that I *want* to see and spend time with. I have things to look forward to, most days. In a nutshell, I'm not "fine" per se, but I'm doing better. Thanks, as always, for your concern, and your friendship. It means the fucking world to me.

Yours,
Riley

Riley fired the email off but then went into his SENT folder to read over what he had written. Had he lied to Sammy? Had he deceived his old friend? No, he didn't think he had. Not technically. Riley *was* still working on the renos to Applegarth, with Gordon Lightfoot and John Fogarty's voices throbbing out of that boom box in the living room as he swept alcoves and replaced rusted door hinges and tore up old tiles. That part was true. And there *were* new floorboards in the living room, and new cupboards in the kitchen, and new paint on the walls. That part was also true.

What *wasn't* true was what his email had implied—that those two things were connected. Because they weren't. Riley couldn't bear to think, let alone mention in an email, that the living room's gleaming new hardwood floor, and the bright new kitchen cupboards, and the paint on the walls, had all appeared *on their own*. It was absolutely fucking insane, but he could no longer mince words inside his own head: Applegarth was *renovating itself*—just like the garden outside was growing vegetables and fruit all on its own. Somehow, when he first noticed these things, he was able to shrug them off, to make flimsy excuses to himself—not about the reason they were happening, because there was no logical explanation, but only about why he had chosen to accept them, or ignore them, or both. Honestly, everything that had happened since he'd moved in here—the repairs, the garden, the intense sexual visions that came to him at night—felt like his *due,* like he was claiming for himself something that had belonged to the men in his family for generations. Living here, in this house, on this land, was paramount to Riley starting a fresh chapter of his life, and he thought that Applegarth was simply *helping him out*, a bit of paranormal assistance as he tried to make the place habitable.

But now, it was obviously the other way around: his modest, perfunctory repairs were but an adjunct to what was happening to Applegarth, a token gesture. The house now seemed to be… to be *coming alive*, turning into a living thing.

It was also happening faster than before, and Riley thought he knew why. It was his visit to the village of Lowfield. It was that damned church, and the book sitting upon its pulpit, *The Grimoire of Shaal*, that was causing things to speed up. He wasn't sure how he knew this, but the mere fact that he had touched that text, read some of its words, had been like a… like a catalyst, an invisible force pulsating out from the woods behind his property, an energy that was accelerating the house's self-repair.

How was this possible? Riley didn't know, but he knew where he might find out. From his place at the computer, he looked over to the other side of the library, to the first volume of his grandfather's grandfather's diary, still sitting on the reading chair's cushion. He hadn't touched that tome in over three weeks, when he'd read its opening entry. He couldn't bear to go back to it, no matter how much his curiosity nudged him along.

Instead, Riley tried to distract himself from it. He'd read one of the obscure, impenetrable books of Canadian poetry that Sammy had sent him. That volume had not only baffled Riley but *annoyed* him by how baffling, how indecipherable it was. What did Sammy see in this stuff? Riley had no intention of reading the others. Instead, he lost himself in yardwork and more home repairs. He stayed clear of the library, and watched TV in the living room instead. He told himself: I hate reading. It's going to take me a long while to come back to that other Riley Fuller's diary. It'll be a long time before I'm ready.

Sighing, he got up from the desk and walked over to the reading chair. He picked up the diary resting on its cushion, and sat down. Then he cracked open its covers.

The tale that unspooled over the next few entries was almost too fantastical to believe. The original Riley Fuller and his brother Robert, with nine-year-old Miriam in tow, had made their promised trek into Lowfield. On its main drag, the trio encountered a villager who directed them to speak to Lowfield's resident preacher if they wanted to learn about their kin. This villager, the diary noted in horrifying detail, seemed to have suffered from a hideous array of birth defects, so bad that they frightened little Miriam. The trio nonetheless made their way to the village church where they met the preacher, one James Robert Fuller. The brothers had known this name, and had always assumed that it belonged to their mother Melinda's *grandfather*, the founder of Lowfield, who was already in his seventies when she had fled PEI for Halifax when her boys were still very young. They had also assumed that this old man would be long in his grave. But no—the brothers learned that James Robert Fuller was in fact a) Melinda's *father*, not grandfather, and b) alive and well and still living in Lowfield at the advanced age of 103.

There was more. One of the ushers attending to this Elder Fuller had suffered from the same birth defects the brothers had seen in that villager on their way in. In the diary, Riley Fuller began referring to this array of deformities as the *Lowfield look*.

A week later, the brothers attended their grandfather's Sunday service in Lowfield. To Riley Fuller's horror, *many* in the congregation seemed to possess the Lowfield look, and it soon became apparent why. James Robert Fuller's preaching was full of strange, sexually charged blasphemies that advocated for incest. These acts, he had reminded his parishioners, helped them all to access something he referred to as the Great Force Beyond—a term, the diary noted, found nowhere in scripture.

Riley Fuller had been *aghast* at this service, but his brother Robert was utterly mesmerized by the old man. He had insisted they accept the preacher's invitation to lunch after the service, where they learned more about the founding of Lowfield and that strange church.

And here, Riley stopped for a moment, letting the open diary rest in his lap as he leaned back in his chair. This was one of the vilest things he had ever read, but he would read on. He wanted to learn more, and knew specifically what he was searching the diary for. He was already more than halfway through the first volume and thought he'd come upon it before long.

Still, he found himself skimming several entries written over the summer of 1862; many of these had to do with dull details of the brothers' import-export business in Montague, and the daily domesticities of Applegarth. But then, a series of accounts seized his eye.

Robert, he read, had stopped attending the Presbyterian church in Glenning. He confessed to visiting Lowfield several times over the last number of weeks. He had begun taking Miriam to Sunday services there. The two brothers fought. There were threats from Riley of abandoning his half of their enterprise on the Island and returning to Halifax. There were pleads from Robert for his brother to understand the transformation of faith he was going through. He had seemed to latch onto the preaching of James Robert Fuller in a kind of mania. One entry was particularly disturbing: late one night, Riley had walked by his brother's bedroom door—the very chamber that Riley himself, here in 1995, used as the master bedroom—and could hear him, as the diary put it, *abusing himself loudly*. Horrified, he had nonetheless paused to listen, and swore that Robert had called out his own daughter's name, Miriam Fuller, during this fit of masturbation. It was so sickening that Riley almost set the diary aside.

And then, a few pages later, the reference he'd been hunting for came. By August, Robert had invited the old man to supper at Applegarth despite Riley's protestations, and while there, the Elder Fuller had made mention of what sounded to the younger brother like a fictitious deity: *Shaal.* The preacher described Shaal as *the sibling of Christ*, which had sent Riley into a tailspin of rage and mockery there at the dinner table. But Elder Fuller and Robert, not to mention the entire townsfolk of Lowfield, believed in this God, who, they had said, held the key to the Great Force Beyond. Strangely enough, during that dinner, Elder Fuller had shown an inordinate interest in the brothers' import-export concern, and it soon became clear why. Robert had, through an antiquarian bookseller in Montreal, learned of the existence of an ancient text called *The Grimoire of Shaal*, and by late autumn 1862 had tracked a copy to another antiquarian, a man named Barlow, in Strasberg, Germany, who was willing to ship the book to PEI for 95 pounds.

And here, the first volume of the journal came to an end. Riley closed the slim book, went into the library's second-storey turret, and put the diary back on its shelf. Then he stared at the other two volumes, sitting upright before him. Should he take down the next one and begin reading it, too?

No. Not tonight. He needed to rest.

Riley left the library, moved down Applegarth's long second-floor hall to the bathroom, and began getting ready for bed. But as he brushed his teeth and then urinated, as he washed his hands and then his face, he felt something come over him. It began like an eddy, swirling low and deep inside his body, before coiling up through him like a snake. Riley looked at his grizzled face in the mirror and gripped the sides of the sink. The house rasped and shuddered all around him, a slow and steady twisting, like the constriction of a boa. The feeling inside him grew, licking at him like a tide. It was an urge, a desire. Darkness had fallen, the whole of PEI now asleep, and Riley's night cravings poured over him once again.

He moved from the bathroom into his bedroom, stripped off his clothes, and climbed between the sheets. As he lay there with himself now lightly grasped in his hand, awaiting the vision he knew would come, he expected to see Jessie-Mac, or maybe Marigold, hovering like a phantom over his bed, a gorgeous and inviting spectre. These visions, a nightly hallucination glowing in his room, had come to feel like just another entitlement bestowed upon him by this house, this land, this Island. It felt like a *right* to see these girls in this way, a right that Riley wanted to exercise through such delicious self-abuse. And why not? He knew that Applegarth was imbuing his forty-five-year-old body with lusts, with pornographic imaginings he had not had in decades. But what did it matter? He was just a man reawakening to his sexual self, was he not? He was harming no one here in this shadowy chamber—not Jessie MacIntosh in her bedroom over in Glenning; not Marigold Burque, rotting away in her cell at the women's prison in New Brunswick for the triple murders she had committed.

Except tonight, it was neither Jessie nor Marigold who visited him in his bed. It was somebody else.

When Riley saw who it was, he recoiled. He tried to take his hand away, but the desire seized him with such startling force that he flinched and then writhed in the bed. The vision descended upon him, and the desire he felt was sweet and runny, even as he revolted against it. *Oh God*, he thought. *Oh Jesus, no.*

The vision was of Miriam. Little nine-year-old Miriam, as he imagined her from those diary pages. Riley felt her small, warm hands running up his thighs as her face appeared over the crest of his gut. He fought that vision with everything he had, but his strength gave out the very instant she looked at him with that soft, sweet expectancy. It was that face Riley imagined as he began to stroke himself. Was this not what Robert Fuller himself had been doing on the night his brother overheard him through the bedroom door? *Oh God, oh fuck,* Riley thought as the pure novelty of this vision overwhelmed him. *This isn't who I really am.* To allow himself to continue, to engage in this vile and, now, incestuous act, felt like a bridge too far, a sin against the very fabric of existence itself. He could not do this. He must stop. He must not submit to what Applegarth wanted him to see, to *do* to himself.

Those young girl's eyes would not let him. They were so intrigued by the show he was about to put on for her, so curious by this unfamiliar act. He stared into those eyes as the intensity rose and burned and threatened to burst out of him.

And it was her soft little mouth he thought of as that bliss did come, and he cried out. It was right there, a mouth hovering over the end of him. It cooed and cackled with pleasurable surprise as pleasure leaped and danced over Riley's belly.

Chapter 18

On a Friday night in mid-June, Riley arrived at the Boar's Head in Montague to meet up with Jack Mackenzie and Dave Campbell for a drink. It had been a while since Riley had set foot in a bar. After the Moncton shooting, he really couldn't show his face in one, at least in that city—and stepping inside the Boar's Head now, he was imbued with a familiarity long forgotten.

The Boar's Head was like any Maritime pub: some local-history knickknacks and the provincial flag hanging on the walls; beat-up mahogany bar with brass taps and rails; shelves of booze bottles against the back mirror; wooden four- and six-seaters in the centre of the room, a few scalloped leather booths along the edges. The night was warm, and Jack had mentioned wanting to sit out on the back deck if they could. Riley headed there now, and was relieved to see that his companions had yet to arrive. This meant he could nab a table in the corner and sit with his back against the deck's rickety latticework wall. He did so, then ordered a beer from the passing waitress and lit a du Maurier.

He was halfway through his pint when Jack and Dave showed up together, and Riley stood briefly to greet them. The waitress zoomed in to take their drink orders, too. After she was gone, Dave finished relaying some story he'd been telling Jack. "So yeah, a developer bought the land last week and plans to turn the soccer field into an apartment complex, so unless town council can figure out where to move the kids, there may be no soccer season next year at all."

"Is that so?" Jack said, not to question the veracity of what his friend was saying, but only to nurse out more details from him.

Riley just tapped his cigarette and listened passively to his friends' banter. The banality of it made him feel like he was living in a perfectly normal time and place, that there was nothing bizarre or even out of the ordinary about his life, his *new* life, here on PEI. They were just three men enjoying a drink together at a bar on a late spring night in one of the safest and most uneventful places on earth.

But when Dave wrapped up his story, he turned to Riley with a smile. "You're awfully quiet over there," he said.

"Oh, well. Just taking it all in."

Dave's smile deepened. "Say, how's your garden of mystery coming along?"

Riley flinched at that, his shoulders juddering in surprise. He had said exactly nothing to anyone about the wild, improbable garden growing on Applegarth's side lawn. Its crops were lush and full now, the carrots and onions blooming, the stocks of corn standing high, the dark, bulbous eggplants lying like huge slugs on the soil.

Jack caught his reaction right away. "Garden of mystery?" he asked.

"Strangest friggin' thing," Dave went on. "Riley here wanted some topsoil when he first moved into that house up there. I asked around a couple places but couldn't score him any. Then one day, some just showed up. Like, poured and raked right into the plots and everything. My guess is somebody must have gotten wind he was looking for topsoil and just dropped some off." He looked at Riley. "Did you ever figure out who that good Samaritan was?"

Riley sipped his pint. "Nope," he said, though he could tell the men wanted him to say more.

"How *is* your garden?" Jack asked.

Riley slowly cleared his throat. "I'm having," he said, "a good growing season so far."

"Glad somebody is," Dave said. "My wife's garden's the shits this year. Even the zucchini isn't coming up yet." He sipped his beer. "Oh, and another thing. I drove by your property the other day, Riley. Holy smokes, my friend. I had to pull over at the sight of it. You've done a *ton* of work up there. The whole outside with fresh paint. New railing on your front porch. New windows, it looked like. You must have somebody helping you."

Riley stewed in his hesitation again. He *wanted* to say something, to let these men in on what was happening at his property. It might sound less crazy if he did. "No, it's just me and the house," he said, taking some first tentative steps. "But it's like… like the property is helping me along, like it *wants* me to be there." He swallowed again. "It, and the property behind it."

As soon as Riley said this, he longed to reel the words back in. Saying such a thing out loud made him sound *more* insane, not less.

But it was too late. Jack perked up right away. "You're talking about that place you mentioned before. What did you call it? Lowfield?"

Riley said nothing.

"What's Lowfield?" Dave asked.

"Well, Riley here claims that it's a deserted v—"

"It *is* a deserted village," Riley finally spoke up, cutting Jack off. "It's about two miles out behind my backyard, sort of in the middle of that big swath of woods between my lot on the Eight Mile Road and Route 319 in Cardigan North. I learned about Lowfield from an old journal I found in Applegarth's library, written by my grandfather's grandfather." Riley traced a finger along the side of his pint glass, making a track in the condensation there. "I've been reading more of that diary. There was some crazy shit that went on in that village back in the 1800s. Some *crazy* shit."

Jack, who had stuck his pipe in his mouth and lit it, leaned in to the table. "Is that so?" he asked with a puff. "What kind of crazy shit?"

Riley was all in now. Was he really prepared to involve these men in the madness he had read about, and seen with his own eyes? Was he ready to share all or part of this, to stop facing it alone? "Like—a cult," he said. "Like the whole village was founded around this really weird, really… warped religion. It was like Christianity, but also not like Christianity. It was sort of pro-slavery, and also talked a lot about incest—dads raping their daughters, sons fucking their moms. Shit like that. And Christ not being God's only begotten son. That he had… he had a brother."

"*Phwore!*" Jack said with a chuckle, pulling away from the table in mock disgust. "You've been drinking some bad 'shine, there Fuller."

"I had some bad 'shine once," Dave said. "Got a teddy of it from the bootlegger in Morell. Messed me up for a week."

Riley lit a fresh cigarette. "I ain't been drinking no bad 'shine."

"Well, I don't know what this diary told you," Jack went on, "but religion's pretty Wonder Bread here on PEI. Always has been."

A party of six, Riley noticed vaguely, had come out onto the deck then, moving toward a table at the other end. He paused for a moment before addressing Jack again. "I'm not shitting you," he said, lowering his voice. "Look, I didn't mention this when I was at your place last week. But…" He took a slow, unsteady sip of his beer and looked at his friends. "But… I've been there. I've been to Lowfield. Hiked out there one afternoon just to see if that diary was telling the truth. And it was. There *is* a village out there, right in the middle of that woods. There's only the remnants of an old corduroy road in and out. You've got to hike in just to find it, but once you do it'll lead you right into Lowfield. The place looks like it's been abandoned since the time that diary was written. Jack, I was there. And I found the church that the journal talked about. I went inside it. Whatever was being worshipped there, back in the 1800s, it wasn't Christianity. It was like Satanism, or something worse." He lowered his voice even more. "The cross at the back of the altar, it was… it was hanging upside down." Riley couldn't quite bring himself to mention that it hadn't been upside down when he first stepped into the church, that the cross had flipped itself around only after he… after he…

Riley was abruptly overcome then with a sense that he was being watched. He looked up from their table and saw someone from the party of six that had just come in standing in the middle of the deck. This person had not joined his friends yet at their table. Instead, he stood frozen and glaring at Riley.

It was Danny MacPherson.

Riley seized up and scowled back at him before glancing over at the party Danny had come in with. Riley could see that it included some of the other friends that Jessie-Mac had been hanging out with that day in the park, including the slim, pretty girl with the pixie cut and dog tags, plus one of the kids who had been with Danny when he came onto Applegarth's property. What was his name? Kevin? No. It was Calvin.

Riley turned his hard, hazel eyes back to Danny, whose own face—framed there by that feathery blond mullet—was tight and fierce and inscrutable. The huge dimple in the middle of his chin had turned a bright pink.

Both Jack and Dave twisted around in their seats to stare at the kid before turning back to Riley. "You know that guy?" Dave asked.

"Unfortunately, I do." Riley dragged hard on his cigarette before raising his voice and calling over to the centre of the deck. "You got something you wanna say to me, Danny?"

But the Calvin kid was already up from their table and at Danny's side, trying to pull him away by the elbow. "Dude, c'mon. What, you gonna mess with that guy again? C'mon. Sit. Sit. Have a drink."

Danny reluctantly allowed himself to be pulled away. But before he got out of earshot, he called over to Riley. "You starting to figure things out, Fuller? You looking for another place to live yet?"

"Go to hell," Riley muttered, turning back to his own table and crushing out his cigarette.

"What the heck was that all about?" Dave asked.

"I don't want to talk about it," Riley replied. He downed the rest of his beer, then wiped his mouth with his wrist. "In fact, I'm going to go drink at the bar. I don't want to be out here with him."

Riley got up from their table, quick enough to surprise Jack and Dave, and lumbered back inside. His friends just looked at each other and shrugged, but then reluctantly followed, telling the passing waitress—herself a touch shaken by the brief burst of conflict on her deck—about their move.

~

Lined up on stools at the bar, Riley smoked maniacally while his buddies just chatted amongst themselves, not sure whether they wanted to hear more about the creepy, incredible story he'd been telling them before Danny showed up, or of the confrontation with Danny itself.

At last Riley seemed to calm down enough to rejoin the conversation. "So where's Jessie-Mac tonight?" he asked Jack. "Those were her friends out there, but she wasn't with them."

"Where do you think she is?" Jack said with a smile. "At the office on a Friday night, of course, working on a story. *Och aye*, that girl is going to toil herself into an early grave." He squinted at Riley. "Did you see her op-ed about her abortion? We ran it in yesterday's paper."

"Yeah, I saw it."

"This is your summer intern?" Dave asked.

"Aye. Jessica MacIntosh. Dick and Roberta's oldest, from over in Glenning. Only twenty and already conquering the world." Jack nodded at Riley again. "What did you think of that piece?"

Riley picked up the fresh beer that the bartender had set in front of him and took a sip. "It was certainly ballsy. A little over the top with the feminism, but she made a lot of good points."

"That's one way to describe it," Jack chuckled, and relit his pipe. "The phone calls about it are already coming in, and I suspect we'll have a slew of letters to the editor for next week's edition. Me, I'm proud of her. Most rookies can't pull off a good editorial, but she surprised me. The piece was well-written, yet really personal, and it showed no patience with PEI being so far behind on abortion access. I actually got her to amp *up* the feminism—the first draft she showed me was a bit mealy-mouthed." The tobacco in Jack's pipe sizzled in its bowl as he took a drag. "And speaking of which, she's working on another feminist-y piece right now. More straight reportage, but still."

"Oh yeah, what's that?" Riley asked.

"Well, we got this call at the office the other week, from some elderly lady over in Cardigan. She wanted to know if we planned to write about the sixty-fifth anniversary of some 'bad business' that went down in the area back then—a string of rapes and missing-women reports and such. Jessie took the call and brought the story idea to me. I'd never heard of this stuff, but the caller was pretty adamant we *should* write some kind of retrospective on it."

"An old lady in Cardigan?" Dave Campbell asked. He furrowed his brow.

"Indeed. She said nobody talked about what happened to those 'poor girls' back then, but we'd 'do well' to write about it now. Anyway, I put Jessie-Mac on it, and she's been doing some research." Jack nodded at Riley. "She brought some of it over that night in my backyard. You remember? It was a pile of her grandmother's letters from that same time period, trying to find any reference to the crimes that were apparently going on."

Riley's brow also furrowed. "Sorry, *what* time period was this?"

"It was sixty-five years ago, so we're talking... 1930. Summer and fall, according to the old lady. We found no allusions to it in the letters Jessie-Mac brought me, so I sent her to the archives in Charlottetown. Apparently, there was surprisingly little written about it in the newspapers back then. Or maybe not surprising. Just a couple of capsule reports about missing persons—all women. And one instance of..." And here Jack paused, as if two things had collided suddenly in his head. "And one instance of a teenage girl reporting to police that she'd been, well..." He looked at his friends. "... violated by her own father. That's strange—we were *just* talking about incest, weren't we?"

Riley's throat went dry. His stomach roiled with a lush, kinetic dread. These things had happened in 1930. He knew that was the last year Applegarth had been occupied—by his grandfather,

James Fuller, who had moved to PEI from Halifax that year following his own divorce.

"Jack..." he muttered.

But Dave Campbell also looked a bit shaken, and he spoke up before Riley could finish his thought. "Jack, *who* was the elderly lady in Cardigan who called all this in?"

"Oh God, let me see." The old guy rolled his eyes up to the pub's wood-panel ceiling. "What did Jessie-Mac say her name was? Something starting with a P, or maybe a K. Mrs. Peters... or Pearing... or Keiring... or..."

"Was it *Keating*?" Dave asked. "Mrs. Keating of Cardigan."

"Yeah, maybe. Maybe, yeah. That sounds familiar."

The two men noticed that Dave Campbell's face had turned white.

"Dave, what is it?" Riley asked.

"The topsoil," he said slowly. "When I called around for your topsoil, one of the people I spoke to was Gladys Keating, over in Cardigan. I knew her son-in-law, Mike Murphy, had a pile just sitting out in his backyard, and I asked if she'd mind sending him up to your place with a couple truckloads to help you out. But when I told her where you were, and *who* you were, she sort of went off on me. Told me there was no way she was sending Mikey, or any other member of her family, up there. She kind of *lost* it, gibbering about stuff I didn't understand. But I do remember: she said something about bad neighbours forcing people to do things they didn't want to do. To make..." And here, his mind churned as he tried to recall the exact phrasing. "To make 'like lie with like.'" He looked at his friends. "That, that could be a reference to..."

"Incest," Riley said. "Jack, is this the woman Jessie spoke to?"

"Well, now I don't know. I'm sort of second-guessing myself. It *could've* been."

"Would Jessie still be at the office working?"

"Oh, probably," Jack said. "She's a night owl, that one."

"Do you gents mind if we settle up our bill and head over there? I want to get to the bottom of this."

"Yeah, me too, actually," Dave said.

And so that's what they did.

~

The three men hoofed it across Main Street to the *Eastern Pioneer* offices, pulling open its glass entry and hiking the stairs to the second floor. They weren't even halfway up before they heard the noise, what sounded like a rock concert, a raucous dance party, shaking the walls. They came into the office to find Jessie not at her desk but in the centre of the "newsroom" floor, flailing around like a maniac. She had her back to them and was bouncing on her feet and swinging her dark hair from side to side as the boom box on the brick ledge behind her desk blared out at full volume.

Riley thought he recognized the band: it was the one that put out that *Monster* album she had shared with him that day in the park. The song playing was frantic, manic, sonic—heavy guitars drowning out lyrics that Riley could barely discern. But the voice of Jessie-Mac's dream husband was unmistakable, that sour, worldly bleating.

She turned around then, but barely startled to see the three men suddenly standing there, watching her dance. In fact, she put on a little show for them, throwing her bent elbows into the air and grinding her hips, then doing one shimmying three-sixty on her heels before strutting over and grabbing her boss by both wrists. "Just taking a little dance break to clear my head!" she shouted over the music. "Here, Jack, join me!"

Riley watched as the old guy, pipe in mouth, allowed Jessie to pull him over to where she'd been standing and then swing his arms from side to side as she tried to get him to groove along with her. Riley could not take his eyes off the lithe, un-self-conscious way Jessie's body jounced around inside its hoodie and jeans.

Jack played along for a bit, tapping one foot ineptly on the floor, but didn't look happy about it. He soon set Jessie's hands aside and gave her nod that said *Thank you for that, darling, but I'm good*.

She sashayed over to the ledge and killed the boom box just as the song came to its abrupt end. For a moment, the silence in the air seemed louder than the music itself.

"Oh hey, Fuller," she said to Riley, out of breath. "I was just about to email you."

"Oh, about what?"

"I have a gift for you!" Jessie went to her desk and hoisted up her canvas kitbag off the floor. She rifled through it briefly before pulling out three CDs, still in their cellophane, and brought them over to him. "Jack mentioned you'd bought a CD player," she said, her face still slick from the dancing. "So I thought I'd help you get your collection started. Here."

He took the three discs from her and flipped through them. One was an extra copy of *Monster*; one was an album called *August and Everything After*; and the third an album called *Everybody Else Is Doing It, So Why Can't We?*—all from bands he'd never heard of.

"Well thanks for that, but you really shouldn't have." Riley meant it. He couldn't imagine Jack was paying Jessie much beyond the province's $4.75 minimum wage, and she'd need every penny for journalism school in Halifax come the fall.

"Don't worry about it," she replied. "I have a buddy who works at the Sam's in Charlottetown, and he got me these at cost. Just consider it a cultural exchange. You know, cross-generational. If you want to flip me a copy of The Mamas and the Papas' *Greatest Hits* on cassette, I guess that would be fine."

This caused Dave Campbell, standing behind Riley, to snort with laughter.

Riley didn't know what to say. Looking over the CDs' covers again, he suspected that he'd hate this music. But still. When was the last time somebody had given him a gift, save for the books that Sammy had sent through the mail? Since the shooting, since his divorce, Riley's birthdays and Christmases had passed virtually unacknowledged—a penance, he figured, for all his treachery. So he found himself oddly moved by Jessie's gesture.

She looked at him expectantly. Should he hug her? Even give her a peck on the cheek? Was that what she wanted? If they were alone, might he even reach across and cup her small hip in his hand and pull her close to—

Don't you fucking touch her. Don't be gross. What's the matter with you, old man? She is twenty and you are forty-five, so fuck the hell off.

"Well, thanks again," he said plainly. "I appreciate it."

"No worries," she replied, then turned back to Jack. "So what are you guys doing here? I thought I'd have the office to myself tonight."

"We need to talk to you about your story," Jack said.

"Which one? I'm working on, like, three at the moment."

"The retrospective about the missing women and rapes from back in '30," Jack told her.

"Who was the old lady who pitched you the idea?" Dave asked. But then he added: "Oh sorry, Dave Campbell. We spoke on the phone last month when you profiled Riley."

"Jessie MacIntosh." They shook hands. "The old lady? It was Gladys Keating, over in Cardigan."

"That's her," Dave said to Riley and Jack.

"When you spoke to her," Riley asked, "did she say anything about me? Or about Applegarth?"

Jessie just shrugged. "No, she didn't. Why?"

"Well, according to Dave here, Mrs. Keating's got some kind of beef with me, or my property. The same sort of beef Danny seems to have. We ran into him earlier, by the way, at the Boar's Head."

"Jesus. Did you guys, like, get into it again?"

Riley nodded. "A little. It was tense there for a sec, but then he backed off."

Jessie just boggled her head. "That is so weird. I don't know *what's* gotten into him."

"We're trying to get to the bottom of this," Jack said. "Riley here thinks some rather bad business went on back behind his property over a century ago, but it may be related to those events in 1930. Did you find anything else about what was happening around here back then?"

"Well, that's why I was in town. After I left the record store, I went to the library for another chance to dig around in the archives from that period. I did find a couple more articles about missing women around this part of the province—but again, the details were scant. Very short pieces with hardly any information in them. It was so *weird*. You'd think a story like that would be big news here on little PEI in 1930."

"Can you call Mrs. Keating back tomorrow?" Jack asked. "See if you can't get some more details out of her, or at least find out what prompted her to put all this on our radar in the first place."

"Already done," Jessie said. "She won't talk to me."

"What?"

"No, she's clammed right up. I spoke to her yesterday, trying to squeeze more out of her, but she got really aloof. *I've already said too much.* That sort of thing. I was, like, why did you even raise this with us if you didn't want to talk about it yourself? By my math, Mrs. Keating would've been in her late teens in 1930—so roughly the same age as those missing girls. She probably knew them. When I insisted she give me *something* else, she started spouting all this baffling stuff. Like how the 'soil is now awake' and how the 'animals are on their hunt,' and she couldn't say more for fear of her safety. I think she's a bit senile, to be honest."

"Yeah, that sounds like her," Dave Campbell said. "She was equally cryptic when I spoke to her."

Jessie turned back to Riley. "Speaking of cryptic, what's this 'bad business' Jack mentioned about your property?"

The three men glanced sheepishly at each other, then looked at the floor.

"Um, that's not something," Jack said to her, squinting over his pipe, "one should really, uh, discuss... in the presence of a lady."

"What, I'm a *lady* now? C'mon, Jack, let me do my job."

"Well, it's not anything confirmed, darling. Just old rumours, really. I don't think that—"

"A cult," Riley said to her. "There used to be another community in this area, adjacent to Glenning, that was founded, like, two centuries ago... on a cult."

"*Now* were getting somewhere," Jessie said. "What kind of cult?"

Riley paused before leveling his hazel eyes at her. They loitered there for a moment, lingering on the hook of her young hip, at the delectable place where her thighs came together inside her jeans, at the fall of her dark hair on the shoulders of her hoodie, at the intense look in those crystal-grey eyes. God, he did want to fuck her. Just once.

Knock it off! You're like a teen again. Seriously, Fuller, what the ever-loving fuck?

"Riley?" she asked.

"A sex cult," he replied. "Only, not like any sex cult you could imagine. Think sick stuff—sick to the nth degree. Maybe the person who committed those crimes in 1930 learned about the cult, and was inspired by it."

"Wow," she said. "Jesus." She gave her head a shake. "So when you say 'adjacent' to Glenning, you're talking about someplace near your property. Right?"

He nodded. "Look, do you know who the primary suspect was in these crimes? From those articles, I mean."

"Not at all," she replied. "Like I said—scant details. But frankly, I'm not too concerned about who it was. I think my piece should focus on the women who got raped and went missing, not the sicko who did all this. I mean, I think that's what Mrs. Keating had in mind when she pitched us this story."

I seriously doubt that, if she's terrified of Applegarth, Riley thought but did not say. Instead, he turned to Jack. "Can we find out if the police had a primary suspect, back then?"

"Well, you're a cop. You know the answer as well as I do. We're talking a Freedom of Information request for their notes, but that could take weeks. Or months. If the Mounties' records even go back that far. I have no idea what policing was like on the Island back in 1930."

"*Can* you try to get that name?" Riley asked Jessie.

"Well, I wasn't planning to. I have five hundred words to play with. Like I said, I really want to focus on the women, on *their* lives and *their* stories." But she looked at Jack, to see if her boss still agreed with that approach.

He paused a moment, but then gave a shrug. "Let's put the request in. I'll show you how tomorrow. If you get a name, it's one sentence in your story. If you don't, it's not the end of the world. Maybe we can make it a two- or even three-parter over the course of the summer, to give the Mounties time to process our request."

"Fine," she sighed. "School isn't planning to teach us FOI requests until fourth year anyhow, so I'll be," and then she sounded downright cheery, "ahead of my class on that front."

Dave piped up then. "Riley, why do *you* want to know who that guy was? What's your skin in the game?"

Riley swallowed as the three of them glanced over at him. In that moment, he didn't want to say. He felt as if he'd painted himself into a corner.

But it was Jessie who figured it out. It was like watching a key fit into a lock inside her mind. "Your grandfather," she said. "You told me, during our interview, that he was the last person to live in Applegarth. Back in *1930.*"

"Oh my God, that's right," Dave said. "I'd forgotten that."

"You think *he* had something to do with all this," Jessie said. It wasn't a question.

Riley swallowed again. Cleared his throat. "Let's just see if we can't get that name."

"You know, you can put in a request as easily as I can. Probably more easily, considering you're a cop yourself."

"Well, let's let Jessie try first," Jack said. "Then we'll see what we see. It'll be a good learning opportunity for you, missy."

"Fine. I'm okay with that." She folded her arms over her chest and jabbed a playful chin at them. "Now you gents need to skedaddle. I still have lots of work to do before I go home."

Riley nodded, turned to go, but then turned back. "Oh, and Jessie, thanks again for the CDs."

"No problem. And just to be clear, I *don't* want The Mamas and the Papas' *Greatest Hits* in return."

He couldn't help but laugh. "Yeah, no, I got that," he said.

~

Back in the pub's parking lot, Dave wished Jack and Riley a good night as he climbed into his Honda Accord, and was soon gone. The two other men hung back for a bit. Jack relit his pipe and Riley sparked up another du Maurier.

"I have something I want to ask you," Jack said, puffing away. "You're free to say no, of course."

"Of course."

"I'd like to see those journals you found. It's not that I don't believe you, but it just seems crazy that something like that was happening around here back then. It boggles the mind."

Riley said nothing.

"And I don't plan to publish anything out of them," Jack assured him. "But I do know a historian, at UPEI, who would be very interested in seeing those diaries. He's published a number of books on Island history, but I doubt he's ever heard of anything like this."

Riley said nothing.

"Would you be willing to share them?" Jack asked. "As a matter of local history?"

Riley took a long, deep breath. "I need to think about that," he said. "I need to finish reading them myself, first."

Chapter 19

June 20, 1995
Dear Diary, or Journal, or whatever the fuck you are,
I wonder if the fact that I'm blowing through so much money means I really am going to kill myself. I once read an article about how suicidal people become cavalier with their cash—just spending it all now, or not caring *how* they spend it, if they're just going to off themselves anyway. Does anyone actually think like that? Do people ever achieve enough certainty about suicide to have it affect their day-to-day banking? Raised by parents who were raised during the Depression, I've had frugality boiled into my marrow. Even on days when I've literally had the Glock in my mouth, I still stress later about counting my pennies and balancing my chequebook. The absurdity of this reminds me of something *else* I once read, a story recounted by George Orwell (one of Sammy's favourite writers) about a condemned man being led to the gallows who still skirts around a puddle in the courtyard so he doesn't muddy his shoes.

It's not that I'm in financial straits just yet. My Off Duty Sick payments, which are sixty-five percent of my salary—thank you very much, unionized labour—are still being deposited automatically into my chequing account, but those will come to an end later this year. Meanwhile, whatever's left of my half of the liquidated assets from my divorce are just sitting in my savings account. I pay for day-to-day things out of chequing, but the bigger expenses, almost all of which are associated with the renos to Applegarth, come from savings.

Like today's planned purchase, for example: I'm off to a furniture store later to order a not-inexpensive dining set for the solarium just off Applegarth's living room. Why am I doing this? I have no clue. Like so many things involving the house, I do them in a kind of pleasant, hypnotic stupor. I'm almost getting used to the magnetic power this place holds over me. At any rate, the money in both accounts will eventually run out, and I'll have to decide what to do before that happens. I could apply for a transfer to the RCMP detachment in Montague, or to the larger one in Charlottetown. Or I could sell Applegarth—at a tidy profit, no doubt—and try rejoining my colleagues in Moncton, though the thought of that makes my stomach sick.

Or I could just shove the Glock in my mouth, pull the trigger this time, and make all of it a moot point.

~

Coming back from the furniture store, Riley turned onto the craggy Eight Mile Road, drove by what passed for civilization in Glenning, and then cruised farther out on that desolate stretch toward Applegarth. With dense and overgrown forests all around, it *was* kind of spooky out here, even now, at the threshold of summer. Maybe old lady Keating was onto something, Riley thought, being afraid to send her son-in-law up here with the topsoil.

He was musing on this as he approached Applegarth—and suddenly saw, even two or three hundred yards out, that something was moving through the trees that bracketed his driveway. In one instant, Riley's eyes widened as a vehicle came backing down out of that lane. In another, he could see that it was Danny MacPherson's butterscotch-coloured pickup truck.

At first the vehicle pulled out and steered toward Riley. But then, at the sight of the Lumina coming up the cratered road, Danny did an abrupt, vicious U-turn—Riley had to brake to avoid hitting him—and went squealing off in the opposite direction.

"Oh mother*fucker!*" Riley screamed, and hit the gas.

The engine thundered as he tried to catch up with Danny, and Riley banged his open palm like a gavel on the steering wheel. *Why the FUCK were you back on my property!?* his brain bellowed. *What is your fucking problem, Danny?* He even laid on the horn, hoping the racket would get the kid to pull over. If he did, Riley was convinced he'd haul him out of his cab and beat the shit out of him, right there on the side of the road. If he didn't, Riley seriously considered ramming the back of the pickup, if he could catch up to it. At this point, he didn't give a good goddamn about anything.

But to Riley's surprise, Danny's truck had a startling amount of pep, and the 1990 Lumina was no match for it. He lost the kid after the northbound turnoff at Albion Cross, and Riley pulled over in the pink dirt next to a rolling wheat field and cursed again.

Sitting there, panting in his seatbelt, Riley had a good mind to race home and write a furious email to Jessie-Mac. *Tell your ex to stay off my land!* he'd say. *Do you have ANY idea what his problem is with me?* But the thought of that caused something to jolt in Riley's head, and his stomach did a crazy loop-the-loop.

Applegarth!

He hit the gas and did his own U-turn, and before long was tearing back down the Eight Mile Road. A vision flooded his brain then. Perhaps Danny had smashed all the windows in the house, or spray-painted a graffito across its side, or, worse, thrown a Molotov cocktail onto its wide front porch, causing the whole wooden structure to burn.

But when he finally reached the house and pulled up its long, J-shaped driveway, Riley could see that the place was fine. Applegarth just sat there with its bright-white clapboard siding, its blood-red gables reaching up into the PEI sky. Riley parked the Lumina in its usual place and got out. The only difference he could see at first was that there was now a note taped to the side door. He was about to go over and tear it off when something else caught his eye. It had rained earlier that morning, a brief but heavy shower, and the grass was still wet.

Through that dew, Riley could see a faint but unmistakable set of foot tracks leading to the garden. He followed them, and soon stood at the edge of the nearest kidney-shaped bed, where his crops towered and flourished and bulged grotesquely, far larger than any fruit or vegetable should have been. He looked down where he stood and saw a single sneaker print in the rusty-red mud. Danny, it turned out, had taken a good gawk at what was growing there.

Riley went back to the house. Danny's note was written on a single sheet of photocopy paper, folded over, and he had taped it to the door by its crease. Riley ripped it down and took it inside.

Sitting at the kitchen table, he unfolded the missive. He could see that there were actually two parts to the note. The first, written neatly at the top of the page, read:

> Dear Riley,
> Running into you the other night at the Boar's Head just confirmed two things for me. One, you <u>are</u> starting to clue in about what Applegarth really is. The way you were talking when I came in, about the history around here, proves that. And two, that you are, despite everything, <u>still</u> living under its roof. What is the matter with you? Please listen to me. You need to <u>sell</u> this house. Get it out of your bloodline. You must have some sense by now of what it did to the men who came before you. It brings out the very worst in every Fuller who has lived here. It cranks up the darkness in them. My grandmother, who is ninety-seven, could tell you stories about what happened around these parts decades ago. She has told some of them to me. Applegarth is a toxic place, and it will make <u>you</u> toxic, if you stay. You know it's true.
> Danny

Under this, he had scribbled the second part of the note, a hastily written PS scrawled with a different pen than the one used above it. Riley figured that Danny must have written the main part of the note at home, then driven over and taped it to the door. But then, on the way back to his truck, he must have glimpsed the garden and walked over to it, saw what he saw, and then raced back to add this post-scriptum:

> Riley: I just paid a visit to your garden. Motherfucker, those crops are <u>not right</u>. What more do you need to see? Leave this place NOW.

Riley folded Danny's note back over. His mind churned like the waters of an estuary, dark, silty, fathomless.

> *Tell your mom the boys all say thanks for a* grrreat *weekend!*
> *This isn't who you really are!*
> *... ti Ghroyan shuun dorn, dos maya Shaal huit, Shaal huit.*

Above Riley's head, the second floor of Applegarth creaked and murmured. This was not the house merely settling onto itself. Something was moving upstairs.

Riley got up and, bringing Danny's note with him, went to the kitchen drawer and took out the Glock. He went to the house's main foyer, to where the winding staircase ascended to the second floor. More creaking and shuffling above, and what sounded like the wind passing over the house, causing it to shake. Riley climbed the stairs and was soon on the landing outside his bedroom door, the very place where, on his first night sleeping in Applegarth, his mind had imagined the corpse of his grandfather, James Fuller, dangling from his noose. Riley looked up. There, in the ceiling above him, was the hatchway leading up to the house's attic, a place that Riley, even now, had yet to visit. Behind the hatch, he could hear more cracking and snapping, more twists of wood on wood, and what sounded like a sigh, like a young girl crying out in anguish, her noises muffled by the door. His heart thundered as he gripped the Glock. He was about to reach up and pull down those hatchway stairs when something to his left caught his eye. Through the master bedroom's ajar door, Riley thought he saw a light move across the back wall there. He turned and stepped inside the room, raising the gun to the flickering shadows.

It wasn't a light. It wasn't a shadow either, but something in between, a darkness that seemed to shine, to emit its own queer radiance. It drew him to the room's far window, the one facing out into the backyard and the woods behind it. Riley soon stood at that window. He soon looked out over that forest. Two miles back was Lowfield, with its rotting corduroy roads, its moldering saltbox cottages, its cursed church, and that blasphemous book, *The Grimoire of Shaal*, sitting on its pulpit. As Riley stood there looking out, the whole forest seemed to shimmer, to come to life with every animal living in its thickets—the fox and the skunk, the crow and the sparrow, the squirrel and the rat. He could hear them all shrieking into the now-glowing air at once, a deafening cacophony.

The portal will open, this time. We will not fail again. We will reach the Great Force Beyond. We will stop anyone who tries to stop us.

And then, just as quickly as it started, the noise ceased. That alien luminosity receded. The house stilled. Riley raised the hand that held Danny's note. He read it over again, but then crinkled the paper into a ball. Going over and setting the Glock on his nightstand, Riley headed back out of his bedroom and down the hall to the library. When he got there, he threw Danny's note without a thought into one of the far, shadowy corners, then turned and stepped inside the second-floor turret. He went to the bookcase against the back wall and pulled down the second volume of his grandfather's grandfather's diary.

~

Settling into his reading chair and cracking the moldy journal open, Riley began skimming the first several entries. Written over the winter of 1862-63, these inclusions seemed altogether duller than what had come before. The other Riley Fuller spent nearly a third of this volume recording the stress of keeping his and his brother's business afloat through their first full winter on tiny "P.E. Island." There were passing reminders of Robert having broken with their Presbyterian church and giving himself over to their grandfather's cult in Lowfield. Riley Fuller had once again bemoaned this threat to his brother's soul, but he wrote of it in much the same way he discussed business negotiations with local farmers and "Charlottetown elites." There was a lack of detail, of reckoning with what all this meant, and Riley found himself breezing over these paragraphs.

But then, finally, he located the phrase he had been hunting for. It appeared in an entry that his grandfather's grandfather had written in late March 1863. *The Grimoire of Shaal* had finally arrived on PEI from Barlow in Strasberg via the broker in Montreal. Robert was ecstatic, and had quickly begun to, as his brother put it in the diary, *parse its satanic syllables*. But they soon discovered that it was Riley, not Robert, who had possessed the supernatural talent needed to decipher that queer language. He had read a single passage aloud to Robert but refused to read more.

Yet, over the coming weeks, a kind of horror had begun to unravel in the area. Twin girls from Glenning had gone missing while out for a hike. Shortly thereafter, a farmer in Georgetown turned himself in to authorities after violating his own daughter one night while sleepwalking. The constable in charge of investigating these occurrences was soon found mauled to death, injuries that could not be caused by any animal indigenous to PEI.

Meanwhile, Elder Fuller and his henchmen (Robert now chief among them) had come to Applegarth on a day in May 1863, pleading with Riley to parse more of the text from the *Grimoire*. He refused, and fled upstairs to his bedroom. The men had stayed anyway, and began chanting from that text themselves. When they did, the younger brother had sensed something come over the house itself. As he put it: *I once again became convinced that those incantations, wafting up from below me, were seeping into the very walls and floorboards and brickwork of Applegarth itself, saturating its every nook and chamber with their otherworldly poison.*

Then, a most shocking revelation: the brothers learned that James Robert Fuller was *not* their grandfather—or not merely so.

He was also their *father*. He had raped and impregnated his own daughter, Melinda Fuller, not once, but twice. The boys themselves had been the progeny of this incest.

At that part, Riley gave out a great wretch of disgust, a whole-body spasm in his reading chair, and threw the diary across the room. It scuttled like a crab across the dusty floor and into the same corner as Danny's note.

He stared at it for a long time where it lay. *Oh Jesus*, he thought. *Oh fucking Christ*. He should burn that journal. Or bury it in the yard. Or throw it into the Northumberland Strait.

But then Riley took a deep breath and rose from the reading chair. Going over, he picked up the diary where it lay. He wouldn't read any more tonight—he couldn't bear to—but nor would he destroy it. How could he? There were so many things still left to learn. There were so many pages in it, and in the next volume, still left to read.

Chapter 20

Danny MacPherson awoke not so much with a jolt as with a sense that he was floating out of his bed. In those first few seconds of semi-consciousness, after he cast off the bed sheets that suddenly felt too weighty, Danny had the impression he was surfing on a heat wave. It seemed to lift him up, to tug him into a sitting position, as if with marionette strings. He became vaguely aware that he was slimy with sweat. Why was it so hot? It hadn't been when he'd turned in for the night, hours before. This was only the third week of June, and it was not unusual, here on PEI, for the evenings to turn brisk after the sun went down, even at this time of year. But the heavy, oppressive temperature that now saturated his bedroom felt like something straight out of late July or mid-August.

With another sense that he was moving involuntarily, Danny swung his legs around to put his feet on his bedroom floor, anxious to touch down on its cool hardwood. But as his toes and heels padded onto the boards, what he felt was not coolness. The floor was warm. No, it was *hot*, like a living body gone feverish. Where was that heat coming from? *I must be dreaming*, he thought. *I must be still asleep*. But if he was, then why was he climbing to his feet, hoisting himself out of his now damp and clammy bed?

The two-storey house he shared with his grandmother, Peg, up on a hill on the outskirts of Montague, was old and did not have central air. On those height-of-summer nights when the house did get hot enough to make sleeping difficult, Danny would break out a couple of stand-up fans—one for his bedroom and one for Peg's—that he otherwise stored in the hall closet. Those fans would sit unused and gathering dust for ten and a half months of the year, but on those truly hot nights in July and

August, they were a godsend. Danny slipped out of his bedroom and went to them now. On his way, he stopped at Peg's ajar bedroom door to check on her. If she were awake and suffering from this furnace-like heat, as he was, he'd ask if she wanted a fan, too. But as he poked his head in and cast his gaze across her dark room, he could see that her own duvet was pulled up to her ears. The only visible part of her was a few curls of her silver hair. She was fast asleep. What's more, he could see her window was closed. Danny frowned at that as he sweated and sweated.

He resumed his stroll down to the closet, and was just reaching for its little brass knob, when he turned his head up to the large bay window at the far end of the hall. Something there caught his eye. Danny paused, licked his now slick and salty lips. It was a light shimmering through the window. Or, not quite a light. It was a darkness that seemed to... that seemed to *glow*. It rippled and shimmered there, as if wafting through the heat itself. What was that?

He ambled through the suffocating swelter toward it, and soon stood inside the bay window's shallow alcove, his thighs pressed up against its wooden sill. Through the window, he could see Petit Point off on the horizon. At this late hour, the waters and shoreline there should have been indistinguishable; but tonight, for some reason, they weren't. For some reason, that dark glowing, that glowing dark, caused the entire inlet to blaze to life as if it were the middle of the day. As usual, the waters off Petit Point were the colour of pewter, but they were also now giving off a tinsel-like glitter, as if illuminated by some unseen sun. Those waters looked beautiful, but they also looked cold, refreshing, like a dunk through them would be just the thing to beat this heat.

Danny thought: *I should go for a swim.*

And then he thought: *Oh, I must be dreaming. Or else sleepwalking. Do people actually sleepwalk? Or does that only happen in the movies?*

It wasn't that he'd never gone night-swimming off Petit Point before, though never quite this late. He and his friends had had lots of bonfire parties down there over the years, and he and

Jessie-Mac, back when they were dating, had even gone skinny-dipping once. Indeed, that night had been the first time he'd asked her to marry him—sort of as a joke, but sort of not. She was in Grade 11 at the time; he was one year out of high school. He loved her then, and... and still did. He still loved her. It *hadn't* been a joke, he now realized, asking her to marry him. He had always been dead serious about wanting to marry her. And still was.

Now, in a full-on stupor, Danny shuffled back up the hall toward his bedroom. The air was hotter, thicker than ever. Sweat rivered down his face and over his chest. He had enough control, enough self-awareness, to check in on Peg one last time. His grandmother was still asleep, still covered in the duvet pulled up high.

Danny returned to his bedroom. He pulled on his socks, his jeans, his favourite AC/DC t-shirt, the one with the sleeves cut off. He ran his hands through his now soaked mullet. Then he went downstairs, stepped into his high-top sneakers on the rubber mat, grabbed his keys, and went quietly out the door.

~

Even with the pickup's windows rolled down and the fan cranked, Danny could not stop sweating. It was like he was infected by a fever, a disease that set his whole body ablaze. He knew on some level that he was now in a trance, that he had the singlemindedness of someone under hypnosis. *I need to get into that water*, he thought, his moist hands clamped tight around the steering wheel. *I need to go for a SWIM and COOL OFF.*

He raced along the pitch-black country roads that ran around the bay toward Petit Point. The air coming in through his open truck windows carried the salty stink of the sea, the funk of low tide. While the smell was unpleasant, Danny couldn't bear the thought of rolling up his windows. He just scrunched up his face and focused on the road. Out here, there was little to see except a couple of nondescript potato fields and a smattering of run-down cottages. A few larger homes sat right along the edge of the shore, but at this hour their windows were black. There was very little life out here, which made it sort of spooky. But still. He knew exactly the bare patch of beach he wanted to reach. It was the same one where he'd asked Jessie-Mac to marry him.

Finally he got there, glimpsing the coppery sand through the parting in the spruce and larch trees that ran along the edge of the road. Danny pulled over and killed the pickup's engine. Getting out, he sensed two things right away: one, that the fishy stench in the air was even stronger out here than it had been closer to home; and two, the temperature seemed to have *climbed* another five degrees. Jesus. His scalp itched from all the sweating; he felt as if he were boiling inside his own skin. *I have to get in that water*, he thought distantly, moving like an automaton as he climbed down into the ditch and then up the other side. *I need to beat this heat.*

Coming through the trees, he moved across a brief set of weedy dunes before descending down toward the water. To his left, well off in the distance, were a few dark, sleepy homes overlooking the shoreline. To his right, he saw the high red cliffs of Petit Point and the pitch blackness beyond them. And, of course, in front of Danny came the gentle inhale and exhale of the salty, briny surf. These waters sparkled coldly in front of him, as if illuminated from within.

Standing on the beach itself now, Danny looked around at the sands. They were pockmarked everywhere by jellyfish—a *lot* of jellyfish. Their purple, gelatinous bodies seemed to laze there on the sand every couple of feet, and in every direction, as if they had rained down from the sky instead of washing in with the tide. Danny knew that these creatures—arctic reds, they were called, or sometimes lion's mane—inundated beaches all around PEI at this time of year. Jessie-Mac even had a nickname for them, *sea bugs*, which struck him as adorable the first time she said it, but didn't now. He had never seen so many jellyfish on a beach, or ones this large. They looked the size of dinner plates, or even vinyl records. *I'll need to find a clear patch of sand*, he thought inside his trance, *if I'm going to strip off my clothes and go for a dip.*

A moment later, he did find such a patch, and was soon pulling his AC/DC shirt over his head and off before stepping out of his high-tops. Next came the blue jeans. On some foggy level, Danny *knew* that what he was doing wasn't right, that it was *strange* to be out here alone, at this time of night, desperately wanting to go for a swim on this sad little stretch of PEI beach. But he couldn't help himself. The heat had forced him here; the water was calling to him. Once his jeans were off, he peeled his socks from his feet, then piled everything into a heap on the sand. He thought for a moment of also removing his boxer shorts, but then opted against it. *I'm not going bare pole by myself,* he thought. *That's just ridiculous.*

And then Danny began gingerly making his way toward the water. With so many jellyfish here, it was like an elaborate game of hopscotch, of "step on a crack, break your mother's back." Only, it was step on a jellyfish and... what? Get the worst sting of your life? These sea bugs, these mounds of plum-coloured jelly, almost seemed to lurch, to ooze toward his feet with each hopping prance he took around them.

As Danny approached the surf, he prepared himself for the bracing clutch of that first, cold wave crashing into his ankles. It was still only late June, and the swimming everywhere on Prince Edward Island—even on its south shore—would be bitterly, uncomfortably cold for another month yet. But that first striking wave shocked him—shocked him, because it *wasn't* cold. It was warm. As warm as bath water. *Oh, this* isn't *right,* Danny thought, even as he waded out into the surf, first to his shins and then to his thighs. *Oh, this is fucked up. I've got to be dreaming. This water should be icy cold. It should take me ten minutes to get this far in.* Another couple of steps and he was at what normally would be the worst part, the scrotum-seizing slap of that first wave at his groin. Only, his pelvis arced into the water with no discomfort at all. Another few steps and the surf was up at his chest. Another few, and his shoulders were in, dropping under the tide's rhythmic undulations.

Danny bobbed there for a while, finally feeling refreshed, thinking about dunking his head under to put an end to its incessant sweating. The water was so pleasant, better than all the times he'd been out here with his friends, even in late August. He stroked out a bit further, until his feet could no longer touch bottom. *This is amazing*, he thought dreamily. *I really wish Jessie-Mac were here tonight. I really wish, even now, after all this time, that she and I could still—*

And just like that, the salty, briny water changed. It was as if someone had flipped a switch. In one instant, the rising and falling waves turned bitingly cold. They turned back to normal.

Danny jolted as he dipped around in the surf. When he did, it was like the spell was broken. His mind came back to full clarity, and he realized that he wasn't hot, had *never* been. He realized that he was bobbing around in the waters off Petit Point in the middle of the night for no reason. That somehow, these waters had *lured* him here.

He looked back and forth across the dark, sloshing surf, and finally noticed what he should have before: that he was now surrounded on all sides by jellyfish. Dozens of them were bouncing on the waves, a thick, glutinous ring of them drawing ever closer on the tide.

Panic gripped Danny. He dog-paddled toward shore, trying to weave around the mass of sea bugs that loomed toward him. One brushed across his right thigh and gave him a sudden, lusty sting. Danny cried out and fought to touch bottom, but it wasn't quite there. A second jellyfish caressed his left buttock before giving him another buzzing, harrowing bite. He cried out again. Another jellyfish loomed over his shoulders, and he bobbed to get out of its way. He felt yet another try to sting him *between* his buttocks, and he screamed out in terror.

But then his feet *did* touch bottom, and an instant later he was climbing out of the dark water and back onto the beach. His eyes hunted around maniacally for the place where he'd left his clothes. Where were they? The current must have drifted him further down the shore.

And that's when he saw it. Saw *them*.

There many, many more jellyfish on the beach, what looked like *thousands* of them, all along the sands there, running forty or fifty feet in either direction. Indeed, there was barely a single square inch not covered by those purple, leaching paddies of jam. Danny gaped at them. All those jellyfish made the beach look like a single, gleaming collop of flesh, a roiling and coiling snake on the sand.

Then Danny did spot his clothes up a bit on the shore, half obscured now by sea bugs. He tried to maneuver his way up and over to them, but there was nowhere to walk. Each time he thought he saw a foot-sized patch where he could step, another jellyfish seeped over and covered it up.

"Oh *fuck off!*" he barked through the black night. "*Fuck off and let me pass!*" He was wholly aware of the ridiculousness of screaming at these things, hoping they'd listen.

But then, to his shock, an answer did come back. It wasn't from the jellyfish, but from whatever was controlling them. Danny froze as he heard it inside his head, standing there shin-deep in the rushing surf.

Three strikes and you're out, Danny. We gave you a chance. Your dear old granny tried to warn you, but you didn't listen. We know that first visit to Fuller was an impulse decision, and that was fine. Your run-in with him at that bar was happenstance, though you didn't need to say anything. You could've just kept your mouth shut and ignored him. But that note you wrote, that letter you left taped to his door, was the last straw. We can't have you scaring him off his land, Danny. We can't have you around trying to stop what is about to come. The portal will open this time. Fuller is going to make it happen. And men like you will not be around to stand in the way.

Danny trembled all over at this voice, a palsy that gripped him from neck to ankles. *Oh, fuck,* he thought. *Oh, fucking Christ.*

Two jellyfish swam up then and stung him hard on the backs of his calves.

Danny screamed again and dropped to his knees in the muddy water. He tried to force himself back up, but a jellyfish took out his right elbow. As he collapsed face down into the surf, another sea bug stung him, this time in the centre of his back. Danny writhed around, trying to get up, trying to get at least his face out of the water. He opened his mouth the scream yet again, and that's when he felt it, a jellyfish, a small sea bug, swim up and *climb* between his lips, between his teeth, and sting him on the tongue. He went down again. Fresh waves crashed over him, bringing more jellyfish in from the sea, piling them atop his twisted, writhing body. They clung to Danny MacPherson like barnacles on a boat.

He was once again a puppet on a string, gyrating like mad as the jellyfish stung him and stung him and stung him.

Part III: The Fruit of a Poisonous Tree

Chapter 21

Riley awoke on a Saturday morning after another short, fitful night of feverish dreams. He had spent the previous evening doing something he'd meant to do for several days now: he'd sat down and listened to the three CDs that Jessie-Mac had given him. Having set up his CD player on the wicker cabinet in Applegarth's living room, he settled into the recliner next to it and kicked back, ready to give these albums a good honest try. He played *August and Everything After* first, followed by *Everybody Else Is Doing It, So Why Can't We?*, and then finished with *Monster*, which he'd already heard parts of and knew he hated. What had Jessie called this? A cross-generational cultural exchange? Riley wasn't entirely unfamiliar with this music, convinced that he'd surfed past at least a few of these tracks on the Lumina's FM dial over the last year or two. But now, having choked down all three records to the end, he arrived at a morose appraisal: they were all sung by a bunch of whiny little bitch-squealers. What did Jessie-Mac—so assured of herself, so comfortable in her own skin—see in these sniveling rockers? What was it with young people today, this whole Generation X, as they were called? What did they have to be so bitch-squealy about?

But later, as Riley roamed the large, spacious house he had inherited, he couldn't get the tunes out of his head. They followed him when he finally turned in for the night; they provided the soundtrack to the intense, vivid dreams that plagued him in the hours that followed. Jessie-Mac made her usual appearance, but, perhaps because of the music, so too did one of her female friends that he'd seen her hanging out with in the park the month before. The girl with the pixie cut and dog tags and nice bum. He didn't even know her name, but that made little difference to the night visions. In them, he had her and Jessie-Mac, together.

Now, the next morning, he staggered out of his bedroom in shorts and t-shirt, mildly revolted with himself and determined to put the night behind him, to get his day started. He came down Applegarth's noisy staircase, went into the kitchen, and put the coffee on. While it percolated, Riley headed outside and down the driveway to its end, where a yellow, tube-like holder for Charlottetown's *Guardian* newspaper stood upright on a metal pole next to his mailbox near the roadside. Riley had gotten the tube installed just the week before, thinking a subscription to the daily would help better connect him to the Island and the wider word. Inside the tube he found the Saturday edition, folded thickly over onto itself. He hauled it out, tucked it under his arm, and carried it back up to the house. On the way, he glanced at Applegarth's front lawn, thinking it was starting to look shaggy and that he might get on the mower later and cut it.

Stepping up the front porch, he chucked the newspaper onto the swing seat there and then went back inside the house to fetch some coffee. After stirring in the milk and sugar, he took his mug out to the porch and settled in on the swing seat. He sipped his coffee with one hand while he unfolded the newspaper into his lap with the other.

There, in the centre of the front page, sandwiched between an update on the construction of the bridge and an economic report from the provincial government, was a picture of Danny MacPherson.

It looked to be his high school graduation photo. In this shot, his long and feathery locks had an almost permed quality to them, and above his barely smiling lips sat a thin, trashy mustache, what some might call a pussy tickler, which he had wisely shaven off in the years since the photo was taken. On his chin, meanwhile, sat that enormous dimple. *You could park a car in it*, Riley thought.

Above this picture ran the headline:

Montague man drowns off Kings County's Petit Point

Riley's blood turned to ice.

His disbelieving eyes fell to the article itself. In one instant, he felt as if he weren't reading this at all, that he was instead still upstairs, still in his bedroom dreaming his raunchy dreams. *This isn't real*, he thought. *I'm still sleeping. This day hasn't actually started yet.*

But as he read on, he knew that it had.

By Raymond Power—Staff reporter
A Montague man has drowned following a late-night swim off Petit Point, the RCMP have reported.

The body of Daniel Eric MacPherson, 22, was found Friday morning by Parks department staff on an isolated stretch of beach just off Route 311. The staff were headed to a cleanup day on Panmure Island when they found a pickup truck parked suspiciously along the deserted road. They stopped to investigate and discovered MacPherson's body on the beach.

RCMP constable Kirby Jarvis said that MacPherson had been last seen in Montague on Thursday evening, and must have gone swimming at Petit Point in the hours between Thursday night and Friday morning.

Mr. Jarvis could not explain why Mr. MacPherson would have decided to go for a late-night swim, considering how cool the evening had been, with water temperatures somewhere in the low teens.

Results from an autopsy, including a toxicology report, will take a few weeks to come in. "We'll determine then what factors, including alcohol consumption, were involved in the drowning," said Mr. Jarvis. He noted that Mr. MacPherson most likely got caught in a rip current after swimming out from the shore and could not fight his way back in.

The death may be especially tragic, as Mr. MacPherson was the sole caretaker of his grandmother, Margaret MacPherson, 97, also of Montague. RCMP confirmed that the woman needed to be sedated upon learning of her grandson's death, and has now been admitted to Kings County Memorial Hospital.

Riley flinched in the swing seat as a splash of hot coffee, suddenly tipping from the cup in his weakened hand, doused his knee just below the hem of his shorts. He cursed and set the coffee down before wiping at the scald with the ball of his fist. Then he took up the newspaper again and reread the article, his heart picking up pace.

Jessie-Mac's got to be devastated by this, he thought. *I should go into town and see if she's okay.*

He read the article a third time, and then something occurred to him. No, more than occurred. A memory came swimming up into his skull then. Danny had drown either late Thursday night or early Friday morning. Hadn't Riley had a dream that night, too? Not a sexy dream, like the one from last night, but another kind. That night vision had been, he recalled now, full of the strange dark light that he was convinced radiated from the woods behind his property—that queer luminance shining out of Lowfield. He remembered that.

He remembered something else. There had *been* something else, in Thursday's dream. Riley pushed hard to evoke it, scouring his brain like an old pan. And then it came to him.

Jellyfish. He had dreamt of jellyfish. An entire sea of them.

Riley set the paper aside and went back into the house to get cleaned up so he could drive into Montague.

~

He parked out front of the *Eastern Pioneer* offices. Main Street was quiet on a Saturday morning, but he knew the newspaper wouldn't be. Jack and his team often worked six out of seven days to put out their weekly paper—with Wednesday, which fell immediately after an issue went to bed, being the only one resembling a day off. Sure enough, as Riley hiked up to the second-floor loft, he found the tiny office in a state that passed for bustling. At a desk to his right sat Jack's wife, whom Riley knew worked part-time selling ads. At the very back of the floor, in his little glass-wall fishbowl of an office, was Jack himself, talking into the phone with great animation. To Riley's left, he saw a woman in a lumberjack coat and rubber boots rifling through folders in a filing cabinet against the brick wall. This, he was fairly certain, was Maggie, the only other full-time journalist on staff. Next to where she stood was the news desk she shared with Jessie-Mac.

Only Jessie-Mac wasn't there. Riley was unsurprised but still disappointed to see someone else sitting in her chair. He was a silver-haired, wrinkly-faced man in a blue turtleneck, an unlit cigarette parked in the corner of his mouth. Looking well into his sixties, the man sat hunched toward the Macintosh computer in front of him, staring at it as if were an alien technology that might steal his soul.

He looked up at Riley. "Can I help you, sir?"

Instead of answering, Riley cast his eyes back to Jack's glass office. The publisher had spotted him coming in and was now beckoning to Riley even as he talked on the phone.

"I'm here to see Jack," Riley said, and the old guy gestured for him to proceed.

Entering the fish bowl, Riley set his lumbering limbs down into the guest chair opposite Jack's desk. As he had done before, he glanced up to the big collage on the office's back wall, the green and red YES and NO stickers from the bridge plebiscite. Jack raised a *Give me a sec* finger to Riley as he finished on the phone.

"Yes... Uh-huh... Uh-huh. No, I get that, Roger. I understand that the Premier has already come out as anti-abor... fine, fine, pro-life. Pro-life. We all know she's not going to shake up the status quo here on PEI. But I'd still appreciate a statement from her. So she can either address this now or she can address this *after* we publish the latest batch of letters to the editor... Okay... Okay, fine. I will call your office on Monday. Enjoy your fishing trip. Sorry I made you late. Thank you Roger."

Jack hung up. He gave Riley a look and a smile before picking up a huge stack of mail sitting on the corner of his desk. "*Och aye*," he said, giving it a jostle. "I swear, I could publish a whole special edition just with the letters about Jessie-Mac's op-ed. That girl has really stirred the pot."

"I bet she has," Riley said. He took out his du Mauriers and lit one.

"Coupling abortion access on PEI with the construction of the bridge, and then bundling it up with her own personal experience, was a stroke of genius—genius! That little lady is going places, let me tell you."

Riley nodded, but then the two men grew silent. Sombre.

"So, Danny MacPherson," Riley said, and swallowed.

Jack nodded solemnly. "Yeah."

"How's Jessie doing?"

"How do you think?" Jack fluttered his lips. "I mean, imagine being twenty and finding out someone you dated in high school is already dead. Christ, I'm *fifty-nine* and the idea gives me the heebie-jeebies."

"So, she's off now?"

"Yeah. Though I practically had to beat her out of here with a stick. Her internship's only eighteen weeks and she wants to work every single day before she goes back to Halifax for school. But I had to put my foot down. She needs some time to grieve."

"Who's that at her desk?"

"That's Jim. Former *Guardian* man, he's been one of our columnists since he retired. I asked him to come in full-time to cover her work, at least for a week or two until she gets herself together."

Riley nodded at that. He was about to ask something else when Jack cut him off. "Actually, I'm glad you're here," he said. "I was going to call you anyway. I assume you saw the *Guardian* story about Danny."

"Yeah."

"There was something about it I wanted to ask you."

Riley felt himself seize up, coil a little inside his chair. He half-expected Jack to lob a question or three about his own relationship with Danny MacPherson. Something along the lines of: *I thought it mighty curious that you two had a wee confrontation at the*

Boar's Head that night, and a week later he shows up dead. Mighty curious indeed. And I hear he came by your property a while back with some of his buddies, and there was a physical altercation between you two. Is that true?

But instead, Jack asked, "Do you happen to know the RCMP mentioned in the story? Kirby Jarvis?"

Riley relaxed a bit. "No. I haven't gone down and introduced myself to the Montague detachment yet." *And may never*, he thought, but didn't say. *My name's still kinda mud with the force, and Jessie-Mac's profile of me probably didn't help, so...* "Why do you ask?"

"Well, Ray Power's piece wasn't bad but there's something about it that's not sitting right with me. I gave Kirb a call to ask my own questions, but he was pretty tight-lipped. Uncharacteristically so. He usually gives me the straight goods. But he said they aren't releasing any more information about Danny's death until after the autopsy results come back, which'll take weeks. So, yeah, something's not sitting right."

"The fact Danny went for a late-night swim in the first place?"

"Well, there's that. Mighty strange, considering how chilly that water would've been. But there's something else." Jack cleared his throat and lowered his voice a little. "Helen and I have a nephew who works for the Parks department. He wasn't on the crew that found Danny, but he knows the people who were. They're already telling tales about what they saw. They say his body was in quite a state when they came upon it on that beach."

"What kind of state?"

"Well, he was in his boxers for his swim, so they could see most of his skin. They say it was all covered in—oh, I don't know, like welts and such. Big, weeping blisters all over him. Like, head to toe."

Riley felt his blood stop flowing through his body.

Jack went on. "Now, yesterday morning was bright and warm, but they found Danny just a few hours after dawn. Not enough time for his body to get a sunburn that would give him welts and blisters like that. But there they were. I thought it weird that Ray didn't mention it in his story."

Riley couldn't breathe. All of a sudden, the vague and oceanic nightmare he'd had on Thursday night, about jellyfish, came back to him with startling clarity. Yes, he had dreamt of an entire sea teeming with them—an army of glutinous, wine-dark blobs undulating in the salty waves, trailing their stinging tendrils behind them like torn skirts. Hundreds of them, thousands of them, swaying in the surf. But there was something more in the dream. He could see it now, burning in his mind's eye. A person trapped among their numbers. Trapped and screaming for his life as the jellyfish stung him dozens and *dozens* of times over.

Jack went on. "Now, I asked Kirb about it point-blank, but he hushed right up. Just stuck to his line, no matter how I phrased the question. *We ain't releasing any more details until after the autopsy.* It was like he was embarrassed that he couldn't explain all the welts on Danny's body. So I figured if you were friendly with him, you might pop by the detachment and start nosing arou—" Jack stopped when he finally looked up into Riley's face. "Jesus, Fuller, are you okay? You look like you're going to puke."

Riley did want to puke. In that moment, he wanted to shove his face into Jack's nearby trash bin and let last night's supper come roaring up.

Jack squinted at him. "Riley, do you *know* something?"

I know Danny tried to scare me off my land, he thought. *And I'm pretty sure Applegarth, and the village of Lowfield behind it, doesn't want that to happen.*

"No," he said simply.

Jack squinted at him again. But then he seemed to let it go, at least for now. "Anyway. That stretch of beach is only a couple klicks from my house. I may go down there after the RCMP are done with it to see what I can see for myself."

"Jack, please don't," Riley said quickly. Too quickly.

Jack perked right up in his chair, his eyebrows sailing toward the ceiling.

"Just, just leave it alone," Riley added. "I'll think about introducing myself to the Montague boys. But in the meantime, do me a favour and hold tight, will you?"

Jack hesitated, still looking suspicious, but then shrugged. "Okay, fine. But don't think about it too long. Something's not sitting right. Ray Power's a decent journalist but he sometimes phones it in. If there's more to the story, I want it for the *Pioneer*."

"Okay," Riley said, but then cast his mind away as far as he could. He had no intention of introducing himself to the boys at the Montague detachment. He had no intention of asking Kirby Jarvis about the welts and blisters on Danny MacPherson's body.

~

Despite everything, Riley decided to cut the front lawn as planned. The day was going to be hot, and he wanted to feel the sun's bright bead on his neck and smell the fragrance of freshly cut grass as he made long, repetitive laps on the ride-on mower. This was normalcy, the safe, familiar sensations of summer borne of a pleasantly mindless chore that had been part of his life since his pre-teens. Riley remembered how particular his father, Thomas, had been about his own lawn, back in Moncton, at the house Riley grew up in. He would often scold his son if he didn't cut it just right. Years later, when he sold the house after Riley's mother had died, Thomas would sometimes drive by the old place and grouse about how poorly the new owners were maintaining it. Riley himself was not so fussy. A lawn was just a lawn, especially here at Applegarth. Like so much around the property, it seemed to take care of itself. But he needed this. Kicking back in the ride-on's plastic seat and thinking about exactly nothing, Riley surrendered himself over to this humdrum task, the almost hypnotic routine of it.

He was about halfway finished when he spotted a vehicle approaching on the Eight Mile Road. It slowed down and then turned into Riley's driveway. He saw instantly that it was Jessie-Mac's beat-up, robin-blue Dodge minivan with the rusted P over the back driver-side wheel well. The high afternoon sun gleamed off the van's windshield as she pulled up toward the house.

Riley killed the mower's engine at the same time she killed the van's. Once the blades stopped spinning, he climbed off and started walking over. As he did, he saw that she wasn't alone. Another girl was with her, hopping down from the van's passenger-side door. In a single moment, he realized that it was one of the other young people Jessie had been with that day in the park. It was the girl with the pixie cut and dog tags. The girl who had made a guest appearance, joining Jessie, in Riley's raunchy night vision from the evening before. He couldn't believe it, the coincidence. But there she was, in the flesh.

He tried not to let his gaze loiter on her, but he couldn't help himself. She, in turn, was not looking at Riley. She was looking beyond him, up the driveway at Applegarth itself. Her eyes lingered on that old, rambling manse in the remote PEI countryside, on its broad front porch and towering Queen Anne turret, its bright-white siding and scarlet gables. But she didn't look impressed by the sight. She looked somehow... unsettled.

Riley turned back to Jessie. Her icy-grey, Cheshire eyes were puffy and red from crying. As she locked onto him standing there at the driveway's edge, he thought that maybe an accusation might come raging out of her mouth. *YOU had something to do with this, didn't you!* she'd bawl at him. *You and Danny had that weird quarrel; you took an instant dislike to each other, right? You nearly got into a couple of fights! So did you have ANYTHING to do with what happened to him on that beach, Riley Fuller? Did you?*

Of course, she said none of this. She just gazed at him with a gentle pleading.

His expression must have said, *I heard the news*, because she ran up to him then and was suddenly in his arms for a hug. Like the one she'd given him after they played scat that night at Jack's, it was a perfectly platonic embrace. But Riley knew that if Jessie had any idea about the sort of fantasies that came to him about her in his bed at night, she wouldn't be doing this. He was tempted to push her gently away, even as another part of him wanted to draw out the bliss of having her body pressed against his.

Instead, he just asked, "How you holding up, kiddo?"

"I'm all right," she replied, and finally let him go. She pawed at her eyes as if in disbelief that they *still* held tears. "Fuck," she said with a throaty murmur. "Sorry, Riley. I can't seem to stop crying. *Fuck.*"

"It's okay. Take your time." He turned then to the other girl and extended his hand. "Riley Fuller."

"Tara Moore," she replied, and shook it.

"Sorry, manners," Jessie said. "Riley, Tara. Tara, Riley. She was friends with Danny, too."

"I'm sorry for your loss," Riley said to her, and the girl nodded once, almost militarily, before placing a hand on Jessie's shoulder and giving it a comforting rub.

He turned back to her. "How's his grandmother?"

"Not great," Jessie replied, pressing her wrist to her nose as if to hold in fresh tears. "They're now saying she had a stroke when they told her. That's why they had to take her to the hospital."

"She's *quite* old," Tara added, "so it doesn't look good. She probably won't ever get to go home."

Riley gave a solemn nod. "Is there anything I can do?"

"No," Jessie said, "but thank you. Listen, that's not why I popped by. I have some news, and I wanted to tell you before I told Jack."

"Oh?"

"Yeah. The Mounties in Charlottetown got back to me late Thursday with an answer to my FOI request."

"Already?" Riley felt his heart go from a trot to a gallop in one second.

"I know, eh? Jack said these things sometimes take months, and sometimes—like in this case—they take three days. I was going to come by yesterday afternoon to tell you, except I…" And here she paused, to collect herself once again. "Except I found out about Danny."

"What, what did the RCMP tell you?" Riley felt his brow begin to sweat. Could these girls see it, beading there on the ridge above his eyes? Could they see him turning queasy?

"So, first of all, there *was* no RCMP on the Island in 1930," she said. "Oddly enough, PEI got its own provincial force that year, modelled on a similar one in New Brunswick, but it only lasted two years. The RCMP replaced it when it was established here in '32, but—miracle of miracles—they inherited all the open cases and archival stuff from the older force. The cops I spoke to were able to pull up the police reports from the 1930 case involving missing and sexually assaulted girls. Those reports have recently been digitized, which made them relatively easy to find. They actually emailed me over a copy. I started going through them earlier today. Oh, and don't tell Jack I'm still working. He'd be pissed if he knew."

"Did they..." Riley began but then paused, needing his own moment to collect himself. "Did they say if they had a primary suspect?"

"They had a person of interest, for sure," Jessie replied. "I wanted you to know well in advance of anything I might publish about this. You definitely don't need any more surprises about your personal life showing up in the *Pioneer*." She looked up at him with her cool, glacier-coloured eyes, and paused as if giving Riley a chance to brace himself. "His name was James Fuller, and he was living here at Applegarth at the time of the investigation."

"My grandfather," Riley said.

"Yeah."

"What... what else did the report say?"

"Lots. It said he killed himself, here in this house, before the provincial force had a chance to question him. When that happened, the rapes and disappearances stopped, which meant word got around the community that it was probably him behind it all along. It also said there were lots more of them, way more than the newspapers of the time had reported. Enough for the cops to do a deep dive into James Fuller's background." She squinted at Riley. "How much do you know about your grandfather?"

"I know he was an Anglican priest in Halifax. I know my grandmother divorced him earlier in 1930, when my dad was just seven years old. I know she moved back to Moncton, her hometown, to raise him as a single mom, and James moved to PEI. I did know he killed himself in this house later that year, although I didn't know why. On those few occasions my dad did talk about James, he just said that there were rumours he was, quote, 'screwy in the head.' That was the phrase he used."

"Did he tell you that James lost his ordained status—was basically defrocked—by the Anglican Church in Halifax?" Jessie asked.

Riley paused. Licked his lips. "No. No, I didn't know that."

"The police investigation indicates that he was stripped of his position in the church after it came to light that he'd messed around with several women in his congregation over the years. He had multiple affairs with multiple parishioners of multiple ages. It was why he was defrocked, and probably why your grandmother divorced him. His 'deviant background'—that's language straight out of the officers' notes—absolutely made him a suspect in the case, especially since the rapes and disappearances started not long after he moved to PEI. Small-town suspicions and all that."

Riley felt as if the entirety of his stomach had just fallen out. He was instantly transported back to the diaries he'd found upstairs in Applegarth's library, and what they described: the sex cult that passed for a church in Lowfield; the sheer degradations that Elder Fuller had instilled in his congregation to open a doorway to the Great Force Beyond. If James Fuller had found and read those diaries in Applegarth's library, as Riley himself had, and if he traipsed back into the woods to find the remnants of Lowfield, and if he had touched and read a few lines of that wretched book sitting on its wretched pulpit in that wretched chapel, then… then what might its powers have inspired in him? Riley's head began to keel, but he fought to keep his composure. "No, I didn't know any of that," he told Jessie.

"Anyway, I doubt I'll be able to include much beyond his name in my story," she went on. "Like I said before, I really want to focus on the women and *their* experiences. Tara here is trying to get me an interview with her own grandmother, who lived in Georgetown at the time."

Riley turned to Tara. "Your grandmother?"

"Yes, sir. She doesn't live here anymore. But she was in her early twenties in 1930, and I've been calling her, trying to get her to open up about what happened back then, for Jessie's story."

"Where does she live now?"

"Ontario. When my parents split up, she followed my dad to Trenton. He's a colonel at the Canadian Forces Base there."

Riley raised an eyebrow. "Oh yeah? I'm ex-military myself. I was at Gagetown in the early seventies, before I joined the RCMP."

"Oh cool," Tara said plainly. "I did Basic at Gagetown last summer, after I finished my first year at UPEI."

Riley couldn't help but grin. "That explains the dog tags."

Tara just shrugged. "What can I say? I want to follow in my old man's footsteps. Anyway. Grams is in a nursing home now and her memory's shot. When I asked her what she recalled from back in 1930, she got all weird on me. Started speaking in riddles and then clammed right up. I was going to ask Dad about it when he came down for his annual fishing trip, but he had to cancel. He's now on mission and *incommunicado*, so I won't speak to him until he's here hunting in the fall. By the time I get him in the woods, it'll be far too late for Jessie's story."

"You hunt?"

She gave him a slant smile. "Yeah, don't let the pixie cut and lip gloss fool you. I know my way around guns."

"What do you hunt?"

"Rabbits mostly. But ducks and geese too, if the mood hits."

Another question suddenly burned in Riley. He grew serious, his hazel eyes narrowing at Tara with inquiry. "Does he ever take you hunting in *these* woods?" he asked, and gestured toward the overgrown forest behind Applegarth.

"No. It's strange. When he visits, he doesn't like coming out here for some reason. I don't know why. He prefers to hunt just beyond Murray River, or else up west. We have our favourite spots." She glanced up at him. "Why do you ask?"

Riley said nothing, but thoughts began to churn, to eddy inside his head. *You say he doesn't like coming up here for some reason. Is it because your grandmother told him to avoid this place, this area altogether? Maybe she said not to ever come this far out on the Eight Mile Road, because there's something bad in the woods here, something worth avoiding. You say she speaks in riddles, but would her words make sense to me, if I heard them? Maybe she spoke of cursed crops growing in cursed soil. Maybe she spoke of animals keeping watch, keeping guard. Maybe she spoke of incest—just like Mrs. Keating did. Surely you know something isn't right out here. Look at Applegarth. Can't you both see that it looks like I've done a year's worth of repairs in less than two months? And if you came even ten feet farther up my driveway, you'd be able to see into my side garden, and what's growing there.*

"Why do you ask?" Tara said again.

Jessie-Mac took a step closer to Riley, her own face now seized by curiosity. "Does this have something to do with Lowfield?"

Riley just blinked at her. Even in the throes of her grief, she didn't miss anything. *Frig she's smart*, he thought.

"What's Lowfield?" Tara asked.

Riley swallowed. "It's nothing," he said quickly, trying to backpedal. "Just a bunch of bullshit family lore, just a bunch of stories. It's nothing." Was he shaking? He was shaking.

Tara threw him a skeptical look. But then her eyes did draw away from him and back toward the house, the garden, the woods beyond. Maybe she sensed that something wasn't right up here, that there was some dark, queer energy radiating from this whole place. Maybe they both sensed it, her and Jessie, and in another moment they'd begin to wonder if this had anything to do with Danny's death.

But Jessie just reached out to squeeze Riley's arm. "Sorry. I've upset you, haven't I? Look, I don't want to dredge up more stuff about your background in a story I'm writing. Seriously. I don't plan to focus on your grandfather. It's really not the point of the piece."

"Okay," Riley said with a nod. "Thank you. I appreciate that."

Tara, who seemed in no way satisfied, who looked like she wanted to hear more about this Lowfield place, nonetheless turned to Jessie and said, "We should probably go. You're going to be late."

Jessie looked at her watch. "Oh shoot. You're right."

"Late for what?" Riley asked.

"I have to pick up my sister from soccer practice in Montague. She finishes in, like, ten minutes."

Riley perked at this. "I didn't know you had a sister."

"Yeah, no. Her name's Kyla. I don't talk about her much. She's a little brat."

"A *bossy* little brat," Tara confirmed.

"Chauffeuring her around this summer was one of my parents' conditions for giving me free rein with their old minivan." Jessie rolled her steely eyes. "As if I don't need it anyway for my actual job."

"How old is she?" Riley found himself asking.

"Kyla? She's twelve going on twenty-five. Seriously, if you know any third-world countries that need a new dictator, I'll gladly mail her there in an envelope."

Another of his frequent, unwelcome thoughts bullied its way into Riley's mind. He tried to fight it, but in one instant it consumed him like a fire. He wanted to imagine then what this Kyla girl looked like. Would she be a twelve-year-old version of Jessie-Mac herself, or something even better? A bright, demanding nymph of a girl, and at the threshold of puberty no less? Maybe Jessie could bring her up here sometime, and maybe Riley could—

He froze. *What the ever-loving fuck? Really? Really? You lecherous piece of shit, what is even the matter with you? Are you insane? This isn't who you really ar—*

It was as if Applegarth itself—that huge, gabled, rambling house, that manifestation of everything toxic about Riley, of everything noxious about the men in his bloodline—reached out and clutched him from behind. Its grip caused all the cells in his body to light up like fireworks. A great energy came over him then, stirring up his mind and enlivening his loins. He knew that, if he wanted to, he could grab both of these girls, Jessie *and* Tara, and drag them shocked and screaming over to the house, to the privacy of the porch, where he cou—

No. No! Fuck off! FUCK OFF! He pried himself away from that thought, from the cinematic delights it promised to play inside his head.

The house settled onto itself then, creaking and groaning loud enough to startle the girls. Riley watched as Tara peered up and over at Applegarth with an uneasy gaze. She squinted at it, as if she had just seen something—or some*one*—move past one of its second-storey windows.

"So, yeah, I should go," Jessie repeated. "I'm already late." Then she raised herself up on the balls of her feet to hug Riley again.

"I'm really sorry about Danny," he said as he came out of his trance and held her in his arms. "If you need anything, you just let me know. Okay, kiddo?"

"I will." When she let him go, Riley saw her eyes had moistened again. She wiped away at them clinically. "And I'm sorry to be the bearer of bad news about your granddad."

"It's okay." Then he turned to Tara. "It was nice meeting you."

She gave another of her militant little nods, but said nothing in return.

Then he watched them both head back over to the minivan and pull open its front doors. He watched as their small, lithe bodies scooted up into the seats. He watched as seatbelts were fastened and the ignition was turned on. *Oh, to be twenty again*, he thought. *To be able to glance at girls like that and not feel like a dirty old man.*

When the van had pulled down the driveway and was gone, Riley turned back to Applegarth. Every molecule of his body wanted to head inside, to go upstairs and into his bed and surrender himself to whatever fresh visions the house had in store for him.

But he wouldn't. He wouldn't give in to that. *This isn't who you really are.* Instead, Riley just wandered back over to his ride-on. He had a lawn to finish mowing.

Chapter 22

June 25, 1995

Dear Diary, or Journal, or whatever the fuck you are,

Lord knows I can say things here, in the privacy of these digital pages, that I can't say out loud to people, or even in an email to Sammy, because it would sound fucking nuts. But let me state, for whatever... force of posterity is reading this, that I believe Lowfield, that empty, rotting village two miles behind my property, had something to do with Danny MacPherson's death last Thursday night. I'm convinced that there are dark forces there that *want* me in this house, that want me in this area. Danny tried to scare me away, and I believe he paid for it with his life.

So this raises the question: why don't I leave? If I *know* that my presence here might cause something terrible to happen, then why don't I flee from this place and never come back? God, the answer will sound so horrible. Despite all that has happened, being inside this house is the only thing that keeps me together. Despite the revulsion I feel after one of my night visions—involving Jessie or Jane, involving Marigold or Tara, or any number of other women, real or imagined—I'm still addicted to them, to the desires that wash over me at night. These urges make me feel powerful, like I have some semblance of control over myself and... and the lives of others around me.

It's becoming evident that granddad James may have felt something similar. For him, it looks like suicide was the only way out. But is that true for me? The Glock is right downstairs. It has made a promise to me, a promise it will keep if I choose that path. But *must* I choose it? I need to understand more. I need to learn more about my family history, and not just what my grandfather's grandfather recorded in his diary from the 1860s. I need to learn more about my bloodline. Granddad James, as far as I can tell, left nothing behind—no diaries of his own, no letters, no record of information at all about his six months living under this roof in 1930. And I learned nothing from his son, my father. Thomas was an expert at keeping his mouth shut, and took many family secrets with him to the grave. So I need to go another route.

To that end, I've reached out for help. Earlier today, I called my uncle Barrie in Moncton—this would be my mother's younger brother. Since retiring seven or eight years ago from his job as an accountant with the city, Barrie has committed his free time almost exclusively to genealogy. I know he's done huge, elaborate trees for his side of the family, but I asked if he'd do a shorter one for me on the Fuller side, if I gave him some leads. He was happy to oblige. He provided me with his email address (*everyone* is getting on email these days, it seems) and I sent him what I had, what I was able to glean from the diaries I found, and from what I know of granddad James, and my own dad, and myself. We'll see what Barrie is able to come back with.

Can I be honest? If I can't be honest here, in these digital pages, then where can I be? I've asked Barrie to do this because I *need* to know that I am in fact the last of my bloodline. No doubt James Robert Fuller sired many children as part of his incestuous cult, but from what I read in the diaries, I somehow know that his daughter, Melinda Fuller, was the only one who ever got out, fleeing Lowfield with her two sons in 1834. Nearly thirty years later, a confrontation fomented between those two sons when they returned to the Island and built this house. I still haven't gone back to the diaries after learning that Melinda was raped and impregnated by her own father, but I am certain that something truly terrible happened in Lowfield in 1863 that cause its *entire population to vanish*. Perhaps they *were* able to open the portal that James Robert Fuller preached of, but it did not result in the effects they wanted. At any rate, my grandfather's grandfather, Riley Fuller, (but not his brother Robert?) must have fled after these events and returned to Halifax. He must have married and continued the line, of which I am a part and probably the last. If other offspring of Elder Fuller's incest *did* escape Lowfield prior to 1863, someone on the Island must have an account, or heard a rumour, or shared an old tall tale, about someone showing the deformities and defects that often come with inbreeding, what the other Riley called *the Lowfield look*. I think I'll ask Jack about it. He seems to know everyone on, and nearly everything about, Prince Edward Island.

On an unrelated note, they announced Danny's wake on the radio this afternoon. It'll be held at a funeral home in Montague on Tuesday, with two visitations: from two to four and seven to nine. Despite my altercations with the kid, part of me wants to pop by during one of those two times. Jessie-Mac will no doubt be there, along with Tara and the other friends in their circle, and I could show them all some support. But another part of me thinks I should stay away. Part of me is fairly certain that, by the mere fact that I am still living in Applegarth, I am responsible for Danny's death. Oh God, what a wretched thought to think.

...

PS: I have just reread this entry, and *once again* I do not recognize the syntax with which it is written. Fuck—the syntax I've written it with. Jesus. This isn't how I express myself in my own head. And as for the vocabulary? "Foment," "demise," "wretched"—these are not terms

I use in everyday speech. What is happening to me? What is happening when I sit down to write in this diary, or journal, or whatever the fuck you are? It's almost like a force possesses me, to help me document what is going on far more vividly than I could express on my own. But why? To what purpose? Am I... Am I actually leaving this behind for someone?

Chapter 23

Maybe it was another sign he'd become middle-aged, because Riley was suddenly very interested in genealogy, something he hadn't given two shits about before. Following the phone call and email exchange with his uncle Barrie in Moncton, Riley had gained an abrupt, burning fascination with his family background and how it intersected with the broader history of Prince Edward Island. Wasn't this the sort of thing that only old folks cared about, he thought, people who were at or near retirement and had lots of free time on their hands? But after his chat with Barrie, Riley found he couldn't stop thinking about it. He knew there was a bigger story—decades or even centuries old, and much darker than he could have imagined—burbling under the surface of his own tale. He craved to throw himself into that flow, to see where those bleak and choppy waters might take him.

And so, a few days later, he made another trip into Charlottetown, to the Confederation Library downtown. He went up to the counter, where a young, pretty librarian was happy to issue him a library card after confirming his address via a phone bill he'd brought from home. Riley got her to take him over to the section that carried books about the history of PEI, which she cheerfully did. Once there, Riley watched as she stood on tiptoes to stretch toward the highest shelf, checking the Dewey Decimal numbers printed on the spines there, and eyed her again as she squatted down to do the same on the lowest shelf. "Nope, none down there," she said, standing back up with a little hop. "Okay, so they're all right *here*," and she made a spread-armed indication of where the section began and ended.

"Thank you," Riley said.

"No problem. Let me know if you need anything else."

"I will." And then he watched as she returned to the front desk and scooped back into her chair with a cute little bounce. *Fuck*, he thought, looking away.

He returned to the section, which was a shelf and a half's worth of books, and began browsing through them. Several of the newer-looking titles seemed to be written by the same guy, a history prof at UPEI, according to his author page. Riley wondered if this was the fellow Jack had mentioned, the one who might be interested in seeing the diaries that Riley had found in Applegarth's library, if he was willing to share them. Riley pulled out the books that looked the most interesting, ones that were both recent and offered a good overview of Island history. He brought his picks over to the librarian to sign them out. She seemed pleased that he'd found so many he wanted to read, and began running them over the scanner for him.

Next, he asked her for something else. "Do you have copies of old newspapers from Halifax?" he said. "On, like, what do you call it…?"

"On microfilm?"

"Yeah, yeah."

"Of course. Do you know what you're looking for?"

He told her he wanted to know if there were any articles from early 1930—say, in the first three months of that year—about an Anglican priest getting defrocked and having to leave his Halifax parish. He gave the librarian his grandfather's name and the name of his church, which Riley had gleaned from the ancient, digitized police report that Jessie-Mac had emailed him. This was very little to go on, but the librarian helped him comb through various indexes—large, leather-bound books—of the various newspapers running in Halifax at the time. Finally, they found a reference to a James Fuller, and cross-referenced it to a mention of the church: they both appeared in an article from the *Halifax Evening Mail* dated February 13, 1930.

"That's probably it," he said.

Next she took him over to the large filing cabinets of microfilm and helped him locate the box that corresponded to the newspaper and date in question. Once they did, they took it over to one of the microfilm machines and she gave him a quick tutorial on it, showing him how to load the small, hand-size wheel of microfilm onto the machine's peg and feed the film itself through the viewfinder. Riley tried hard not to stare as the librarian explained how the various knobs and buttons worked, how to spin through the newspaper pages quickly until he found what he was looking for, and how to focus and zoom in and print, if he wanted. Then she left him to it. The slightest hint of strawberry shampoo lingered in her wake.

Riley felt his heart pick up pace as he began, whirring through the first few weeks' worth of editions of the *Halifax Evening Mail* in 1930. It took a while, but he finally found February 13. He slowly began to move through the day's pages, their columns of dense text and old-timey advertisements, hunting for the story that would mention his grandfather. At long last, he found it. It was like magic, how a person's name and the name of a church, listed in tiny print in a leather-bound index, could lead you to a sole page, sixty-five years in the past, in a newspaper that no longer existed.

The story, he could quickly see, was not about James Fuller per se. It instead announced that his replacement, a Father Joseph Callan, would be taking over the parish as of the next Sunday, February 16. The article included details of Father Callan's background and a photo of him shaking hands with a parishioner. The Anglican priest looked to be in late middle age, with a doughy face and severe eyes. Only at the very end of the article did Riley find the reference he was looking for. The story stated that Father James Fuller had abruptly left the church the previous Sunday, February 9, and that the entire congregation "wished him well in his future endeavours." There was no mention of him moving to Prince Edward Island, but there was, Riley could see, a small photograph, a simple thumbnail headshot of his grandfather, embedded in the story's final paragraph.

Riley positioned the photo into the centre of the viewfinder and turned the knob that would zoom in on it. He nearly winced at what he saw.

It was essentially his own face, captured there in grainy black and white. Yes, the man in the picture was more than a decade younger than Riley; and yes, his facial hair was of the period's Clark Gable style—thin and dainty, as if drawn on with a pencil, in stark contrast to Riley's own scruffy and graying beard—but otherwise they could have been twins. They had the same hard, narrow eyes, the same pinched mouth that looked unaccustomed to smiling, the same stovepipe neck. It was eerie, how closely genetics had rendered their basic appearance.

And then Riley had a flight of pure imagination comingling with what he already knew of James Fuller's story, the trajectory from his old life to his new one, here on the Island. The police report had said he'd been defrocked after having multiple affairs with multiple women in his Halifax church. They must have been going on for years. Perhaps Riley's grandmother, whose name he knew was Cecilia, had found out about the affairs when they had first begun. Perhaps she—a young mother by this point, and terrified of a husbandless future—had given James every chance to break the relations off, to redeem himself. And perhaps he did for a while. But maybe the affairs resumed, and Cecilia found out, and that was the last straw. She left him, fleeing to her hometown of Moncton by early 1930 with Riley's dad, Thomas, who would not yet have turned seven, in tow.

And James, now stripped of his career and of his family, spiraled down into some dark place. And it was there, perhaps, where he found the deed to Applegarth, sitting among papers inherited from his own father years earlier, who in turn would have inherited it from the original Riley Fuller. And obviously James had travelled to PEI to check the old manse out, just as Riley himself had. And just as Riley had, perhaps James had become enamoured of the place. He began fixing it up, installing contemporary plumbing and electrical—even Dave Campbell had known this when he'd given Riley his tour of Applegarth. And perhaps the house had helped James along, as it had with Riley, making those magical, mysterious repairs that allowed him to move in under its roof. And like Riley, perhaps James began having dreams at night, raunchy, filthy visions once he did.

Perhaps he too had found the diaries in Applegarth's library. Perhaps he too had trekked out to the deserted village of Lowfield, and found *The Grimoire of Shaal* sitting on its pulpit in that horrible church. Perhaps he had turned the pages of that book, found them warm to the touch, like a living thing, and perhaps he had recited aloud some of the incantations he found inside. Just as Riley had.

And perhaps... and perhaps impulses came over James Fuller then, a man Thomas had always heard was "a bit screwy in the head." And soon girls around the area began disappearing, or getting raped. But maybe other things, more inexplicable things—involving local animals, involving crops growing in the soil of that garden—began to happen. These phenomena would be frightening enough to terrify the young women of the area, to the point where they would tell their children and grandchildren, *for decades*, to stay away, to not go that far out on Glenning's Eight Mile Road. And perhaps James was overcome with a sickening guilt over what he had triggered, or perhaps that nascent, ragtag motley of provincial police was closing in on him, and he decided to kill himself as a means of escape.

But... but... he must have done something else first. Stricken with shame over all that he had wrought, James had most definitely put the deed to Applegarth in a trust for young Thomas, which he would be given access to when he came of age. But maybe the trust came with instructions: sell the property unseen and use the proceeds to give yourself a leg-up in life if you wish, but whatever you do, stay away from that land, from that whole wooded, isolated area of PEI. And Thomas... so emotionally closed off, so bitter at what life had dealt him, so obsessed with becoming a "self-made man"—just let the deed languish in his own estate for decades. Maybe he meant to sell it at some point; maybe he forgot about or ignored the deed because he wanted nothing to do with the screw-up excuse for a father who destroyed his childhood with his appalling behaviour back in Halifax.

And then Thomas died suddenly of a stroke, in 1991, and the deed passed on to Riley as part of his estate. And so here Riley was on PEI, his own life on the mainland shattered by his own deviancy, and he was now reliving everything he imagined James going through. It wasn't just their faces that were identical. It was their fates. It was—

"Do you need any additional help?" the librarian, looming suddenly over his left shoulder, asked him.

Riley flinched in the chair.

"Oh *sorry*," she said. "I didn't mean to startle you." And she touched his arm.

"I'd like to print this page," he said quickly. "Sorry, can you show me how again?"

"Of course." But before Riley could zoom back out from the picture of James, the librarian glanced up at it. "He's handsome," she said. Then she turned to Riley. "Oh wow, he looks like you." And she gave him what Riley could only interpret as a flirty little smile.

"Sorry, I'm in a rush," he said coldly, shoving down that sudden impulse, the urge that seemed borne from the very plaster and boards of Applegarth itself, to grab this poor, unsuspecting girl and have his way with her, right then and there at the microfilm machine. "I need to get out of here," he added, and was pleased to see her smile slip away like something on the tide.

~

He decided to stay in the city for lunch. Once finished at the library, Riley drove over to a pizza place he'd heard about, one housed in the former Charlottetown jail. It was a large, imposing brick building located on the edge of downtown. At each red light on the way, he kept peeping over at the stack of books sitting on the Lumina's passenger seat. He wanted to read them right away, to unlock their mysteries. *What, am I turning into Sammy?* he thought. *Am I becoming a bloody bookworm?* Still and all, when he got to the restaurant, he decided to take the tomes in with him.

Soon he was sitting in a booth, munching away at a glistening Hawaiian pizza and some garlic bread he'd toasted himself at a garlic bread bar in the corner, and perusing the books once again. As he spot-read certain chapters, Riley felt both a familiarity with and ignorance of the information captured on its pages. It was like they summoned up a knowledge he had passively absorbed in some high-school history class, retaining the information just long enough to write whatever essay or exam had corresponded with it. *When am I ever going to use this stuff?* his teenaged self had no doubt thought, and yet here he was, thirty years later, ravenous for these stories and timelines, the narrative arc that bent across centuries.

Naturally, it all began with the Mi'kmaq people, who inhabited what was now called Prince Edward Island for millennia, part of a larger region they called Mi'kma'ki. Their name for this island was *Epekwitk*, which future European settlers would pronounce—or, Riley supposed, *mis*pronounce—as *Abegweit*. (He did know this term. It was the name of one of the passenger ferries that crossed between PEI and New Brunswick every day, and which would be taken out of service once the bridge was completed in a couple of years.) The books quickly moved on to settler history. Jacques Cartier was the first European to lay eyes on the Island, in 1534, and by 1604 the French had colonized the entire Maritime region, calling it *Acadia*, and giving *Epekwitk* the French name *Île Saint-Jean*. Again: all terms that rang vague bells in Riley's head. The French eventually established the settlement of Montague, on the eastern end of the Island.

By the eighteenth century, the French and English were going hammer and tongs over their various colonies around the world, culminating in the Seven Years' War, between 1756 and 1763. At the war's conclusion, France formally ceded Île Saint-Jean to the British as part of the Treaty of Paris. But the British—*In the spirit of a gracious victor?* Riley wondered—kept the Island's name, albeit in English: St. John's Island. By 1767, a surveyor named Samuel Holland had carved up the Island into sixty-seven lots of land for the crown, which allocated them to supporters of the current British monarch, King George III, via a lottery. Riley's grandfather's grandfather had alluded to this in his diary. The lots would, for the most part, stay in the hands of these

English and Scottish landlords, and their descendants, for more than a century, sparking what came to be known as the absentee landlord controversy among local settlers. Riley paused over this part. He knew that phrase, too. Hadn't Dave Campbell called him that while giving Riley his tour of Applegarth? He must have been riffing on a term of local history, but it was true: Riley *was* Applegarth's absentee owner, just as his father had been before him.

By 1769, St. John's Island ceased to be part of Nova Scotia and became its own colony. Over the next fifteen years, its first governor, Walter Patterson, began a campaign to attract a wide array of settlers to the colony, including those from Scotland and Ireland, as well as loyalist refugees from the American Revolution. It was from this last group, Riley had learned from the diaries, that James Robert Fuller and his cult had come from. The twenty-five-year-old preacher, perhaps too extreme for even the most mystical faiths of New England, had brought his followers up to the colony in 1784 and settled in Montague. Riley hunted through the books that had indexes for a reference to the 1781 slavery law that, he learned from the diaries, had attracted Fuller here, but saw none. He also hunted the indexes for a reference to Lowfield, but again found nothing. Still, from Applegarth's diaries, he knew Fuller and his cult ran afoul of settlers already in the Montague region, and so Patterson's successor, Edmund Fanning, allowed them to settle on a boggy, isolated swath of land nine miles away, directly on the border between lots 53 and 54. It was here, the diaries said, that they founded the shunned village of Lowfield in 1790.

The books went on. By 1798, the British government allowed Fanning to change the colony's name from St. John's Island to Prince Edward Island, in honour of the fourth son of King George III, Prince Edward Augustus, the Duke of Kent. (Another chime of familiarity rang in Riley's head: he knew that one of the main arteries in Charlottetown was called Kent Street.) By 1825, slavery was outlawed on PEI—that *did* get a mention in one of the older books—and yet Riley knew that the bizarre religious practices in Lowfield continued regardless. The "coffles of Christ could take many forms," James Robert Fuller would tell his congregation.

Finally, in 1853, PEI's local administration attempted once and for all to resolve the absentee landlord controversy by enacting the Land Purchase Act. Though ultimately unsuccessful, it did liberate about a third of the Island's acreage from absentee landlordism, and Riley knew that this allowed the original Riley Fuller, and his brother Robert, to inherit a sublot of land upon which they built Applegarth a decade later. What exactly happened after that, in 1863—as the gulf between the two young men grew—Riley still didn't know. He hadn't returned to the diaries since learning that horrible family secret, that the boys' mother, Melinda Fuller, had, as a young teen, been raped multiple times by her own elderly father, and thus, James Robert was both the boys' grandfather *and* their father. It was too vile to even contemplate. Yet, that year, 1863, must have been pivotal, must have been a prominent demarcation between what was and what would be on PEI, because something significant occurred in Island history a year later.

That event, of course, was detailed across many pages in each of these books: the Charlottetown Conference, held in September 1864. It was originally meant to be a discussion about Maritime union, but with the inclusion of politicians from Upper and Lower Canada (modern-day Ontario and Quebec), it morphed into a talk of amalgamating British North America into a single new nation. Indeed, this slapdash conference became—according to the locals at least—the catalyst for Canadian Confederation itself. Consequently, it had become a load-bearing detail in the Island's tourism narrative. Summer had barely begun and yet Riley had already seen the young character actors in period garb strolling the streets of Charlottetown's historic district to greet visitors and share this history. Eighteen sixty-four was treated like a magical year on the Island. But by then, the real magic, the dark forces engulfing that cursed village thirty miles from Charlottetown, was already over. Whatever had happened in Lowfield to cause its residents to vanish, and for the original Riley Fuller to flee back to Halifax and never return, had already occurred. Within another decade, PEI would formally join Canadian Confederation, finally resolving its land question with an $800,000 influx of cash from the new government to buy out the last remaining absentee owners. Applegarth, meanwhile, was left to rot on its secluded property outside Glenning, until James Fuller showed up in 1930. And the rest, as they say, was history.

Riley looked up from the books to realize he'd eaten his entire pizza, and the waiter had come by to drop the bill off unnoticed.

Chapter 24

The Canada Day weekend came, but Riley stayed in the house. An email arrived from Sammy, wishing him a happy celebration and asking what he had scheduled for the big day. Meanwhile, both Jack and Dave called, leaving invitations on his answering machine to join them in their respective holiday plans, which included barbecues and fireworks and such.

Riley ignored it all. A cloud of depression, as thick as any he had experienced, fell on him in the wake of reading those history books and seeing a picture of his grandfather in that newspaper. He was beginning to connect the dots, to see how his lurid family background was linked to the history of the Island itself. How could he look people in the eye now? How could he face the random strangers he'd encounter in Glenning or Cardigan, in Montague or Petit Point? Where were their pitchforks and flaming torches? Why hadn't they, like Danny MacPherson before them, shown up on his property trying to scare him off? Maybe because they didn't understand their own history. People rarely did. But that might change if Jessie-Mac could get her story together and publish it in the *Pioneer*. That was clearly what the old lady in Cardigan, Mrs. Keating, had wanted.

So instead, Riley spent his days in Applegarth, roaming its rooms and alcoves. He rearranged the furniture in the solarium. He flipped through old, moldering books in the library. He spent an afternoon in the dirt basement, moving the stack of cinderblocks from one end of the space to the other for no discernible reason.

And at night, as he headed toward bed, he would pause on the second-floor landing to listen to the groans and shuffling, the creaks and whimpers coming from behind the attic's hatchway in the ceiling. *Those are my tenants*, he'd think. *Whatever is up there, I was once their absentee landlord. But not anymore.*

By Wednesday, groceries were getting low, so Riley broke his self-isolation and drove to the Sobeys in Montague to do a big shop. He was back in the parking lot and just loading his purchases, big fistfuls of plastic bags, into the Lumina's trunk when he looked over and saw a group of three young people climbing out of a Honda that had parked near the cart corral.

One of them was Tara Moore.

She froze when she saw him. Observing her for a moment, Riley thought: *Yes, the pixie cut* is *deceiving. Even if she hadn't said anything, even if I hadn't noticed her dog tags, I might have guessed that she's had some military training. The way she stands, the way her eyes try to both look everywhere at once and focus on the most immediate threat. I think she and I are cut from the same cloth. We're both... we're both warriors, in a sense.* The two other girls looked downright mousy by comparison.

Riley slammed the trunk shut, stuck a du Maurier in his mouth and lit it, then walked his cart over to the corral as casually as he could. Tara's eyes never left him. He shoved the cart in with its brethren and then walked over.

"It's Tara, right?" he asked, pointing with his cigarette. "Jessie's friend. How are you?"

She stared at him for a long time before speaking. "Did you *know*?" she asked coldly. That sudden, icy accusation caused a paralysis to fall over Riley, turning every muscle of his body to water. "You *did* know, didn't you?" she added.

He looked from her to the two other girls, now staring sheepishly at the parking lot pavement.

"What... what are you talked about?"

Tara's face pancaked with disbelief. "What, are you kidding? Have you been living under a rock for the last three days?"

"I've been battling the flu," he lied. "Haven't been out of the house since Friday."

She looked at her friends, then back at him. "So you don't know about the girls?"

He just blinked. "What girls?"

Tara gave an incredulous huff, but then told him what would be, under any other circumstance, an unbelievable story. She said that the Montague RCMP had picked up a girl on Sunday night, a thirteen-year-old wandering the side of the highway near Pooles Corner. Barefoot and wearing just her nightgown, she was deeply disoriented. "They took her back to the station and got her to calm down enough to tell them what happened," Tara said. "She claims her father came into her bedroom that night and raped her."

Riley kept his face stone still, but his whole body felt like it was keeling to the left, a ship about the capsize. *This isn't happening*, he thought. *This is not happening. You're still back at Applegarth. Maybe you're in bed, dreaming. Any second now these girls will start peeling off their clothes, and this parking lot will turn into a big, comfy mattress, and the four of us will—*

"And then, like, two hours later," Tara went on, "it happened again. They picked up another girl, one wandering the side of the road just outside Georgetown. This one was sixteen, but told the same story. She said her father had come into her room in the wee hours that night and raped her right there in her bed. The two men are now in custody."

"And these may not be the only cases," piped up one of Tara's friends. Riley was too distraught to even bother asking her name. "I have a younger cousin at Montague High," she said. "She told me that one of her girlfriends *lost her shit* one day in Health Ed class about a month ago. My cousin said they had just begun a unit on incest and birth defects, and this girl started screaming and crying out of nowhere. The teacher had to send her to the office. My cousin approached her at lunch to see if she was okay, and the girl eventually admitted what was going on. She said that her older brother had 'messed around' with her about a week earlier. The health class lesson on incest had set her *right* off. The girl was so ashamed and embarrassed that she hadn't told anyone at the time. But my cousin says that, in light of what happened Sunday night, the girl is now thinking about coming forward to the police."

Riley reeled on his feet. He flicked his half-finished du Maurier to the pavement and rested his hands on his hips to steady himself. "The men taken into custody..." he began, almost in a trance, turning back to Tara. "What, what did they tell the police?"

"Nobody knows for sure," she replied, "but I've caught a few rumours floating around. Just in the last day or so, I heard that they were both distraught themselves, and gave this kind of quasi-confession. They both said, independent of each other, that they thought what happened to their daughters," and here Tara scoffed again, "had happened *in a dream.* Can you believe that?"

All the blood drained out of Riley. Suddenly, his new life here on PEI—the house, the land, his fresh chapter, that second chance he had worked so hard to grasp for himself—felt as ephemeral as sets on a stage. Yes, that was it. The sense of comfort and belonging that washed over Riley every moment he was under Applegarth now felt fake and flimsy, something that could be wheeled away to expose the darkness hiding underneath. The news that Tara was sharing with him could mean only one thing: that his future here, his future *anywhere*, was now under threat. *This is not happening*, he thought. *This is not fucking happening.*

Tara must have noticed his face going ashen, because she took a step closer to him. "So I'll ask you again, do you know anything?"

"How... how could I?"

"I don't know. But I find it pretty strange, Mr. Fuller, that Jessie-Mac is trying to write a retrospective about a bunch of rapes and disappearances and acts of incest that happened back in 1930, and finds out that the main suspect was your grandfather. And then *you* move here sixty-five years later, and similar shit starts happening again. How do you explain that?"

"I... I can't." He swallowed. "Where is Jessie now?"

"Still at home," Tara replied. "She's trying to convince Jack Mackenzie to let her return to work. Trying to convince him *not* to spike her retrospective, and also to assign her to cover these new cases. She thinks they can be part of a series of stories—stories about, *you know*, the secrets girls keep." Tara looked hard into Riley's face. "So you have *nothing* to say about this?"

"I, I don't. I don't... know what you want me to say."

"What's Lowfield?" Tara asked, abruptly shifting gears.

Riley felt the paralysis, that looming sense of loss, come on all over again.

Tara just continued. "Jessie brought it up when we popped by your place after Danny died. I remember asking you then what Lowfield was, and I remember your bullshit answer. I also put that question to my grandmother, by the way, out in Trenton. *What's Lowfield, Grams?* Can you guess what happened when I did?" She eyed him up and down. "You can, can't you. She *went fucking hysterical*. Like I had just tapped something she'd refused to talk about, or even think about, *for decades*. This little old lady in her eighties, who probably hasn't raised her voice in thirty-five years, started screaming at me. She kept saying, *The soil out there is bad, the soil out there is bad, stay way, Tara-girl, stay away from that place.* When I asked her what place she was talking about, do you know what she said, this old woman who sometimes can't remember what the nursing home fed her for breakfast? Who hasn't lived on PEI in years? She said, *Don't go north of 319. Don't go south of the Eight Mile Road.* That's what she said. Now correct me if I'm wrong, Mr. Fuller, but north of Route 319 and south of the Eight Mile Road is that big wooded area out back of your property. Right?"

Riley was beyond words.

"So I'll ask you again: What is Lowfield? What is out there? If you know something, you should say something." She paused to give him a chance to speak, and when he didn't, she went on. "Look, girls are getting *raped*. I'm starting to wonder if this Lowfield place has something to do with it. I'm also starting to wonder if it had something to do with Danny's death." She caught the flicker in Riley's eyes. Caught it instantly. "Look, I know you've become friends with Jessie-Mac, so think about this: What if what happened to those girls happens to Jessie's sister, Kyla—or even to Jessie herself? I don't know if you've noticed, but she's pretty much," and here, she motioned to her friends, "the centre of our wheel. She's the hub that brings us all together. We're very protective of her. So if all of this *is* connected, you need to say so."

Riley wiped his dry mouth and raked his fingers through his beard, never taking his eyes off Tara. Then he said the one thing he *didn't* believe, the one thing he thought might protect himself, protect Applegarth, and everything it meant to him. He said the one thing that always felt reflexive whenever girls and women levelled accusations like these.

"I think you're blowing this out of proportion," he lied. As soon as he saw the reaction on Tara's face, he wanted to take the words back, to reel them home, but it was too late.

"All right, you know what? Fuck you," Tara said. "Girls are getting *raped*. That's a fact. You just going to stick your head in the sand about this? Jesus, you're a cop. If you give a shit, you should do something. Otherwise, go fuck yourself." Then she marched passed him and headed toward the Sobeys' doors. Her two mousy friends reluctantly followed. Riley just stood there, alone in the parking lot, watching them go.

Later, as he drove home to Applegarth, his heart thundering in his chest, he couldn't escape the feeling that returned to him then, the feeling that this was just another of his dreams, a sensation of otherworldliness, of inaction. He *knew* this emotion, this place inside himself, the awareness that something horrible was unfolding, and that he might be the only one with the power to stop it, but could *not* bring himself to act. It was fear, plain and simple, but one masquerading in excuses and prevarications. He simply couldn't shake off that dread, push through the fog of its lies, and find the courage he *knew* he had, somewhere in reserve.

Worse, Riley knew he'd had this exact feeling before. Oh, yes he had. He had felt it before, and not that long ago.

Chapter 25

For some reason, he could always recall the exact date and time of his last proper conversation with her: Wednesday, September 15, 1993 at about six in the evening. Riley was in his squad car at the time, cutting across John Street to get to Mountain Road, where there was a gas station he liked to fuel up at. On the way, he passed a park where he saw her sitting on a bench near the sidewalk. He nearly didn't recognize her at first, on account of what she was wearing: a creamy pink chambermaid's uniform, almost like hospital scrubs, and a pair of very cheap but comfortable-looking white sneakers. As he slowed and then parked in front of her, Riley thought the pink uniform made her look like some sort of confection left behind on that green-painted bench—a cake, maybe, or a delicate meringue spun out of coloured sugar and egg whites. Good enough to eat, he thought.

He climbed out of his vehicle, adjusted his utility belt, and walked over to her. Perhaps by old instincts, she had followed the cop car with her eyes the moment it had come into view, her shoulders and face tensing. But when she saw it was him—no doubt glimpsing that familiar hazel stare beneath the shining brim of his policeman's cap—she let go a big, toothy grin.

"Officer," she said with a *faux* respectful nod as he approached.

"Evening, miss," he replied, one corner of his mouth curling upward. "Are we being law abiding this fine day?"

"Well, *I* certainly am," she smiled. "I can't speak for *you*."

He hadn't seen Marigold Burque in sixteen months, not since he had broken things off with her at that Tim Hortons. She had changed a bit since then. She'd put on some weight, he noticed, but in a good way—her breasts were bigger, her face fuller, warmer. Sitting with her back straight as a rod on that bench, she also appeared more confident than he remembered, like someone slowly getting her life together. Riley had heard the rumours, that Marigold had gotten off the streets of Moncton shortly after he had ended things with her, that she had returned to her hometown of Bouctouche for a while but was now back in the city and had gotten herself a job, as a chambermaid at the Red King Hotel on Mountain Road. The pink uniform, degrading as it was, seemed to verify this good news.

"You wanna sit?" she asked, moving aside the remnants of her supper, what looked like a quarter-pounder combo from a nearby McDonald's.

He did, and did. They began chatting, and Marigold confirmed the gossip. Sure, the job cleaning rooms at the Red King was horrible—low pay, hard and often disgusting work, lots of split shifts—but it was something. She told him she'd be going for her GED soon, and then the sky would be the limit for her.

As she talked, Riley thought that, no, the uniform wasn't degrading after all. She looked pretty in it. Professional. A young woman, maybe on the bottom rung of the workforce now, but ready to claw her way up to the second-bottom rung, and then the one after that. His old attraction to her flooded his bloodstream then. She really was quite striking in that uniform. He could just eat her up, put every inch of her in his mouth.

"What time is it?" she asked, and then, without permission, grabbed his wrist and pulled it toward her so she could see the watch strapped there. "Oh shit! I gotta get down to the bus station. I'm catching the last one to Bouctouche tonight."

"So, listen," he said as they stood, "do you want to go for coffee sometime? Just to chat or… whatever."

She didn't hesitate. "I can't. Riley, I have zero free time now." She told him that she spent her every day off down in Bouctouche. The Red King rarely gave her two in a row, but it didn't matter. Even if she had only twenty-four hours, she always caught the first bus she could down there, and the last bus she could coming back.

"Why?" he asked. "What's in Bouctouche?"

But her gaze went slantwise and she didn't answer at first. For a moment, Riley thought that there must be a guy, somebody closer to her own age that she'd met and started dating down there. Which was fine. It was what she probably needed, and definitely deserved. But when she leveled her eyes back at him, something told Riley that, no, it wasn't that. It was something—or some*one*—else.

"Oh, you know," she said finally. "My people."

"I miss you," he told her. "I wish we could just hang out somet—"

"Say, how's your marriage?" she asked with a sly jut of her chin. "You and your wife doing better these days?"

He stared at her for a second, a bit dumbstruck, but then gave her a slow, piteous nod. He got the message loud and clear.

"It was good seeing you, Marigold."

"You too, Riley." No hug. No kiss on the cheek. She just sent him on his way.

~

How *was* his marriage? *That's a very good question, Marigold*, he thought snidely in the days and weeks that followed. How *had* things been with Jane in the eighteen months since Riley had stepped out on their union? He felt the heft of that guilt every day; the months that passed did nothing to abate it. It was like a rope, with one end tied to a cinder block and the other around his waist, threatening to drag him down to the bottom of the sea.

The guilt manifested itself in strange ways. Riley could not abide even the most fleeting compliment sent his way. About a week after seeing Marigold in the park, he got a commendation at work and didn't even bother telling Jane about it. In November, work announced the date for the annual RCMP Christmas party and Riley made moves to ensure he got scheduled to work that night. This too was a kind of penance. He had loved Christmas parties all his life but now he wouldn't allow himself to feel the festive spirit.

And besides, the work party had changed this year. Due to budget cuts, spouses were no longer invited; it was for staff only now. What's more, they had to move the party from its usual venue, the ballroom at the Sheraton, to a conference room at the Red King Hotel on Mountain Road. That sealed it for Riley. So instead, he just volunteered to work that night, part of a bigger effort to keep Christmas as drab and uneventful as he could—just as he had done the year before, his first as an adulterer.

~

Barely a day passed after the Christmas party before a tale began circulating around the Moncton RCMP detachment. Something had happened at the Red King in the hours after the shindig. Riley was not wont to take part in or even listen to such locker room banter, especially among the younger, dumber officers. These guys, Riley often thought, were well on their way to becoming the same cruel, feckless cop that Dale Sloka had become. But Riley couldn't help eavesdropping as the story made its way around the desks in the bullpen and at the watercooler.

Apparently, after the official event ended at midnight, a crew went up to a hotel room that one of the officers, a young cop named Doodnaught, had booked, to keep the party going. And going it went, long into the night, as a group of officers drank and smoked and carried on with each other. The older cops eventually drifted home, until it was just Doodnaught and two other young guys who kept partying well after dawn. Their reveling went so deep into the morning, in fact, that a young, pretty chambermaid eventually arrived to do up the room, and the boys invited her in to join them when she did.

Riley's ears perked up like a fox's when he heard this part.

The chambermaid, or so the talk went, wasn't just pretty. She was *smokin' hot*, was how Doodnaught put it. *Smokin' hot*. In fact, the boys could tell, just by the look of this girl, by the vibe she gave off, that she was a real goer. The three drunk cops offered her some booze, which she declined. They invited her to stay and party with them, which she also declined. She told them she'd come back later to clean the room, but by then Doodnaught was using his large, solid body to block the door.

This chambermaid, or so the story went, also had a real mouth on her. She tried to wisecrack her way out of the situation, which the boys didn't appreciate. One of them, a kid named Smith, apparently got right in her face and asked her a rather nasty question about her sexual history—specifically whether she'd ever been in a situation like this before, with three guys at once. Much to their surprise, the chick slapped him, slapped this officer of the law right across his face, and so Doodnaught marched over and slapped her back, hard enough to knock her onto one of the room's double beds.

The three cops got on the bed with her then. She fought against them for a while, but then resigned herself to what was about to happen, probably because it was something she had always wanted anyway. After all, the boys thought, wasn't this every slutty chambermaid's fantasy? It was amazing, Doodnaught quipped, how easily the bottoms of her uniform, so much like hospital scrubs, came down. She even raised her hips off the duvet a little while she struggled, which they took as a big green light.

So all three guys had a turn with her, and she grew more pliant with each than the last. When they finished, the girl hauled her pants back up and hurried out of the room without so much as a thank you, returning to her cart of fresh linens and cleaning products in the hall. She never did come back to straighten up the room.

Riley listened to this yarn in a kind of stupor. *This didn't happen,* was his first thought, a natural, knee-jerk reaction. *Or, if it did, it didn't happen the way these fuckwits describe. Why would they brag so openly about it if it did? Don't blow this out of proportion.*

Are you not going to say something? another voice countered. It belonged, of course, to Jane. But Riley just looked around the bullpen as this anecdote, its lurid details, unfurled. Some of the cops laughed along with Doodnaught; others just cast their eyes down and said nothing. But nobody spoke up. So neither did Riley.

Can you at least try to contact Marigold? Make sure she's okay?

But Riley couldn't bring himself to do that, either. Who's to say, he thought, that it was even her? Maybe she's not the only smoking-hot chambermaid at the Red King.

You're a coward, Riley Fuller. For all your bravado about courage and law enforcement, about running toward danger and protecting the public, you have no spine. No fucking spine at all.

He wasn't sure if that was Jane's voice this time, or his own.

~

A night a week and a half after the Christmas party, Riley was doing paperwork at the Main Street detachment. He decided he wanted some fresh air, so he took a smoke break outside, in the back parking lot, despite the fact that it was cold out and there were flurries corkscrewing out of the sky. He put on his officer's coat and officer's cap, went out the back door, and sparked up a du Maurier. Riley wanted to be alone, but was only two drags in before three other cops joined him in the cold, lighting up their own cigarettes. It was Sloka, and Doodnaught, and another officer, named Nadon, an older cop just four months away from retirement. Riley stood silent as they began their banter: Fuck this, and fuck that, and fuck those fuckers. Riley would recall later that only one of these men, Doodnaught, had actually been in that hotel room on the morning after the Christmas party.

He was just listening to Nadon talk about a recent golf trip he'd made to Texas when Riley saw a figure hurry across the shadowy sidewalk beyond the parking lot's chain-link fence. In another instant, this person veered through the open gate and raced up across the snowy parking lot toward them.

In another instant, he saw that it was Marigold Burque. Her face, inside her jacket's hood, was an absolute furnace of tears and rage. He saw it was the same flimsy, pathetic jacket she'd been wearing on the night he rescued her from her trip to "go see Queen Victoria."

In another instant, she raised her right hand, which held a Beretta 92.

None of them had any time to react—to react as she fired into what looked like, from her perspective at least, an anonymous gaggle of cops.

POP! POP! POP! POP!

The fourth of these shots had been intended for Riley, but she must have adjusted her aim, flinching her hand a split second after he turned and she glimpsed the hazel eyes beneath his cap's brim and realized it was him. The bullet, intended to take him out, instead screamed an inch past his left ear, breaking the sound barrier a fraction of a second before it cleaved off half of Sloka's face. Sloka had already taken a shot in the chest, and now collapsed like a sack onto the pavement. The other two officers were already down, already dying in the drifts. The air was peppery with the scent of gun powder.

Marigold leveled her weapon at him again, her face wet and gibbering. Riley stared into the barrel of the Beretta, probably borrowed from one of her old street buddies. Riley had his hand on his own piece, still in its holster at his hip, but against all reflexes and his training, against all common sense itself, he did not draw his sidearm against her. He couldn't bring himself to. Part of him, he realized later, *wanted* her to shoot him.

If she was going to, it would happen in another second. But instead, her elbow bent and he watched her tuck the gun's muzzle under her chin and turn her face up to the black sky, to the flurries weeping furiously out of it. Riley came to life then. In two quick strides, he was upon her, yanking the gun out of her hand and throwing it to the ground. Then his arms were around her, her body pressed to his, her small, warm mouth at his neck.

"Oh Riley… oh fuck… oh fuck, Riley… fuck, oh Jesus, oh FUCK, Riley…"

He just put his arms around Marigold and held her. He pressed his mouth tight to her cold forehead inside her hood, a fruitless attempt to comfort her.

They held each other as the snow swirled around them like warp-speed stars. It was a moment just for them. A moment before Marigold was arrested and charged with three counts of first-degree murder. Before the media circus started and reporters began asking why Riley hadn't pulled out his service weapon and shot her, why he instead held her in his arms. Before the whole province went into mourning for the three innocent police officers gunned down in cold blood. Before Marigold was convicted on all counts, and they locked her up for life.

For that moment, it was just the two of them, standing there and holding each other in the flurries swirling all around. That was how the dispatcher found Riley and Marigold when she came running out to the parking lot at what sounded like shots ringing through the night.

Chapter 26

July 11, 1995
Dear Diary, or Journal, or whatever the fuck you are,
Much to my surprise, Uncle Barrie has already come through with the Fuller family tree I asked him for. He emailed it to me this morning. In his note, he said he had needed to make a trip over to Halifax late last week anyway—there is a golf shop there that his wife likes—and while in town he popped by the archives, the library, and even a couple of cemeteries, to either gain or confirm certain details for the tree. I offered to at least pay for his gas but, Barrie being Barrie, wouldn't hear of it.

At any rate, the tree he sent me is by no means complete, but it does provide some very interesting—and, I'll admit, frightening—particulars about my bloodline. I should point out that I did not give Barrie the name "James Robert Fuller" to research for the very top of the tree, for a few reasons. I already know from the diaries that Elder Fuller was born around 1759 in Gloucester, Massachusetts, fled the American Revolution with his cult, and migrated to the British colony that was then called St. John's Island, in 1784. I also know that he most likely died in—or vanished from?—Lowfield in 1863 at the unfathomable age of one hundred and four. I can also infer from the diaries that he most likely sired dozens of children over the course of his life, many through acts of unspeakable incest with his own kin. But these offspring, I have little doubt, also vanished with the rest of the villagers of Lowfield following whatever happened there in 1863. Obviously, I didn't want these details muddying the waters of Barrie's work.

So we begin instead with Melinda Fuller. My uncle must be some kind of wunderkind when it comes to research, because he was able to independently confirm various details I found in the diaries but never shared with him. I have copied and pasted below the tree straight from his email. The notes are his:

Melinda Fuller. b. July 8, 1815 (Lowfield, PE), d. April 2, 1857 (Halifax, NS).
This gal appears to have moved to Halifax around 1834 and raised her two sons as a single mother, which would have been quite something in the mid-19th century. If the dates below are correct, she had her first child at age 14. Is that right?

|

Robert James Fuller
b. January 12, 1830 (??? Lowfield, PE?)
d. ??? 1863 ???
m. Claire Applegarth (1831—1860) May 8, 1852 (Halifax, NS)

|

Miriam Fuller. b. June 27, 1853 (Halifax, NS). d. ??? 1863 ???

>Riley Robert Fuller (this is, as you've indicated, your direct descendent) b. April 29, 1832 (Lowfield, PE). d. August 1, 1906 (Halifax, NS)

What's interesting about these two brothers is they appear to have been self-made men. Despite being raised by a single mother, they managed to found an import-export business in Halifax in 1854, while they were both in their early twenties, probably in response to a new free-trade agreement with the United States that launched that year. By the end of the decade, the company had grown into a major concern, since, according to archive documents, the brothers sold the business in 1862 for £4,500, which would have been a tidy sum back then.

Is this when they moved back to PEI, do you know?

At any rate, the move didn't appear to take for your great-great grandfather. Records show that Riley Fuller returned to Halifax before the end of 1863 following the death of both his brother and his niece that year (do you know what happened?) and reestablished himself in the business community there. He married Amanda Jones (1844—1905) on August 14, 1869 in Halifax.

|

Clayton Riley Fuller

b. October 9, 1870 (Halifax, NS). d. December 6, 1917 (Halifax, NS) m. Isabella Gardner (March 19, 1872—December 6, 1917) July 18, 1896 (Halifax, NS)

As you can probably guess from the death dates above, both Clayton and Isabella died in the Halifax Explosion of 1917. According to their obit, their son (your grandfather), James Fuller, was away at university at the time, studying theology at King's College in Windsor, NS at the time of the explosion.

|

Robert "James" Fuller

b. May 6, 1897 (Halifax, NS). d. October 31, 1930 (Glenning, PE) m. Cecilia Gagnon (1900—1934) August 12, 1922 (Halifax, NS). div. January 1930

Like his grandfather before him (and his grandson after him, har har), James seems to have moved to PEI for a fresh start, following his divorce from Cecilia in 1930. Queerly enough, he killed himself on Halloween later that year. Do you have any sense as to why?

|

Thomas Riley Fuller
b. November 23, 1923 (Halifax, NS). d. January 10, 1991 (Moncton, NB) m. Ellen-Mary Smith (that's my sis, God rest her soul!) (June 29, 1927—September 1, 1986), August 14, 1948 (Moncton, NB)

If the dates above are correct, does that mean that your dad was an orphan by age eleven? Thomas never talked very much, but I did hear Ellie say once that he'd been raised mostly by an aunt in Shediac. Anyway, as you well know, your dad served in WWII from 1942 to '45, then returned to Moncton to work in a shoe factory until retiring in 1980. Despite what had clearly been a hard life, Thomas didn't follow the family tradition of moving to PEI for a fresh start (har har).

|

Riley Robert Fuller (that's you!)
b. February 19, 1950 (Moncton, NB) m. Jane Kendell (1952—) May 28, 1977 (Moncton, NB). div. August 1994. No children.

And as the guy on the radio says, Diary, or Journal, or whatever the fuck you are, you know the *rest* of the story.

There are a number of details in this tree that have sent a chill through my blood. Chief among them is the mention of Lowfield itself, despite the fact that neither the PEI history books I checked out of the library nor any map I've found make mention of it. Barrie clearly got the name from the obituaries of Melinda Fuller and the original Riley Fuller when they were published in

1857 and 1906, respectively. He has question marks around both the birthplace and death of Riley's brother, Robert, and around the death of Robert's daughter, Miriam. Why? Because there would have been no obituaries for them. He got the year 1863 from me. Whatever happened in Lowfield that year was not publicly recorded.

Speaking of history, until now I had no idea that my grandfather, James, lost both his parents in the Halifax Explosion of 1917 while he was away at university. Perhaps having them both die on the same day when he was just twenty years old contributed to him becoming "screwy in the head," as my father had always put it.

There's more. Uncle Barrie makes reference to our "family tradition" of moving to Prince Edward Island for a fresh start. I am the third in my line to do this—the *fourth*, if you count Elder Fuller himself. Barrie makes light of this custom in his notes, but it is no joke. It cannot be a coincidence. There is something that has drawn my bloodline to this seemingly idyllic island cradled in the Northumberland Strait, a dark force luring us here, generation after generation.

There is another non-coincidence to make note of: the reoccurring instances of an only child. Robert and Claire, Riley and Amanda, Clayton and Isabella, James and Cecilia, *and* my mom and dad, all had one child apiece. Are we to believe that this is just happenstance? Or is there another, more cosmic force at play? A force that lures a single offspring to PEI to pass on the horror? Does a lone descendent attempt, every few decades, to open the portal mentioned in the diaries? Again, it alarms me to see that potentiality laid out here in black and white.

But most chilling of all is how first and middle names move through this tree like genes, like a birth defect passed from one branch to the next. Look closely. There are so many different combinations of "James,"

"Robert," and "Riley" throughout my lineage. Should I take that as a sign as well? Imagine it. The original Riley Fuller flees PEI after the horrors of 1863, just abandons Applegarth and moves back to Halifax alone. He meets Amanda Jones at some point thereafter and marries her in 1869. They have a child a year later, a son they name Clayton. In the ensuing decades, perhaps Riley refuses to talk about what happened during his time on PEI, about the death of his brother and his niece. But then Clayton has a son of his own, and he and Isabella name him *Robert James*. How did Riley, now a sixty-five-year-old grandfather, react to that? The name must have triggered some terrible memories for him of that twisted old preacher spewing blasphemies from his pulpit in Lowfield, whose name was *James Robert*. I envision Riley beseeching Clayton to reconsider what he named his own son, that doomed child, and not being able to tell him why.

I need to learn more about exactly what happened in 1863. Even Barrie raises the question in his notes to me. I have been avoiding the diaries for a while now, ever since learning... well, I've already said what I learned. But I need to go back to them. I know, from when I first took them down from their shelf, that the last volume ends abruptly on Sunday, September 13 of that year. The last entry I read was dated May 23. I need to bite the bullet and read as many of the entries in between as I can stomach. I have the diary right here, and plan to get back to it just as soon as I finish this entry.

There is, I will say, one ray of hope from the tree that Barrie sent me: i.e., how it ends with those two words, about Jane and me. Yes, it's now a relief that we did not have any children. The bloodline ends with me. But do you want to hear something weird, Diary, or Journal, or whatever the fuck you are? I remember, back in the day, that she and I had discussed kids' names when we still thought it possible to have some. And I swear to

Christ—or is it Shaal?—that one of the leading contenders for a boy... was James.

How fucked up is that?

~

Riley returned to the diary, picking up where he left off. In early June 1863, more horror had struck the area: a farmer in Glenning had died under mysterious circumstances. The journal speculated that the man had met foul play after confronting a neighbour about his decision to join Elder Fuller's cult in Lowfield. Indeed, the congregation there had *swelled* with locals since the arrival of *The Grimoire of Shaal* that spring. Meanwhile, the school year had ended a week early after several girls stopped showing up to the one-room school that little Miriam Fuller attended. Officials had suspected an outbreak of influenza, but Riley Fuller thought he knew the real cause.

In July 1863, Elder Fuller had made it official: Robert would succeed him as the head of Lowfield's church. Through Robert's ramblings, Riley had learned of a strange phenomenon, something his brother kept calling "the taproot"—*draatis* in the queer language of the *Grimoire*—which, Robert had claimed, sprouted in the basement of Lowfield's church. Riley had decided to break into the church late one night to destroy that cursed book before it could do any more harm to the community. But he was nonetheless lured to the basement by the same glowing darkness that Riley himself, there in 1995, had witnessed. His grandfather's grandfather had descended into the church's basement and saw this taproot, but refused to describe it in his diary—the thing had been horrific beyond words.

By late July, Robert—ready to replace Elder Fuller as the leader of Lowfield's church—had demanded that his brother buy him out of his half of their business. Riley agreed. He was ready to flee PEI, and had begun making plans to do so.

Riley was about to read more, but was yanked out of the diary by the sound of the phone ringing. He could hear its robotic cry from the other end of Applegarth's long second-floor hallway, where the upstairs extension sat in its charger on the nightstand in his bedroom.

He set the diary down and went to answer it, hustling across the hall and poking himself through the bedroom door. He grabbed the extension just as the answering machine downstairs kicked in. Through the receiver Riley could hear his own voice, its bland recorded greeting, and he pressed 9 to cut it off.

"Hello?" he said.

"Riley?"

"Yep."

"Hi. It's Jack at the *Pioneer*."

"And Jessie-Mac. I'm here, too. We've got you on our new speaker phone." Their voices sounded tinny and distant, as if talking to Riley from the bottom of a well.

Riley greeted them pleasantly, asking if Jessie was now back to work full-time after her bereavement leave. "I am, and it's a good thing, too," she said. "Tonight's production night and the paper's a bloody mess. I honestly don't know how Jack and Maggie ever got through these nights without me."

"Too true, too true," Jack said with a chuckle. "I'm going to miss this little lady when she goes back to school in the fall."

"How are you holding up, kiddo?" Riley asked her.

"Oh, I'm... okay," she replied, her voice reserved. "I've started to accept that Danny's really gone. I think I could move forward, you know, *in my mind,* except..." And here she paused. "Except things are getting... Riley, they're getting really *weird* around here."

"Weird how?" he asked.

"Well, that's what we're calling about," Jack said. "Do you have a minute?"

Riley settled onto the edge of his bed. "Of course. I've got all the minutes in the world."

"So we got a fax here this morning," Jack said, clearing his throat, "from the Montague RCMP. Riley, they've arrested a man, a potato farmer over near Brudenell, for sexually assaulting his own daughter. The wife caught them together last night and turned him in."

At those words, it felt as if Riley's bedroom had turned upside, that gravity itself had suddenly betrayed him. He just blinked as he held the phone to his ear, feeling that same sensation he'd gotten talking to Tara that day in the Sobeys parking lot wash over him again: that these walls, this house, this *fresh start,* was about to be pulled out from under him. His life in Applegarth would soon be under threat, because his life in Applegarth was... was *causing these things to happen.* "How... how old was the girl?" he asked, trying to keep his voice steady.

"Twelve," Jessie-Mac answered. "Same age as my sister, Kyla, in case you're keeping track. Thing is, this is like the third or fourth instance of incest we've heard about in as many weeks. I talked to my friend Tara the other day and she told me a few stories she's heard."

"I ran into Tara myself," Riley said very tentatively, "at the Sobeys. She... she told me some stuff, too. Really disturbing shit."

"I know. Fuck. I mean, here I am trying to finish a retrospective about what happened back in 1930, and the same sort of stuff is unfolding now. Riley, it's starting to freak me out."

"Now, I'm not a superstitious man," Jack added. His Scottish brogue seemed to thicken, right there on the phone. "I don't believe in God or ghosts or the occult. I don't believe in fate *or* faith, or anything supernatural. I'm a newsman and I believe in facts. But the fact is, we started learning about what happened all those decades ago, *and* what is happening now, at the same time you learned about that sex cult in the diaries you found in your house. It can't be a coincidence, Riley. You can't tell me it is."

"I won't," Riley said.

"So I'm asking you again: do you mind showing us those diaries? I still want to see them, now more than ever."

"I haven't finished reading them myself," Riley replied. "I've got about six weeks' worth of entries to go, but it's taking me a while. There's some really messed-up shit in them. About my family. My family history. It makes them hard to read."

"I realize that," Jack said. "And I know you want to learn the truth, especially about what happened around here with your grandfather in 1930. So I'll offer you a trade."

"A trade?"

"Yes. I've done some digging around in the last week or so, talking to old timers and such, asking them questions on the sly. About incest. About inbreeding. Now, as far as I can figure, PEI has never seen anything on the scale of what happened with that Goler family over in Nova Scotia. Do you know that story?"

"Of course."

"So nothing like that—which contradicts what you're reading in those diaries *and* what we're learning about the events of 1930. So I pressed people at bit harder, and finally got a name. There was a man who lived around these parts decades ago, a fisherman who had birth defects consistent with inbreeding."

"Really?"

"Yes, sir. What's more, he would've born shortly after the period your grandfather lived in Applegarth."

Riley's mouth went dry and fell open with a click. "Are you fucking kidding me?"

"No, sir. His name is Obed Marsten, originally from Lower Montague. Story goes he worked boats off the wharf there starting in his mid-teens but left more than thirty-five years ago, driven out of the community. Apparently his deformities—the *reason* for his deformities—has made him the subject of ridicule since he was a kid. He now lives like a hermit way up west, beyond the town of Tignish, in a little place called Fleshers Pond. It's just about as far from Lower Montague as you can get and still be on PEI." Jack took a breath. "Now, obviously, I'm not going to send Jessie-Mac up there to interview him."

"Exactly," Jessie cut in. "I mean, what am I going to say? *'Tell me, sir, are you the product of your mom getting raped by a family member back in 1930?'*"

"But I can give you directions if you want to go find him," Jack said. "I think you do. He may be able to fill in some of the blanks you've been struggling with. And in exchange, maybe you'd share those diaries with us. You could drop them off here at the *Pioneer*'s office after we get this latest issue to bed."

Riley thought about this, but not for very long. "Deal," he said. "Only, I don't want them leaving Applegarth. Those journals are a part of this house. You can come here and take notes as you read them, but I don't want them leaving the property." Just as Riley said this, the house settled onto itself, murmuring through its plaster walls and floorboards. When it did, an idea, not sane, not welcome, emerged in Riley's head. He spoke before he could stop himself. "I've been meaning to have you guys over anyway. What would you say to a dinner party here?"

"That sounds fine," Jack said. "Jessie?"

"Yeah, I'd be up for that. Never been to, you know, a *grown-up* dinner party before."

"Great," Riley said. "Should we say Friday night?"

"Okay," Jessie replied. "Should we bring, like, food and stuff?"

Riley bristled at that even as he smiled. "What? No. I can cook." When she gave a light laugh, he added, "Jessie, I've been living alone for nearly a year and a half. I can cook."

"Sure," she said. "But the thing is, I'm a vegetarian."

"You're a...?"

"A vegetarian. You know, someone who doesn't eat meat."

"Oh."

"Yeah, I know. It's been driving my parents nuts for five years now. But it's fine. I can pick up a veggie pizza for myself and bring that."

"No, no. I can make you something." Then another involuntary thought pressed into Riley's head as he stared up at Applegarth's walls. They seemed to be moving in and out of focus, to be pressing down on him. "I have a whole garden full of vegetables out there," he said. "I can make you something out of that." His blood turned cold as these words left his mouth against his will, against his better judgement.

"Great. What do you have?"

"I don't know. Carrots, peas, cabbage, eggplant—"

"*Ooh*, eggplant please. That's my favourite."

"Eggplant it is." But then he paused. "Only—how do I cook it?"

She gave another light laugh. "Oh, you know. Just poke some holes in it, put it in a pan, and throw it in the oven like a roast."

"Sounds easy enough," he said. "Jack, you okay with steaks for us?"

"Perfect," Jack replied. "I'll bring the whisky."

"Great. We'll have some drinks and eat, and then I'll show you the journals."

"Fine and dandy," Jack and Jessie said almost in unison, the latter mock-mimicking the former.

Neither of them thought to ask why Riley was growing a vegetable in his garden that he didn't know how to prepare.

Chapter 27

Riley's first realization, as he set out the next morning with Jack's directions scrawled on a scrap of paper, was that Canada's smallest province wasn't that small at all. To drive from Glenning, near PEI's eastern edge, to Fleshers Pond, close to its western-most tip, was going to take him a full two and a half hours. Riley would never have guessed, prior to moving to PEI, that any two places on the Island could be that far apart. His second realization was that the idea of this journey was slightly insane. Did he really plan to drive that far just to show up unannounced on a stranger's doorstep? Riley couldn't find Obed Marsten in PEI's slim phonebook—perhaps the old hermit didn't own a phone—but even if he had, what would Riley have said to him after looking him up and calling ahead? What did he plan to say *in person*, for that matter? The best he could imagine was some wobbly half-truth about doing research into his family's presence at the other end of the Island, a personal history curious enough to approach a stranger about it out of the blue. But what if the old guy wasn't even home when Riley finally arrived? Would that make this long trek a waste of time and gas money?

On this point, Riley thought no. He had moved to the Island more than three months ago now, but he had yet to spend much time up west. He figured if you're going to call Prince Edward Island home, you should know it tip to tip.

So he set out on his journey, driving first toward and then around Charlottetown, moving further westward, all the way to the other end of Island, past the community of Tignish, where he then jogged a hard left at some bleak rural intersection and then out toward Fleshers Pond. The day was grimly overcast, the sky the colour of a roasting pan and threatening rain.

There wasn't much to Fleshers Pond when he finally got there, which made following the last of Jack's directions relatively easy. He located the Old Arsenault Road off Route 14 and banged a left onto it, driving down its length toward the wide expanse of water, the Gulf of St. Lawrence. The first part of the road was paved and there were some nice and newer-looking cottages dotting the land out here. A couple of them were even two storeys high and had windows as tall as two men, giving their owners a panoramic view of the sandy, indented coastline. But the pavement soon dropped away and it became a scarlet dirt road closer to the water. Its mud was wet and splashed up like blood into the Lumina's undercarriage, and the uneven road jounced and jostled Riley behind the wheel as he searched for his destination. Out here was all weedy, desolate dunes and ugly Queen Anne's lace growing in the ditches. The wind had come up. The day looked cold, despite it being the middle of July.

Then he found the place he was looking for, near the end of the Old Arsenault Road, right before it T-boned at a lonely, empty beach. It was the smallest house Riley had ever seen, really just an aged, dilapidated shack sitting in a rocky field. Its flaking grey paint gave the house the same hornet's nest look that Applegarth used to have, and an even greyer chimney climbed like a small, blunt tower out of the centre of the roof. Riley was relieved to see a gentle plume of smoke spiraling from that chimney and toward the sky. In the unpaved driveway sat a rusted-out pickup truck that looked from the 1940s, and next to it, on what passed for the side lawn, was a pile of beaten-up mussel traps.

Riley pulled into the driveway and parked behind the pickup. Turning off the Lumina's engine, he sat there for a moment, not sure what he would—or *could*—do. His heart picked up pace a little. He tried to rehearse some introductory lines in his head, but nothing would come.

Riley looked up at the house. Through its sole front window, he saw a shape move past, causing the light lace curtains there to rustle. A moment later the front door opened and a man waddled out onto the stoop. He looked to be in his mid-sixties and wore a plaid work shirt under suspenders hooked into plain brown corduroys, the bottoms of which were tucked into gum rubbers squeezed onto his feet. He crouched a little to stare with suspicion at Riley through the Lumina's windshield. To Riley's eye, the man looked a bit like Danny DeVito when he played the Penguin in that *Batman* movie. His torso, like so many men's in late middle age, was all gut and no hips, and he didn't appear to have a neck at all. What's more, there was something not quite right with his skin. It looked downright oily, fishy almost, as if he had just climbed out of a filthy, briny body of water. His thinning grey hair, badly in need of a wash, lay matted around his skull like the tendrils of a monster.

Riley climbed out of the Lumina, closed the door, and took a couple steps toward the stoop. This much closer, he could see that the man suffered from what his grandfather's grandfather had called *the Lowfield look*. The man's left eye seemed four times larger than the right, and the right eye practically drooped down his cheek like a tear. The man's mouth appeared full of blunt, crooked teeth, like tiny gravestones rising out of uneven earth. And even from here, Riley could see the most-telling feature of all: the man's left index and middle fingers, nearly identical in their long length, were fused together into a kind of flipper, an amphibious appendage, with a lone yellowed nail rising out of the tip like a hook.

"You Obed Marsten?" he asked.

The man's large, Cyclopean eye took a walk all over Riley, and his mouth opened like a watery cave. "Je Zeus fuckin' Christ!" he exclaimed, and took one step down the stoop. "Holy mudder a mercy. Look at cha—just look at cha! Ye cornholin' son of a whore. Ye carpetbaggin' cocksucker from parts unknown. Just look at cha, standin' in my driveway as if birthed from *Satan's own arsehole*."

Riley flinched a little, taken aback by this unexpected greeting. He pivoted his shoulders and balanced his weight on his dominant leg, a fighter's stance.

"Well, ye might as well *come in*," Marsten added, as if this idea were the biggest imposition imaginable. He climbed back into the shack, leaving the door open for Riley in his wake. As he did, Riley could see that the man's shoulders and spine were covered in a wide, veritable bakery of back fat, but his butt was the size of an apple.

~

"You'll have tea?" Marsten said. It wasn't really a question. The old fisherman filled the kettle at the sink in his tiny kitchen and moved it to the woodstove in the centre of the room while Riley made his way toward the table. His eyes couldn't help but cast around Marsten's modest hovel even before he sat down. Fastened to the kitchen wall was a piece of wood carved into the shape of Prince Edward Island, with a row of tiny pewter spoons dangling from it on pegs. Below this was a wicker rack holding stacks of ancient-looking magazines, periodicals of local history and musings with titles like *The Islander* and *Them Times*. Beyond this was Marsten's "living room," which was just a couch shoved against one wall, covered in ratty and faded quilts and overlooking a tiny TV with tinfoil wrapped over the tops of its antennae. Next to this was a large bookshelf stacked helter-skelter with old books and newspapers and more magazines. On the side opposite was a doorway leading to the smallest bedroom Riley had ever seen. Even from here, he thought he could smell a pungent, old-man funk emanating out of that chamber. He turned his gaze away and finally sat at the kitchen table. It was covered in cracked and dusty plastic, as if laminated, and where the table butted against the wall sat an old metal alarm clock the size of a fist and painted green. Depicted on its face was a mechanized robin trying to pull a worm out of the ground with its mouth. Each yank of its head was timed to the ticking seconds—*click… click… click*—as if the robin were doomed to spend an eternity pulling that worm out of the ground.

With the kettle set to boil, Marsten wobbled over to the table, wrapped his deformed hand around the spindles of one of the other kitchen chairs, and leveled his distorted gaze at Riley again. "Je Zeus fucking Murphy," he said. "Ye *do* look just like him—or like he woulda, had he lived to yer age. The spittin' image. I didn't really see it in that photo of youse printed in Mackenzie's paper, but I see it now. By Christ I do."

"What... what are you talking about?"

"Oh, for fucksake. Can't ye *guess?*" Marsten turned and did his penguin shuffle over to the bookshelf in the living room. He dug around for a while before pulling out a copy of a newspaper. He also yanked out what looked like a very old photo album and tucked it under his arm.

He came back to the table and slapped the newspaper in front of Riley. It was the issue of the *Eastern Pioneer* from back in May with Riley's picture and profile on the front page. Of course it was.

"The spittin' fuckin' image," Marsten repeated.

"You're talking about my grandfather."

Marsten nodded once.

Riley squinted at the fisherman suspiciously. "Tell me something: how old are you? When were you born?"

"March 19, 1931," Marsten replied. "You do the math."

"Well, I don't need math to tell me you were born *after* my grandfather killed himself. So how do you know what he looked like?"

"What, are ye *thick?*" Marsten maneuvered the photo album out of his armpit and onto the table. "Compliments of me mudder," he said, and threw the album open and began flipping, its pages cracking and peeling apart as he did. Finally he stopped to reveal a black-and-white photo of three stern people standing in a field: two men with a rather homely young woman in a summer dress between them. Their eyes were squinting in the sun.

Marsten pointed his flipper at the woman and tapped its yellowed nail on the plastic. "Me mudder," he said. He then pointed at the older of the two men. "Her fadder." Then he pointed at the younger of the two men, whom Riley recognized instantly. "Your grandfadder," Marsten said. Then he slowly moved his flipper back to the first man. "*Me* fadder." That huge, Cyclopean eye bore into Riley again with a blink. "This photo was taken in August of '30. You do the math."

The kettle on the stove began to scream.

~

"Do ye take milk and sugar, cocksucker?" Marsten asked as he prepared the tea at the kitchen's tiny counter.

"Both, please," Riley said as he turned pages in the album, unfazed now by the fisherman's rote vulgarities. There were several pictures of James Fuller in this old book. It was alarming to see those images, to see a face nearly identical to his own staring up at Riley from behind the album's cellophane.

"What I wanna know," Marsten said, bringing the tea over, "is... who's *yer* fadder? Me mudder never mentioned the Fuller man havin' any kids."

"He did," Riley replied. "A seven-year-old son, named Thomas. James left him back on the mainland after his divorce."

"That cornholer was *married*?" Marsten belched in disbelief. "By Christ's third nut, I don't believe it."

Riley just shrugged as if to say, *Well here I am*. He tilted his chin up at Marsten. "Your mother fell in love with James, didn't she? I think I can see that in these photos."

"Aye."

"So what do you know?" Riley asked. "About what happened in 1930?"

"Everything," Marsten replied. "Me mudder told me everything, once I was old enough to ask. I wanted to know why I was like *this*." And here, he raised his greasy, fish-like flipper. "And she told me. She said a mainlander moved into an old abandoned house on the outskirts of Glenning. She got to know the guy, fell in love with him. But he discovered something truly awful out in the back woods behind his property. He was drawn to it. He showed it to her, showed it to her fadder. There was some kind of... ritual they did out there, together, and it unleashed something bad in the air. It took the cap off, as it were. Soon, brudders and fadders began to do unspeakable things with their own sisses and dodders. Word crept around the community about what was causin' it. But aye! They couldn't stop it. By Christ, if anyone confronted the Fuller man about what was goin' on, something foul befell that person. Torn to bits they were by *unearthly* animals protecting what was out there, in the woods. That village. That *church*. Now, whenever I hear about a suspicious death down east, I can't help but raise an eyebrow. Like that… that kid who died on the Petit Point beach last month. Tell me, do ye know anything about that?"

Riley looked at the old fisherman, but then looked away.

"Ye *do*, don't cha," Marsten said, grinning sinisterly.

"What else did she tell you?"

"I already said—*everything*. She shared tales, by God. She said the Fuller man told her that the old house in Glenning could *repair itself*. Started to, the minute he set foot in it. She said the house held him in its grip, stirred up all these queer dreams and unholy desires within him. Turned him into a *prevert*… well, more of a *prevert* than he already was, be *my* guess. But once he heard about all these people dyin', the Fuller man became awash in guilt. Ended up offing himself on Halloween that year. Hanged himself right up in that house's attic. After that, me mudder came to her senses—though she'd already fallen preggers to her own fadder by then. Wanted to abort me, she did, but such ideas made people squirrelly here on PEI. Still do."

"So, you learned all this as a young man and left the area out of shame? Moved as far away as you could while still staying on the Island?"

"What? No. Fuck no! I got nuthin to be shamed about. Not *my* fault she diddled her own dad. No. I left because of what I learned was in that woods. After the Fuller man offed himself, the cap went back on and everything started returning to normal. But still. I didn't want to live anywhere near that place. Toxic, it is. Toxic to the extreme."

"You're talking about Lowfield?"

"Phwore!" Marsten bellowed, flinching away. "Oh, by the hairy three balls o' Christ, how that name still chills me. Je Zeus fucking Murphy. Now you listen to me, cocksucker. You listen good. This ain't no folk tale or ghost story for tourists. This ain't Captain Kidd's treasure or girls gone missin' off Goblins Hollow. No. You want to understand Lowfield? You want to understand the… the *thing* that lives in the basement of that church? Then here." At this, Marsten got up from the table and shuffled back over to the living room bookshelf. He pulled out what looked like a coffee-table book and brought it over.

"This. This here is the closest I've come to seeing it explained."

He showed the tome to Riley. It *was* a coffee-table book, commemorating the fifth anniversary of the Chernobyl disaster. Its cover was a collage of photographs: a blown-out nuclear reactor; a pile of protective gear sitting in a dusty heap; a gaggle of Soviet scientists in face masks and lab coats.

"I don't understand," Riley said. "What does Chernobyl have to do with Lowfield?"

"It *don't*. Not a thing. It's a whatchamacallit—an *analogy*. Think of that place, that village, that *church* out there, as radioactive. Just like *this* place." And here he tapped the cover of the book, again with that awful flipper-nail. "After the disaster, the Soviets built a cap to put over that blown-out reactor, a big lead sarcophagus to keep the radiation in. Otherwise, it woulda poisoned most of Europe. But only an idiot would spend any time near that area, even now. It's still a bad place nine years out—and will be ninety years from now, and nine hundred. Now imagine someone had the power, just by their presence, their... *proximity* to that cap, to take it right off. To lift up the lid of that sarcophagus. Why, it would set the whole area back to near where it was in '86 when the plant first blew. You understand my analogy now? Lowfield is like that. The Fuller man discovered that his own grandfadder couldn't stop *his* brudder from exposin' the core, so to speak. That fucker opened a door to another world, one that wants to poison this one. The signs come when it happens. That old house starts to repair itself. The soil o' that land grows crops it has no business growin'. Animals 'come violent to protect the thing what's out there in that woods. And men start to feel ungodly desires and have queer, lustful visions. To act on them creates a charge, a power impulse that blows the door wide open."

Riley just stared at Marsten, a bit shattered by how much he knew of what had started happening since April. "What, what takes the cap off?" he asked, though he already knew.

Marsten just glared at him. "What, are you some kind of *moron*? Your bloodline, of course! If any Fuller from your line comes near that place, I figure it all starts up again. I figure it already has. When I saw this here profile of you in Mackenzie's paper, I nearly shat my pants. I thought: Oh Christ, it'll start up again, all the horrors that me mudder told me about." When Marsten said this, it made Riley think of Gladys Keating, who also knew tales from 1930. Who also freaked out after seeing Jessie-Mac's profile of him.

Marsten's oversized eye loomed once again at Riley, bearing down on him like a moon. "Tell me about this here 'summer intern,'" he said, as if he'd read Riley's mind, and tapped Jessie's byline on the *Pioneer* article, "this… *chickee* who came out to interview ye. Has she started showing up in yer dreams yet?"

"Shut up," Riley said.

"She *has*, hasn't she?" Marsten cackled.

"Shut the fuck up."

"You've been cornholin' her in your dreams! I can tell just by the flush on yer face. Oh, it *is* startin' up again. You're 'renovating' that house? Horse pucky! It's renovating itself. And that kid who died at Petit Point? Maybe he tried to scare you off your land and ran afoul o' some jellyfish out there fer his trouble. Mudder always said the jellyfish were some bad back in 1930. Oh, it is *starting up again*. If you're still around by this time next year, maybe the whole Island will be poisoned, and every fadder will be cornholin' his dodder by Christmas. Hell, maybe when they finish that bloody bridge, that fucking 'fixed link' in a couple years, the poison'll spread to the mainland. Me, I'll throw myself into the Strait by then."

Riley was now slumped in the kitchen chair, his head down. The two men said nothing for a moment. The only noise was the *click… click… click…* of the robin trying to get its worm, and the spit and crackle of the woodstove.

"So… so how do I stop it?" Riley finally asked.

"Oh well, you could off yourself," Marsten said. "That'd be the simplest way. I got a shotgun under me bed if you wanna borrow it. Just go do it out in the dunes. I don't want ye makin' a mess on me floor. I mean, I'd kill ye meself, except," and here, his voice grew almost woebegone, "I'm too *dumb* to cover it up, and I'm too old to go to jail."

Riley just shook his head. He had no answer for the old man, no rebuttal.

"Yer the fruit of a poisonous tree," Marsten said. "You gotta tear the root out."

Riley flashed his stiff gaze back up at the fisherman. "The taproot?" he asked.

Marsten flinched again, but then nodded. "Aye. That's a good word for it."

"What if I... what if I *literally* tore it out? What if I went back to that church, went into that basement, and killed whatever... *thing* lives down there?"

"Oh ye could, I suppose. But ye won't. If ye think yer lustful desires are bad now, sleeping under the roof of that house, just wait till yer standing before that *thing*, that taproot. Mudder always said the Fuller man and her fadder couldn't control themselves after the three of them went down into that basement. Took turns with her, the men did. Had a whore of good time, 'pparently. A *whore* of a good time. No. Ye won't kill the taproot. The pleasure it infects ye with, the lustful desires, will be too much to turn your back on. No. Best bet is to off yourself. Sooner as opposed to later, be my guess. More girls'll get raped the longer you wait."

"Well, you've been incredibly unhelpful," Riley said, and abruptly got up from the table. "Thanks for the tea."

He moved toward the door, was just reaching for the knob to get out of there, when Marsten called over. "Hey, cocksucker."

Riley paused. "Yeah?"

"Tell me, have ye got any sprouts o' yer own?"

Riley hesitated again, but then said, "No. My wife and I tried, but we had a bunch of miscarriages. We're divorced now, as you read in that article. So no, no kids."

"Are ye *sure*?"

"Of course I'm sure."

"Good. Cuz if ye did, you'd have to off them before ye offed yourself. You can't leave any part of the root behind. Ye gotta be the last in yer bloodline. Otherwise, that house'll lure whatever offspring ye do have back here, and the cap'll come off again. That'd be my guess."

I don't know if I believe you, Riley thought. *I sometimes think that if I'd had some kids, or even just one, none of this would be happening, because I wouldn't be here. And besides, I'd probably be a better man than I am.*

But he said none of this. He just opened Marsten's door and lumbered back down into the muddy driveway and to his waiting Lumina.

Chapter 28

July 13, 1995
Dear Diary, or Journal, or whatever the fuck you are,
It is midnight here, and I have finally limped into Applegarth's library to put this entry down after several aborted attempts to scrape myself off my bed. I have never felt like this before, at once utterly spent and yet somehow manic, somehow *electrified*, as if a low current hums through the very core of me despite what I've been doing to my body for the last several hours.

Obed Marsten used an analogy when I visited him yesterday in Fleshers Pond. He compared Lowfield—not inaccurately, it turns out—to the Chernobyl nuclear disaster. But since then, I have come up with an analogy all my own, one that feels more precise.

Applegarth is the cheese, and Lowfield is the trap.

I realize that now. I realize that I began sniffing at that cheese, nibbling around its edges, in those days and weeks after I first set foot in this house. Each repair and reno represents another bite. Each day that I have felt more comfortable calling this place home, more unable to leave, represents me putting additional weight on the tray that holds the cheese.

Earlier today, the trap finally sprung.

I didn't want to do it, Diary, or Journal, or whatever the fuck you are. All afternoon, I sat out in Applegarth's backyard, parked in a cheap lawn chair, smoking maniacally with one hand and grasping the Glock with the other. With each finished cigarette, I put the gun in my mouth or under my chin. Believe me, I came very close to pulling the trigger—maybe closer than I ever have before.

But in the end, I decided that Obed Marsten was wrong. He'd have to be. Surely I could go back out there, to that deserted village in the woods, to that *church*, and the kill the thing living in its basement, that taproot. I would not be overcome with, as the old fisherman put it, lustful visions and unholy desires. I'm better than that, I told myself. I can do what needs to be done. I will kill it, ending whatever threat my presence here has caused. Then I could let myself stay in this house, and live my life, and no longer be a risk to anyone.

And so, as I did back in May, I set out for the village of Lowfield. And this time, I brought my Glock.

The two-mile hike through that forest felt more arduous, seemed to take longer, than it had even back in May. (The smokes and the booze are catching up with me, I guess.) Though the height of summer now, the woods felt almost chilly as I tramped and trounced around through its thickets and brambles, the ageless hardwood reaching endlessly into the sky. There was an unmistakable scent of rot in the air, becoming stronger the deeper I went in. The trees and grass seemed to almost *crawl* with fauna, as they had back in May—crows and squirrels, chipmunks and rabbits, and things unseen that slithered and bounded through the dense brush that tried to thwart my every step. The animals, I now knew, were standing on guard for the thing living out there in that woods. They watched me with their black eyes as I made my way toward it, the Glock tucked into the waistband of my jeans.

Finally the forest began to change, as it had before. Untouched hardwood gave way to spruce timber. The last remnants of that corduroy road, thick wooden planks now mushy with rot, appeared at my feet. I followed the path that emerge, and I could soon see the deserted old cottages, those saltbox structures, peeping through the trees like giant toadstools, like huge, poisonous mushrooms. I moved into the clearing and was soon walking through Lowfield's weedy, ancient avenues, the air unspeakably still. Before long, I stood before that church. Its door was still agape from where I had pried it open two months earlier.

I fished the Glock out of my waistband and held it poised and ready as I made my way up the church steps and squeezed myself back inside. The smell was nearly indescribable. A mossy, earthy stench of decay, far stronger than it had been during my first visit. It was like a grave had been opened. I pulled my shirt up over my nose and kept the Glock ready as I made my way across the church's warped and filthy floor toward the main part of the chapel. I actually thought: *This will be easy. The stink of this place will keep me focused.*

I stepped up to the altar. The gold cross at the back still hung upside down; the giant purple bloodstain still clung like a shadow to the back wall, the relic of some violence that occurred here more than a century ago. I moved toward the arched door that I knew from the diary led into the basement. But even as I did, I felt my head begin to turn, an involuntary pivot to my left. My eyes locked onto the tall pulpit there with its two books resting on that wide, ornate lectern. I moved toward it, a great desire swelling up inside me. A desire to set eyes once again on *The Grimoire of Shaal*.

There it sat, open on the pulpit, next to the King James Bible, just as I had left it. I stepped closer, my eyes falling toward its bastard text. I couldn't help myself. I felt the Glock go slack in my hand as I lowered it to my hip. Blinking, I took a step closer. And then I caught another glimpse of that book's cosmic, alien prose.

"Ji'agga thon. Ti morel'hin thos Ghroyan. Ghroyan e Shaal shoiut das mual. Mual dagoth e purin."

I didn't just read these words. I spoke them aloud. And when I did, the whole church lit up with that dark light, that toxic, radiating glare that I have seen so many times in my dreams.

I turned then, to face the archway at the end of the altar, leading to the stairs that would take me down into the basement. That horrific light seemed to rise from it, to bloom out like a rose. I walked to its centre, feeling every tendon and sinew in my body come alive. The Glock was barely an afterthought in my hand as I stepped onto that antechamber's landing and then around the rail that led to a descending set of stairs. Down I went, down into a dark that wasn't *really* dark, but a beaming black light that called to every molecule of my body.

I descended trance-like into that dungeon, that unholy gizzard. I could not close my eyes as I was led across its dirt floor, my flesh practically sizzling on my bones. One step closer and I stopped, standing stiff as lumber in the whirls of that light.

And then I saw it, Diary, or Journal, or whatever the fuck you are. Oh God, *I saw it*.

I will put my description down here, in my diary, because my grandfather's grandfather, that *other* Riley Fuller, could not in his. It looked like the root of a giant tree twisting and snaking through a large hole in the dirt floor. Only, it didn't look like wood. It looked like living flesh, a muscular purple, veiny and thick, and pulsing with quick, manic spasms, as if some unseen fluid were pumping through it in mad jerks. It appeared almost wet, almost glistening in the dark light it cast, as if it had just passed through something viscous. Don't ask me how I know, but I could tell that it was just one root of many, a single pipeline that had managed to pierce through the fabric of existence and into our world. Imagine a giant tree uprooted and turned upside down. Now imagine those exposed roots like the tentacles of a beast, a cephalopodic creature larger than the universe itself, and you are staring just one tiny tip of it. That's what I saw.

Shaal. Shaal opens the portal for us. Feel his energy awaken your every desire.

And how he did. I felt almost reborn as I bathed in that light. I tucked the Glock back into my waistband, and then raised both hands up and spread my fingers wide.

Obed Marsten *was* right, it turns out. This *was* like standing near an open reactor core. Only, instead of poisoning the cells of my body, it was rejuvenating them. I felt my mind grow clearer and more peaceful than it had in *years*; it was like I could see through time itself, could exist in past, present and future all at once. I felt my heart flower outward and burn, full of unfettered passions I had never known. My body heaved upward, wanting to leap out of my clothes, wanting to spring forth and surrender itself to that bright darkness, those undulating shadows of light. This is what Shaal wanted for me. This what Shaal was manipulating me to feel.

But Marsten's taunts and accusations raced into my head then. He was right about something else, but in that moment I wanted to prove him wrong. I had come here to kill that... that *thing*, and I was convinced I would— no matter how much pleasure and peace it brought me. I reached down toward the butt of my Glock, there in my waistband, but my hand... my hand *moved past it*, and lingered somewhere else. Oh, Diary, or Journal, or whatever the fuck you are. Oh Jesus Christ. Forgive me. I braced not the pistol, but *myself* in my hand, and the sheer bliss, the runny, delicious ache that coursed up through me was like nothing I had ever experienced. The firm but gentle grip of my fingers upon that tented, swelling knot, the very taproot of who I am, was an indescribable ecstasy. Immediately I was coated in revulsion. Fuck, it was disgusting. I disgusted myself.

No! I thought. *Dammit, no! This isn't who I really am!*

I threw my hand away and yelled at that tentacle, a bellow from the very tips of my toes.

The root writhed then. Writhed, and came slithering toward me.

I fled. Back across the basement floor. Up those steps and onto the landing. Out to and off the altar, down the aisle and through the doors of that church that led back outside. I hustled over the wide, weedy avenues of that empty, rotting village, and practically flung myself back into the woods when I reached its edge. My forty-minute hike home through that forest was *nothing*—I was barely winded when I finally stumbled out into Applegarth's backyard. I moved like a shark through water toward the house, and threw open its main doors when I arrived.

Up the stairs I went, its wooden boards popping like cannons under my weight. I cast myself into my bedroom and upon my bed, stripping off my clothes as I fast as I could.

Know this, Diary, or Journal, or whatever the fuck you are. I took no pleasure in what I did next. Four or five strokes of my hand, vicious and immediate, and it was done. Only, it wasn't done. A moment later, a *half-*moment, the desire roared up in me again, and I took myself back in my hand. Visions of Jessie-Mac and her little friend, Tara, that pixie-cut warrior, floated over my bed. I lingered with them and did what needed to be done.

And then, a moment later, the passions washed over me anew. It was like they had never left. I was now in Shaal's full grip and He wasn't going to let me go. I thought of Jane during my next explosive thrusts, but was given barely a minute's reprieve once I was done. Then I thought of Marigold, of the way she was when we first met, all youthful eagerness, all girlish experimentation, and how ravenous we were for each other. I exploded again, my cries practically shattering my bedroom ceiling. But no relief came, and so I imagined the two of them—my wife *and* my mistress—together, and thrashed and spasmed around on my bed once more.

On and on it went. For hours. I imagined friends' wives and work acquaintances. I imagined strangers I'd seen on the street. Soon the room was hot and steamy and stank of my seed. I had battered myself raw, practically bleeding into my hand. Each climactic cry was followed by a cry of despair, a plea for mercy.

Finally, enough relief came for me to stop. I lay there weeping in my soiled, debauched sheets, my chest heaving, my face and shoulders and the pillow beneath my head befouled with my own spend. How much time had passed, I didn't know. But the sunlight outside my bedroom window was gone; summer's long, loitering dusk had given way to night. Eventually, I peeled myself off my mattress and sat up on the edge of my bed. I soon pulled my clothes back on, not even bothering to clean myself up first. Then I rose and shuffled like a zombie down Applegarth's long hall to the library. Flopped into this chair at the desk, lifted off the plastic shroud covering this computer and put it on the floor, then booted up the machine to document what had happened.

And now that I have, I can already feel the desires coming over me again. Oh God—what am I going to do? Can I never leave this house, because of what I've become? I've been rendered into something I'm not: an insatiable beast, a demon, a *prevert*, as that vulgar old fisherman had called it. *This is not who I am*.

What am I going to do? Jessie-Mac is coming over here with Jack tomorrow night for dinner. Will these hungers subside by then? Will I be able to keep them to myself if they're not? Will she be safe here with me if I can't?

Oh Jesus. Oh fucking Christ. I have never felt this utterly alone.

Chapter 29

It had rained hard overnight, and by the time Riley stood in his garden the next morning to pull out some vegetables for his dinner party, the soil wanted to suck the sneakers right off his feet. Both kidney-shaped plots were a muddy red soup now, the Island dirt like gooey pools of blood that squelched and popped with each step he took. Still in a jelly-legged stupor from the night before, he nonetheless moved around the verdant rows of what he had grown here—what this land, he corrected himself, had grown *for him*. He stooped to lift leaves and examine his yields, trying to make a decision in his fogged-out brain. What would go well with his and Jack's steaks and Jessie-Mac's eggplant? Not the snow peas. These were grotesquely huge now, dangling on their thin vines like big green fingers with eight knuckles each. He yanked a parsnip out of the dirt instead, but saw that the thing had gone full mutant, looking like a gnarled, bone-white hand freed from a fresh grave. He chucked it aside. The carrots were a bit better. They were only forked at their tips, like a snake's tongue. He went with these, as well as three ears of corn, chucking them into the empty and washed-out ADL ice cream container he'd brought out from the house. His mother always said that the sign of a healthy meal was how many colours you could get on your plate, and these would do nicely.

But now came the question of Jessie's eggplant itself. Riley wandered over to its patch near the edge of the first plot, near the sundial. Beneath those wide, lobed leaves, he could see the massive eggplants, dark and slug-like, growing low to the soil. He squatted down and pushed the leaves aside. Which eggplant should he pick? Considering it would be her main dish, he opted for the largest one, which was nearly the size of a loaf of bread.

He pulled it free from its stem, the sinews cracking and tearing as he yanked, the bloody-red mud gurgling up from under his sneaker as he put his weight down.

He looked at the dark yield, moved it around in his hands. He'd never prepared eggplant before. What had Jessie said? *Just poke some holes in it, put it in a pan, and throw it in the oven like a roast.*

Riley lifted it to his face, pressed his nose against its smooth black skin. It had a strange, unfamiliar smell, one that made him flinch back and grimace a little. What *was* that? It was... it was like the hint of something feral seeping up through the eggplant's flesh. Mild, for sure, but unmistakable.

Well, whatever, he thought, still hazy in the mind, still sore between the legs, and tucked the eggplant under his arm and carried the ADL container with the other vegetables in it back toward the house.

~

While he waited for his guests to arrive, Riley prepared as much of the meal as he could. He peeled and chopped carrots and placed them in their pot of water. He husked the corn. He seasoned the marinated steaks and put them on a plate to transport them to the barbecue. He lay the eggplant flat in its roasting pan atop the stove and preheated the oven. He was just thinking of washing up what few dishes he'd generated when he saw, through the kitchen window, Jessie-Mac's baby blue minivan, with its badly rusted sides, pull up his driveway. He watched her park and turn off the engine before climbing down from the cab.

She was wearing a dress.

Even from here, he could make out the formality of its details. It was a deep royal-blue number, shining and satiny, mismatching the fainter blue of the van, but a perfect complement to Jessie's jet-black hair and icy grey eyes. It was also shoulderless, with a tight bodice up top and loose pleats below, which ended just above her pale knees. On her feet, he could see she wore a pair of open-toed shoes with small blunt heels. All in all, it was exactly the sort of outfit a twenty-year-old might wear to what she imagined a grown-up dinner party to be.

In her hands, she carried a box of Timbits.

She was heading toward the front porch, but Riley knocked on the kitchen window's glass and motioned to Applegarth's side door. She nodded, turned in that direction, and walked gingerly, almost clumsily, across the grass in shoes she was not used to wearing. Riley set the wash cloth down and moved through the wide wooden arch that led to the foyer.

"Sorry, this is the main entry to the house," he said after opening the door and welcoming her in. "I'm trying to get in the habit of using it. It's okay. Leave your shoes on."

"Thanks," she replied. "Sorry I'm early. But I brought dessert!" She handed him the box of Timbits via its tented cardboard handle.

"Thanks." He set it on the Cherrywood table by the door.

"Holy *smokes*, Riley," Jessie said, moving past him and deeper into Applegarth's foyer. She took a moment to absorb the nineteenth-century opulence all around her—the gleaming hardwood floors, the polished and ornate staircase leading to the second floor, the intricate wainscoting above their heads. "This is like a whole new house," she marveled. "When I was here in May, the place was practically falling down. How did you do all this work in just two months?"

"I… I can't explain it," he said honestly, his eyes downcast.

"Well, it's impressive," she said. "I'm *impressed*."

When he looked back up at her, he saw that she was looking up at him. Perhaps she had just realized how badly she'd overdressed for this evening. Riley himself wore a ratty, wrinkled golf shirt and blue jeans, the hems of which were still muddy from that morning's trip to the garden.

"Aren't you going to comment on my outfit?" she asked.

"You look… nice," he said, trying not to stare.

Jessie rolled her eyes at that but then smiled. She moved across the foyer and through the other wide wooden archway, the one leading into the living room, and he followed her. It was like she knew where to go. She found the wicker cabinet with the boombox on top and the stack of CDs she'd given him piled next to it.

"Ooh, did you listen to these?" she asked, picking each one up in turn.

"I did," he replied, sidling up behind her.

"And?"

"Oh well. They weren't really my cup of tea."

This statement had no bearing on her actions whatsoever. Jessie powered up the boombox and popped its lid. She cracked open one of the CD cases, plucked the disc out, and navigated it carefully in before closing the lid again and pressing PLAY. He saw that she'd chosen the album *August and Everything After*. Riley grimaced when, following a lengthy, languid riff of guitar chords, the mopey, bitch-squealing voice of the band's front man filled his living room.

When Jessie turned back around to face him, Riley realized that he was standing too close to her. While she was busy feeding the CD into the player, he had stolen a drawn-out look at her bare shoulders, at the dark hair that spread out over them, at the way the dress's bodice hugged the angles of her soft, narrow back. Now, with her facing him again, he took one full step in reverse, which only made Jessie furrow her brow at him.

"Riley, are you okay?"

"Sorry," he said, clearing his throat. "It's been a rough couple of days."

She nodded. "So you heard?"

He froze. Stared at her again. "Heard what?" he asked.

Jessie just blinked at him. "You *didn't* hear...?" she said. "About yesterday."

"What about it?"

"There was a murder over in Georgetown. Early yesterday morning, a girl was found... raped and strangled in the park behind the playhouse there."

"*Jesus.*" And in an instant, the room began to spin. "How... how old?"

"Eleven. Her older brother confessed to everything, and the RCMP have taken him into custody. Riley, this is, like, the third or fourth girl to be attacked by a man in her own family in recent weeks. What the *hell* is going on?"

Riley struggled to speak, and could only echo the words he'd said about Applegarth's renos. "I... I can't explain it." He wiped his mouth with his hand. "Are you, are you writing an article about what happened?"

"No. Jack has assigned this one to Maggie. And my retrospective piece is officially spiked. We can't publish about what happened in 1930 when all the same shit is going on right now. It wouldn't be in good taste." Her eyes narrowed at him. "Unless the two are connected?"

In that moment, Riley knew it was over. He realized that everything was finished for him now. Not just his peace of mind here in Applegarth, or his future on PEI, but his life. His *life. I don't even want a future for myself*, he thought, *if this is the shit that's going to weigh on my conscience*. Riley grew certain that he *could* do what needed to be done, that he *would* go through with it, if he were alone right now. He could make himself alone. He could ask Jessie-Mac if she'd mind stepping back outside for a minute. She'd be confused by that but ultimately comply. She was, after all, only twenty. Once she was safely out on Applegarth's stoop, he'd saunter into the kitchen, open the drawer, pull out the Glock, load it, shove it in his mouth, and pull the trigger. She's hear the shot, but by the time she came running back in, his brains would already be on the wall.

More girls'll get raped the longer you wait, Obed Marsten had crooned at him.

"Riley?" Jessie's bright grey eyes probed his face. "You okay?"

He just gave her one stiff nod.

"Look, people are starting to freak out," she went on. "Including me. And there are more cops around now, called up from Charlottetown. There's a tension in the air that I've never felt around here before. Why are these things happening?"

And just like that, his conviction left him, blown away like so much dust on the breeze. He *did* have something to live for, didn't he? He was a man who deserved a second, a third, a *fifth* chance, was he not? Applegarth settled and creaked. "Could be copycat stuff," he replied, losing his nerve. "One person commits a crime and it gives others ideas. You're more likely to see that sort of thing in big cities, but it could happen here, too."

"You don't believe that," Jessie said. "And neither do I. This has something to do with Lowfield, doesn't it? I think we need to start talking seriously about what's out in those woods."

Riley swallowed. "I'd like to wait till Jack's here to do that," he said. "I think he would have some—"

And just on time, they heard a car pull up Applegarth's driveway and park. Riley went to the door and Jessie followed him. He opened it to see Jack climbing out of his Honda after fishing something from the bucket of the passenger seat. He shut the door and turned around, a bit flustered. Cradled in one arm, like a baby, was a bottle of Scotch.

Riley and Jessie came out to greet him. "You made it," he said.

"I did. Missed my turnoff twice. You really are out in the middle of nowhere here." Jack turned to Jessie. "Holy smokes, girl, you look some good. *Och aye*, you clean up *right* nice." Jack himself wore plain brown slacks and a short-sleeve work shirt, the breast pocket choked with pens and a notebook

Jessie smiled and gave Riley a glance that said, *See*, that's *how you compliment someone.*

"This is for you," Jack said to Riley and handed him the Scotch. It looked expensive.

"Thanks. Are we cracking this open tonight?"

"That depends," Jack said. "Are you drinkin' hard or hardly drinkin'?"

"Well, if *this* is what's on offer."

"Ah fuck," Jack said, growing abruptly mournful. His thoughts had no doubt returned to the murdered girl in Georgetown. "We bloody well need a drink."

~

Riley gave Jack a quick tour of Applegarth's ground floor, starting with the living room and solarium (he discreetly pressed STOP on the CD player as they passed), with Jessie trailing behind and still in awe of how much work Riley must have done on the house. Jack was equally gobsmacked. He knew this old place had sat empty for decades, but now it looked practically new. Riley did not extend the tour to the second floor. He worried that, once in the library, Jack would ask to see the diaries, and Riley was still building up the nerve to share them. Instead, he led Jack and Jessie into Applegarth's huge kitchen, showing them the pantry, the cabinetry he'd had installed, the original kitchen table now miraculously restored. He took them out to the front parlour and inside the turret. Then he led them back and into the dining room, where the long table inside was already set for dinner.

"Wow, it has a door that closes," Jack said of the dining room. "You don't see that very often."

Riley nodded. "I know the trend these days is to take out doors and knock down walls and open everything up, but I might keep it. I like it this way." He set the Scotch down on the table and motioned for them to sit, then returned to the kitchen briefly to fetch some rocks glasses and an ashtray. He returned and distributed the glasses while Jack cracked open the bottle. He poured a generous glug in each.

"*Slainte*," he said.

"Here's mud in your eye," Riley added, and they did a cheers. Riley lit a du Maurier then and offered the pack to the others, but they demurred. He took a hard drag and then asked, "So what can you tell me about this girl killed in Georgetown?"

"Her name's Stacey St. Clair," Jessie said. "Kyla has a friend who knows her." She let out a slight murmur of discomfort. "Sorry—who *knew* her."

"The cops arrested her brother, Jeff, late yesterday afternoon," Jack added. "Maggie said it came as a complete shock to everyone out there. He's a good kid, apparently. Plays hockey. Mows lawns in the summer. Goes to Bible camp, for Pete's sake."

"His only other run-in with police," Jessie went on, "was five years ago when he got caught spray-painting a bad word on the side of his school. But it was Bart Simpson stuff, a one-off. Otherwise, his nose was completely clean. No trouble to anyone."

"Exactly," Jack said, and took a gulp of his Scotch. "So what would possess a boy to do something like that to his kid sister?"

Riley took another harsh drag on his cigarette, then cast his hazel eyes up at them. "I think 'possess' is the right word."

Jessie-Mac turned ashen, but Jack was already shaking his head and leaning away from the table, folding his arms incredulously over his chest. "I won't believe it," he said. "I won't bloody believe it."

"Jack, will you please listen to him?" Jessie said.

"No."

"Jack, c'mon," she pressed. "It isn't just Jeff St. Clair, okay? It's a bunch of men all around Kings county. I've talked to my friend Tara. This is *happening*."

But Jack just continued shaking his head.

"Jack, look at me," Riley said, parking his cigarette in the ashtray. "I'm going to show you the diaries later, after we eat. But I want you to know: it's all true. Everything they say. I don't want it to be, but it is."

"Did you track down Obed Marsten?" Jack asked, clearly holding out for a logical explanation.

"I did."

"And what did he have to say?"

Riley hesitated, but then told them everything, giving an unvarnished account of what the vulgar old fisherman had relayed to him—the stories, the explanations, the theories. By the time he finished, the bottom half of Jessie's face was cupped in her hands, and Jack's were laced over the crown of his head, his mouth gaping.

"I know it's a lot to absorb," Riley said. "Why don't we take a break? I'll go finish putting on supper." When he got up from the table, neither of them acknowledged it. They just sat there, stunned. "Jack, how do you like your steak?"

He took forever to reply. "Well done," he said finally, his voice trance-like, as if he'd seen a ghost. "Cook the fuck out of it."

~

Riley went to the side of the house, to the small concrete slab he'd had poured there about a month earlier and where a small barbeque he'd purchased now sat. He cranked the propane and lit the barbeque, watching the blue donut of fire gasp to life under the grills. Giving those iron racks time to heat up, he went back into the house to fetch the plate of steaks from the fridge. He brought it out and, after a few moments, forked the marbled slabs of meat onto the now hot grills. Then he closed the lid and went back inside.

In the kitchen, Riley located the largest pot he owned, put the ears of corn in it, and began filling it with cold water from the sink before carrying it over to the stove to join the pot of carrots he'd prepared earlier. He cranked the burners to get them going, then turned his attention to the eggplant nestled in its roasting pan. With the oven already preheated, all he had to do, according to Jessie, was poke a few holes into that dark mass of flesh and then pop the pan in. He grabbed a large knife out of the knife block and stuck the tip into several places to break the skin. Riley expected to find dry resistance there, like one would find in an uncooked zucchini or tomato. Instead, the knife sank into what felt like goo, and a small glob of viscous material, brown and sickly, oozed up from each slit. The tawny substance ran down the side of the eggplant like tears and carried with it the same alien smell it had while still on the vine. It was more pronounced now, pungent. *Is that supposed to happen?* Riley thought. *I don't know eggplant at all. Is it supposed to look like that, to smell like that?* He examined the large piece of fruit again. *It must be fine*, he thought. *It's straight from the garden. It has to be okay.*

He yawned open the door and set the roasting pan in the centre of the lower rack before closing the oven again.

~

Back in the dining room, he found his guests sitting in relative silence, their faces pale. Jessie had barely touched her shot of whisky, but Jack was clearly on his second slug. Riley resumed his seat and looked at his friends. A lengthy moment passed before he spoke.

"So yeah, that's what Obed Marsten told me," he said at last.

Jessie-Mac looked up at him. "So I don't think you should *kill* yourself," she said with a gentle shake of her head. "I doubt that's going to solve anything, do you?"

"I don't know," Riley replied. "Marsten seemed to think it would."

"Now hang on a sec," Jack piped up. "Let me get this straight. Are we to understand that your grandfather, while living in this house in 1930, found the diaries that *his* grandfather wrote back in the 1860s? Same as you did? And they led him to Lowfield, same as you?"

"That's right."

"And while he was mucking about in that church with Marsten's mother, he read that book and was inspired by it, managed to convince her father to have sex with her? And inspired others to do the same with their family members?"

"No, Jack, that's not what I'm saying. Listen to me. The book is not written in English. It's not 'inspiring' anyone. It's… like, casting a spell, which opens up a sort of doorway in the basement of that church, and has allowed that… *thing*, that taproot, or whatever it is, to come through into our world. Marsten said it was my presence, the presence of my bloodline here, that makes that possible."

"Oh fuck," Jack said, leaning back from the table again. "Oh bloody hell. We're all drinking bad 'shine now. This is nonsense. Bloody *nonsense*."

"Jack, look at me. I know you're searching for a logical explanation to all this, but I'm telling you there isn't one. Some things are beyond our ability to explain." But Jack just refolded his arms over his chest and gave another disbelieving shake of his head.

"What if you sold Applegarth?" Jessie asked. "Got it out of your bloodline and just moved into Charlottetown, or back to Moncton even? Would that put an end to all this?"

Riley shrugged. "Maybe."

"So then why don't you do that?"

Riley looked at her, but then looked at his lap. He took a long, slow breath. Felt the weight of his decision, the heft of consequence, bear down on him. "This house... it has a grip on me. I, I can't explain it. But when I first set foot in here, after the dust had cleared from the Moncton shooting and my divorce, I felt like myself for the first time in forever. This house... *does* that for me, every moment I'm under its roof. It would be very hard for me to let that go."

"But at what cost? How many more people have to get hurt? These girls are *children*, Riley. What if it happened to my sister Kyla? She's twelve. What if it happened to *me*?"

More girls'll get raped the longer you wait.

The house suddenly settled again, creaking and snapping as if under the strength of an unseen wind. This did not even startle Jessie-Mac.

"Riley, what if I get raped?" she asked, noticing him flinch. "What will you think then?"

He looked at her, at those cat-like eyes boring into him. Her face seemed so young and yet so wise. A strand of dark hair formed a question mark on her brow. Her shoulders looked so tender under the dining room's chandelier light. *I have lost so much already. You have no idea. Don't take this away from me, too.*

"I should go flip the steaks," he said, and got up from the table.

~

Riley stopped by the kitchen to set the carrots and corn to simmer, then grabbed his stainless-steel tongs and took them out to the barbecue. He flipped the now grease-weeping slabs of meat, their underbellies already nicely charred, before putting the lid back down. Returning to the kitchen, he set out a serving dish for the corn, one for the carrots, and another for the steaks, before hauling down the oven door and checking on the eggplant. The pan, Riley noticed, had somehow shifted a few inches from the centre of the rack. It was closer to the oven's left-hand wall now and... and further up toward the front than it had been when he set it in there. *That's strange*, Riley thought. *That's fucking weird*. He nabbed an oven mitt and moved it back.

Grabbing a few items he'd forgotten while setting the table earlier—the butter dish, the salt and pepper—Riley headed back into the dining room and caught a snippet of Jack and Jessie's conversation.

"—is that what he said?"

"Well, he's right there," Jack replied. "Ask him."

She turned to Riley. "Did you tell Jack exactly where this Lowfield place is? He says it's in that big swath of woods between the back of your property and where it ends near Cardigan North."

"That's right," he replied, setting the items down and resuming his seat. "The village was built right on the border between Lots 53 and 54 of the Island. If you started walking south from my backyard through the woods, you'd pass Lowfield after nearly two miles, and after another half mile or so you'd come out the other side, there at Route 319. Do you know it?"

"Sort of," she said. "It's really just a service road, right? I don't think that stretch of it is even paved."

"It's not. I've been down there. You drive through some dense woods on a red-clay road and come out the other side to a couple of old potato fields. There's literally nothing else back there."

Jessie looked at him, then glanced at Jack. He glanced at her, and then they both looked at Riley.

He got their meaning.

"*No*," he said emphatically.

"Oh *c'mon*," she replied. "We could go after supper. That's, like, ten minutes away."

"And then a half-mile hike through dense woods after that," Riley said. "It'll be dark eventually. No. I will show you the diaries after we eat, but I am *not* taking you guys out there."

"Oh for fuck's sake," Jack said, pouring them more whisky. "*Och*, Riley, what do you think is even out there, lad?"

"I *know* what's out there. Believe me. And this isn't something you can just write about for your little paper."

"I'm not interested in this as a journalist," Jessie countered. "I'm interested in this as a *woman*." She caught then how they were staring at her. "Don't look at me like that. You know what I mean. Girls are getting *raped*. Something in that woods is causing it. Your *presence* on this land, Riley, is causing it. That's what Marsten told you, right? I have a twelve-year-old sister. Don't you think I have a vested interest in trying to stop what's happening?"

He wouldn't look at her.

"*You* could stop what's happening, by selling this land and moving away. But you won't do it, will you? You'd rather stay here, all alone in this giant house your ancestors built, sitting around and stewing in your own past, your own pain. And that's somehow better than stopping people from getting hurt? C'mon, Riley. You're better than that. Please tell me you are."

He wouldn't look at her.

"You need to sell this land," she said. "You need to sell Applegarth and move the fuck aw…" But then she stopped, her words drifting off. Riley looked up to see a gradual, tentative dawning come over her face then. A key was attempting to fit into a lock. A puzzle piece was nearly slipping into place. He watched as her grey eyes gently darted from side to side as she tried to parse the realization emerging in her mind.

Danny.

She's just about to think of Danny. He tried to convince me to sell Applegarth, too. He tried to scare me off this land. She knows that. I told her that. And now he's dead.

Riley rose slowly from the table. "Dinner's ready," he said.

~

With serving plate in hand, Riley fetched the steaks off the grill and killed the barbecue. He brought the meat back into the house and set it on the counter. He drained the carrots and put them in their serving dish, then tonged out the corn and did the same. Jack emerged from the dining room to help Riley get everything onto the table.

"Poor thing's upset herself," he said, taking the steaks in one hand and the corn in the other. "This has been hard on her."

Riley just nodded. "I know. Go on. I'll follow you in."

Jack headed back into the dining room while Riley donned the oven mitt and went over to fish the eggplant out. He hoisted the roasting pan onto the stovetop and examined the large fruit inside. Its time in the oven had caused the eggplant's purple-black skin to wrinkle and pucker, but otherwise it had maintained its structural integrity. It looked like a roast. Yet Riley could see, through the little slits he'd made with the knife, that a lot more of that viscous material had seeped up and out. It ran like shit-coloured tears down the sides of the eggplant. What's more, cooking it had not killed that bizarre, unfamiliar odour. It had done the opposite. That stench filled the kitchen.

Is it supposed to look like that? Riley thought. *Is it supposed to smell like that?*

He just shook his head. Grabbing a spatula, he transported the eggplant onto a wooden cutting board, then carried it and the dish of carrots into the dining room.

Inside, he found Jack had served up the steaks and corn and was now back in his seat. Jessie, meanwhile, was just staring absently out the dining room's window facing the east side of the property.

Riley set the eggplant near his own plate and then grabbed his fork and knife. "So… what do I do here?" he asked her.

"Oh, just cut it like it's a ham," she replied, turning a casual glance to the eggplant. "It'll be fine, R—"

But her words stopped in her throat when she saw the brown liquid oozing out of her dinner. Jack too had paused, freezing with his whisky glass halfway to his mouth. He looked around the room, baffled, and gave the air a sniff. "That smell," he said. "I… I *know* that smell. What is that?"

Riley just shrugged, and then approached the cutting board with his fork and knife poised over it.

When he did, the eggplant rolled off the cutting board and away from him.

The three of them looked at it, at first more flummoxed than afraid. It was like a magician's trick, an illusion. Their faces ignited into flares of bewilderment.

Without really thinking, Riley reached further across the table and tried to stab the eggplant to lift it back onto the cutting board. But as the knife came down, the eggplant rolled again, this time across the table toward Jessie's plate in one sickly, human-like lurch.

Two sets of chair legs screamed on the floor as both Jack and Jessie climbed to their feet, staring transfixed at the eggplant. Riley watched as the large piece of fruit began to... began to *squirm* on the table, to bend and shift and throb like a beating heart. Through the slits in its skin, more of that greyish-brown substance came discharging out, faster, thicker, as if the eggplant's innards were slowly boiling over. The mess of it began to pool there on the table.

The stench moved through the room like fog, and Jack was finally able to place it. He hadn't smelled that dense, hormonal odor in decades, but it came back to him then in a freshet of memory—a *trio* of memories, actually: the arrival of his three youngest children in an upstairs bedroom of his house. *Home births with a midwife*, he'd told Riley the night they'd played scat. *You can't beat it with a stick. Caught them myself as they came into the world.*

He was smelling *vernix*—the greasy, cheesy film that coats a baby as it comes gushing out of the womb. He was smelling afterbirth.

The rocks glass slipped from Jack's hand. It hit the hardwood and went off like a bomb.

The sound did not jolt Riley or Jessie-Mac from their paralysis. Indeed, the three of them stared mesmerized, too afraid to move, as the eggplant's throbbing and twitching grew more frantic. Its two ends were trying to touch, thus sending its middle pulsing upward toward Jessie, beating faster and faster, as if overcome with spasms, as if something inside were trying to get out. *Stab it*, Riley told himself. *You have the knife, goddamn it—stab the fucking thing.* But it was too late.

The eggplant exploded then, dousing Jessie's pretty summer dress in a yellow-brown sludge. She screamed as it hit her like a slap across the breasts.

Chairs toppled noisily to the floor as the three of them recoiled from the table. Yet they could not look away. The hole in the eggplant was a mouth now... or something else. It resembled a flower trying to bloom, a tulip trying to open. It pulsed, again and again, faster and faster, with what could only be described as... as *contractions*.

And then, finally, the eggplant expelled something onto the table. It came sliding out on a great tide of fluid.

The three of them stared at it, frozen. At first, Riley thought it looked like a grotesquely oversized snail freed from its shell. But no. In an instant he could see he was wrong. It wasn't that at all.

It was a human fetus.

It lay there, palely purple against the dark mahogany of the dining room table. It stayed motionless for only a moment, and then its tiny hands and feet began to twitch. Riley watched as the fetus grew more animated and started to sit up, to climb to its haunches. It turned its monstrously small face towards them then, and opened its mouth, prying its lips apart through the vernix. The lusty cry it gave was a cross between the hiss of a cat and a pterodactyl's scream.

Its tiny blue eyelids began to flicker like candles, and soon the fetus was ungluing them from the vernix, too. With eyes now open, the thing on the table looked up at them, at Jessie-Mac. That gaze—so sharp and cold—was unmistakable. They all recognized it, instantly.

It had the same icy-grey eye colour, the same Cheshire stare, as Jessie-Mac herself.

It also had Danny MacPherson's dimple in the middle of its chin.

The fetus hissed at Jessie again, louder than before.

This noise was immediately joined by another, a rattling from the table. The three of them glanced down at their plates. The cobs of corn were starting to throb as well. Two rows of kernels on each were pulling apart and clicking together, again and again, like chattering teeth. Meanwhile, the carrots, still in their serving dish, began to bounce and jostle like Jiffy Pop, trying to leap over the sides.

That was enough for Jack. He screamed, rounded the table, shoved past Jessie and Riley, and threw himself out the dining room door. Jessie went hurling after him, her throat giving off a sound of nauseated disgust. Riley dropped the knife and fork, heard them clatter on the floor. He took one last look at the fetus as it glared up at him—its face was so *knowing*—and then he too abandoned the dining room, slamming its door hard behind him.

He would never open that door again.

~

They fled into Applegarth's backyard, spreading out where the lawn met the woods, the three of them together and yet somehow... *alone*. Jack was hyperventilating, his face gone fuchsia beneath its salt-and-pepper beard, his hands on his thighs, his torso heaving like he was having a heart attack. Jessie, meanwhile, just stood stalk-stiff on the grass, paralyzed by revulsion, her summer dress ruined, her head down, her black hair now hiding her face. Riley stood nearby, his mouth cupped in both hands. His eyes were trying to be everywhere at once.

The three friends stood there on the grass, not saying anything for what felt like a long time.

"Riley..." Jessie-Mac finally whispered, her head still down. She said his name as if from a state of hypnosis.

He approached her cautiously.

"Riley... Riley..." Through the curtains of her downcast hair, he could see her soft throat take a deep swallow. "That was my baby," she said. "That was my baby, wasn't it? My... *aborted child*..." She was practically vibrating with repugnance.

He put his hands on her bare shoulders in an attempt to steady her and was just about to speak when she looked up at him, her face a piazza of tears. "Everything you told us was true," she muttered. "Every last bit of it, right? We're in danger, aren't we? Kyla, me, all the girls of this area. We're in danger of... of... men possessed. Of men controlled by that *place* out there," and she nodded toward the woods. In that moment, Jessie no longer looked like a crackerjack student journalist, a sharp and clever twenty-year-old trying to carve out her place in the world. She looked like a kid. A terrified kid.

"Listen to me," Riley said, panning his face toward hers. He was vaguely aware that Jack was drifting over to them. "Hey, hey, listen to me. I don't know what that... that *thing* out of the eggplant was, okay, but it was *not* your baby. Jessie, look at me. Look at me. It wasn't. You *know* that. The house is *messing* with you. Messing with you because you're trying to get me off this land. Because you're trying to convince me to lea—"

He stopped himself, but it was too late. His words caused the key to finally slide into the lock inside Jessie's mind, the puzzle piece to slip into place. Suddenly, she wasn't a kid anymore. In one instant, she became a furious young woman, driven to a place beyond anger, and teeming with a sense of purpose.

"*Danny* tried to get you off this land," she said. "*He* tried to convince you to leave. Did the house mess with him? Did that *thing* out there mess with my ex?"

Riley kept his hands on her soft shoulders, but he pitched his gaze away.

"Riley, did that thing out there *mess with my friend?*"

"*Stung*," Jack said, startling them both. They looked over to see that his face was no longer pink, but a ghastly pale. "He was stung to death. I didn't tell you but... but I ran into the coroner yesterday at the Tims in Montague. He gave me... gave me the inside scoop. On Danny's autopsy. The kid didn't drown. There was no water in his lungs. The coroner said it looked like... like he'd been *stung* to death, by jellyfish. But that's not possible. It would take dozens of them, or hundreds, stinging him all at once. I didn't think that was... that was possible yesterday. But now...?"

Jessie turned back to Riley, her expression full of rage and accusation.

"I can kill the taproot," he said before she could speak. "Jessie, I know I can. I've *been* there. I can do what needs to be done."

"Then *why haven't you?*" she wept.

He paused, made like he was about to say something else, but then looked away again. A deep, crimson shame collared his throat and burned up behind his ears.

And it was like she *knew*. Like she and Jack both did. Not the particulars. Not his possessiveness over Applegarth, not his sense of entitlement to a second chance at life. And not the night visions, the nocturnal lust that visited him in his bed. But a *sense* of these things. A sense of exactly what power this place held over him.

She flapped away from Riley then, prying free of his gentle grasp and taking a full step backwards.

"Jessie, c'mon..."

But she turned then and began walking up the rear lawn toward the driveway and where her minivan was parked. Riley called to her but she did not stop. She opened the minivan, climbed in, slammed the door, and gunned the engine. A moment later, she yanked the gear shift into reverse, and the vehicle sank down Riley's driveway and onto the Eight Mile Road below.

He turned to Jack then. Turned to him for a sense of solace, of camaraderie and brotherhood. But the old newsman was just shaking his head and rubbing the back of his neck. "I'm out," he told Riley. "I'm done. I'm out. I'm sorry, Riley. You've been a good friend, but that's it. I'm done. I'm out. I'm *out*."

And then he too headed up the back lawn to the driveway, to his waiting Civic. Riley watched him go. In that moment, he realized that Jack had completely forgotten about the diaries. Or, perhaps more accurately, he no longer had any desire to read them.

Part IV: Burn It Down

Chapter 30

It was now the apotheosis of summer, a day so bright that the July sun cast wild, mesmerizing pictograms behind his eyelids whenever Riley closed them. He had them closed now as he sat parked and idling in Applegarth's driveway, the Lumina's windows down, the stereo up, the rubber steering wheel beneath his hands practically scalding in the heat. From the car speakers, Bruce Springsteen sang "Prove It All Night," a jaunty, jouncing tune that would normally flood Riley with adrenalin, with a desire to move his body, to get shit done. When in doubt, he was forever telling himself, always go back to Bruce. Bruce was True North. Bruce saw who you really were. Bruce reminded you of what you knew but kept forgetting.

Yet, in that moment Riley was not flooded with adrenalin or spurred to action. His eyes were closed, his head bowed, his hands cupping the top of the wheel in a limp clasp. He was so exhausted, so soaked in traumatic memory, as to be on the cusp of weeping.

His errand that Saturday morning into Cardigan had been a simple one, yet it still took a lot out of him. He had driven to the Irving gas station at the crossroads there, greeted by its ads for barbecue propane and bags of ice, by its welcoming three flags—the Canadian one, the four-treed PEI provincial flag, and the Stars and Stripes, for the tourists—flapping in the hot breeze atop tall flagpoles on a concrete island. As Riley went about acquiring his purchase, he cast his gaze out over the parking lot, now animated by the motifs of summer. Three scrape-kneed kids with skateboards were sprawled on the grass near the concrete island and eating Freezies. A convertible with four girls inside had pulled in to fuel up. The girls looked even younger than Jessie-Mac and were all impossibly beautiful in their bare-shouldered summer tops and floppy hats—probably rich kids from Charlottetown, Riley thought, on their way to a beach day at Basin Head or Panmure Island. Behind them at the pumps was an RV with Pennsylvania plates, the dad at the nozzle, the mom yelling at one of their kids who had gotten out—a boy in a green Ninja Turtles tee-shirt and orange board shorts, his crewcut marred by a preposterous rattail—that no, it was too early to get an ice cream from the gas station's dairy bar. Beyond the parking lot, the Cardigan River glittered majestically. If this was the apotheosis of summer, then that parking lot was the apotheosis of normalcy, a bland snapshot of life on PEI, utterly ignorant of the sight, the incomprehensible horror, that had unfolded in Riley Fuller's dining room twelve hours earlier. The very thought of these strangers being unaware of what he had seen with his own eyes left Riley utterly enervated.

He opened those eyes now, reached up and turned the ignition off, stopping Clarence Clemons just as he began his sax solo. From the Lumina's ashtray, Riley plucked a cigarette with one drag left, took that drag, then crushed the smoldering butt out on the tray's metallic lip. Then he got out of the car, slammed the door behind him, and went to the trunk to fish out his purchase.

All across the Island on this July morning, people would be lugging out various tools to their gardens to help with the tending—rakes and spades, hoses and sprinklers, bags of fertilizer and mulch where needed, and, perhaps most notably, watering cans. For Riley, no other garden implement quite said 'summer' the way a watering can did—the sloshing weight of it, how that heft would lighten in your hand as you sent out blooms of water across your plants, the way the can pared so nicely with a wide-brimmed hat to protect your head from the hot, lazy sun.

Today, he carried a very different kind of can to his garden. It too had a sloshing weight.

He stood at the edge of those kidney-shaped patches and panned his gaze over what was growing there. The tall corn stalks held grotesquely huge ears of corn, their dense, sinewy skins almost neon green in this light. The bulbs of onion and garlic growing in the soil looked like giant eyeballs yanked out by their nerve stems.

The leaves of his beets, swaying in the hot breeze, struck him like the tendrils of jellyfish on the hunt for something to sting. And the eggplants in the corner looked more horrific than ever—fat, sluglike things, ready to crawl through the rows toward him and spew up something putrid from their smooth, black bodies. How did Riley fail to see these monstrosities for what they were? How could he have served his friends food that grew out of this toxic soil, this malevolent, blood-red dirt?

He began to douse the crops. The smell that came out of the yellow nozzle was oily, synthetic, acrid. With each greasy splash, the fruit and vegetables, their vines and leaves, all seemed to flinch away, as if terrified by this unwelcome presence in their patch.

When he finished, Riley set the can—still about a third full—onto the grass, then lit a fresh du Maurier. He took a long, single drag as he stole a final look at these ghastly, alien yields. Then he flicked his cigarette into the centre of the first patch. The flame that burst from its glowing tip looked almost like a halo at first, a ring of destruction, but soon transmogrified into great gulps of fire that climbed and spread and consumed everything in their path. Leaves curdled out of existence, vines and roots crackled and spat, whole chunks of vegetable and fruit ruptured under the flames. Riley moved to the second patch, lit another du Maurier, and did the same.

Soon the sky welcomed two billowing columns of greyblack smoke, the air growing rich with yet another scent of summer in the country, the woodsy, peppery smell of a controlled burn. Riley stood there watching it for a long time, how the dancing flames moved almost in syncopation, like a flock of orange starlings fluttering and swaying across his garden. He stared deep into that fire and could see shapes emerge out of what was destroyed. Strange icons danced in front of his eyes and formed into what looked almost like goblin faces, gibbering mouths that screamed at him from the flames, pleading to stop this annihilation and put them out. It was hypnotic, how the crops changed into something even more sinister as they charred down toward nothingness.

Riley lit another cigarette and smoked it, then another, and then another, puffing away as his garden crackled and popped, chucking each butt in as he finished. He stayed there until both patches were reduced to two smoldering scars on the land. The black chunks of char looked almost speckled in snow by the white ash that coated them.

When he was sure the fire had burned down completely and posed no threat to the stretch of woods rimming his property, Riley picked up the jerrycan off the grass and sauntered back toward Applegarth, that cursed and haunted home.

~

He sat at the kitchen table for what felt like hours, his long legs stretched listlessly out in front of him, his clothes reeking of smoke, and stared trance-like at his closed dining room door. He had not gone back in that room since last night, and would not go back in there, not ever. *Let the food we left behind spoil and then rot away*, he thought. *The steaks and the corn, the carrots and the husked-out eggplant can break down into clots of mold for all I care. I will never set foot in that room again.*

He knew why. He could *hear* why. That... that *thing*, disgorged from the eggplant, was still in there. Riley could hear it mewing behind the door, crying out to him with its little mouth. *You and Jane wanted a baby*, those tiny wails seemed to say. *Now you have one.* From his place in the kitchen chair, he listened to the small sound of the thing slapping down onto the hardwood after climbing off the dining room table. He heard it skitter like an insect toward him, its miniature limbs tapping along the floorboards until it reached the closed dining room door. The thing whimpered again and began scratching at the door like a cat wanting to be let out.

You're not real, Riley wanted to think. *You're not fucking REAL.* But he knew that wasn't true. The fetus was as real as whatever was up in Applegarth's attic, lurching and moaning behind its walls, sounds that had kept him awake all last night. He still had not set foot up there, even after *three months* in the house.

Between the attic with its noises, the unfinished, dungeon-like basement, and, now, the sealed dining room, the house felt much smaller, more claustrophobic, than Riley ever thought possible.

He had to get off PEI. It was as simple as that. Riley knew that the Wood Islands ferry to Nova Scotia was only thirty minutes away. If he left now, and caught a ferry in good time, and drove over to New Brunswick without stopping, he could be on Sammy's doorstep in Fredericton well before dark. He could just show up at his best friend's house and ask to be taken in. Sams would do it, too, no questions asked. He'd receive Riley into his home with a smile and an arm around his shoulders, saying, *Of course you're welcome here. What took you so long, asshole?*

Do it. Just fucking do it.

Riley got up from the kitchen table. He turned his back on the closed dining room door. He didn't even bother to go upstairs and a pack a bag, not even his toothbrush or a change of clothes. He just stepped into his sneakers in the foyer closet, grabbed the Lumina's keys, and went out to the driveway. He didn't even lock Applegarth's doors behind him before climbing into his car and taking off.

~

Except.

Except thirty minutes were long enough to have a good, solid think about what he was about to do.

As he drove over to Cardigan, down through Montague, and then south along the creepy, wooded stretch of Route 315 that led all the way to Wood Islands, something came over Riley. He thought that he should give PEI one last viewing before he left it behind forever. Maybe instead of catching the ferry at Wood Islands, he should drive all the way toward the western end of the province and then catch the ferry at Borden, which would take him directly to New Brunswick. From there, he'd be less than three hours to Fredericton and Sammy's doorstep.

And so, when he reached the fork in the road at the end of Route 315, he veered right, onto the westbound highway toward

Charlottetown, rather than left toward the ferry terminal. From there, the drive to Borden took nearly ninety minutes, more than enough time for Riley to stew in certain thoughts, certain feelings. He felt them coming on like a wave of nausea. He cranked up Bruce from car's tape deck, but it did no good. A growing unease, all of his old anxieties, came washing over him again. He turned the stereo off and drove in silence for a while. It was like the farther he got from Applegarth, the more he reverted back to his old mindsets, the person he used to be. He hated that person. He hated who he had been. And now, was he seriously driving back in the direction of Moncton, of that life? Was he seriously turning his back on the calm and settled mind that Applegarth offered him? The thought of doing that, of putting miles of distance between himself and his property, what *belonged to him*, made him physically unwell.

By the time he passed the turnoff to Victoria-by-the-Sea, Riley was making excuses inside his head for what he was about to do. The Lumina needed fuel, and Riley, having missed lunch (and breakfast, and supper the night before) did too. Never mind that he could have stopped for gas in Borden. Never mind that he could have gotten a bite to eat in the boat's cafeteria during the forty-five minute crossing. He was already making up his mind.

He soon arrived at another fork in the highway—the left side veering south toward the Borden ferry terminal, the right swinging north up to the tiny city of Summerside. Riley veered right, as if the Lumina were drawn in that direction by a magnet. Twenty minutes later, he was gassing up at an Esso station in a spot called Read's Corner. Ten minutes after that, he was sitting in a Summerside diner and ordering a whole mess of food from the waitress who served him. Riley wasn't sure whether he'd be able to eat, or whether he'd keep down what the girl brought him if he did. He was now utterly awash in a sickening paranoia, to the point where he asked the waitress if he could move to the far booth, so he could sit with his back to the wall. He had done this sort of thing many times in the wake of the Moncton shooting, tried to do it in the cafeteria of the ferry on the way over to

PEI back in April. The waitress was happy to oblige him, as there was only one other party in the diner at that hour of the afternoon. Riley glanced over at them after he shuffled into the booth. It was a couple, the guy clearly a middle-aged farmer, dressed in a plaid work shirt and chewed-up John Deere cap, sitting across from his jowly, potato-titted wife at a table near the windows. They kept glancing over at Riley after he settled into the booth, kept staring at him, perhaps nervous about the cold glare in his eyes, by the sour, seething expression on his face. *What the fuck are you looking at?* he wanted to call over to them. *Why don't you mind your own goddamn business?*

His huge order eventually came, but Riley could only pick away at it, his appetite shot.

He wanted a drink, but the diner wasn't licensed.

He wanted the Glock, but it sat in its kitchen drawer back at Applegarth.

He smoked five du Mauriers in a row and then called for the cheque.

~

Outside, in the sun-soaked parking lot, he stood leaning against his car, smoking even more, trying to calm the mind that was now a torrent inside his head. *This* was who he really was—a shattered man, deeply ashamed of himself, deeply afraid that people who looked at him could see straight through his sullen guises and into the dark core of his true self. That feeling, he knew, would only get worse if he returned to the mainland. He might not make it all the way to Sammy's. He might lose what grip he had left while on the road, might steer the Lumina suddenly into oncoming traffic before the divided highway began, might swerve into a huge, fast eighteen wheeler coming up the other way, and put an end to this once and for all.

Despite everything, he couldn't bear the thought of doing that.

He chucked away his latest cigarette and got in the car. He peeled out of the diner's parking lot and headed back toward

Read's Corner. There, he did not turn south, toward Borden. He headed in the opposite direction, toward the northern shore. He went up past Kensington and past Stanley Bridge, went through Cavendish and North Rustico, around to Oyster Bed Bridge and zigzagging to Tracadie, and then on to Saint Peters Bay before heading south back down to Glenning. He had basically done a lap around Prince Edward Island.

He pulled up Applegarth's long driveway and parked near the main door. But as Riley turned off the engine and let his hands fall to his thighs, he realized that this place, this house that had renovated itself into a home for him, frightened him just as much as the mainland did now. He couldn't bear to go inside. He couldn't face the man he would become within those walls. *I am nowhere*, he thought. *I am in some in-between place, trapped inside a version of myself that does not exist. I am not this man, nor that man. I am neither. I am no one.*

He sat like that for a long time, refusing to even get out of his car.

~

Eventually it got dark. Through the Lumina's open driver window, Riley listened as the woods all around his house grew cacophonous with the sounds of the night—the drone of crickets, the buzz of mosquitoes, the squeal of cicadas. Several times, he reached for the ignition and tried to turn it, to bring the car to life again and reverse it back out of this driveway. But each time, his hand returned limply to his lap.

It was his bladder, rather than his conscience, that ultimately got the better of him. He scrambled up out of the car and, instead of going into the house, wandered over to his now blackened garden patches. Riley stood at the edge of the first one, unzipped his jeans, and took himself out. His piss was like a drill, grinding into the scorched earth with surprising force before bouncing in a mist off the stone sundial, now reduced to a charred hunk on the ground. As he urinated, Riley stared into the vast, dense forest in front of him. The forest stared back, seemed to shift and rustle with the presence of living things. Foxes and squirrels, raccoons and crows, all the animals of the earth, gathered here to stand on guard, to protect the thing in the woods, the doorway to the Great Force Beyond, and the man who acted as its key.

Riley zipped himself back up. He crossed the driveway and approached Applegarth, but then paused. He looked up, *all* the way up, to the house's third storey, to the attic that he had yet to set foot inside. It had a small port window sitting above even the highest of the high red gables.

And there, through that port window, he watched the same dark light he'd seen in the basement of Lowfield's church begin to rise and radiate out of the glass. The sight of it took his breath away, turned his limbs to ice.

And then a face appeared in that window. It seemed to be the face of a young girl, her blond hair smeared across her brow in sweaty clumps, her cheeks pallid, her eyes glowing a deep yellow through the dark. That face pressed itself ghoulishly against the glass at Riley.

He raced back to the Lumina and climbed inside. His heart was pounding as he reached for the ignition and turned the key. *Am I too late to catch tonight's last ferry to Nova Scotia?* he thought as he slammed the vehicle into reverse. *If I am, then fuck it. I'll just sleep in my car in the terminal parking lot and catch the first boat in the morning.*

He tore backwards down the driveway, squealing his tires as he straightened up out on the Eight Mile Road, and made a beeline for the same route he had taken earlier in the day before he'd changed his mind.

Yet, Riley had driven less than a hundred yards when he saw something appear in the swell of his headlights. It came shambling up the shoulder on the other side of the road toward him. He slammed on his breaks and pulled over. At first, he thought it was another ghost, another apparition emerging out of these ancient, anguished woods.

But then he saw that it was a person, a little old lady, dressed in nothing but a minty blue nightgown and slippers.

She was hunched a little as she shuffled her way through the now pitch-black night toward Applegarth, the only destination this far up the road.

Riley put the car in park but left the engine running, the lights on. He got out, looked back down the dark, tree-lined corridor behind him, and then crossed. He soon stood in front of the woman as she ambled up the weedy, red-clay shoulder. She halted at the sight of him and lifted her eyes to his face. Those eyes, he could see, were seething in their sockets, poached in a look of determination. When she saw him, the old woman slipped her right hand behind her back, like a child trying to hide something from its parent.

In that moment, Riley somehow knew that this was Mrs. Keating of Cardigan. Mrs. Keating—the eighty-something-old lady who refused to send her son-in-law up here to share some topsoil with Riley. The little old lady who had called in the story idea to the *Eastern Pioneer* for a retrospective about all the terrible things that had happened to the women of this community back in 1930. *Good God*, Riley thought, *if that's true, she's walked up here from Cardigan. Jesus. That's, like, four miles.*

He was about to speak, but then her watery blue eyes swelled as she recognized him, probably from the picture that appeared in Jessie's profile of him back in May.

"Mrs.... Keating?" Riley asked tentatively.

"*Sisterfucker!*" she belched at him. "Daughter-raping monster! Fuck you. *FUCK YOU!*"

In those few scant moments before things turned completely horrific, Riley allowed an almost comical thought to pass through his brain. *I don't have a sister* or *a daughter, you old bag. Maybe that's my problem.*

"Mrs. Keating, please..."

"No one listens to *'old ladies'!*" she spat, as if talking to herself. "Nobody wants to hear our stories. Nobody wants to hear the truth! They just want to sweep it all under the rug. *That's* what they's want. Don't talk about the past. Don't dreg up the dark stuff. But the dark stuff has started up again. Oh, by Jesus it has. Ever since you, *Fuller man*, moved into that there," and she raised her left hand and flapped a finger in the direction of Applegarth, "that there *house!*"

"Listen, you need to calm down," he told her. "Why don't you get in my car and I'll drive you home. We can talk about things on the w—"

But her face crumbled into anguish then, her mouth a black, jabbering hole at the bottom of her face. "Tells me to calm down, does he? Tells me! When girls are getting' disgraced by their own kin? Well *fuck you, Fuller man! Fuck you straight to hell!*" And at this, Mrs. Keating raised her right hand, revealing what Riley had suspected she'd been hiding there all along. It was a huge kitchen knife, no doubt taken from her knife block at home. She rushed at him with it, her slippers flapping against her heels as she did.

Riley moved lightly into a fighter's stance and caught her right wrist with his left hand just as the knife was coming down, bracing it a few inches above his shoulder. In one instant, he could tell Mrs. Keating was moving to knee him in the groin, and so he placed his left hand between her collarbones and gave her a gentle push. The idea was to get her to back up a step or two so he could pry the knife out of her hand, but her little frame was so light that she pinwheeled backwards under the force of his shove and fell onto her scrawny duff on the road's edge. She looked up at him from the dirt with an expression of hate, and then started to scramble back to her feet.

But Riley was no longer looking at her. He was looking beyond her, at the dense, ancient woods lining the side of the road. The shadows were out of range of his car's headlights, and yet they started to glow just the same. Those shadows started to glow like a galaxy of stars.

He saw them before Mrs. Keating did. They moved together, as one, dashing out of the thickets and slinking like snakes into the ditch. The old lady must have caught something in Riley's eyes, because she turned then in her nightgown to face the ditch just as the creatures came streaming up out of it and towards her. Foxes. Squirrels. Raccoons. Dozens of them, pouring out of the forest in a great gush of fur and clicking claws. In another instant, they swarmed around Mrs. Keating's feet. She screamed, a wild and panicked aria that cut through the empty night. Raising her knife, she went to slash one of the creatures with its blade, but Riley watched as a red-tailed fox leaped into the air and sank its jaws into her wrist, dragging her hand down toward the ground. The old lady screamed again as she toppled over. And then they were on her, sliding across her shoulders and up to her neck, like a mink shawl coming to life.

Riley could not move, could not speak. He just watched as the animals of the forest overwhelmed this woman, pouring over her like a swarm of bees, clawing and biting and snapping at her. It happened so fast. There was a horrible tearing sound, like gristle being wrenched off of bone, and then a great geyser of blood spurted up from the swarm, splattering the creatures' fur. They licked and chopped at it maniacally, and then went back to their work. Riley could see only Mrs. Keating's ankles and feet now, sticking out from under the horde like the Wicked Witch of the East's out from under Dorothy's house. Those feet flailed and gyrated for a few seconds before growing still. It was over just as quickly as it began. The swarm, moving as one, dragged what was left of Mrs. Keating down into the ditch and then up into the woods. Another moment and they were gone, leaving an eerie silence in their wake.

Riley, his own eyes now blazing, his body tremulous, turned to look back down the Eight Mile Road. There, in the blaze of his car's headlights, he saw a row of more creatures blocking the way. Their eyes burned into his with their sickly glow.

No one threatens you, they said. *No one scares a Fuller off this land. We won't have it. Now go back, Fuller man. Get back in your car and go back to Applegarth, to where you belong.*

And that was what Riley did.

Chapter 31

A heavy rain fell on the morning after the animals had dragged Mrs. Keating into the wood, washing away any trace of her on the cracked and puckered pavement, on the narrow shoulder, in the ditch. What had happened to her wasn't a dream or a nightmare, as much as it felt like one to Riley. A day passed, maybe two, and there were soon reports about her disappearance on the radio. He even watched from Applegarth's library windows as an occasional squad car passed by on the Eight Mile Road. But no, his Montague-detachment colleagues were not going to find any physical evidence of Mrs. Keating up here. Not anymore.

Another day passed. Maybe two. Time seemed to be losing its integrity for Riley, its sense of dimension. Yet he still knew time passed. Knew it for two reasons.

One, that the noise coming from behind Applegarth's closed dining room door had stopped. That... that *thing* in there, birthed out of the eggplant, had ceased its caterwauling, its scratching to be let out. It sounded as if the fetus had finally crawled into a corner of the room to die.

And two, that the sounds coming from the attic, far above the dining room, had gotten worse over several nights. Much worse.

All spring and summer, Riley was able to dismiss those noises—the shuffles, the scraping and shudders that reverberated out of that space—via a hank of logic he pulled out of his mind. It was birds nesting in the rafters, he told himself. Rats scuttering behind the walls; the wind passing through a broken windowpane. He was also able to dismiss the sight he had seen on his first night in Applegarth, of his grandfather, James Fuller, dangling in his noose from the attic's pull-down steps, as nothing more than the flight of a roused imagination.

No longer. The shuffling was now clearly a series of loud lurches, a banging behind the walls. What he mistook for wind through the rafters was now, obviously, a heavy human moan. Since Mrs. Keating's death, since Riley had looked up from the driveway before he left and seen a young girl's face pressed against that port window, the noises had grown loud enough to keep him awake at night.

He finally decided to go up there.

It took him all day, whatever day this was, but Riley soon stood on the landing outside his bedroom door. He stared all around the space that had created the silhouette, the apparition of his grandfather. Then he reached up to pull down the stairs leading to the attic. At first he thought they might resist his overture by the sheer fact of their age. But then they came down with a thunderous rattle, their brass bolts and hinges squealing against the ironwood planks of those steps.

He ascended them, their stairs' frame wobbling under his weight, and when he got to the top, he pushed open the double doors there after turning their small ceramic knobs. Climbing up and onto the attic's floor, the first thing that hit him was the hot, stale air, almost sauna-like as it trapped half a summer's worth of heat up here. That warmth felt almost unnatural, as if Riley were now standing inside the body of a living being. It reminded him of what it felt like to touch *The Grimoire of Shaal*.

The second thing he noticed were the rafters, so intricately laced above his head. As he looked up, Riley expected to see another apparition of James, as this was likely the place where he did hang himself, on October 31, 1930 at the age of thirty-three. Wasn't that what every cheap horror movie and dime-store tale of the macabre had prepared him for? Wasn't he expecting to see his grandfather's bloated, purple face staring down at him with bulging eyes as the noose twisted his neck at an unholy angle?

There was nothing up there but motes of dust. They swayed through unseen currents of air and the fading sun that passed through the port windows.

Riley moved his gaze out over the rest of the attic's wide, empty expanse. It was like a barn loft up here; dirty floorboards, unloved walls, a few bits of rotting furniture scattered here and there. He swallowed, then moved over to the port window on the west side, the one facing the driveway, the one at which the young girl he *knew* he had seen up here would have been standing. He lowered his face toward the glass. Through its grimy pane he could just make out the Lumina parked in the driveway three storeys below. Then he looked around the sill and the floor where he stood. The dust was undisturbed. There was no evidence that anyone had lingered here on the night Mrs. Keating was killed.

Riley turned back to the attic, and saw the girl standing in the middle of the floor.

He retreated at the sight of her, flinching back against the window hard enough to nearly put an elbow through it. All the blood draining clean out of his body in a cold gush. Riley groaned from the bottom of his lungs. The girl, he could see, was just sort of floating there, hovering in a bladder of light, the same dark luminescence, cosmic and eternal, that he had witnessed in Lowfield. He could see that she was wearing a neck-to-ankle dress hanging off her narrow, delicate shoulders. The dress, with its yellow-green floral patterns and outmoded pleats, looked dated, almost vintage. It looked very... nineteenth century.

He recognized this person. He knew this child. It was Miriam Fuller, the niece of his grandfather's grandfather. Perhaps she didn't appear as she had actually been, but only as Riley had *conjured* her in his mind's eye, as he had imagined her while reading the other Riley Fuller's diary, and during that night, that horrifying, mortifying night vision when... when she had come to him in his bed.

Against his every instinct, he took a step closer to her. When he did, the girl rotated her face toward him, the joints of her neck cracking like old stairs as she did. That face was half rotted, split and blistered everywhere, the skin the colour of a soiled mattress. The girl's hair was matted across her brow as if with sweat. The yellowy stones of her eyes just glared at him with an inscrutable look.

He was about to speak to this apparition, to say something to acknowledge its presence, when that watery sack of light around her began to grow. Riley watched as it tripled in size, then tripled again, filling almost the entire attic with its radiance.

Riley looked up and stared. Behind Miriam, hobbling up toward them from the front of the attic, he could see another shape, another female form taking long, lumbering steps toward him. It took a moment for this specter to materialize there on the floorboards. But when it did, he recognized her, too.

Oh Jesus, he thought. *Oh Jesus fuck.*

It was... it was Marigold. It was Marigold Burque—here in Applegarth. She stood before him, dressed in her orange prison jumpsuit, its serial number stitched on a small white panel above her breast. Only, it was not Marigold as Riley had known her, the lithe, sharp-tongued twenty-four year old who had charmed him, who had stolen his heart three and a half years earlier. No. It was not *that* Marigold. This Marigold appeared to be in late middle age, her crow-black hair now a steely grey, her face broad and jowly, her belly sagging, her hips wide and square. Yet, despite her startling age and unexpected heft, Riley could see that she did not look well. In fact, she looked very, very sick. He immediately noticed that there was something wrong with her face, her throat, her hands. They were the colour of tea, a brownish-yellow tinge that appeared almost corrosive. That colour, that tinge, made her look like she was dying. She *was* dying. There was some unseen force, a rapidly spreading cancer, beginning to eat her body from the inside out. Somehow he knew that, could *tell* that just by the tint of her skin.

She too looked at him with an impenetrable expression, as if she wanted Riley to do something, do something now, even though he had no idea what. She floated there before him, the girl he had allowed himself to fall for, now a woman decaying down toward death.

"Marigold..." he whispered, stretching out his hand to her. "Marigold... please..."

But she stepped aside, away from his reach. He looked beyond her, to the very front of that wide, long attic. The sachet of light had turned into a tunnel, swirling and churning its otherworldly colours, a luminosity from another dimension, the

Great Force Beyond. Riley sensed that power now, that energy. He believed that, if he went into this tunnel of light, he could know things he had no business knowing, and travel to places beyond this present moment—back to the past, to the history of this house, but also... also to the future. Yes, that was possible as well.

A shape appeared then at the very end of the tunnel, moving out of its long, swirling wall to stand before Riley's eyes.

He cringed from it for a moment, from the sudden arrival of this third phantom in the attic. But then he settled his gaze upon it. From this distance, there at the mouth of the tunnel, he couldn't make out much detail of this new apparition. It seemed very far away, its face obscured in shadow, its body flickering in and out of the tunnel's swirls.

And yet, even down that long corridor of time, he could tell certain things.

This new presence was also female. Somehow he knew that. Somehow he could tell that it was a young woman—maybe not as young as Jessie-Mac, but, unlike the vision of Marigold that appeared here, still very much in the prime of her life. Despite the distance and lack of detail, he could tell this young woman had a certain attractiveness, a certain confidence. There was an assuredness to her posture, an almost cocky jut to her hip.

But he could also see something else. He could see that she had one hand on her stomach, resting there almost protectively. And then she turned to stand in profile to him. And when she did, Riley glimpsed the slightest, gentlest bump at her tummy. A smooth little mound just above her hips.

This apparition, it seemed, was pregnant.

Riley took one step forward in that tunnel, a step toward the future. And then another.

But as he did, the house gave a sudden, violent judder. It wasn't just the structure settling onto itself. It was like every plank and board was twisting at once, a long, conscious, faltering heave, as if Applegarth was doing everything it could to stop Riley from approaching that presence, that impregnated phantom at the other end of the glowing corridor.

And then, as if in response to this abrupt rebellion, the vision vanished. The corridor of light, and the being at the end of it, was gone. So too were Miriam and Marigold. Before Riley knew it, the attic was just an attic again—dusty floorboards, unloved walls, sticks of old furniture scattered hither and yon.

Riley looked around. Looked at the emptiness, and felt more alone than ever.

His knees gave out beneath him. And before he could stop himself, he was tumbling down into a dead faint.

Chapter 32

More time passed. A day. Maybe two.

Riley managed to bathe, to dress in fresh clothes. He eventually drove to the Sobeys in Montague for groceries, though he would not make eye contact with his neighbours as he meandered the aisles and acquired his items. Everyone appeared to be on edge, thanks to the rape-murder of Stacey St. Clair of Georgetown, and, now, the disappearance of Gladys Keating of Cardigan. His first instinct was one of self-preservation. Riley wondered whether he was in actual danger, here among these people. He wondered whether he'd be the victim of mob justice, if the community was starting to connect the dots between his presence in eastern PEI and all these horrible things that had begun happening. His second instinct, though, was of profound concern for this community. Riley glanced at these shoppers and checkout girls as they glanced at the floor. Were other horrible things happening, he wondered, behind the closed doors of their homes? Things you could never discuss in the supermarket aisle with your neighbours, your friends, people you'd known all your life? Were fathers looking at their daughters differently? Were brothers eyeing up their sisters, sons their moms, overcome with a lust borne out of that otherworldly radiation seeping from the old woods out beyond Glenning?

The thought made him sick.

Yet, despite his revulsion, Riley felt no desire to make another try at Wood Islands, either on his way into Montague or on the way back out. His grocery run took less than an hour, and he soon found himself back inside Applegarth, ensconced within its long, ornate hallways and opulent chambers. The house was like a mother's womb that welcomed him back. It kept all that literal, visceral *sickliness* he felt each time he thought of leaving at bay.

How does one escape Prince Edward Island? he found himself asking once he'd eaten his first proper meal in days and then returned to the library upstairs. *How does one break free from the force that holds me here?*

That question brought him back to the Fuller family tree that his uncle Barrie had sent him. He thought of all those repeated names passing through his lineage like a defective gene— *James... Robert... Riley...* or some combination thereof. He knew from the tree that his grandfather's grandfather, that *other* Riley Fuller, had managed to escape PEI. He had fled the horror of Lowfield in 1863 and returned to Halifax, and lived there for decades afterward, until his death in 1906. He'd gotten married and had a son. He had lived a whole other life after PEI. How did he do that? How did this house, this land, not lure him back?

He was ready now, after nearly two weeks of avoiding it, to return to his grandfather's grandfather's diary. He had only a handful of pages left to go in the final volume, and Riley now hoped that those pages may explain how the other Riley Fuller managed to flee this place and never come back.

He went to his reading chair and picked up the journal, tented open at an entry in early August 1863, and sat down with it to read. Here, his grandfather's grandfather had travelled to Charlottetown to secure financing from the Bank of Prince Edward Island in order to buy his brother out of their business. He was approved, and it had looked as though the transaction would go through without conflict. But matters had grown complicated when Robert discovered that it was Riley who had broken into the Lowfield church earlier that summer. After learning of his brother's visit to the taproot, Robert became convinced that it was Riley, not he, who must lead Lowfield's congregation in order to open the portal to the Great Force Beyond. Naturally, Riley had refused. Yet Robert had insisted, saying that if his brother wouldn't step up to lead, the cult would force Robert to rape little Miriam, his own daughter.

At this threat, Riley had decided to join a growing rebellion in Glenning against what was happening in Lowfield. The community was clearly up in arms. Yet, a curious thing had happened during a meeting in early September when talk turned to actual violence. The farmers in charge of this uprising had asked their wives and daughters to leave the room. At first, these women refused. They had *wanted* to join the fight against Elder Fuller's cult—they had the most to lose, after all, if the *Satanist in Lowfield*, as the journal put it, was not stopped. Riley Fuller himself had come to believe that the women *must* join the fight, that the rebellion's success depended on it. The men, after all, may not have been able to resist the incestuous, sexualized aura that now seemed to permeate that whole cursed village. Yet the rebellion's leaders had been adamant: matters of ultimatum and violence were no place for women, they had said, and, much to Riley's despair, these wives and daughters were denied a place in the insurrection against Elder Fuller, and had been shuffled to the sidelines.

And now Riley turned the page and came upon the final entry in the final volume of the diary, dated 13 September 1863—which was the first entry he had encountered after discovering these journals back in April. He looked down at the manic block of text, so cryptic the first time he had laid eyes on it, but decidedly less so now. The rebels had gathered at Applegarth. They had brought some weapons with them, but, they soon realized they didn't have enough. During the lull when they raced home to collect more, Riley had stolen away to Applegarth's library to jot down this last entry in haste. He had known a great supernatural threat awaited them in Lowfield, but was resolved to face it. The wives and daughters had come as well, once again pleading to take part, but once again, the men in charge had refused them. Riley was nearly certain that the rebellion would fail as a result of this decision, but they had to push forward with it nonetheless. And here, the diary had ended abruptly as he was summoned back outside Applegarth to join the fray.

Riley closed the slim volume and stared at its leather cover. So many questions remained. What happened on that day when the weapon-wielding mob stormed into Lowfield? The confrontation likely turned violent—the giant, ancient bloodstain on the church's altar was evidence of that. And some supernatural cataclysm must have occurred, causing the entire populace of Lowfield, along with Robert Fuller and his daughter Miriam, to vanish into thin air—or, perhaps more accurately, into the Great Force Beyond. But the other Riley Fuller somehow escaped with his life, managed to flee back to Halifax as planned, and lived out his remaining decades there. Following Robert's death, Riley Fuller would have gained full ownership over Applegarth, but he did not sell it. He kept the house in his bloodline, and it got passed down to his son, Clayton Riley, and then *his* son, Robert "James," and then *his* son, Thomas Riley, and then to Riley himself. Passed as if coded into their very DNA.

He got up from the chair, moved into the library's turret, and set the diary back onto the bookcase with the other two volumes. They stood reunited in their neat row, an ominous chronicle of the past, as if waiting for their next reader.

Chapter 33

July 25, 1995
Dear Sammy,
Sorry it's been more than a month since my last email. No, I'm not avoiding you, haha. This old house continues to... how do I put it? Eat up my life, I guess—to the point where I still don't feel comfortable hosting company here, and may never. I realize summer is passing fast and that you and Joan are anxious to visit before the school year starts. But I don't think that's a good idea. Sorry I can't be more specific.

But yes, I will admit, my reluctance has something to do with the stuff you've been seeing on the news recently. Thanks for asking about it. The murder of that girl in Georgetown and the missing old lady in Cardigan have got this entire community on edge. There are more cops around than usual—that is to say, *any*—and there is a tension in the air you can practically taste. As strange as it sounds, Sams, I blame myself for what's going on. I think I'm a bad omen on this place. Some things have come to light over this spring and summer about my family's history here. I can't go into details, but it is all very... *complicated*, to the point where I think I shouldn't have moved here at all, no matter how much it feels like home.

To be honest, Sam, I am still, after all these months, completely adrift. You may be surprised to know that I've actually tried to get off PEI a couple of times over the last week or so, but this Island *literally* won't let me leave. I'm not sure where I'd go if it did. Not back to Moncton, definitely, but not anywhere else, either. I feel utterly gutted these days—gutted like an old house, stripped bare of everything that had once given it meaning.

To answer your other question, I don't know *what* I'm going to do—from a practical standpoint, that is. My ODS benefits and my savings are both going to run out soon. I can't imagine ever returning to active duty, but I can't imagine doing anything else, either. Most days I feel like I shouldn't be here, or anywhere, at all.

I shouldn't exist.

Before I sign off, Sams, I need you to know something. Your friendship has meant the world to me. You stood at my side through all the shit with Marigold and the shooting, and with what happened afterwards, with Jane. You have been the last rat to flee the sinking ship that is Riley Fuller, and I am grateful for that. I love you. I know it's weird when men say that to each other, but it's true. I fucking love you to death.

I'm sorry, Sam, for the pain I've caused so many people, and continue to cause. I wish things had worked out differently.

Yours,
Riley

Chapter 34

Not ten minutes after Riley hit SEND on that email and then logged off the dial-up modem, the phone at Applegarth began to ring. Its shrill, robotic wail sounded almost alien to Riley now; it had been a while since anyone had called.

As he moved into the living room to answer the phone, Riley just assumed it was Sammy calling from Fredericton after reading his email. That message had been the closest thing Riley had written to a suicide note, and he braced himself now to confront what would surely be a tidal wave of concern and admonishment from his best friend.

"Hello."

"Riley? Riley, it's Jack Mackenzie. At the *Pioneer*."

"Jack." Riley found himself awash in relief, in delight even, to hear that warm Scottish accent on the line. He hadn't seen or spoken to Jack since the dinner party. After what had happened, he figured he never would. Riley tried to imagine the old newsman at his typewriter, attempting to articulate what he had seen unfold in Riley's dining room for a story in his paper. Of course, he wouldn't. He *couldn't*. That horror seemed to shatter Jack's entire world view, and certainly how he saw the community he'd be reporting on for nearly thirty-five years. *I'm out*, he had told Riley. *I'm done. I'm out.* And Riley wondered whether *anything* of substance would appear now in the *Eastern Pioneer*—about what had been happening this summer, or anything else. He wondered whether Jack was done with it all. "I'm so glad you called," he said to him. "I've been meaning to reach out to you. I... I don't know what to say, frankly... about what happened here the other night, but—"

"She's gone missing," Jack said. His Highland brogue warbled as panic passed through it like voltage.

Riley swallowed. "Mrs. Keating?" he asked. "Yeah, I saw the news report. Jack, I'm not sure how to begin. A month ago, you probably wouldn't have believed me, but after what happened in my dining roo—"

"No, not her," Jack said. "I'm not talking about Gladys Keating. But Christ, Riley, if you *know* something you should go to the RCMP. I mean, you *are* the RCMP. What the fuck is the matter with you?" He barely took a pause. "No, I'm talking about Jessie-Mac. Jessie-Mac has gone missing, too."

And everything just fell out of the bottom of Riley then, as if his very life force splashed like water onto the floor below him. He stood there, just a husk of a man now, the cordless phone limp against his face.

"What?" he said.

"It's production night and she's not shown up for work. She'd *never* miss production night. Not for anything."

Riley's mouth went dry. "Maybe, maybe she got a flat tire?"

"For eight hours? Riley, I called her place twenty minutes ago, and her mother said Jessie left the house *late this morning*. She said she went to run… to run an 'errand,' but never came home. She was supposed to pick up her sister from soccer practice at two o'clock before coming to work, but she didn't show up for that, either. Which she'd also never do." Jack's voice was picking up pace as he spoke. No doubt various horrible scenarios were running through his mind. "Riley, she's missing. She's *fucking missing*."

"Okay, look. We can call the cops if you want, but they usually need twenty-four hours to pass before—"

"I didn't tell you the other thing," Jack cut him off.

Riley closed his eyes. "What other thing?"

"Jessie came into work yesterday right upset. And I mean *fuming*. She'd had a huge fight with her father that morning. Which she'd never, *ever* do. She and her dad are like this."

Riley's head dropped, his brow now pressed against the back of his free hand. "What… What did they fight about?"

"*What do you think?* What do you think she *caught him doing* the night before?"

Riley said nothing. He could find no words.

"Now you listen to me," Jack went on. "She's been threatening to go find that... that *place* out in the woods since your dinner party. She's been mustering up her courage to see exactly what is out there. You follow me? Then, two nights ago, she catches her father leering at her sis` as he sends her off to bed. Catches him touching his daughter in a way no father ever should. So what do you *think* she's done, Riley?"

Riley didn't have to reply. He knew. He could remember the look of determination on Jessie's face, clear as glass, during the dinner party. He could remember what she had said to him before that... that *thing* had come squelching out of the eggplant. *What if I get raped?... What if it happened to my sister, Kyla?*

"I'm going to find her," Riley said. "Jack, do you want to come with me? I can pick you up."

"No, sir. I've got a newspaper to put out."

"Jack, c'mon. Your paper can wait." Then he paused. Lingered on the question that had been on his mind this whole conversation. "Are you, are you planning to write about all this?" he asked. "About what you saw in my house, and everything else that's been happening this summer?"

"Are you *insane?*" Jack said. Then he confirmed Riley's worst suspicion. "I have a good mind to shut this whole enterprise down. I mean, how can I write about this community now, after seeing what I've seen, and knowing what I know? No. No, Riley. Nothing about this summer is *ever* going in the pages of the *Pioneer*. I just want to write about local politics and the construction of the bridge and be done with it. I just want to bury myself in work tonight."

"Jack, please don't. Please come with me. This is Jessie-Mac we're talking about."

The silence on the line felt eternal. "No," Jack said finally. "No, I am *not* going out there. Go ahead and call me a coward if you want. I love that girl like one of my own kids, but I am *not* going out there. Not after what I saw in your dining room. I am scared out of my fucking mind."

"Jack..."

"You're the cop, Riley. *You* fucking fix this. You brought this thing here—"

"I did not. It was here long before I was."

"Yeah, well, you woke it up. You woke it up just by coming to the Island, didn't you?"

If any Fuller from your line comes near that place, Riley remembered Marsten saying to him, *I figure it all starts up again.*

"I'll find her," Riley said.

"You better. And you call me when you do. Do you hear? And I mean the *instant.*"

"I will," Riley replied, not realizing until later that this was a lie.

~

He reckoned she didn't try to enter Lowfield via the woods out back of Applegarth's property, otherwise he would have seen her, would've spotted her parents' minivan parked out where his driveway met the Eight Mile Road. If she had planned to go in that way, maybe she would have knocked on his door first, to demand that Riley come with her. But she hadn't. So instead, Riley drove around, to the southern side of that deep forested area, to the deserted, unpaved stretch of Route 319 that they had discussed at the dinner party.

He took the Glock with him, fetching it out of its drawer in the kitchen and putting it in the Lumina's glovebox.

Now, as he approached his turnoff just north of Cardigan, his mind began to flicker through what was most likely starting to happen. It had been eight or nine hours since Jessie-Mac had left the house, five or six hours since she had failed to pick up Kyla, and half an hour since Jack had called her house and told her parents that she hadn't shown up for work. Her parents would be starting to panic—especially after everything that had been going on in this community, the disappearance of Mrs. Keating and the rape-murder of Stacey St. Clair in Georgetown—and had probably made their first call to the police.

Or maybe everything was fine. Maybe Jessie had had a real 'errand' to do earlier and ran into one of her friends while doing it, maybe that Tara girl, the military chick with the pixie cut, and maybe they got to talking about this or that, maybe got engrossed in a conversation and just lost track of time. Or maybe Jessie had received an email that morning from a journalism-school chum in Halifax who had gotten herself into some pickle or other, and Jessie's 'errand' was to drive all the way there on the down low and help her out. Neither of these scenarios, Riley knew, was likely. Jessie-Mac may only be twenty, but she took her job and her responsibilities to Kyla seriously, and wouldn't do either of those things.

And besides, would she want to leave her sister alone too long with her dad now? After what she had seen?

Still, as Riley made his turnoff, passing a big Catholic church on the corner and then a couple of lonely potato fields further up, he held out hope that there was still a logical explanation for why nobody had seen or heard from Jessie all day. Soon, dense and ominous woods appeared on either side of Route 319, and eventually the pavement dropped away and the road turned to red dirt. The forest grew even thicker, the trees pressing close along the road as it narrowed. Riley clutched the Lumina's wheel, pleading with whatever god he believed in that he'd see nothing out on this now creepy and isolated stretch, that he'd find no trace of Jessie at all.

But then he saw it. A vehicle sat parked up on the shoulder ahead, gently listing toward the weedy ditch. The late-day sun glared and glinted off the vehicle, obscuring what type it was for a moment, and these were the final two or three seconds when Riley allowed himself to believe that this was not Jessie's minivan. This was some *other* car or truck, parked inexplicably out in the middle of nowhere.

His heart sank an instant later as the sun's rays cleared and he could see that the metal frame in front of him belonged to a sky-blue Dodge Caravan.

Riley pulled up behind it, killed the Lumina's engine, and got out, taking the Glock with him as he went. Another brief blast of hope: maybe this was *another* minivan, not Jessie-Mac's. The vehicle was certainly popular these days—they seemed to be everywhere on the roads. Maybe this one belonged to a fisherman or a hiker, somebody who had decided, for whatever reason, to park on this obscure rural route and then hike southward toward the Cardigan River. Did that make sense? Was that even possible?

But as Riley walked up along the vehicle, his gun at his hip, he saw the familiar sign. A patch of rust, thick and scabby and in the shape of a P, sat over the minivan's back right wheel well.

Fuck, he thought. *This is her fucking van.*

And then he was calling her name over and over, a staccato panic as he stepped down into the ditch and up into the woods, heading northward. He continued calling her name as he stumbled through brush and around thick trees. The sun bowed out now, and the air grew almost cool. The forest was alive with sounds—the drill of a woodpecker, the natter of squirrels, the rustle of long weeds as unseen foxes bounded through them. He hollered Jessie's name over this din, longing to hear her young voice call back through all that wild and ancient flora.

How long would it take to reach Lowfield moving northward from Route 319? Riley was convinced that the village couldn't be more than a half mile in, but it seemed much farther, now that he was making the trek. Even with his hiking boots on, his ankles struggled around roots and long grass and wild ferns that stood in his way. The trees above him seemed to rattle their branches like bones. He was overcome with the same feeling he'd had the first time he'd tried to find Lowfield—that the village wouldn't be there at all, that it was a mere phantasm of the mind, a fiction told in the rambling diary of a man long dead.

But finally the woods began to thin, and soon faint traces of a corduroy road that should have long rotted away began to appear beneath his feet. He followed it, walking deeper into what was now an obvious clearing in the woods, its corners obscured in shadow. The first moldering cottages began to appear on his path, their greyish black siding dim in this light. Oily windows stared out at him like eyes. The air grew almost too heavy to breathe. Riley held his Glock up, swung it from side to side, though no enemy stood in his path.

And then he came upon that clapboard church in the centre of the village, walking up from behind it rather than the front, as he had the other times he'd been here. That rotting chapel stood like a bleak edifice against the sky. Riley paused for a moment, his heart racing as he looked up at the church, at its unwavering steeple. He came around the side of the building then, heading toward the front, and looked up at the stain glass windows greeting him as he passed.

They were glowing. Those ornate panes were pregnant with that unearthly dark light.

Draatis sh'un maul, he thought in a language he did not speak. *The taproot awaits me.*

He came around the front of the church, climbed its stairs, and squeezed himself through its still wrenched-open door. He walked in, calling Jessie's name as he moved through that stale, noxious air. Every fibre of his flesh began to tingle as he moved toward that light. His hand lowered the Glock to his thigh as he stepped into that small cathedral. He moved slowly up the centre aisle between those rows of old, decaying pews. The light was guiding him to the altar, to the archway that led down into the basement. The pulpit ahead, tall and ornate on its stage, almost seemed to *burn* in the light—burn like a torch, or a beacon pointing to the path ahead.

Just before he stepped up onto that altar once again, Riley turned and saw something heaped onto the first pew there. His breath hitched with an agonizing choke as he realized what he was looking at.

It was a pile of clothing. A pile of clothing strewn on the pew: a pair of girl's blue jeans, Capri-style, their legs folded over each other; a burgundy tee-shirt bunched up in one corner; a pair of balled-up lavender panties; and a small bra of dark navy, one strap dangling over the pew's edge. Below the pew, on the church's rotted wooden floor, sat an upturned set of women's sandals, kicked off in haste.

Oh Jesus fuck, Riley thought.

He turned back toward the altar, toward the archway leading down into that gullet of a basement, into the very throat of Hell. And that's when he heard it, a heavy sound abruptly trilling and blundering out of that mouth and piping into his ears like liquid.

It was music. Music was playing in the basement below his feet.

The sound was instantly incongruous: a contemporary piece of pop music playing suddenly in this archaic and decaying house of worship. Riley found himself moving up onto the altar and toward that sound, that archway. The tune grew louder as he approached. In another instant, he recognized the lead singer's voice: it was the same simpering vocalist that Jessie had joked about wanting to marry. But Riley didn't recognize this song. It wasn't off the album, *Monster*, that she had given him back in June. It was, perhaps, off another record. He paused to listen to the track. Slow, echoing strums of acoustic guitar formed its backbone, buttressed by a languid yet grandiose orchestra cutting in every few seconds. The lyrics seemed to be a set of innocuous rhetorical questions, yet they still sent a volt of fear racing up Riley's spine. He stepped through the archway and onto the landing leading to the basement, and the song grew louder still.

"Jessie-Mac?" he called down the stairs, hollering above the music.

"Riley?" her own voice called up, sweet and hospitable. "Oh, hey. You're here. Come to me. Come down and see."

He froze, forgetting to breathe, his hand tightening around the Glock's grip.

"Seriously, it's all right," she said, her voice floating up through the billows of dark light that unfurled out of that basement. "It's pretty awesome, actually. Better than I imagined. Come on down. Don't keep me waiting. I want to see you. I want *you* to see *me*."

Help her. Fucking help her. What are you waiting for?

This was the voice he wanted to listen to. He tried to ignore the other voice in his head, and the accompanying images that flickered across his mind's eye. He tried to ignore the swelling erection that pressed suddenly and painfully against his jeans.

Help her. Just. Fucking. Help her.

He took one step onto the descending stairs, and then another. They creaked and twisted, just like the staircase in Applegarth.

"That's it," Jessie said. "It's okay, Riley. Don't be afraid. You're going to love this. Trust me. Do you trust me?"

He went down and down, until he reached the bottom. He rounded the corner and stepped into that wide basement, moved through its flowing blooms of dark, alien luminance.

There, against where the back wall should have been, he found Jessie-Mac. She floated in a huge, boundless ocean of light, its radiance churning out towards him. She was maybe eight inches off the floor, her arms spread out in a wide, welcoming cruciform, her feet together and pointing downward, revealing toes painted a bright, cute red. What she looked like in this position, Riley thought, was unmistakable. She looked like a key. A giant key ready to be turned.

As Riley approached, the Glock up and quavering in his hand, he could see that the taproot had coiled itself around her, slithering wetly across her thighs and over her hips, behind her back and up between her breasts, then around her throat like a noose. Something appeared to be moving inside that thick, fleshy stem, pumping through it in quick, manic spasms. Jessie seemed oblivious. Her head was back a little, her mouth open, her eyes glowing vacantly, yet wildly, *brilliantly*, with that dark light. Her cheekbones flickered with it from the inside, like a Jack-o-Lantern's. The music, meanwhile, played on, trapped in a loop, reduced to its thrumming acoustic centre and overlaying electric guitar riff. The knuckle-dragging drawl of it egged Riley forward.

"It's amazing," Jessie said, a talking scarecrow in front of him. "Oh Riley, do you know what I can see from here, from this… *threshold* of the doorway? I can see through time itself—past, present *and* future, all at once." She gave out a light, girlish laugh. "God, it's so delightful. I've gotten the Great Force to play me some R.E.M. yet to come. I've been rocking out to it all afternoon. You know, they still put out some pretty decent albums later on, before they broke up for good in the 2010s."

"Jessie..." he muttered, drawing closer to her, the Glock shaking lightly in his grasp.

"But then I got tired of the new stuff," she said, "and I wanted to play an old favourite. This one's the first track off the first album of theirs I ever bought. I love this tune. It's called 'Drive.' It's the song that was playing the last time Danny and I ever made love, before we broke up. I always associate this song with *fucking*."

Riley's heart engorged with terror even as his erection raged in his jeans. Despite the throbbing, snake-like root that constricted around her body, Jessie was as gorgeous naked as he always imagined she would be. Though he fought to stop himself, Riley allowed his eyes to fall from her face and take a hungry gander at her small, lovely breasts, her flat stomach, her soft, pretty pubis. All of it, together, was absolute perfection. Even Marigold herself, at the height of her affair with Riley, hadn't been *this* beautiful.

"Do you like what you see?" Jessie asked. "It's okay, Riley. Come over here. Make love to me. Please. The *draatis* and I want you to, and so do you. Don't be afraid."

Riley held his ground even as a fierce desire surged up in him like a jet stream. His brain filled with a thousand vicarious sensations, all the pleasures he had imagined with her in dozens of night visions while under Applegarth's roof, now just a moment away. It was like a pair of unseen hands were pushing him from the small of his back toward her. But Riley fought with everything he had against that riptide, literally digging his heels into the church basement's dirt floor.

R.E.M. played on.

"Oh, what, you're going to be coy now?" Jessie asked. "Riley, I've caught you staring at me, like, *several* times. You were—what's that old chestnut?—*undressing me with your eyes*. Admit it. You've wanted this from the first day we met, when I came out to interview you. Come on. *Please*. I haven't been fucked all summer. What are you waiting for? It's not like it'll be weird. I'm not your mom, or your daughter. *Jesus*. There's nothing incestuous about it. That'll come later, when I get down from here and go home to seduce my dad. Maybe Kyla and I will seduce him together. I've *always* wanted to be in a threesome like that. In the meanwhile, why don't you and I just give in to what we've both wanted since the spring."

"Jessica, if you're in there," Riley called over tremulously, "if you can hear me, I need you to fight against this. Fight against it as hard as I am right now."

"*... as hard as you are right now,*" the Jessie-thing floating in front of him mocked, her mouth bending upward into a jackal's grin.

At these words, the taproot began to constrict again, moving like a locomotive across her body. That wet, fleshy branch crawled down her spine with aching slowness, down lower than her spine, causing her torso to arch upward, her head to tilt back, her tits to point toward the ceiling. Somehow, the root managed to wrap one coil around Jessie's right thigh and one around her left. And then it pulled them apart with delicious ease.

"*Ohh fuck,*" she moaned off into space. "*Ohh JESUS that feels good...*"

And Riley nearly gave in then, nearly stumbled over to her beneath the clumsy weight of his lust to unbuckle his jeans and pull them down and take Jessie right there. Every cell of his body wanted to. Shaal was making sure of that. He could feel the beast's coercion seeping into his every molecule and thrusting away all his resistance.

But then Riley did stop himself, and would not step forward. Instead, he brandished the Glock downward, pointing it at the thickest part of the root, where it seemed to be coming up out of the floor, right where that enormous bath of dark light had started. It took his whole will to do this. Pointing the gun at that meaty stem felt like pointing it at his own throbbing flesh.

When he did, the entire taproot seemed to flinch, to tighten, to squeeze Jessie like a python. She let out a noise then that was not pleasure. The music ceased abruptly, casting the basement into a chilly silence.

Do NOT pull that trigger, a voice boomed suddenly in his head, one as deep and vast as the universe itself. *Do not wound me, or else I will take away this girl, my offering to you, forever.*

Riley hesitated under those words, his finger flickering like a flame over the trigger.

Do not call my bluff, Fuller man. Do not tempt me, gunwielder. I will act. Her life means nothing to me. Do you hear? I made the entire populace of this village vanish in a single flash when I grew displeased. Don't think I won't do the same here.

Riley watched as a *second* root came slithering out of that ocean of light. It slowly crawled up Jessie's body and then spiraled itself around the top two-thirds of her face, covering it like a mask. A wretched, galloping desire, an unholy physical passion unlike any Riley had felt, surged through him as she donned this meaty blindfold. He stood on the precipice then: to touch her, to take her, to fuck her, to relieve and release himself into her, to extinguish this blissful agony before it split him in half at the waist.

Help me, Fuller man, the voice persisted. *Do as I command you. Help me through the door. I am so close now—even closer than I was with your grandfather, and his grandfather before him. Accept this gift from me, this young and supple girl. Don't force me to take her away.*

A third root came flopping out of the light, and then a fourth, and then a fifth—slimy, pulsing trunks of flesh. They each seemed to have a mind of their own. A couple of them reached up under Jessie and tilted her backwards a little, and the root that was wrapped around her legs moved in unison with this action, spreading her thighs apart even further and pushing her knees toward her shoulders. She stiffened in this stirrup-like position, paralyzed and helpless before Riley's raging desire.

Take her. Take her NOW, gunwielder. Do as your god commands you!

At these words, Riley looked up, looked up beyond Jessie, and saw it. Saw *them*. Two giant eyes, shaped like diamonds, were staring at him through the light behind Jessie. These eyes, he could see, were part of a face as large as the church basement itself. More roots wriggled out of that light, and Riley saw that they were not roots at all. They were tentacles. An entire *beard* of tentacles, a cephalopodic *nest* of them, writhed on that face, and the huge diamond eyes glowed above it. That squid-like visage was trying to squeeze itself through a hole, a narrow doorway in the fabric of existence itself.

You are Shaal, Riley thought. *You are what Elder Fuller called the sibling of Christ. You go by other names as well, don't you? Endless other monikers across the dimensions of time and space. But here, you are called Shaal.*

Riley noticed that his hand with the gun had slid back down to a resting position next to his leg. Fighting with everything he had against the furnace of his lust, he raised the weapon once more.

Do not wound me, gunwielder, Shaal said. *Shoot me and I will take this girl away. Fuck her now, or I will take her away. You have no choice. Give in to your body. Give in to the delicious images that dance, even now, before your mind's eye. Give in to what you* really *are, Fuller MAN.*

The weapon trembled in Riley's hand as his fingers struggled to return to the trigger.

All the tentacles seized up then and descending upon Jessie, coalescing around her. This seemed to break her trance, her paralysis, and she screamed out. Screamed out in agonizing terror. The sound of it shattered Riley's heart.

"Help me!" she called out blindly beneath the tentacle that covered her eyes. "Is there somebody there? Oh Jesus. Oh Jesus, help me. Somebody please fucking help m—" But then another tentacle swirled around her jawline and shoved itself thickly into her mouth, prying it wide open as it oozed down into her throat, its veiny underbelly pulsing as it did. Riley heard the snap of a bone.

That *finally* got him moving. He reached out with his free hand to grab her, but his fingers only grazed her soft, bare hip. Before he could get any purchase on Jessie, Shaal hauled her away like a toy taken from a child, and then a great blast of light exploded through the basement, knocking Riley clean off his feet. He flew briefly through the air and then landed hard on his back. The wind was knocked out of him but he still managed to hang on to the Glock. He sat up and raised it, raised it just as the light vanished and the basement became a basement again, pitched in cobwebs and darkness. He squeezed off three shots anyway, and they were bright and thunderous in that space. But the bullets merely tore into the back wall, sending bits of earth and stone flying through the shadows.

In the eerily living silence that followed the gun's reports, a panting and desperate Riley realized two things as he sat there on that dirt floor.

One: that he was alone. That Shaal had briefly retreated. That Jessie was gone.

And two: that his lap was wet. At first, Riley thought he might have shot himself with the Glock by accident. But as he patted his free hand down there desperately and felt no pain, he realized it was something else. The front of his jeans were soaked through... with semen. The denim there was sodden with the stuff.

Then Riley screamed. He screamed, and screamed, and screamed.

Chapter 35

July 26, 1995
Dear Diary, or Journal, or whatever the fuck you are,
I cannot, will not, document here what happened last night in Lowfield. To do so would be to relive it, which would break me all over again. Why recount Jessie-Mac's death—and she *is* dead, I have no doubt about that; she died in a manner so horrific, so beyond human comprehension, that I cannot bring myself to recall it now—for the sake of posterity? Fuck posterity. Fuck all that stuff. My grandfather's grandfather wrote of ghosts from the future haunting this house, but is that true? Who is reading this? Who am I writing this for? Is it the girl I saw up in the attic? Not the spectre of little Miriam Fuller, with her rotted-out face; not the older version of Marigold, with her dull silver hair and wearing a prison jumpsuit; but the *other* one, the one in the prime of life and who looked to be... pregnant? Is that her? Is that *you*? Are *you* reading this? Do *you* want to know, do you *need* to know what happened to Jessie MacIntosh? Are you there? And if you are, then why haven't you revealed yourself to me?

This will be my last entry. I'm going to kill myself with the Glock after I finish here. The end of this story is not yet told, but I don't care. An email from Sammy arrived while I was out, but I won't even open it. The Montague RCMP will find Jessie's minivan out on the 319, either later today or tomorrow at the latest, and they may even come around here to question me, but I'll be long gone. They'll find my body and put a narrative together, though it won't be the correct one. A few of the locals may have a different story, a more *accurate* story, to tell, and they'll pass it around amongst themselves, for years to come. It'll be literally unbelievable, but people will still heed its warnings. *Don't go north of 319. Don't go south of the Eight Mile Road. And whatever you do, stay away from that old, decaying house on the outskirts of Glenning.*

Yes, I suspect it'll be a very long time before anyone—even the cops—sets foot on this property again.

Chapter 36

He decided to do it out on the porch.

After finishing his final diary entry, Riley shut off the computer, placed its plastic dust cover over it, got up from the desk, and headed downstairs. He went into the kitchen, opened the drawer where he kept the Glock, and took the weapon out. It was still loaded, missing just the trio of rounds he had fired uselessly into the wall of that church basement the night before. Moving through Applegarth's long, large kitchen toward the front parlour and the porch beyond, Riley passed the dining room, its door still closed tight against the rest of the house. There was now a clear and pervasive stench seeping out from the sealed frame as the food left inside—not to mention the corpse of the thing that had come birthing out of the eggplant—rotted away in the late July heat. Riley was relieved he would never have to smell that smell again.

Out on the porch, he sat himself down into the swing seat, laid the gun across his thigh, and looked out over the wide expanse of his front property. The day was hot and clear, the sky a lazy blue, a warm westerly wind rustling the tall birch and spruce trees that rimmed his land. All around Prince Edward Island, locals and tourists alike would be enjoying this perfect day. The ferries arriving at either end of the Island would be disgorging long lines of cars—boat traffic, they called it—full of vacationers anxious for a break. The waters of the northern shore would finally be warm enough to swim in, their beaches crowded. On the streets of Charlottetown, people would be eating the local ice cream in waffle cones and staring up at big billboards advertising the cheesy *Anne of Green Gables* musical that played every summer at the Confederation Centre. Here, in the less-touristy end of PEI, the Eight Mile Road was quiet as ever, almost desolate. Minutes passed and not a single car drove by. The trees and the grass of Riley's land, the scorched soil of his garden plots, all seemed to have resigned themselves to the inevitable.

He thought about smoking a final du Maurier but decided against it. *Don't want to give myself lung cancer*, he joked to himself without smiling. Then he racked the slide, pulled in a breath, and looked up to take one final glance at the world.

And that's when he heard it. The faint, susurrus-like sound of a vehicle approaching. The Eight Mile Road was not empty after all. Riley watched as a car appeared abruptly through the trees before braking at the end of his driveway and swerving onto his land in a mad squeal of tires.

The car was a Honda, one that Riley had seen somewhere before. In fact, he nearly mistook it for Jack's Civic. But as it tore up his laneway in a cloud of red dust, he realized that it was a different model and colour. He watched it pull up tersely and park behind his Lumina. A moment later, four girls climbed out of its doors.

It was Tara Moore and her entourage of friends. Of course, *that's* where he had seen this car. It was hers. It was there on the day she had confronted him in the Sobeys parking lot.

Riley watched as they looked around his property before approaching. He stood up, the swing seat banging against the porch's back wall, the gun now dangling limp and nearly forgotten at his thigh. The four girls rushed across the front lawn toward him.

"*Where is she?*" Tara bellowed as the quartet arrived at the porch's railing. Riley looked down at them and noticed something right off the bat. Three of these four girls were carrying guns of their own, brought over from the car. Tara had a pistol in her hand, and the girls at her left and right each had a hunting rifle slung over her shoulder. The fourth, who hadn't been at the Sobeys that day, carried no weapon at all.

"Fuller, *where is she?*" Tara screamed at him again. "Her parents are going *insane*. Do you *know* something? Did she… did she…" She pointed toward the back of Applegarth. "Did she go out into that woods, to see that… that *thing* for herself?"

Riley cleared his throat to speak, but then lowered his head. His eyeballs began to blaze in their sockets, and his neck flushed with shame. "Tara... I don't know... what you think..." he stammered.

"Oh fuck off," she spat at him. "I know what's out there, okay. I *know*. I finally got my grandmother in Trenton to talk, after she heard on the news what's been happening around here. She told me *everything*, everything she knew, about what happened here in 1930—and before. So don't bullshit us, Fuller. I *know* what Lowfield is, and I know what... what *lives* under that church out there. So I'll ask you again: Where the *fuck* is Jessie-Mac?"

Riley looked up at her, at all of them, and then his eyes began pissing tears. He felt them stream down his face in thick, salty rivers. "I'm so sorry," he said through his now sodden and trembling lips. "I'm really sorry. I tried to stop it, to help her, but I... I couldn't..."

All four girls gave a cry of anguish that branded Riley's ears like tattoos. Tara threw both her arms up and pressed the balls of her hands into her temples. The pistol rose above her pixie cut like a single grey-black horn. "Oh fucking Jesus..." she cried as she swayed from one foot to the other in grief. "Oh fucking Christ..."

Oh fucking Shaal, you mean, Riley thought. *There is no Christ back there in that woods.*

Then, just like that, Tara's demeanor hardened again, and she fought to regain her composure, her stoicism. This reminded Riley of what she had told him, that she'd had training; that she'd done Basic at CFB Gagetown; that she was from a military family, in fact. She was cut, or so Riley believed, from the same cloth he was. A warrior. A defender. They were both what Shaal might have labeled *gunwielders*.

As if sensing his thoughts, Tara looked up at him with searing eyes and then nodded to her friends. "We're going back there," she said. "*We're* going to deal with that... that *thing*." Riley eyed up these girls again. They all looked to be the same age as Jessie had been—twenty, or thereabouts. Yet, standing on his front lawn, they somehow looked like a militia. A small army of angry young women.

Tara spotted his Glock then, and nodded at it. "You have a gun as well. That's good. We're short one. Give it to Jennifer." And she nodded to the friend at the end, the one who didn't have a gun.

Riley turned to this Jennifer. She was a short, stocky girl with dense, curly hair and a pug nose. Despite the heat of the day, she was wearing a cardigan, a grey and navy thing with snowflake patterns knitted through it. It was buttoned up tight, almost ill-fitting, against her breasts and gut. To Riley, it seemed like the sort of outfit worn by a grown woman who still slept with a teddy bear at night. Yet, there was nothing child-like or gentle about this person now. She looked ready to kill, that she would just as soon eat Riley's face as speak to him.

"Pass your weapon," she said, her voice like ice.

He let out a nervous huff. "Look, I'm not just giving you girls my gun."

"Yes, you are," Tara said, and he turned back to her. "We need it. Do you have any other weapons here we can use?"

"No, I don't. And I'm not giving you this one—"

"Yes, you are," she said. "Pass your weapon, Riley."

He blinked at her. "*No.* You... you can't just take my gun."

When he said this, it reminded Riley of something that had happened the year before, when the RCMP had put him on Off Duty Sick following Marigold's shooting rampage. A supervisor, still grieving the officers murdered, had come by Riley's house, after all the paperwork had been submitted, to confiscate his service weapon. There was an unspoken but definite concern that Riley might harm himself or somebody else. His colleague's visit that day had been awkward and awful. Both of them knew that a police officer's gun was an extension of himself, a part of his identity, and to relinquish it, no matter the circumstances, was humiliating. It immediately felt like a kind of amputation. And yes, Riley *was* a risk to himself, but to give up his service weapon like that just made his depression darker, fiercer, as the full scope of what had happened finally sunk in.

He felt the same sensation coming on now.

"Listen," he said slowly, "I can't just…"

"Pass your weapon," Tara said again, her voice steely, her still-wet, still-grieving eyes locked onto his.

Riley ran his free hand over his beard. "Look, I'll take you out there myself. You girls don't know what you're facing, okay."

"And you do. You tried to face it a couple of times, didn't you? And you *couldn't*." Riley stared into Tara's face as it joggled up and down at him caustically. "Yeah, asshole, we *know* what you've been failing to fight against. I talked to Jessie-Mac *two days* before she went missing. She told me what happened up here during your little dinner party. But she also told me what you've been unable to do, even in the face of *everything* that's happened. She told you that girls are *getting raped*, and you did nothing. You still couldn't bring yourself to let," and here, she motioned to the big rambling house he had inherited from the men in his bloodline, and the surrounding property, and what lived in the woods behind it, "any of this go. So between that, and the stories my grandmother finally shared with me, and what's been happening around here this summer, we *know* what you can't fight against."

Another reminiscence came to him, something he had read in those last entries of his grandfather's grandfather's diary. What had that *other* Riley Fuller called it? The network of whispers. Of women sharing things among themselves to keep each other safe. The stories they passed along in hushed tones. The women of this area had wanted to join the fight against Shaal even then, in 1863, but their menfolk wouldn't let them.

"You have had your time," Tara went on. "You have had your chance. Now it's ours. You couldn't bring yourself to stop this, to resist whatever hold this place has over you. You couldn't do what needed to be done. So we will. *We*," and she motioned to her army of girls, "will do this, not you. So I'll say again—pass your weapon."

Riley swallowed and let his head fall, casting his eyes down at his feet. "Tara…" he muttered, "… please…"

"Pass. Your. *Weapon*."

He looked up. Gave a long, slow sigh. Then flipped his Glock around and offered it to her handle first.

She took it in her free hand, shoved her own pistol into the waistband of her camo shorts, and immediately began a tutorial for Jennifer on how the Glock worked. As Riley watched this from the porch, watched the expert way Tara navigated around and explained his weapon to her friend, he felt something grip his insides. A slow, aching urge. Behind him, the old house creaked and shuttered, cracked and settled. The freshet of lust that bloomed up in Riley as he watched Tara, watched her easy skillfulness with his gun, was warm and runny and sweet. She *was* quite striking, he thought. Maybe not as pretty as Jessie-Mac had been, but close. And made more attractive, of course, by the leadership she was showing as she prepared her friends for combat. A vision rippled across his mind then—of him saying something, anything, to convince these other girls to go take a walk while he and Tara went into Applegarth together, to go hand-in-hand up its winding wooden staircase to his bedroom and—

Danny MacPherson's voice boomed inside his head. *This isn't who you really are!*

Tara glanced up at Riley then. She caught the expression on his face, but couldn't quite interpret it. Despite her shrewdness in so many areas, she still seemed unable to fathom that a forty-five-year-old man would look at her in that way.

"Do you have any more ammunition for this?" she asked.

"Are you really planning to *shoot* the thing living under that church?"

"You got a better idea?"

He blinked at that. He had had a better idea, before they came tearing onto his property.

"Do you have more ammo or not?"

"Of course," he said. "It's in the house."

"Well then why don't you go get it?"

Her insolence stung Riley, and he nearly told Tara to go fuck herself. But the way she was glaring at him, the way they all were—still seized up in their fury and sorrow and grief over

Jessie-Mac, and wanting to do something about it—made him change his mind.

He slunk back into the house like an obedient dog and went to the kitchen drawer to fetch the box of bullets. He brought it back out to the porch and was just about to pass it to Tara, like an offering, when he saw something. An animal suddenly came racing out of the woods and across his lawn toward them. At first Riley thought it was another red-tailed fox. But then, in one fraction of a second, he realized that it was something else—something not of this world. It looked like a cross between a fox, a raccoon and a... and a *person*, a Frankenstein hybrid that had no business existing. As its paws pattered maniacally across the grass, Riley saw that they looked almost like human hands. The animal's mouth, meanwhile, was full of razor-sharp teeth that glinted in the sunlight.

And this animal's eyes, he could see, glowed with the same dark light that he'd witnessed in the church.

The girls turned to where he was looking, saw the beast sprinting across the grass toward them, and screamed. The four of them recoiled together against the rail of the porch, and Tara fumbled to yank the pistol out of her waistband. It wouldn't come free. But then Jennifer, a novice with a gun just a moment ago, raised her weapon just as the animal leaped up and rocketed toward Tara's throat. She fired. The thing's body bent in midair like a U, and then fell back to the ground in front of them with a heavy thud. It twitched for just a second before growing still.

The girls were on the cusp of hyperventilating as they stared down at the now-dead thing that had come out of the woods to kill them. No, it was no animal of this earth. It was some great grotesque beast, a demon from the cosmos beyond—half animal, half human.

Tara composed herself enough then to grab the monstrosity by its hindquarters and carry the dead and bloodied thing to the forest's edge. With a great heave of her arm, she threw the animal back into the woods from whence it came.

Then she returned to her still-trembling friends, her face a bright fire of rage and determination. "Let's go," she said, and turned.

The three other girls hesitated, but then joined her as they headed toward the back of Riley's property. He waited a moment, but then trailed after them as they worked their way into the woods.

~

It turned out to be a smart move on Jennifer's part, to wear a winter cardigan for this long July hike. The mosquitoes and blackflies, the slapping birch branches and scraping spruce, didn't seem to bother her as much as they did Tara's other two friends, whose names, Riley had learned, were Mandy and Kim. They had worn simple sleeveless shirts for this nearly two-mile trek through dense forest and were obviously regretting it. Less than fifteen minutes in, they looked like they wanted to turn back, even as their hunting rifles lay unshouldered and lightly resting in their hands. Tara, who was still in the lead, had her pistol up and was strangely calm as she surveyed the woods with it.

"It's towards your right," Riley called from the rear when he saw that she was veering them off course.

"How much farther?" Mandy called out, her voice quaking with fear.

"We're not even halfway," Riley replied dourly over the sound of snapping branches and droning mosquitoes.

A strange, awful rattle, as loud as a siren, rose up in the woods then, and all five of them halted in fright. The noise pierced their eardrums and seemed to be coming from every direction at once. It wasn't quite the squeal of a cicada. It sounded more like a large plastic shaker full of beans clattering ferociously through the branches overhead.

"What the *fuck* is that?" Jennifer asked. Riley's Glock was practically bouncing in her hands as she raised it up in a defensive posture.

"There!" he yelled, and pointed to a large tree off to their left. Something was slithering down its trunk toward them, twirling around it like the swirl in a barber's pole. Its body was long and furry, its tail furrier still, a greyish-brown, toupee-like mass bringing up the rear. Claws clittered in the bark as the thing made its rotations around the long trunk. The animal was obviously a squirrel, and yet was not. For one thing, it was as large as a cat. For another, it had, at the very end of that dense bushy tail, what looked like the rattle from a rattlesnake.

It paused halfway down the tree and shook its rattle again. The noise sent a chilling reverberation through the woods. Then the squirrel-like thing perked its head up toward them. They could see that the beast had an almost human-like face, and one that Riley recognized. It sort of looked like *his* face, a faint but unmistakable resemblance in chin and cheekbones, in the ridge of the brow. The likeness was marred only in the eyes, which were glowing blackly at the group as they stared. The thing let out a hiss—the same pterodactyl-like screech that the fetus in Riley's dining room had made at Jessie-Mac.

The girls didn't scream this time. Instead, Kim just raised her rifle, pointed it at the tree, looked briefly through the scope, and fired. Her first shot missed the squirrel-thing, and instead dug a quick and furious trench through the bark above it. The animal was on the move again, racing down the tree toward the brush at its base. Kim pulled the bolt back to drive another round home, re-aimed, and fired again. This time she caught the beast between its tiny shoulders just as it approached the ground. A pulpy mesh of blood and fur spat up onto the bark, and the thing dropped in an instant, falling dead away into the thickets below. The forest seemed to hold on to the echo of Kim's shots for whole seconds, spreading them for a quarter mile all around.

"Let's keep going," Tara said after a moment, her voice shaky but determined.

Another ten minutes of trudging through the woods, and then Mandy let out a deafening holler. She had put her hiking boot down into a small mound of wet mud in the undergrowth, and when she pulled it back up, something was attaching itself to her boot's rubber treads. Long, stringy worms, mottled in purple and white, writhed up suddenly over her boot and laced themselves around her ankle like the fingers of a hand. This time she did scream, scream like she was about to be sucked into the earth, which, in that moment, it looked like she was. She hauled her foot away a good three feet, but the worms just came with her, holding on for dear life as they stretched out of the ground. Jennifer staggered over through the brush, grabbed Mandy's arm and pulled with one hand while she aimed Riley's Glock with the other. She fired and fired and fired into the mud until the magazine in the handle was empty. The worms that had grabbed hold of her friend were now reduced to a mush. Mandy yanked her foot free and then dashed the worms off her boot with mad strokes against the forest floor. Tears were streaming down her face even as she told everyone that she was fine, that she was fine, that she was okay.

Tara took out the box of bullets, which she had stored in the left cargo pocket of her shorts, and chucked it at Riley. "Help her reload that thing," she said of Jennifer's Glock, and he obeyed.

It took nearly an hour, but finally they had reached the clearing that Riley knew would soon appear. Up ahead, he could see the first hint of the rotted-out corduroy road leading in to the abandoned village. The girls saw it too, and they paused to stare at it quizzically. Riley understood their confusion. How could an old road from the 1800s that still exist out here? Wouldn't the boards, the very nails that held them in place, have decayed long ago? That thought reminded Riley of what Obed Marsten had told him, about how Lowfield was like Chernobyl, leaking a sort of radiation into the air and soil. It was a kind of dark energy from another dimension, one that might keep a corduroy road from decaying back into the earth, that might make a house two miles away repair itself should the right person take up occupancy inside it.

"We're nearly there," he said to the girls. "Keep going."

They nodded nervously and stepped through the brush toward the clearing, toward the road. But as they did, something rustled through the undergrowth all around them. It was like a huge, noisy applause passing through the grass and leaves and weeds on the ground. The girls screamed again—they couldn't help themselves. Looking all around at once, they saw what had suddenly surrounded them on all sides.

Hundreds of mice were moving through the undergrowth toward the group. It was unreal, the sight of them. The mice formed what looked like a giant carpet on the forest floor, their bodies climbing over one another to take up a position against this invading force in their woods. Everyone tried to back up, but there was no place to back up to. The mice were everywhere, and moving in fast.

"You better start *shooting*," Riley yelled out, regretting more than ever that he had surrendered his gun.

Tara complied, aiming her pistol downward and firing into the mass of mice. A swath of them scattered, more from the noise than from the bullet ripping into the earth, and for a moment it looked like that lone shot had cleared a path into Lowfield. But then Mandy screamed as two or three mice scurried up her legs and onto her back, their tiny feet digging into the skin beneath her shirt. She began smacking at herself, trying to get them off her. Kim ran up and began pulling the mice from her friend's back as if they were leeches, throwing them to the ground in wild chucks of her hand. Then she unshouldered her rifle and fired into the cloud of fur and teeth on the ground, and another patch of the mice scattered back into the woods.

"C'mon, let's g—" Tara began, but her words were cut off by Jennifer's sudden shriek.

They all turned to see what was happening to their friend. An entire swarm of mice had begun streaming up her legs and clawing their way onto her cardigan. Jennifer spun around and around, like a dreidel, flailing madly as she tried to get them off her. A large mouse had scampered down her arm and was gnawing at her wrist, trying to get her to drop the Glock. Several of the mice had climbed up into her thick, curly mane, and when Jennifer spun around once more, she suddenly looked like a Medusa, only with rodents for hair instead of snakes. *If she drops to her knees, she's done*, Riley thought, the memory of Mrs. Keating's death sharp in his mind. *They'll overwhelm her and that will be that.* Yet Riley did not move to help the girl. It was like something in the forest was holding him in place.

It didn't matter. Her friends were right there. Kim and Mandy began yanking mice out of Jennifer's hair and off her back and legs while Tara fired and fired and fired her pistol into the crowd of creatures trying to surge at them. She dropped the empty mag out of the gun's handle with swift expertness and loaded a fresh one in. But by then, the mice had backed off, cowering into the underbrush from whence they came.

"Jenn, are you okay?" Tara called to her friend without turning around, her eyes still scanning the forest like mad.

"I'm, I'm f-f-fine."

"You sure?"

"Mm-hmm."

"You wanna go home? We can turn back if you like."

"*Fuck no!*"

So together, the four girls marched into the clearing, and Riley followed them. Their guns were up, pointing everywhere at once, as each noise that passed through the trees and bushes and weeds struck them as an immediate threat. To Riley's ears, the forest had never been this loud before. It was like the entire woods had come alive at their presence.

Soon they were on the corduroy road, stepping over its mushy, sodden logs, and Lowfield emerged in front of them. "Which way, Riley?" Tara called back.

"The church is in the centre of the village."

They walked up the main thoroughfare, passing the old rotting cottages nearly lost to towering weeds, and that's when it hit them: a stench like nothing Riley had ever smelled before, a noxious, pestiferous funk that seemed to clog the very air they breathed. The girls grimaced and lowered their faces halfway into their shirts in an attempt to block it out. This smell, this odour of decay, had not been here the other times Riley had hiked into Lowfield. The air had been both clear and calm on those treks, the forest almost silent.

It was almost like the place was now in rebellion.

He followed the girls as they came upon Lowfield's church near the village square. They froze when they saw it. The oily, dirty windows were ablaze in that same dark light they had all seen in the eyes of the animals that attacked them. It was like the church was burning from the inside out.

"Is it, is it *on fire*?" Kim asked.

"No," Riley replied. "That is from Shaal, the thing you've come here to fight."

The girls huddled together for a moment, perhaps each waiting for someone to give them permission to turn tail and flee. But nobody did. Riley watched as they stood together in anger, and then took their first tentative steps onto the stairs that led up into that rambling church. Riley followed them, followed as they squeezed their way into the pried-open door and stepped inside the narthex.

He trailed behind them as they moved through the glowing archway and into the nave. He listened as they screamed at the sight of what they saw.

Up ahead, through the long aisle running between the pews, they could see that something had come bursting up through the dusty, rotting floor of the altar. It was a hole the size of a car, and there was no other way to describe what was writhing up from inside it. It was a mass of thick, fleshy tentacles—twelve or fifteen feet long. They flailed around as if they each had a mind of their own. The same light that had taken Jessie MacIntosh glowed all around this nest of limbs, casting the upside-down cross hanging on the wall behind it in a halo of luminescence.

Riley felt the memory, the sudden trauma of what had happened the night before, come over him then, and he drew his eyes away in fear. Desire overwhelmed him like a flow of magma, and he grew instantly repulsed by what his body wanted in that moment.

"*Kill it*," he yelled at the girls. "Hurry up and fucking *kill it*."

With this prompt, Jennifer stepped forward first. She raised the Glock and pointed it at the altar. But before she could squeeze off a shot, one of the tentacles came eeling down the aisle, as quick as lightning, and slapped the weapon out of her hand. A second tentacle seized it before it even hit the floor and dragged it backwards, toward that shattered stage, and then disappeared down the hole.

My gun! Riley thought. He gasped. *My fucking gun. Just like that, my fucking gun is gone!*

He had no time to process the loss of the thing, for a third tentacle had gripped Jennifer around the leg and was now pulling her toward the hole, toward the dark light. She screamed in terror. The other girls raised their weapons and fired. The tentacle's thick stem burst in a gush of black, glowing blood, and Jennifer scrambled free of the severed limb now divorced from its stump. She pulled the thing off her and threw it down. The other girls, meanwhile, fired again as those alien limbs came lurching toward them, and with each blast the tentacles withdrew backward and down into the hole. More tentacles came, but more bullets sent them back. Riley recalled then what Shaal had said to him, the threat he had made. The thing was afraid of being shot. It was, in the end, flesh and blood, and was terrified of bullets ripping through it.

Soon the girls were out of ammo. A final tentacle came curling up the aisle, ready to seize at least one of them and haul her into the pit of the basement. Riley watched as the four girls tackled the root and began tearing at it with their bare hands, ripping it apart like animals feeding. More of that black, glowing blood spurted up. The girls screamed as they were doused in it, but they continued to rip and tear and pull the tentacle apart until it grew still. Riley just watched as the stump fell like a dead thing back into the altar, and the girls cursed and screamed at it as it did.

Then the church was quiet. The dark light first faded, and then was gone. Up ahead, beyond the gutted altar, the cross hung right side up once more. The four girls, meanwhile, were still huddled in the aisle together and weeping in each other's arms. Riley thought he heard Tara mutter something to them, though he couldn't quite make out what. Was she asking her friends for a promise? Was she beseeching these girls for a pledge over what they'd do if it turned out Shaal *wasn't* gone, if that... if that *thing* down there, under the old, rotting church, ever came back? If that *was* what she was asking, the girls seemed to accept it, to nod their reluctant agreement.

Riley stood there, waiting for the lust, the desire, to drain from his body. It horrified him that it would not. He was *sickened* to realize that the lust lingered, that he wanted to take on all four of these girls at once, right there on the floor of this filthy, shattered church. He looked up and saw the pulpit at the edge of the altar, obscured by motes of dust that fell there. Two books, he could see, still sat upon its lectern. The King James Bible and *The Grimoire of Shaal*. The latter was still open and glowing faintly through the falling shadows.

"Tara…" he muttered, and tried to point. He wanted for her, for them all, to see that damned book on its pulpit, and to go over there and rip it apart with their bare hands, as they had that final tentacle. But this plea would not come, could not escape his mouth. It seemed stuck in his throat as lust continued to coil through his body like a snake.

Tara… girls… you need to, you need to go up there and rip that book ap—

But before he could speak, the four of them climbed to their feet and came back up the aisle toward him. They shoved past Riley without a word, as if he weren't even there, as if he hadn't been the one who had led them to this moment. They walked from the nave arm-and-arm and out into the narthex. Riley was about to join them when he turned back to the altar, to the gaping hole there. He stared at it for a moment. Through the fresh, prominent silence, he thought he could *just* hear something rising up out of that pit. It was… it was *voices*, calling out in pain. People in darkness begging for help, pleading to be set free of the beast that had hauled them off to the Great Force Beyond. He thought he heard Jessie-Mac's voice among them.

Or maybe it was just the wind. Maybe it was the old church settling onto itself, the way Applegarth often did. Riley turned his eyes back up to the pulpit, to where the *Grimoire* lay, its otherworldly glow pulsing weakly through the chaff like a lighthouse lamp through fog. *If you won't ask the girls to go tear that book apart,* a voice in his head asked, *will you not go do it yourself? Will you not take your lighter and* burn *that thing to ash?* But he already knew the answer. He would not. He *could* not. Riley knew that no Fuller male could ever bring harm to that book. Every muscle of his body rejected the thought. It was as if the cocktail of lust and cowardice and self-loathing that that tome imbued in him would... would stop him from harming the thing that harmed himself—and *others*—the most.

Riley turned away and lumbered back out to the narthex, trailing after the girls. They had already squeezed their way out the door, and he soon followed them. Back on the main thoroughfare of Lowfield, he found that the forest had stilled, and that the smell of decay was gone. Did that mean that Shaal was dead? Or just retreated, back through His doorway, and resuming His slumber just beyond the rim of reality?

Riley tried to catch up to the girls. By the time he did, he could hear that their weeping had turned to hiccupy laughter. They were almost *joyous* in their success. They held each other close, as friends do. They were together, ready to hike back out of that woods as one, while Riley walked behind them, alone.

Chapter 37

He almost expected to come staggering back out of the woods with the girls to find Applegarth reverted to some previous state, the greying, crumbling papier mâché-like mass it had been when he first laid eyes on it in early April. If Shaal was dead, if the portal was closed and its dark energy sealed off, would the house not have transformed back into a flaking, dilapidated old manse sitting out in the vast rural emptiness of eastern PEI?

Of course, it had not. As the five of them climbed out of the forest and came up behind the house, Riley could see that all his work from the spring and summer was not lost. Applegarth's clapboard sides were still a bright and cheerful white, with the gables high above them gleaming sharply in red. The roof still had all its shingles; the windows were clear and clean. Sauntering around to the front of the house with the girls, he found the porch railing intact and well-maintained, the swing seat still hanging against the back wall. The front and side lawns of the property were still pleasantly manicured, the driveway still paved. Shaal or not, Applegarth would need years, maybe decades, to decay back down to the state it was in on the day Dave Campbell had first taken Riley out here to see it.

Tara and her friends said nothing to him as they headed back to the Honda and began loading their weapons into its trunk. Whatever giddy hysteria had come over them following their confrontation with Shaal was now gone, and they had returned, all of them, to a state of pure and abject mourning. Kim, Mandy and Jennifer climbed down into the passenger seats with faces soaked in tears. Tara just stood at the now-open driver's door and stared at Riley for a moment. There was nothing complicated about the way she looked at him. It was a plain and simple hatred. *I hear you, sister,* Riley thought as he stared back from his place at the driveway's edge. *I hate myself, more than you could possibly know.* At that, Riley once again remembered that his Glock—the promise it had made to him, the escape hatch it had offered—was gone, dragged down into the pit, into the Great Force Beyond, like so many other things.

Can you leave me a gun? Riley almost asked Tara. But he could tell, just from the expression on her face, that she would not brook a single word from him. He watched then as she did something entirely unexpected, entirely unladylike. She turned her head, hauled her messy, snotty tears back inside her face with a snort, and spat with great drama onto his property. Then she dropped down behind the wheel, slammed the door, gunned the engine, and reversed back down onto the Eight Mile Road.

Riley watched them go. What would those four girls say of this day? Who would they tell about it? Likely no one, at least directly. At least for a while. The risk of danger, even now, was just too high. Poor Jessie-Mac's parents would have to live with the idea that their daughter had just vanished into thin air. Just as hundreds, thousands, *millions* of girls had done before her. Knowing some version of the truth would put them—and Kyla—too much in peril if they ever came poking around up here, on this property at the arse end of the Eight Mile Road, or in the woods behind it.

And yet, Tara and Jennifer, Mandy and Kim, *would* say something to someone, eventually. Or so Riley thought. It might take years, but they would tell stories to their female friends, to their sisters, if they had them, and certainly to the daughters they'd likely bring into this world one day. They would tell them to watch. To guard. To see the signs when they came, of what men were capable of when that dark light, those malevolent urges, entered them.

He had no doubt about that.

~

Back inside the house, Riley sat on the couch, his eyes wandering without purpose around his living room. He looked up at the plaster walls and old wainscoting above him. He looked over at the TV and VCR in their stand, at the wicker cabinet next to it with the boom box on top. The three CDs that Jessie-Mac had given him were still there, still stacked one on top of the other. Riley couldn't bring himself to chuck them out, or even to touch them. To disturb those albums now felt, somehow, like a desecration of her memory.

At that, the guilt swirled around inside him once more, fresh and tart. *I should have never surrendered my Glock to that Jennifer girl*, he thought again. The weapon's absence felt sharp, almost like a taste in his mouth. *I guess I won't be shooting myself*, he thought. Riley suspected that there wasn't enough time now to go into town and buy a new gun. The police would probably be here before the day was done. They'd come to ask him questions—about Jessie's disappearance, about Mrs. Keating's, and, maybe, about other things that had happened in the last few weeks, especially if they had already spoken to Jack, which they no doubt had. Riley was most likely a person of interest now, and a couple of RCMP officers might arrive—in the next hour, or the next minute—to ask him their questions.

It will have to happen another way, he thought.

He got up from the couch, shuffled out of the living room and across the main foyer, and into Applegarth's kitchen. The cupboards and counters there looked fresh and bright, the tile floor beneath them gleaming. Riley, for the life of him, couldn't remember whether he had installed these things or whether they had installed themselves. He wondered if the power Lowfield held over this house, the spell it cast, was broken now that Shaal was dead, or at least retreated behind His portal door. The house had spent all spring and summer healing itself like a living thing, had protected itself and Riley from those who would do them harm. Would it still? *Only one way to find out,* he thought.

Riley squatted down and opened the cupboard doors beneath the sink. He reached all the way to the back and found what he was looking for, the empty bottles of Jim Beam, that Sweet Lady Bourbon, that he had planned to take in for deposit but hadn't yet. He grabbed one, along with a rag he had hung over the pipe in there. Riley stood back up and felt in his pocket. The lighter for his du Mauriers was still where it always was.

He went outside. Found the jerrycan near the mower, where he'd left it after burning the garden. Without so much as a thought, Riley lifted it up and steered its yellow spout over that small glass mouth, filling the bottle about two-thirds full with gasoline. Then he soaked the rag with some as well. Then he grabbed a can of motor oil and poured a little of that into the bottle, too. Then he stuffed the rag into the mouth with his thumb, as far as it would go.

Riley went around to the front of the house and stood before the porch. With its broad, white-painted sides and tall turret, Applegarth seemed even bigger now, a full-on mansion, an Island monolith older than the nation of Canada itself. *Burn it down*, Riley thought. *Burn this place right to the ground. You've lost everything, anyhow, so what's one more thing?*

He took out his lighter, sparked it up, and navigated it over the damp rag. As he did, Riley once again recalled the day that Dave Campbell had first taken him up here, and how he had suggested that Riley put out his cigarette as he wrenched open Applegarth's front door, for fear he might set the place on fire. Riley almost laughed at the irony of that, now.

The rag caught in a great whoosh and Riley took one step forward and then hurled the bottle as hard as he could, like a pitcher throwing a fastball, at the porch. That incendiary device flew briefly through the air before smashing against the porch's back wall, just to the right of the swing seat, the opposite side to where the plaque that said "Applegarth" hung. Riley almost expected the flames to dash out horizontally, leaping and dancing and engulfing the porch in a second or two, like they might in a movie. Instead, the fire crawled up and down the wood siding in a three-foot-wide vertical strip next to the swing seat. Black-grey smoke billowed up the wall and crawled like a hand across the ceiling of the porch before funneling up and forming a smudge on the bright blue sky. *Burn*, Riley thought as he stepped closer to the railing. *Burn, you hateful piece of shit, and set me free.*

But then he felt it. A sudden shift in the atmosphere. A slow but unmistakable settling of the house. A long, thick, fleshy lurch of something coiling in the soil beneath his feet, and in his chest. Riley watched in horror then as the flames lapping at the house first flattened and then extinguished entirely, as if by magic, as if someone had doused them with invisible water from an invisible hose. What was left behind was a sizzling, smoking strip of charred wood, a blackened scar on the face of Applegarth. That was all. In another second or two, even the smoke was gone.

Well, that's that, Riley thought, his shoulders slumped. Another tear broke free and rolled down his bearded cheek. He wiped it away bitterly. *That's my fucking answer.*

~

Back inside, Riley went clopping down into Applegarth's unfinished basement, that huge, shadowy crypt. He pulled the chain that ignited the ceiling bulb. In the splash of unnatural light it cast, he spotted the stack of unused cinder blocks he'd come upon during his first visit down here, most likely left over from some project of his grandfather's. He went over to stand in front of that stack, pausing there a moment to think through what he wanted to do. He grabbed one of the blocks, held it like a case of beer in his hands, gave it a little bounce, felt its weight tug at his wrists. *Yeah*, he thought. *Yeah, this'll do just fine.*

He took the block upstairs and set it carefully against the wall near the main foyer doors. Then he went back into the kitchen and pulled open his junk drawer, which was two drawers down from where he'd kept the Glock. From it, he fished out a strong and lengthy piece of twine bundled up near the bottom. Standing back up, he untangled the twine, then wrapped the ends of it around his fists. He gave that thread a good sturdy tug, a manly snap. It held. *Yeah*, Riley thought. *This'll do, too.*

He thought a bit more about what he wanted to do, and where he wanted to do it. At that, Riley pulled three more items out of his junk drawer before closing it up: a pen, a notepad, and some Scotch tape. He took these and the twine back out to the main entry and set them on top of the cinder block. He stepped into his sneakers and tied them up, then looked around that huge, opulent foyer, that welcoming space into his home. On the side of it, the baroque staircase ascended to the second floor. Up there was his computer under its plastic covering in the library, holding that last email from Sammy, which Riley still hadn't even opened. *Oh well,* he thought. *Sorry about that, Sams. But this is the way it has to be. Obed Marsten was right. This is the simplest thing I can do, and the* only *way out. I hope you'll understand.*

Riley opened the door leading outside. He hoisted the cinder block with the items on top and navigated it onto the stoop, then closed and locked the door behind him. Why? What was the point? There was none, of course. Just an old habit. Just the muscle memory that comes with having a home.

He picked up the cinder block and carried it and the other items over to his Lumina. He set them in the bucket of his passenger seat and shut the door. Then he came around to the other side of the car before taking one last look at Applegarth. He froze when he did. Despite its bright-white sidings and gleaming red gables, despite its wide, homey porch (now marred by that big vertical burn mark) and its towering turret, Applegarth looked like a place no sane person would want to step inside. Riley thought then that perhaps the police *wouldn't* pay a visit up here after all. Even they might get the willies coming this far up the Eight Mile Road, to say nothing of everybody else living in the area. Maybe rumours would go around about this place after the local RCMP put their narrative together about what happened to Jessie-Mac, and everyone—cops included—would just stay away. Riley had a vision then, of the house sitting undisturbed forever, of his belongings inside—the clothes and appliances, the food in his fridge, even the abandoned meal still rotting away in his sealed-off dining room—going untouched, sitting still and gathering dust as the house decayed all around them. It might take a century or two for the materials comprising the house—the wood and the nails, the stones and the tiles—to fully return to the earth from whence they came, but Riley was convinced that would happen, once he was gone. The spell would be broken.

He climbed behind the wheel and started up the engine. He back out onto the road, and set off in the direction of Petit Point.

~

Along the way, in spite of himself and what he was about to do, Riley was struck yet again by PEI's bland, peaceful beauty. The Island was in the full bloom of summer now, and he was glad that these coves and inlets, these rolling farm fields, were some of the last sights he would ever see. As he drove past them, Riley was surprised to find that he was thinking of Marigold Burque, sitting in her New Brunswick jail cell. Suddenly, he was missing her, missing her horribly. In that moment, Riley found himself actually *praying* that Marigold's time in prison wouldn't be a life sentence after all, that she might get out one day and see sights as lovely as the ones he was seeing now. She deserved that. She deserved another chapter to her life—for more than *he* did, he now realized. He had spent the last year and a half clinging to a second chance that really didn't belong to him. She, by contrast, *deserved* an opportunity to put behind what had happened on that December morning in the Red King Hotel, and what she had done in response, and live with some semblance of peace. And to see beauty, *true beauty*, like these idyllic little vistas of Prince Edward Island. Might that happen? Might she get another chance to start her life again? Despite the vision he'd seen in Applegarth's attic, Riley really hoped that she would.

He pulled the Lumina along the side of a deserted road at Petit Point, its wheels grinding in the gravel, and parked. This was, he knew, roughly where Danny MacPherson had met his death a month earlier, and there seemed to be some kind of justice in that. *I should've ended this long ago*, Riley thought. *But it ends now. I am the last of my line. Jane and I could not have children, so there is nobody after me. Whatever is lying dormant in Lowfield right now will stay dormant forever, once I'm gone.*

Riley reached into the passenger bucket and took up the pen and notepad. He thought about what he wanted to write. Should it be a long, rambling missive full of apologies and self-excoriation?

No. That wasn't what he wanted. He instead settled on eight simple words. He didn't understand why they were so important, especially after what Jack had told him during their last conversation. The old newsman said he couldn't bring himself to document anything about what had happened this summer, and Riley wanted to keep it that way. He just couldn't bear the thought of there being yet another record of him, of his behaviour, somewhere out in the ether. So he just jotted those eight words in a vertical line down the page, hoping they'd somehow find their intended audience.

> Jack,
> Please
> don't
> write
> about
> me
> again.
> Riley

Once done, he tore the page out of the notepad, grabbed the Scotch tape from the bucket, and fastened the note to the Lumina's steering wheel.

Then he got out, came around the car, and opened the passenger door. He hoisted the cinder block onto the ground and untangled the twine. He shut the car door and, again, on reflex, locked it before tucking his keys back into his pocket. Eventually, someone would come by and report a 1990 silver Chevy Lumina abandoned on the side of the road, and the RCMP would come and investigate. They would run the plates and draw their conclusions. They'd come up with some official narrative tying Riley's act to Jessie's disappearance, or something. Riley didn't care now what the story said. He just didn't want Jack making a public record of it.

He took the twine and tied an end tight against one of the hand holds of the cinder block, and then tied the other end, just as tight, around his waist. He snapped the twine a few times to make sure it would hold. Then he lifted up the block, once again carrying it like a two-four of beer, and walked it and himself down into the ditch, up through the trees, and over onto the sandy, coppery beach beyond.

Frig, it is pretty out here, Riley thought as he shambled out over the stony sand and toward the water. The evening tide was just coming in, the surf loud in his ears. As he stared straight ahead into the water, Riley recalled then some factoid from the world of literature that Sammy had once shared with him. He had told Riley the story of a lady novelist, an early feminist over in Britain somewhere, who had killed herself back in the forties by filling her pockets full of stones and walking into a river. At the time, Riley thought that was a pretty fucking sissy way to go. If she was such a feminist, why didn't she stick a gun in her mouth and blow her face off, like a man? But now, he understood that decision. Understood it in its totality. The water was gorgeous, and gorgeously inviting. It wanted to suck you in, to pull you down, to embrace you in its salty, swaying beauty.

The surf splashed him, first against his shins, then against his knees. Riley turned to his right and took one final look around. Up along the point in the distance, he could see a small line of houses. He was pretty sure Jack's place, with its mint green siding and huge back deck, was among them. Maybe he was out there now, drinking a Scotch and wishing he had somebody to play scat with.

The water crushed into Riley's crotch, cold and bracing. He held the cinder black tight against him. A wave slapped over it and struck his sternum. He walked out farther and farther, ignoring the cold. The water touched his shoulders, and then his throat.

And then the sea bottom dropped away entirely, and he went down. Down into the depths, where the jellyfish live, and other tentacled things, and the great old gods that put them there. Riley took a desperate, needful gulp, and welcomed them all into his lungs.

Epilogue

Dear Patrick,

Greetings from sunny Montague, PEI. Oh Pat, this place really is charming. So much more relaxed and chilled out than Toronto. Did you see the pics I threw up on Insta? I don't know how I'm ever going to go back to my St. James Town neighbourhood. Check that—I don't know if I ever *will* go back. You may not believe me, but this whole area is, well, starting to feel like home. It's almost like I've lived here before. Isn't that *strange?*

I popped by that craft brewery here in Montague that I mentioned in a previous email, the one in the building that used to house the *Eastern Pioneer* newspaper. They have a nice little restaurant up on the second floor and I had lunch there today. You would've loved the guy who served me, Pat. His name was J.J. and he had the most luxuriant handlebar mustache I've ever seen. Seriously, it looked like someone had grafted the Bat Signal onto his face! I'm not normally into that sort of thing, but the dude was super cute, I won't lie, and he was more than a bit flirty with me as he took my order. I eventually found myself asking if he knew anything about the community newspaper that had been in this building before the brewery was, but he said no. He said he'd only been working at the restaurant three or four years and knew nothing about what had been there before. Then I asked him if he'd ever heard of a local reporter named Jessica MacIntosh, who used to work at the paper. He just shook his head, said he'd never heard of her, but of course *MacIntosh* is a very common name around these parts. Then he asked for *my* name, and flirted with me some more, and then asked for my number. I gave it to him, naturally—I mean, what the hell!—and we're planning to meet up later tonight.

But then the weirdest thing happened, Pat. After J.J. went back behind the bar, I glanced over and saw this woman sitting at a table on the other side of the restaurant staring at me with just the *dirtiest* look. Like, a full-on laser beam of disgust. I was shocked. She was maybe fifty years old, one of these middle-aged women who may have been attractive back in the day but sort of resembled a bullfrog now. Even from this distance, I could see she was wearing a sort of hunting vest, even though hunting season is six months away, and she also had on this tiny, beady, mannish-looking chain around her neck, the end of it tucked into her forest-green tank top. I swear, she was looking at me with something like… like *loathing*. It was so strange! She must have overheard my conversation with J.J., and I guess she was offended by our blatant flirting and how easily he got my number. I almost called over, *Oh, I'm sorry, Ma'am, did you have dibs on that guy? Bit young for you, isn't he?*, but I didn't want to make a scene. I tried to ignore her as I ate my lunch, then I settled my bill with J.J. and told him that I'd see him later. As I gathered up to leave, I noticed that the woman was *still* staring, *still* seething there in her chair at the sight of me. She hadn't even touched her meal. She just glared at me, almost hypnotized, like she was on the cusp of getting up and coming over to say something to me. God, it freaked me right out.

Best,
M.

~

Dear Carolyn,
Yes, obviously, that's what I need to do. Once I have confirmation from Charlottetown—hopefully there'll be

a death certificate the coroner can send me—then I'll proceed with exactly that sort of claim. Thanks so much for your help. I don't know yet whether this will fall under PEI's local probate law or its Estates Act, but I'll let you know. Curious stuff, eh?

Anyhow, thanks again for your help. If I send you a draft in the next few days, will you read it over and make sure I've crossed all my t's and dotted my i's?

Best,
M.

~

Dear Karen,
So good to hear from you! I guess Pat's been filling you in a little about what's going on with me. I'm still on PEI, still on a mission to learn everything I can about my father and the property he owned in this area, but I'm running into roadblocks at every turn. I'm struggling to find people who were living around here at the same time he was, and those who were are staying pretty mum about it. I get the sense that something really... I don't know, *awful*, happened in this community around that time, though I can't seem to figure out what. I understand that people in a small place like to keep to themselves, but it's weird that I can't find *anyone* willing to talk to me about happened thirty years ago. It's almost like the few people who know took a pledge never to speak of it.

On a completely unrelated note: I found a fuck buddy! His name is J.J. and I met him at a brew pub here in Montague. We've been hooking up the last few nights and having *lots* of fun.

Ack! Who even am I? I've turned into *such a slut* since coming to PEI. Oh Karen, don't judge me! LOL.
xoxo,
M.

~

Dear Carolyn,

So, news: Mary Kwon, the property lawyer who is helping me at this end, has made a rather interesting proposition. Like I mentioned, she's been practicing here in Montague for the last eighteen years, and in Halifax for fifteen years before that, and is now ready to retire. She has taken a real shine to me since I first approached her for help—has in fact become almost like a mother figure in the brief time I've known her—and here's what she's suggested: provided I get admitted to the Law Society of Prince Edward Island, would I be interested in taking over her practice? She has lots of connections around here, and her business earns her a very respectable living. Would I be willing to step in and take it over once she's ready to call it quits later this summer?

Carolyn, this would be huge. It might actually be the solution to all my problems. As much as I love you guys, I cannot bear the idea of returning to Toronto. I am absolutely enamoured of PEI now and really want to stay here, permanently. What Mary is proposing is a chance to do exactly that. It's also a chance to practice the type of law I trained for. What's more, if what I'm planning with my father's property works out, if it actually comes through, legally speaking, well… that would seal the deal, wouldn't it?

What do you think I should do? Carolyn, you're the smartest lawyer I know and I really trust your opinion. Do you think I have the guts to leave my life in Toronto behind and get the fresh start I've always wanted somewhere else?

Love,
M.

~

Dear Patrick,

So, something strange has happened. The other day I went into Charlottetown to pick up some documents for my claim, and while there I decided to pop into the library downtown, sort of on a whim. I was curious about finding old issues of the *Eastern Pioneer* from around the time my father was living on the Island. I wanted to see how that paper covered some of these awful news stories that I saw from that period. I got the librarian, this knowledgeable old lady who looked like she'd been working there forever, to help me pull the issues up on microfilm. And do you know what? There was almost *nothing*, hardly any mention at all, of the horrible stuff that seemed to unfold in that community during the period in question. The newspaper barely covered it. Isn't that *weird*? I asked the librarian if she knew anything about this weekly paper from decades ago. She said yes. She said she could remember that it was run by an old Scottish guy, for *years*, and that he had become a kind of personality on the Island, someone that everybody knew. Only, she said that he really lost his "zest for journalism" in the later part of his career, and the newspaper's quality went right downhill. She said everyone on the Island who read the paper noticed it. I asked when that happened, and do you know what she did? She looked at my microfilm screen and said, "You know, I think it occurred around the same period you're reading about." Isn't that *weird?!*

And then, coincidently enough, my new fuck buddy here, J.J., discovered something *else* about the paper for me. He knew I was curious about the *Eastern Pioneer*, and so he took it upon himself, sweet guy, to start asking around Montague about it. He eventually tracked down this older gentleman—oddly enough a property lawyer, like me—who is retired and living in nearby Brudenell. Apparently, he was *friends* with the Scottish fellow who ran the paper. But when J.J. went down there to chat him up, the old guy got really uncomfortable. He didn't *want* to talk about the paper, or his friend, and certainly not about the time period that my father was living here on the Island. J.J. eventually squeezed out of him that one of the women who went missing that summer *worked at the newspaper*, and that after that happened the old Scottish guy was never the same again. He lost his passion for news, for life, for everything. J.J. tried to get the name of this woman, but by then the old guy had shut the conversation down. It was just too difficult for him to talk about.

Oh Pat, do you think that missing woman might have been Jessica MacIntosh, the intern who wrote the profile of my father? Oh man, this is getting more and more curious!

M.

~

Dear Mary,
Okay, I think everything is in order. I've copied and pasted the text for my formal request to the municipality below for your review. A lawyer friend in Toronto has already gone over it, but just take a look and make sure you think I've included everything we need for my application. I'll drop off my big file of documents to your office this afternoon, but I have to say, I think our case is air tight. The fact that RIBC has already approved my request and given me access to his accounts is a very good sign.

Mary, I cannot thank you enough for everything you've done for me. You truly are a "tough old Chinese broad," and I appreciate the diligence—and the friendship—you've shown me over these last weeks. I'm still not sure what I ever did to deserve all this, but I'll take it. As for your business proposition, I accept! This is exactly what I need in my life right now. I've come to love eastern PEI and have been hunting for a reason to stay here indefinitely. Thank you for providing me one. And I appreciate that you'll still be around and able to mentor me as I take over your practice.

I also want to address the *other* question you raised in your email. So, okay. Yes, I have been inside the house itself—a few times now. Do you think this will impact my application if word gets around? I hope not. I hope everything is a foregone conclusion and it won't matter. In the meantime, what can I say in my defense? Squatter's rights? Finders keepers? Oh God, if my law professors could hear me now, they'd take my degree away! Mary, don't be mad, but I'm actually planning to spend my first night under Applegarth's roof *tonight*. I'm so excited! I went to the big camping equipment store in Charlottetown and bought a sleeping bag, a cooler and some flashlights. You probably think I'm insane, but there is just something about that old mansion that calls to me, that makes me want to sleep under its roof, and for some reason tonight feels like the perfect night to do so for the first time. The house is actually in really good shape inside—surprisingly so! Though I will say, if my application is successful, the first thing I'm going to do is get some exterminators to come in. There are clearly some huge critters living in the walls, and especially up in the attic. I've heard them lurching and shuffling around up there. If they're birds, or rats, or worse, they must be huge, based on all the noise they make. (Oddly, though, I have found very few droppings throughout the house. Weird, eh?)

Anyway, take a look at the text below and let me know if you have any edits or suggestions. Thanks again, for everything.

Best,

M.

★★★

To Whom It May Concern,

Further to my inquiry to the municipality of Three Rivers, PE on 17 April, please find enclosed my full and formal application to the matter discussed. I am seeking a complete resolution and disposition at your earliest convenience. The following is a summary of the facts associated with my claim, which the accompanying documentary evidence verifies and supports:

i. That the property, colloquially referred to as "Applegarth," located at the far eastern end of Rural Route #4, the Eight Mile Road, in the former municipality of Glenning, was deeded in the name of one Riley Robert Fuller, originally of Moncton, NB.

ii. That Riley Fuller died intestate in July 1995. At the time of his death, it was believed that he had no surviving blood descendants or declared heirs to the assets of his estate. Please find enclosed a copy of his death certificate, as well as documentary evidence that:

    a. verifies Riley Fuller's intestacy; and

    b. confirms he had no other blood descendants or declared heirs.

iii. That "Applegarth" was deemed *bona vacantia* following the death of Riley Fuller in July 1995, and eventually escheated to the municipality of Glenning in 2002. Possession of the property was subsequently transferred to the newly formed municipality of Three Rivers following amalgamation in 2018.

iv. That I am, in fact, the biological daughter of Riley Fuller, and his sole blood descendant. Indeed, I am the progeny of a brief extramarital affair he conducted with one Marigold Burque, originally from Bouctouche, NB, in the winter and early spring of 1992, and I was subsequently born in January 1993. Please find enclosed documentary evidence supporting these facts. As to the nature of Riley Fuller's intestacy, I can confirm that he was unaware of my existence at the time of his death in 1995. Please note that I am willing to sign an affidavit outlining why, despite Riley Fuller and I not knowing each other, I have his last name rather than my mother's.

Based upon these facts, and pursuant to the *Prince Edward Island Probate Act, Part IV s.93 (1988)*, and pursuant to Section 10 of the *Prince Edward Island Provincial Administrator of Estates Act*, I hereby make a formal claim to the ownership of Applegarth under the principles of **consanguinity**.

Please note that I have already established a precedent in my assertion of consanguinity over the assets of the late Riley Fuller. The Royal Imperial Bank of Canada has tentatively approved my stake to three unclaimed accounts he left behind: RIBC chequing account 05064-5012133, currently valued at $1,545.28; RIBC savings account 05064-7054679, currently valued at $4,509.52; and RIBC-RRSP investment account 03804537-3, currently valued at $123,612. These accounts will be transferred to my name pending final approval of the RIBC branch president in Moncton, NB. All associated documentation to the facts surrounding this assertion of consanguinity are enclosed.

I understand that Applegarth has sat unclaimed, and indeed untouched, since the death of my father thirty years ago. Both the former municipality of Glenning and the current municipality of Three Rivers have made token attempts to sell the property over the years, both to locals and to off-Island residents, to no avail. I believe that it is a good house, and a good piece of property, and it deserves to be occupied. Should this application be successful and I am declared Applegarth's rightful owner, I intend to make it my primary residence and restore it to its former glory.

Thank you for your consideration. I hope to hear from you soon.

Yours sincerely,
Melinda Fuller
Date: 28 April 2025

ACKNOWLEDGEMENTS

A big thank you to my dad, Ron Sampson, my wife, Rebecca Rosenblum, my dear friends Art Moore and Sara Heinonen, and my former literary agent Brenna English-Loeb, for all their help with this book at various stages and drafts of its development.

An especially huge thank you to Kelly Daniels of Moncton, for opening up about his experiences as an RCMP officer and with post-traumatic stress disorder.

And a big thanks to Chris Needham at Now Or Never Publishing for taking on this book.